GRIM

AND

BEAR IT

JULIETTE CROSS

UNION
SQUARE
& CO.

NEW YORK

UNION
SQUARE
& CO.

NEW YORK

UNION SQUARE & CO. and the distinctive Union Square & Co. logo are trademarks of Sterling Publishing Co., Inc.

Union Square & Co., LLC, is a subsidiary of Sterling Publishing Co., Inc.

ISBN 978-1-4549-5367-8 (paperback)

For information about custom editions, special sales, and premium purchases, please contact specialsales@unionsquareandco.com

Printed in Canada

2 4 6 8 10 9 7 5 3 1

unionsquareandco.com

Cover design by Jenny Zemanek
Cover images by Shutterstock.com: antonpix (raven); Drawlab19 (cupcake); javarman (ombre); Kate Macate (ribbon); Merfin (herbs); Gorbash Varvara (butterfly bottle); WinWin artlab (skulls)

For Kevin, Justin, Jacob, Noelle, and Jackson
My heart and my home

PROLOGUE

~HENRY~

When I was little, I often escaped to the garden behind my father's sprawling fifty-acre estate. Like everything else in his life, he kept pristine gardens. Toward the center, there was a long bed of wildflowers that attracted a particular kind of butterfly. The wings were yellow with delicate black trim. Beautiful. For some reason, this happened to be a place where I was never disturbed by the dead. I'd watch the golden-winged insects flutter about happily, mindlessly, and bask in their effortless beauty.

Certain Native American tribes said that a yellow butterfly was a spirit of hope and guidance. I wasn't so sure about guidance, but they'd always lifted the weight of my gift as a necromancer. For a short while. I'd found solace in the butterfly garden far too many times to confess to anyone. When I'd had to leave my father's house, I went into a period of mourning, bereft of my yellow butterflies.

Then one day, while I was standing outside of Ruben's bookstore on Magazine, a woman stepped out of a shop and walked down the street, her lengthy blonde hair streaming down her back. I'd felt it like a punch to the gut. I remember sucking in a painful gulp of air the second I laid eyes on her, knowing at long last I'd found my butterfly garden again.

Only, she wasn't a garden. She was a woman. A witch. A breathlessly stunning, beguiling one who began tormenting my dreams with aching frequency from that very day. As I watched her now, I wondered, not for the first time, if she was in fact my hope and my guide. Because wherever she went, I helplessly followed.

CHAPTER 1

~CLARA~

THIS WAS IT. I WAS TOTALLY DOING THIS. NO GOING BACK NOW.

I marched up the shaded walkway of Henry Blackwater's two-story mansion on St. Charles Avenue, the imposing front door drawing closer.

Well, maybe a little going back.

I turned around and paced down the pavement away from the house, weighing the possible outcomes.

What's the worst thing that could happen anyway?

He could say no. Or he could tell me he wanted nothing to do with me. I could discover that I've been completely wrong that he feels the same.

Then you know what would happen? I'd fall into a deep abyss of utter despair. I'd lock myself in my carriage house apartment and cry myself sick while eating praline ice cream and peanut M&Ms and watching *Ever After* on loop. Then I'd never venture out into public, much less daylight, ever again. I'd curl up in a fetal position and wither away in my chocolate-stained, pink satin pajamas.

But that wasn't going to happen. No, ma'am.

An elderly woman peered over the roof of her car and the hedge separating Henry's front yard from hers. Her concern for me, or possibly my mental state, rolled over the shrub and wafted right into me.

I waved and smiled. "All is well," I assured her with a sharp nod, though that didn't seem to allay her worry for me, the woman muttering and pacing up and down her neighbor's walkway, holding a pastry box.

Exhaling a breath and widening my smile, I walked past the Greek columns onto the portico and up to the regal wooden door engraved with tree branches and birds along the edges. A raven was carved in the top corner, a sentinel observing visitors on this doorstep.

I smiled at the wooden raven and gave him a wink. I was *not* wrong.

Balancing my box of cupcakes in one hand, I readied myself to ring the doorbell, smoothing my magenta miniskirt and hardening my resolve. Step one in Clara-gets-Henry was about to happen whether the universe was ready or not.

Or maybe tomorrow will be better.

As I was about to return to my car, I jumped as a bolt sounded on the other side and the heavy wooden door swung open. The jarring sight of *him* slugged me hard in the chest, but I somehow remained upright.

Every time I saw Henry, my body's immediate response was to wilt and melt into a puddle at his feet, which were bare at the moment. Dear Goddess above, even his bare feet were beautiful.

"Hi, Henry." I beamed brightly, admiring his deep purple aura that seemed to match his brooding intensity.

"Clara," was all he managed to say, his dark eyes wide with surprise, that deep, smoky voice of his threatening to tangle my tongue into knots.

But before I could become an inarticulate dummy on his doorstep, I spilled my intentions.

"I hope you don't mind me showing up at your home. I asked Gareth, and he gave me your address. There's something important I wanted to talk to you about. May I come in?"

For a moment, he simply stared and blinked at me. I reached out with my Aura senses, but still . . . nothing. My magic had been a wonderful companion throughout my life, always showing me who needed help and guiding me by revealing the emotions of others in my vicinity. But Henry? Not a thing. Not a tiny inkling of emotion other than what I can read on his expression. Like normal people had to do. It was horrendous.

At the moment, the emotion I was discerning was sheer shock, which wasn't a surprise as I had just bombarded my way into his home. After all, he hadn't invited me. But that was the problem. He was moving too slowly, and I had no patience, so like Jules had advised me several months ago, I was taking matters into my own hands.

Rather than wait for him to answer my request to enter (the way it was looking now, that might be a rejection), I stepped up and into the doorway. Henry took a sudden step backward, widening the door.

"Come in," was all he managed to say, his brow pursed in confusion.

I loved analyzing his emotions, trying to absorb them the way I did others. Though my magic never once tingled to reveal what I could see in everyone else, my skin still zinged in response to his nearness. There was an energy around Henry that drew me like a dragon to her golden treasure. I wanted to swoop in and hoard this sensation for eternity.

When he closed the door, I took a moment to look around. His house was bigger and grander than ours in the lower Garden District. Even though Henry's personal exterior—typically well-worn jeans and a black T-shirt like now—never screamed money in any way, he apparently had some. And this house suited him.

It wasn't sleek and posh, but more ornate and interesting, still reeking of beauty in a unique sort of way. A Henry kind of way.

The chandelier in the foyer was a black, antique wrought iron fixture with candle-like lights. The walls were covered in a deep red brocade pattern, extending up the wall of the curving, white marble staircase, which was also tread in a red-and-gold Persian rug.

He led me down a hallway to his left, and when I thought—*hoped*—he'd veer off into the spacious living room with a gigantic, baroque fireplace and loads of colorful artwork, he kept walking until we reached his kitchen. Yet again, it took me a moment to soak in my surroundings.

The countertops were black marble, the cabinets white with detailed filigree, and a giant copper hood sat over the stove. Again, there were more black wrought iron light fixtures, giving the large room an even grander effect.

"Your kitchen is so beautiful."

Prickles of awareness finally drew my attention back to Henry, who had settled himself back against the farthest countertop from me. He simply stared, devouring me with that same unreadable expression on his lovely angular face.

For a second, I did the same, absorbing his beauty—the perfect line of his sharp jaw and strong chin, the slant of his dark eyes and straight nose, the tattoos covering his arms and peeking out of his T-shirt at the neck. There were some dark spiky tips belonging to a much larger tattoo on his chest that I longed to see. And touch.

I was tactile. And that was a problem at the moment because I couldn't simply wander freely through his home, looking at and caressing everything. Nor could I close the distance between us, lift up his shirt, and trail my fingers over the ink attached to those spiky ends sprouting out of the collar of his T-shirt. I had to rein in my normal behavior as much as possible or I might spook him.

"You're probably wondering why I'm at your house?"

He merely nodded.

"I hope you don't mind I showed up here unannounced. I thought it best we talk in person."

I walked closer, noting his body stiffening against the counter as I came. He braced his hands on the black marble behind him.

I stopped a few feet away, still holding the confectionary box in both hands. "I know your secret."

That's when emotion finally flitted across his face, shock and a touch of fear. Rather than let him stew, I bolted ahead.

"I know you're RavenOne, my biggest fan on my blog for the High Tea Book Club."

He remained fixed and unmoving except for a slight lift of his cleft chin. "How do you know?"

Smiling wider, I admitted, "I wish I could say it was my psychic ability but, unfortunately, I don't have as much of that gift as Violet." I shrugged. "She told me it was you."

Frowning at the memory of her sarcastic demeanor in that conversation, I remembered when she'd added, *"It's so obviously him, Clara. Anyone could figure it out."*

But it hadn't been obvious to me.

I recalled the raven carved into his front door, playing guardian over his domain. Tentatively, I asked because I needed confirmation, "It is you, isn't it?"

Another solid, single nod from the paragon of rough beauty.

"I knew it," I said more to myself. "That's why I'm here," I told him. "You always have such good insight into the books that we're reading that I want you to join our book club."

One dark brow arched high, disappearing beneath a swoop of sable hair. "You want me to join a romance book club with you and your widows," he said as a statement, not a question.

"Don't be all superior now. There's nothing wrong with a man admitting that he enjoys reading romance," I teased, noting his pale complexion suddenly flushed pink.

"I'm not being superior," he argued. "It's just that . . ." Then he lost his words, his gaze trailing down my body.

I preened under the attention. I'd taken great care to pick out the most pleasing outfit for my figure—my favorite magenta miniskirt with a white flowy top that dipped at my cleavage. I'd worn my hair down since he seemed to enjoy looking at it. I wondered what it would feel like to have his hands in it.

"On my blog, you show a keen insight into matters of the heart," I observed. His complexion turned darker still. "And the ladies have all agreed they'd enjoy a masculine point of view. It seems unfair you only offer insights into our books after we've already discussed them. We'd all like you to be a more interactive part of the club rather than simply making comments afterward on the blog."

"Your widows all want me in your book club?" Again with the questioning arched brow that had me squirming a little, a hot sensation pooling between my legs.

I hadn't realized until this moment that, apparently, I was aroused by arching eyebrows. Henry's at least.

"They're not all widows, actually. And yes, they do want you to join us. But"—I stepped closer—"especially me."

The tension between us stretched taut like a bowstring, the air thick as we gazed at each other.

"You won't disappoint me, will you, Henry?"

And so here it was. If he had any feelings for me whatsoever, he couldn't deny me now. He had to join the book club, which would lead to stage two of getting my man. But if he told me no at this moment, then I'd have my answer. And my sisters and I had been wrong in that he liked me too.

I trusted my sisters, but putting my own feelings out there without being able to detect how the other felt was like flying a plane blind. My magic was my navigation system by which I walked through life. With Henry, I couldn't ever tell. Waiting for his reply was sheer torture.

Finally, when I thought I might faint onto his kitchen floor from suspense, he said, "I'll join."

A huge breath of air left my lungs. "Wonderful!" I beamed, trying to calm the giddiness swirling through me.

While I was doing cartwheels on the inside, I held myself together by a thread, trying not to reveal my profound relief and joy that this was going to happen. Once I had him in the book club, I'd seduce him the only way I knew how. Through books.

"I also brought you a little thank-you gift, as well as a welcome to our book club."

I thrust out the open box of cupcakes in my hands. Henry flinched like I'd tossed a nest of snakes at him, his back fully pressed to the countertop.

"It's just cupcakes." I laughed. "This is my very own recipe, including the frosting. Whipped cherry."

He blinked, his near-black eyes rounded with an emotion I couldn't place. And that was what drove me absolutely mad about this man. Of all the people to draw a total blank on my emo-detector, it had to be him? It was like Goddess was playing a nasty joke, probably cackling at me from her heavenly lair.

"Really, Henry. They taste so good."

I took a single step closer. He stiffened, his knuckles whitening, bracketed on the black marble countertop behind him. The veins in his hands rippled as he gripped tighter, the muscles in his arms flexing. I tried not to get distracted by his lovely full-sleeve tattoos, but it was more than a little difficult to stay focused while standing this close to Henry Blackwater.

He seemed almost scared, even though his expression and dark gaze—ever fixed on me—hardly had changed since I'd walked through his front door. I decided to speak softer, maybe come across less threatening. Vi said I could sometimes appear aggressive when I was excited. And I was so very excited standing in his kitchen, basking in his delicious essence.

I glanced down at the perfectly iced pink cupcakes. "This one is my favorite. Strawberries and cream."

He gulped, his Adam's apple bobbing, his eyes never straying to the box of cupcakes. Though I couldn't detect his emotion, I certainly understood the meaning behind the piercing, primal look in his dark eyes. That's when the devil took me. It happened from time to time. Vi said I had a demon inside me that liked to come out and play on occasion.

I lifted a cupcake out of the box and took another step closer, holding it out to him. "It's sweet and creamy, Henry. I promise. Don't you want to lick my cupcake?"

He made a strangled sound in the back of his throat, his eyes blinked heavily, and his chest caved with a gusty breath. For a fleeting few seconds, he seemed pained, almost tortured, then suddenly it was all gone. Like a switch had flipped. The look of agony vanished, replaced by something altogether more terrifying—resignation and a hard wickedness that made me quiver with desire.

He shoved off the counter and straightened above me, forcing me to tilt my chin up. Holding my gaze, his own dark as pitch, he finally spoke. "Yeah, Clara. I wanna lick your cupcake."

I was going to faint. I was. It was going to be so embarrassing, but I couldn't even breathe as he took the cupcake from my hand, his rough fingers grazing mine. Without ever breaking my gaze, he lifted the cupcake to his mouth, darted out his tongue, and licked a big glob of pink with the tip of his tongue.

Stars above! Even his tongue was beautiful.

"Mmm." He closed his eyes a second and swallowed. "You're right." That rarely seen, enigmatic smile of his quirked one side of his mouth. "Sweet and creamy."

Then the front door opened and slammed, both of us jumping at the sound. I twirled a step away from him and watched as his younger brother, Sean, waltzed into the kitchen. He slowed his steps when he saw me, his cranky expression morphing from annoyed to devious in a millisecond.

His aura was a deep shade of red. Sean had a fiery temperament, and his aura reflected that. But it was the level of anger I'd detected right before he walked in that had me concerned.

"Hello there, Blondie," he said, sauntering up to the island and propping his elbows on them. "You brought us cupcakes?"

Henry abruptly closed the lid after he set the licked one back inside. "They're mine, so keep your grubby hands off."

Sean grinned wider. "And why are we getting house calls from the lovely Clara Savoie?"

"I had something to talk to Henry about," I answered, my magic pushing me to fix him. "Who are you so angry at, Sean?"

He lifted off the counter and headed for the fridge. "Nobody."

"What happened?" snapped Henry.

"Nothing." Sean opened the fridge.

"That same asshole?" Henry pushed.

Sean shrugged and pulled out a box of cold pizza from DeAngelo's.

"Did you hurt him?" Henry's voice had risen exponentially.

"No. But I should've broken his fucking hands this time." He pulled out a slice of pizza and tossed the box on the counter. "The arm healed too quickly from his last little fall."

"Sean." Henry was beside him now. "You stay away from that fucker, you hear me?"

"Kind of hard when he's in almost all my classes," he said around a muffled mouthful. "Mm. This is good."

"I'm serious." There was an edge to Henry's tone that sounded more like fear than anger, but I wasn't sure who or what he was afraid of.

Still not as tall as his brother, Sean rolled his eyes and looked up at Henry. "Relax. It's fine."

Even while he said it, his red aura vibrated with threads of black. That was troubling. Without even thinking, I stepped closer and put my hand on Sean's shoulder, washing him with a joy spell. Instantly, his aura brightened again, the black receding.

His smile reappeared when he looked down at me. "Thanks, Blondie."

Then he picked up the pizza box, one slice still half-eaten in his other hand, and sauntered back toward the living room I hadn't gotten a close enough look at.

He called over his shoulder. "Got some icing on your lip there."

Henry wiped the back of his hand across his mouth.

"There's nothing there," I told him. "He was teasing you."

Henry combed both hands into his hair with exasperation, a look I'd never seen on him. I couldn't help but stare because I wanted to know all of his moods, catalog all of his emotions, know the way he looked and sounded as he experienced them.

It was fascinating to me that my magic didn't tabulate and tell me everything about him like it did for other people. It also made him more intriguing. But that was just the tip of my attraction to him. Henry was darkly beautiful, inside and out.

Though he pretended to be indifferent, he cared deeply for his brother and his cousin, Gareth, my sister Livvy's boyfriend. There was something about Henry's rough edges that made me want to smooth them.

"Thank you," Henry grumbled, his broody frown in place. "He can be"—he waved a hand toward where Sean had marched off—"difficult."

"It's okay. He's fine. I didn't detect anything too bad."

Though there had been that strange striation of black weaving through his aura for a moment, it had vanished when I spelled him with my magic.

Henry stared at me, that quiet pensiveness sinking in again. Knowing I was ahead and should count my blessings that this all came off the way I'd wanted, I figured it was time to leave before he tried to change his mind.

"Well." Beaming up at him, I clasped my hands in front of me. "I'll see you on Thursday at my house. Three o'clock. Don't be late. The ladies are looking forward to meeting you."

His mouth hung open as if he were going to protest, but I sashayed out the kitchen toward the hallway.

"I'll let myself out. See you Thursday!"

I gave him one more smile over my shoulder, but he didn't notice. His gaze was decidedly lower than my face, and that had me singing merrily all the way home.

CHAPTER 2

~HENRY~

SHIT. FUCK. DAMN. MOTHERFUCKING HELL.

I chewed my nicotine gum so hard I thought I might break my own jaw as I headed down the sidewalk, closer to Clara's. I hadn't wanted a smoke this badly in months. Actually, I hadn't needed the gum for a few weeks, the cravings all but vanished.

But the mere thought of walking into the Savoie house for the first time, for the purpose of spending a few hours with Clara, had me about to crawl right out of my skin. I was so fucking nervous it was ridiculous. The absurd part of my current manic state was that Clara was the only one who eased the constant edginess I felt from my magic.

Gareth would point out it was from me blocking my magic, not the necromancy itself. Our aunt Lucille had taught me how to build wards to cage my own magic at a young age.

The constant ward-building didn't drain my energy, but there were side effects. Anxiety was the main one, but also the feeling that I wasn't quite whole. The problem was that I'd rather live this life of a half-grim than face the demons that waited in the dark.

The irony of being nervous now as I drew closer to Clara's house was that I never craved a cigarette around Clara to calm my nerves. I didn't crave anything . . . but her.

Glancing down at my clothes as her house came into view, I wondered if there was a dress code for this thing. I worried for a split second that my Iron Maiden T-shirt with the band's skeleton mascot, Eddie, wielding a bloody axe might put off the widows. I hadn't thought about it until this minute.

"Too late now," I muttered as I opened the gate to the Savoie house and walked up to the front door like I belonged here.

Belonged. Here. I couldn't shake the feeling that somehow I did. No matter how hard I tried to extract my obsession with Clara from my brain and body, it had only increased exponentially the more I knew her.

I'd tried a thousand times to convince myself to stay away from her, to not give in to this fanatical fixation I had on the pretty, sweet witch who haunted me day and night. I knew how fucked up I was. A necromancer who hated ghosts. Who hated his magic. And she didn't deserve someone as screwed up in the head as me. Or damaged. She deserved, I don't know, a knight in shining fucking armor.

Of course, the thought of her with anyone else sparked the blackest of thoughts, stirring my deep grim magic to brutal wakefulness. That fucking werewolf Rhett always flirted with her, and I'd imagined beating him bloody too many times to count, which was utterly insane since Clara wasn't mine.

Still, that meant nothing to the dark monster who lived and breathed inside me, who purred his approval every time Clara came near. The one I kept chained behind magical walls, thanks to my aunt Lucille. My monster wasn't the same as Gareth's.

My cousin's creature was entirely different than mine. Perhaps not entirely, but a grimlock's beast wanted destruction and blood, visceral satiation from carnal and vengeful thoughts. He was most closely related to our evil forefather who created us by mistake. That's what dabbling in blood magic and human sacrifice can do—create an entirely new species of beings. The grimlock's monster constantly craved dark desires.

Not mine. He simply wanted me to travel to the netherworld, spend all my time in the death realm, and incinerate evil souls. No biggie, right?

I flinched at a sudden flashback of shrieking screams, black eyes, and smothering, suffocating pain. My hand went to my chest on instinct, the memory so far away but also too near.

After shaking that nightmare off, I knocked on the door, but then a new horror dawned on me. Was I supposed to bring something? A cake or wine? The book?

I'd read the historical romance she'd messaged me about through her blog, now that she knew I was her number one stalker—I mean, fan—to let me know what book to read for today. I'd actually felt far too much connection to the hero of this one, a little disturbingly so.

Before I could worry about one more fucking thing, the front door swung open and my entire soul sighed.

There she stood in all of her stunning, brain-hazing beauty. It hurt to look at her. And yet, I couldn't tear my eyes away if I tried.

She wore a dress today, a pale blue one that was pretty but no comparison to the shade of her eyes. The brightest blue on the clearest day. Like the days I used to spend in the butterfly garden.

"Henry!" she gushed, smiling easily with nothing but joy lighting up her face.

How did she do it? How did she live so honestly with every single emotion radiating off her like that?

"I'm so happy you came," she said with enthusiasm as she wrapped her hands around my forearm and pulled me inside.

I tried not to focus on the intoxicating sensation of having her hands on me. Instantly, the edgy tension vanished, just as it always did when she was anywhere within my radius.

Without saying a word, I let her tug me into the Savoie's family den off the foyer where four sweet-looking old ladies stared at me.

"Ladies, I'd like to introduce Henry Blackwater. Please welcome him to our club."

"Hello, Henry," said the one with glasses and kind eyes. She wore a bright yellow sweater and held her glass of tea with dainty hands.

"Glad you finally decided to grace us with your presence," said another on a chaise next to Yellow Sweater.

"Martha," chastised another woman with a round face and a plate of petit fours on her lap, a pink-iced one in her hand, "that's no way to greet our new member."

There was a silver tea server and little porcelain cups and saucers. Next to the tea setting were two silver, three-tiered trays stacked with little sandwiches, macarons, scones, and petit fours.

I recognized the scones and petit fours as those from Queen of Tarts, the bakery across from the Savoie's pub, the Cauldron, on Magazine Street.

"Thank you, Evelyn," said Clara, guiding me to an empty chair next to another one near the fireplace, which wasn't burning. The weather had finally taken a turn toward spring sunshine and seemed to be sticking to it.

"You can sit by me," she added in a whisper like it was a secret.

Clara was a heady combination of sweet and seductive. I wasn't sure if she was aware just how beguiling she was with her wide blue eyes, easy smiles, and fine-as-fuck body. Not to mention that divinely attractive cloak of honesty and kindness she wore at all times.

"Thanks," I muttered, noticing the copy of *The Taming of a Highlander* by Elisa Braden sitting on her chair. "Was I supposed to bring the book?"

"No, that's okay." She took her seat next to me and held the book on her lap. "Let me introduce everyone before we get started. This is Deborah."

"Hi, there." A petite brunette with short hair waved before biting into a cucumber sandwich.

"This is Evelyn and Martha." She introduced the nice one and the not-so-nice one. "And this is Fran."

"How do you like your tea, dear?" asked Fran, now pouring me a cup.

I didn't want to be rude and admit I never drank the stuff. "Plain is fine."

"I'm sorry you won't meet Miriam." A definite somber note slipped into Clara's voice as she told me, "She's been ill." Then she faced the group, saying with more brightness, "But I'll be sure and bring her a plate from today's club meeting."

Martha narrowed her eyes and pointed her teaspoon at me. "You sure don't look like a guy who would like to read romance."

Now I was getting the shakedown from intimidating grand-mas. This was new.

"Martha, we aren't going to be judgmental," Clara stated evenly.

"Quite frankly," I told Martha, "you don't seem the type who would either."

Her ornery glare lightened. She gave a little huff of laughter. "Touché, Mr. Blackwater." Then she sipped her tea.

"Now that we're all settled," began Clara, taking on a more official tone, "let's begin with the heroine. Did we like her or not like her?"

"I adored her," cooed Fran. "She was so perky and sweet." Then she passed me my teacup. "Here you are, dear."

I nodded a thank-you and settled the dainty cup on my knee.

"Kind of a lost dreamer," added Martha, then squinted at Clara, "though there was some appeal to that, I suppose."

"Well, they were a perfect match, though, weren't they?" Deborah chimed in, taking a second sandwich off the tray. "They had that opposites-attract thing going for them in spades."

"Opposites?" snarked Martha. "They lived on different planets, those two."

"But still perfectly matched, I agree," added Evelyn.

"Why were they perfectly matched?" asked Clara.

No one answered, all of them sinking into pensive silence.

"I don't know how to explain it . . . ," said Fran. "They were like two puzzle pieces cut from different cloth but fit together like they were made for each other."

"I agree," said Clara kindly, "but that still doesn't answer the question. *Why* did they fit?"

Another thoughtful silence.

"Henry?" Fran dragged me into the conversation while I'd been trying to sink into invisibility, wondering why the hell I had agreed to come. "What do you think?"

All eyes swiveled to me, even Clara's. I couldn't look at her while I ruminated over the question. Because I knew exactly why the characters Kate and Broderick fit together so perfectly. But saying it aloud was like confessing a secret desire.

Clearing my throat, I sat straighter in the chair, the teacup rattling on my knee. "Martha is right," I started. "Kate is a dreamer. Broderick brought her out of that dreamworld and into reality. He gave her something solid and real to hold on to. But for him . . ." I licked my lips, staring down at the tea, the pale peachy liquid steaming. "She was the only one who could soothe him after what he'd gone through. The balm to his old wounds. He didn't know why, but she was the one who made the pain go away and made his heart start beating again. Made him want to breathe and live rather than just exist from day to day. She became his whole heart that he could no longer live without."

It was completely silent when I finally lifted my gaze to the room to find all of them staring at me in various expressions of surprise and shock.

Clara shifted next to me, her presence the only one I was completely attuned to. "I-I think Henry's right," she said softly.

"And while Kate might have been a little aggressive in her pursuit of Broderick, he was certainly the one to do the conquering in the end."

"He can conquer me anytime," said Deborah, snagging a scone. For such a tiny thing, she was putting it away.

"Hear, hear," giggled Evelyn.

And now, I felt completely awkward and uncomfortable. The sound of footsteps coming from somewhere down the hallway and drawing closer put me more on edge. Clara's twin sister, Violet, passed by the open entrance to the den, heading toward the front door.

"Hi, ladies." She waved, passing on by, but then froze mid-step and turned toward us, staring straight at me, obviously taking in my presence among the High Tea Book Club with a frilly teacup on my knee. Then she burst into laughter and walked on toward the front door, muttering, "Priceless."

"Don't worry about her." While the ladies started chattering about something else, Clara leaned toward me and whispered, "I think you fit in just fine with us."

Violet's comment or obvious laughable reaction to me sitting in this room among the elder ladies and Clara didn't bother me one bit. The only thing that was currently driving me to distraction was Clara's delicate hand sitting lightly on my knee as she leaned in and surrounded me with her drugging scent. Why was it she could touch me unawares, and panic never took root? Rather the opposite, actually.

She was the only one beyond Gareth or Sean who I could stand to touch me. Her touch felt . . . right.

Dragging my gaze from the sight of her hand on me, I turned and looked at her, her face far too close. And far too distant. "I'm not worried," I assured her.

Her smile faltered before her gaze dropped to my mouth, her eyes sultry, and the reaction my body had to that was more than worrisome. It was downright fucking maddening. I could *not* get a hard-on in this room with the High Tea ladies.

As if Clara could read my mind, she sat back in her chair suddenly and turned everyone's attention to the plot of the story, guiding the group in a further discussion that I barely had enough sense to pay attention to.

After an hour of mostly admiring Broderick's feats of heroism, heart, and bedroom abilities, my first book club was over. The ladies chatted while they gathered their purses.

Martha looped her giant purse over an arm. "Clara, tell Miriam I'll be by tomorrow to see her." Then her gaze shifted to me. "I suppose having a male perspective among the group isn't as bad as I thought it would be."

"Thank you? I guess."

"You're welcome, Blackwater." She headed with the others toward the foyer and front door.

"Don't forget, everyone. Next book is *When Beauty Tamed the Beast* by Eloisa James. I ordered paperbacks, and they should arrive at your houses in a few days."

A round of thank-yous echoed in the hall as they left. Then I was alone with Clara, watching her box up what was left of the sandwiches and sweets.

"You aren't bringing those to the homeless, are you?"

Clara had a habit of parading down to the tent city under the overpass to hand out boxes of leftovers from her tea club or from Sunday dinners with the family. For the most part, she was never in any danger. Except that one time she stumbled into a drug deal gone bad, and I had to knock them out for knocking her unconscious. I stayed hidden afterward but waited until she woke a few minutes later to be sure she was okay. Good thing my instincts told me to follow her that day.

"Not today," she replied with a smile. Always a smile. "I'm bringing them to Miriam."

"Would you like some company?"

When her eyes brightened, there was a pinching sensation in my chest. "I would love that."

After helping her carry the dishes to the kitchen and taking the box of leftovers for her, we left through the front door without running into any more Savoies. I don't know why, but I exhaled relief at that.

Maybe I thought they'd ask me, *What are you doing here?* And I'd wonder the same. But the truth was, I'd enjoyed being here. More than that, I felt like I belonged here, wherever Clara was.

"I parked at the Green Light." Ruben's vampire den adjoined the back of his building where his bookstore was. "It's a short walk."

"I know." She walked beside me, her soft gaze flicking to mine. "Are you still working there even while Ruben is away?"

"Yeah. Devraj is in charge right now. He keeps me busy."

"So what is it that you actually do for Ruben?"

Why did I not anticipate this question? Not that I was going to lie to her, but it was rather unconventional. A little weird. "I do a few things for him. Mainly, I work the Green Light, the crowds outside the bar."

It was actually a vampire den, one of many in the city that catered to vampires seeking blood-hosts for the night.

"So you lure in humans for the vampires?"

She asked it without any accusation, which was new. But expected from Clara. She wasn't the judgy type.

"Yes and no." Compelled to keep her safely away from the street, I guided her with a hand on her elbow so we could switch places on the sidewalk. "The only humans allowed into the Green Light are those who know who and what we are. Who know what they're potentially getting themselves into by entering a vampire den. But yes, I'm there to tempt humans and even other supernaturals into giving in to those cravings. To go into the club and walk on the wild side for the night."

"Interesting."

"Sounds a little degenerate when I say it aloud."

"No. You're simply being who you are, using your magical skills to your own advantage. You're not spelling anyone or forcing them to go inside. Everyone makes their own decisions under temptation, and they're responsible for whatever outcomes there are."

We waited at the corner for the light to change so we could cross to the other side. I faced her. "But I am sort of the devil on their shoulder."

Her mouth slid into a smile I hadn't seen on her before—a mischievous one. All the blood rushed to my dick as she aimed that look at me.

"Everyone needs a devil on their shoulder now and then. It's good to be bad sometimes."

I shoved my hands in my pockets to minimize the obvious bulge in my jeans. Because now my imagination was running wild with all the ways I'd like to be bad with Clara Savoie.

"But I also scan the potential customers going into the Green Light to be sure they have no evil intent. That's a gift all grims have."

"Really? That's so interesting." She said it sincerely, not in a sarcastic way. "I love that you do that. You're sort of a guardian of the Green Light as well."

Uncomfortable with the compliment, I decided to change the subject. "Gareth told me you don't experience any effects from grims because you're an Aura. Is that true? You don't feel anything when I'm near you?"

I clamped my jaw shut, realizing that last question was stupid and suggestive. That's not what I'd meant. But then she surprised me again, her wicked smile widening.

"Yes, Henry. I feel something."

Thank fuck the light changed because I was at a total loss of words, trying to rein in my salacious thoughts.

"But as to a grim's darker aura, no, I don't feel what others do around you. Also"—she frowned as we turned down the side street next to Ruben's bookstore, Rare Books & Brew—"I can't read your emotions like I can others."

Thank fuck for that. Now I knew why she didn't turn and run in the other direction every time we bumped into each other. Because my fanatical obsession with this girl would terrify her if she actually knew how bad it was.

I didn't have to respond because we'd reached my car. I gestured toward the passenger side and opened the door for her.

"Nice," she commented as she ducked in on the passenger side.

My old black Mustang wasn't as pretty or sleek as Gareth's car, but it suited me. Understated, rough around the edges, but powerful.

"What's the address?" I asked as I settled into the driver's seat and cranked it up, watching to be sure she put on her seatbelt.

"It's not far. Head toward the upper Garden District. She doesn't live far from you, actually."

I headed up Magazine toward St. Charles Avenue.

"So what else do you do for Ruben?" she asked, somehow knowing that being a lurer into the club wasn't my sole job.

"I give him information—intel—that he needs."

"Like what would he need?"

I'd never shared this with anyone other than Gareth or Sean because it was somewhat of a secret, but I also found myself wanting to tell her anything she wanted to know.

"As a grim, I have lots of contacts and tech that can keep tabs on vampires."

"Like that vampire tracing app that helped Devraj find Isadora when she was kidnapped?"

"Yeah." I glanced over, but she didn't seem upset talking about the incident. "That was one of Gareth's apps. But I also have a few grim contacts through Obsidian Corp."

"Isn't that the company your dad is CEO of? Take a right at this coming light."

Surprised, I glanced at her as I maneuvered over and flicked on my blinker. "You know who my father is?"

Nausea soured my stomach as I took a deep breath to ease that instant reaction to him.

Her expression turned shy, which gave me the strangest urge to protect her for some reason. She didn't need to be shy with me, and I didn't like that unsure, almost frightened look on her face.

"I kind of researched you a little," she said, turning her face toward the window.

Nothing but genuine joy filled me at the thought of her *researching me* and the possible motivations for it. "What else did you find out?"

"Practically nothing, really. You know you're almost nowhere on the SuperNet?"

I grinned, nodding, as I slowed my car down for the bumpy residential street of single and two-story bungalow-style homes.

"I only found that out," she added huffily, "because I plagued Jules till she gave me information."

"You wanted to know more about me?"

Yes, I sounded like a lovesick schoolboy flirting with his middle school sweetheart, but I honestly couldn't help myself. It never dawned on me that Clara might be interested in me too. Not enough to hound her sisters for information.

"Of course. It was Livvy who told me something, though, that I liked very much. Pull over at that yellow house with the white trim." She pointed off to the right.

"What did you find out?" I asked as I parked on the side of the street in front of the house.

"That you quit smoking," she said on a breathy exhale.

I shoved my car into park and turned to look at her. That was a mistake. Her wide-eyed gaze devoured me, trailing over my face, neck, and chest, flickering lower before jumping back to my face. I'd never told anyone why I'd stopped smoking, but it didn't take a rocket scientist to follow the signs to figure it out.

Clara had told me in a conversation outside of Empress Ink that she loathed smoking because it could cause cancer. No grims had ever died of human disease, but it was the other thing she said that day that had lit a fire under me to quit the habit.

I remembered the day specifically because Clara was behaving the way she always did with me. Friendly and sweet and kind like she was with everyone else while she knitted scarves around the trunk of a crape myrtle tree outside the tattoo shop. Yeah, this was typical Clara behavior. But then her attitude changed.

After her sister Violet had walked up, said a few words to us, and then gone into her tattoo shop, leaving us in privacy, Clara's usual chatter turned decidedly more intimate. More so than she'd ever been with me before.

She'd mentioned that she dated a guy once who smoked, and kissing him was like licking an ashtray. She couldn't date him anymore after that. And then she went into this diatribe about how much she enjoyed kissing. I remember her words exactly when she said, "To me, kissing is more intimate than fucking. Though I like doing that a lot too."

I'd coughed so hard on cigarette smoke that I almost choked to death. By the time I'd finally caught my breath, more than shocked at her blunt words, she'd gathered her knitting stuff and was standing on the sidewalk, her bag over her shoulder.

"Anyway, Henry," she'd told me. "I *really* think you should stop smoking."

Then she turned back toward home, leaving me with an achingly hot view of her walking away.

So here she was sitting in my car, reminding me of that day she'd made a suggestion that sounded very much like an invitation to kiss her one day.

Swallowing hard, I confirmed what she knew. "I did quit."

For you.

Her smile returned tenfold, hitting me like a thunderbolt. "I'm so glad you did." Then she opened her door with her box of leftovers for Mrs. Ferriday.

And I followed. I would always follow.

CHAPTER 3

~HENRY~

I STARED AT THE COMPUTER SCREEN, MY MIND DRIFTING WHILE THE software updated on Ruben's office computer. Because of the sensitive information, both financial and personal, on his office database, he preferred that Gareth or I personally handle any software changes or updates. We were the ones who'd installed his hacker-proof firewall.

So here I was, the day after my first High Tea Book Club meeting, upgrading software and replaying every moment of yesterday on loop in my head. Since she'd shown up on my doorstep, demanding I join her club and eat her cupcakes, my obsession with Clara had dialed up to terrifying levels.

I couldn't stop thinking about her. This was nothing new, but usually it was mild, wistful daydreams. Now she was a fiery fantasy burning through my blood and my brain 24-7. I shifted my dick in my jeans, frustrated with my lack of control of even my own thoughts when it came to her.

Knock, knock.

Ruben's office door opened, and Sal poked his head in. "Hey. There's some lady up front, asking for you."

Frowning, I asked, "Who?"

He shrugged, his mouth tilting into a grin. "Don't know. But she's hot as fuck. I don't mind keeping her company if you don't want to."

Sal wasn't talking about Clara. Number one, he knew who she was and wouldn't call her *some lady*. And two, I'd knock his fucking teeth out for talking about her like that. But Sal was a chatterbox, and it was good to see him back to his normal self.

He and Roland arrived back from England not that long ago. They'd been with Ruben and Jules on their trip, having run into quite a bit of trouble over there. Sal had almost died and had spent a few months recovering before he and Roland returned. So I guess I should be glad he was back to normal, being himself again.

Still, I didn't know what lady would be looking for me, and I was a very private person.

"Where is she?"

"In the lounge in the bookstore. Waiting."

The bookstore had been closed while Ruben was gone to England, but he'd told Sal and Roland to open it back up for a few hours a day, at least, since he was delayed in returning to the US. Since Sal had recovered but still was told to take it easy, he'd taken on the job to manage it until Ruben could hire a new manager. He'd fired the old one, Beverly, before he left for England with Jules. Good riddance too. Beverly was a snake in the grass if I'd ever seen one.

I headed back down the hall from Ruben's office toward the bookstore with Sal following and stopped to look through the partially open office door. His lounge was an elegant space surrounded by shelves of classic and special edition books, forties-style music filling the space.

"Which one is she?" I whispered.

Sal caught that I didn't want to be seen. "That one," he said low.

He pointed to a tall, attractive Black woman, dressed in a sleek cream blouse and billowy sage-green pants. Her hair was cut short, styled straight, which accentuated her beautiful face.

"I don't know her," I told him. "Tell her I'm busy and see what she wants."

I stepped back into the shadows as Sal exited, leaving the door half open before walking across the lounge area. She stood near the wall where a local artist's colorful abstract work hung, observing it. Ruben often allowed artists he admired and whose work fit his decor to use his lounge as a sort of gallery to sell their works.

Though Sal spoke low from across the room, my supernatural hearing picked up the whole conversation.

"Sorry, ma'am. I thought he was in the offices, but he must've left already."

A frown pinched her lovely brow. "I see. Any idea when he'll be back?"

"Afraid not. Henry doesn't work regular hours for Ruben. Can I ask what this is regarding?"

"I'm a friend of his father's. I wanted to talk to him for a few minutes."

My father's? She was dressed too posh to be a personal assistant sent on an errand, though Peony dressed like a Parisian model most of the time. Grims typically preferred the armor of fine clothes and superior style to reflect the power within, especially my father, which was why I preferred jeans and old T-shirts.

"Could I leave him a note?" she asked Sal.

"Sure. Follow me to the cashier."

She walked with long, confident strides behind him. Sal slipped her a piece of stationery from the front desk and she took her time writing something, then folded and sealed it in an envelope, passing it to him. After she left, I stepped out of the office and met him at the cashier's desk.

He handed the letter over, and I opened it immediately. The script looped in a long, elegant scrawl.

Henry,

I'm a good friend of your father, Silas. I know that you two have been estranged for many years, but I'd like the chance to talk to you about him. About the man he is now. If you would please call me at the number below, we could set up a time convenient for you. I hope to receive your call.

Sincerely,
Beatrice Plath

"Bad news?" asked Sal.

I realized I was scowling down at the letter. A good friend of my father's? Since when did he befriend humans? When I was a child, he always seemed to think them beneath his notice.

"No," I finally answered. "It's nothing."

I stuffed the note in my back pocket, intending to throw it away at home. I didn't want Sal nosing through the trash to discover my private business.

"I'll check on that software update later. Will you lock up Ruben's office for me?"

"Of course," Sal answered as I left the bookstore and headed to my Mustang parked outside.

I wondered if my father had told her what kind of car I drove so she'd know if I was here. Why the hell was he sending women to track me down? To appeal to my softer side? Maybe he was smarter than I thought.

Driving home, I tried to figure out what angle my father was taking in sending his *good friend* to talk to me. For the past two years, after he'd started a monthly attempt to reach me, I'd been deleting his texts unopened and refusing to answer or return his calls.

I wasn't interested in his excuses for hand-delivering his oldest son to a monster in an attempt to train me as his personal necromancer. I would never have any interest in joining him at Obsidian Corporation, so I didn't know why he kept trying.

Surely, he'd put that woman Beatrice up to finding me. Why was he so desperate to mend our relationship now?

Sean.

I scoffed as I pulled into our driveway. Of course. He'd used his many spies at Obsidian Corp to watch us and had discovered that Sean was showing signs of latent magical abilities.

"Fuck."

Sean's car was in the driveway, which it shouldn't be. It was two o'clock in the afternoon. He should be at school.

I found him in the kitchen, stuffing a fast-food burger into his mouth.

"What are you doing home?" I snapped.

He continued chewing and muffled, "Mr. Pruitt let those of us who aced the semester go since they were reviewing for midterms." He sipped his coke. "I'm exempt from the midterm. What bug is up your ass?" He took another giant bite of his burger.

I sat on the stool next to him and faced him. "What about that Baylor kid? He giving you trouble?"

He scoffed, unperturbed. "Always. But I can handle it."

"Sean," I said in a sincere, concerned voice. "It's important that you not get entangled with him. You know why, right?"

"Yeah. You and Gareth have talked me to death about it."

"You don't seem concerned at all."

"What am I supposed to do exactly? I don't even know what the fuck is happening to me."

Sean's cavalier attitude was laced with an undertone of frustration and anger. I understood that feeling all too well. When I was a boy, I couldn't grab hold of and control my necromancy either. I didn't even want to have the so-called gift.

After the incident, I learned to block my magic altogether. Holding the shields up now was like muscle memory, except for the residual fatigue and depression. Sometimes, I'd fall into a gloomy state from the pressure of holding back my dark essence and the necromancy magic that longed to course freely through me. During these times, Gareth and Sean were always there for me. Just like I'd always be there for them.

"Gareth is going to teach you everything you need if and when it manifests," I assured my brother.

We all knew that it was truly only a matter of when. And that's what I was afraid of.

Most grims were simply techies with varying degrees of telekinesis and supernatural strength. I'd breathed a sigh of relief when Sean didn't manifest abilities as a necromancer. No ghosts showing up at his bedside at age five like me. But I'd never even thought he might have latent power, showing up now in his late teens. It happened sometimes, but it wasn't the norm.

"Anger will trigger it though, Sean. And not in a good way. I don't want you to hurt yourself or someone else."

Latent grimlocks were extremely unstable. Their dark power had been suppressed for some reason, unknown to any of us, and when it finally broke through, it could be terrifyingly dangerous. When it happened to Gareth, he'd murdered someone.

"I don't want what happened to Gareth to happen to you. And I sure as fuck don't want the GOA or our father to find a reason to take you away."

The Grim Office of Authority was basically the underground law enforcement for all grim criminals. Grims were allegedly subject to the High Coven of every region, but because we operated on our own terms outside the supernatural covens, we had our avenues and offices to handle our own problems. If it was a grim-only issue, then the GOA would handle it before a High Coven could get involved.

Sean sighed and wiped his mouth with a napkin. "I'm fine, okay? That asshole Baylor gets me pissed off on a daily basis, but I'm used to it. There's nothing he can say or do to me to make me lose my cool."

"Promise?"

"Promise."

I reached over and squeezed his shoulder. "I just worry about you."

"I know." He smiled. "You worry too much."

That was the fucking truth.

"What you need to do is go get laid." He grinned. "And I know a pretty blonde who delivers cupcakes who would happily oblige you."

I stood from the stool and smacked him on the back of the head. "Fucker. Go study."

"Don't need to. I'm so fucking smart I'm skipping all my midterms."

What an arrogant ass. Reminded me of our father.

My father.

I wandered back to my home office, wondering about the woman and what my father was up to, sending her to me. After pulling the letter from my pocket, I read it again as I walked over to my desk.

Who was this woman, and why was she working for my father?

Determined to put thoughts of him out of my mind, I shoved the letter in my desk drawer and heaved a sigh, wanting to return to the only object of my thoughts that brought me real, profound happiness.

Clara.

CHAPTER 4

~CLARA~

"No, sir! Give me that." I snatched my sandal from Diego as he shoved the heel into his mouth. "No chewing on shoes." His bottom lip quivered, so I scooped him up into my arms. "Don't cry. You'll break my heart. Violet!" I called, walking toward the kitchen.

You'd think I was talking about a pet puppy, not Evie and Mateo's oldest baby. Diego actually had an industrial-strength dog's chew toy as his teething ring. It happened to be shaped like a bone, which only made him look cuter as he gnawed on it. It already had tiny teeth marks all over it.

His triplet siblings Joaquin and Celine didn't have Diego's nonstop chew obsession or his powerful jaws apparently. Diego also happened to have little canine teeth that extended from time to time.

Evie had freaked out the first time she saw them, as did we all since we thought he was trying to shift or something. Werewolves didn't shift for the first time till puberty hit, and the triplets weren't even a year old.

Mateo had smiled proudly and said that some children whose wolves were extremely dominant showed themselves in ways like that long before they ever shifted for the first time. Apparently, Mateo was the same as a baby.

While Joaquin's eyes glowed gold sometimes, revealing his inner wolf, he was much more chill. He was the calmest of the three by far. Celine was excitable and loved to laugh. Diego was a Cat 5 hurricane. I was terrified of when he learned to walk, having visions of him tearing from room to room like that cartoon character the Tasmanian Devil.

"Where's Diego's chew toy?" I called out again.

"I put it in the freezer," said Vi, walking toward me with the cold rubber dog-bone. "He likes it cold. Here you go, little man."

Diego snatched it up with a giggle and shoved half of it into his mouth.

"Good goddess above," she scolded. "Don't choke, son."

"Aww, now he's happy." I ruffled his dark curls and carried him back into the living room with Violet following me. "Is it time for their bottles?"

"Not yet. Evie said they'd likely be back from the grocery before the next feeding."

Celine was asleep on a blanket on the floor, her chubby legs bent and her little booty sticking up. She had a binky with baby Yoda's face on it in her mouth, her strawberry-blonde curls partly covering her face. Z—our nickname for our elderly black cat named Zombie Cat—was curled up beside her, purring contentedly.

Joaquin was sitting up with one of those baby sensory boards in front of him. He stared intensely at the cogs and wheels that fit together, like he was processing their purpose and how they worked. He probably was. That little one was super smart.

Joaquin was special. While Diego's aura was a deep blue and Celine's was a reddish-orange, both beautiful and vibrant like the souls who inhabited them, Joaquin's was unique. His was gold at the center and green on the outside.

That happened sometimes when people's moods changed suddenly or they were feeling so many emotions at once that their aura reflected the variance. But for Joaquin, his aura remained a dual magical shell. Glittering and bright. Calm and lovely.

I suspected, but hadn't yet mentioned it to anyone, that Joaquin wasn't only a werewolf. I'd bet anything that we'd see some warlock abilities develop at some point in the next year.

"How was the book club the other day?" asked my sister with heavy snark before she plopped on the sofa and planted her bare foot close to Joaquin.

He glanced down, patted Violet's foot as if reassuring her he was fine, and then went back to staring at a block puzzle he'd already figured out.

"If you're referring to my first club meeting with Henry, it was amazing."

I sat down on the floor with Diego between my legs. We had to watch him carefully because even with a rubber chew toy that was considered unbreakable, he still tended to break off tiny pieces, which were a choking hazard.

"Uh-huh. And where did you two sneak off together afterward? Did you finally get to maul your grim?"

"Vi." I arched a brow at her. "I think it's best we take it slowly."

"Slowly? You've been obsessed with him for like a year, and I think he's been stalking you for way longer than that."

"It's not stalking if it's mutual, Vi." I played with Diego's long dark curls. "Stop making it sound so negative."

"I didn't mean to. I'm just saying you need to take this relationship to the next level."

"He's become a member of High Tea Book Club as I wanted. That's step one."

"What's step two?" She wiggled her toes at Joaquin, which distracted him for about three seconds before he went back to contemplating the puzzle.

"None of your business."

"Oh, ho! Now you have to tell me. This sounds juicy."

It was. Quite juicy on my part, but I wasn't telling her or anyone. And I needed to find another way into his house without barging in. Showing up on his doorstep once without being asked was fine, but doing it a second time looked desperate. I wasn't desperate. Not yet.

For some reason, Henry wasn't sure if I liked him or not. So my plan was to be extremely obvious, giving him plenty of doors to walk through without actually throwing myself at him. He certainly got the hint the other day when I'd told him I was glad he'd stopped smoking.

"What is that look for?" asked Violet.

"Again. None of your beeswax."

"Fine, fine. Don't tell the one person in the world you should never keep secrets from. I'm just glad you're getting this ball rolling finally. The rest of us are tired of watching y'all stare at each other with heart-eyes all the damn time."

I gasped. "He stares at me that way?"

She snorted and rolled her eyes. "You two are truly clueless, aren't you?"

My phone buzzed on the sofa, preventing me from further comment. Reaching over without disturbing Diego, I picked up the phone.

"Oh no," said Violet. Her face was stricken as she stared at my phone.

"What is it?" I asked, noting Miriam Ferriday's name on the screen.

Violet extended her hand, expression soft and sad. "Let me answer it for you."

I clicked the button to answer. "Hello?" I was already shaking because I already knew. My sister's psychic abilities had told me before I heard the person's voice on the other end.

"Hello, Clara." It was Miriam's niece, Rachel, who'd been staying with her while she'd been ill.

Closing my eyes to stem the tears already welling there, I asked, "Yes?"

"Aunt Miriam's gone. She passed quietly in the night. I wanted to reach out and tell you." Rachel's voice was hoarse, likely from crying. "I don't have the arrangements yet as I wasn't . . . I didn't expect this to happen."

"I'm so sorry," I said, pushing a comforting spell outward but knowing it wouldn't reach through the phone even as I pressed a hand to my chest. "I'm so sorry, Rachel."

"Thank you." She sniffed. "If you could tell the other ladies, I'd appreciate it. I can't—I just can't."

"It's fine. I'll take care of that. I'll tell them."

But it wasn't fine. My heart splintered at the thought that I'd never see sweet Mrs. Ferriday with her bold scarves and her perky personality again. I'd never hear her sweet laugh or feel her warm hugs again.

"Thank you," Rachel said quietly.

She hung up. My hand dropped into my lap. Violet was suddenly there, kneeling on the floor and pulling me into a hug. "I'm sorry, Clara. I know you loved her so much."

"I just saw her two days ago."

I'd heard people say something similar whenever they lost someone. Like they couldn't believe they'd seen them so recently, yet somehow, they were simply no longer with us. Perhaps if we spoke our disbelief to the universe, we'd be told it wasn't real and our loved one was still on the earth, not gone, having disappeared into the beyond.

"I know." Violet hugged me tighter.

I clenched my fists in her shirt and cried. "I can't believe it."

"Shh." She rocked me gently. "I know it hurts." I couldn't do anything but sob into her shoulder, remembering my last visit with her.

She was paler than normal. The recent kidney infection from her lifelong diabetes that she'd struggled to manage made her face puffy. But she smiled when she saw Henry waiting quietly in the hallway. She patted my hand, her fingers bonier than they'd been two weeks before, and then whispered, "It's about time."

Mrs. Ferriday had known about my deep infatuation for Henry. She was the only one of the club I'd confided in. Though sick, she seemed happier and in better spirits this week. She'd even donned one of her silky green scarves, knowing I'd stop by with the leftovers from the book club.

I sucked in a breath. "She said she'd see me next week."

"I'm so sorry, sis. I wish I was you and could give you one of those spells you always give us."

Violet continued to shush me and hold me, but the sorrow only increased, and my heart kept on breaking.

CHAPTER 5

~HENRY~

I'D LEFT THE HOUSE THREE SECONDS AFTER I'D HUNG UP WITH VIOLET, after she'd told me about Mrs. Ferriday and Clara's current state.

She needs you.

Those words slashed like daggers through flesh and bone. I barely took a moment to wonder why she needed *me*, how I could possibly help. The only words that meant anything to motivate my current high-speed trace across town during daylight were the ones *she—needs—you.*

Clara was hurting, and she needed me. That's all that mattered.

Supernaturals were forbidden from using magic in the presence of humans to keep from exposing ourselves, but I knew that no one could see me at this rate of speed. They wouldn't even see the blur as I passed, only feel the sudden breeze that whooshed by. And I didn't give a shit if some supernatural snitch caught me. I sure as hell wasn't taking the turtle-slow route of driving my car when Clara was in pain.

I hit a rainstorm a few blocks from the Savoies, but it didn't stop me from appearing suddenly in the Savoie's driveway. I stared up at the landing of Clara's carriage house apartment above their garage. The rain was steady, soaking me through my jeans and T-shirt.

Without waiting, I rushed up the staircase and knocked. There was no answer.

"Go on in."

Snapping my head around, I found Violet standing at the bottom in a white raincoat.

"Isadora tried to spell her, but nothing seems to be helping. She wanted to be left alone, but I know she'd want to see you."

What did I say to that? I'd never even properly met Violet. And here she was telling me that Clara was inconsolable, but somehow *I* could help.

"How do you know that?" Rain dripped from the tips of my hair and down my face, the air charged with something that lit my skin with buzzing electricity.

Violet snorted and tilted her head. With an arrogant lilt to her voice, she said, "I'm a psychic, grim. And I know my sister." She flicked her hand. "Go on in. The door's open."

Again, without thinking but moving on instinct, that deeper need to soothe Clara's pain urged me past my hesitation about overstepping. I opened the door and immediately heard her soft crying. Her pain felt like a scythe gutting me up the middle.

My sweet Clara in distress, in turmoil. It was beyond any pain I'd felt before . . . well, almost any.

"Clara?" I called into the small, candlelit living room of the apartment.

A lump of pink moved on the sofa, and Clara's beautiful face flushed with tears and sadness appeared out of a fluffy cloud of pillows and blankets on the sofa.

"Henry?" She sounded shocked, which was better than the heartache I'd heard in her crying as I came in.

"Yes." I grabbed a kitchen towel on the counter of the small kitchenette and quickly wiped my face, hair, and hands, then tossed it back on the counter.

She sat up, pushing out of the covers. I bit back a groan at her in a tiny satin set of pink pajama shorts and tank.

"Why are you here?" she asked, standing and—thankfully— wrapping the pink blanket around her body.

"I came to—"

What did I come to do? I didn't think about it. I'd simply run out my door like a maniac and raced in grim reaper speed—which happens to be as fast as and sometimes faster than vampires—to her aid. But what was it I could actually do?

Offer her condolences? False platitudes?

You could offer her more, the darkness whispered.

"She's dead, Henry."

"I know."

Then she was in my arms, her pink softness drowning me in ecstasy.

"I'm wet from the rain. I'm sorry," I protested weakly.

"I don't care. Please hold me."

For fuck's sake. Hold her? I'd burn the world for her.

Wrapping one arm around her waist, I held her close while coasting a hand up and down her back. She cried harder.

Thunder crashed, lightning split the sky, and the rain poured heavier. The darkness that lived deep inside me, behind a door that had apparently cracked open, hummed in appreciation of the violent storm. And not because my monster was a pluviophile, but because this wasn't a natural storm. He liked it, almost like it was made for him.

Lightning streaked again, a purple-pink flash out the windows, coinciding with Clara's next sob on my shoulder. The dawning realization of what was happening struck me dumb.

Grims knew everything. Or we liked to think that we did. But I'd never heard of this before.

"I'm so sorry," she finally said between a hiccup as she pulled away and shuffled back to the sofa before sinking down. "I shouldn't cry all over you."

"I don't mind."

She could do anything to me. I would never mind.

Again, I was struck senseless because I realized she'd basically attacked me with her embrace, and yet I felt no panic or fear. None at all. If anything, it soothed me even more to have her so close.

What a strange and remarkable sensation. To feel what I'd longed for after so many years.

"Please sit down." She pulled a Kleenex from the box and wiped her eyes and nose, then gave a little laugh. "I must look such a mess."

I wasn't going to sit on her sofa and get it soaking wet. Instead, I knelt in front of her on the floor, trying to come up with something to say that didn't sound frightening or obsessive. So I couldn't say anything about her appearance. She didn't look a mess. She looked like a fucking goddess, like a dream in pink satin with long blonde waves caressing her shoulders, breasts, and hips.

Hell, she was an angel born solely to torment me. And I was the demon who craved nothing more than to mark her with sin.

Dragging myself from my own depraved thoughts, I thought about the best course to get her mind off Mrs. Ferriday. She'd obviously been absorbed in grief too long, and I understood the damage self-indulgent melancholy could do to someone.

"Clara." I planted my hands on my thighs, sitting back on my heels. "Did you know you could change the weather with your moods?"

She glanced outside, the rain subsiding again as her tears stopped falling. "Yes."

"Do all Auras do this?" ·

"No." Her brow wrinkled in concentration. "Jules said there was an Aura in our family, a great-great-aunt who had the ability. It's rare." She shrugged a shoulder. "But I never saw much good in having it."

I huffed a short laugh. "It's extraordinary."

You're extraordinary.

"Do you think so?" One side of her mouth lifted, the closest she'd come to a smile since I barged into her apartment.

"Yes." I held her gaze. "Weather is powerful."

She smiled wider, and my heart lurched, beating harder against my rib cage. "Maybe so. But rain and sunshine doesn't do much in the magic world. It's just a symptom of my magic."

"That's untrue. It's a fact that weather can affect people's moods, can even cause depression when it's dark and rainy for too long."

"Hmm." She tucked a long stand of hair behind her ear. "I suppose it would be helpful if I could actually summon the weather, change it at will. But it's never been more than an aftereffect of when I'm particularly moody one way or another."

"Have you ever tried to summon the weather?" I asked.

"No." She stared down at her lap where she was picking apart the fresh Kleenex she'd pulled from the box. "Seemed no reason to try."

"If you keep crying, you could flood the streets of the Garden District soon enough."

New Orleans was built in a bowl, most of the city below sea level.

"You're right." She nodded, biting her lip as a fresh wave of grief seemed to overwhelm her. I'd reminded her why she was crying in the first place. Another tear slipped.

Unable to control myself, I shifted up onto my knees, eye-level with her on the sofa. I reached up, heart hammering, and touched my fingertips to her cheek and jaw, then wiped the tear with my thumb.

"Please stop crying, Clara."

Her eyes—glassy and wide and glacier-blue—sent an electric current straight through me, igniting every atom in my body. Flames lit me up from the inside.

Brushing my thumb over the apple of her cheek again, I whispered, "Let's not rain on the neighborhood all night. It could cause flooding and trouble."

"Okay."

"So you'll stop crying for me?"

Why I thought she'd do anything because I asked it, I have no idea, but she lifted her small hand and pressed it to the back of mine on her cheek. "Of course, Henry. I'll do whatever you ask."

The energy heating my blood and urging me to lean forward and finally cross that invisible line to kiss her was overwhelming. Crushing.

Kiss her. The sibilant whisper from the depths of the dark called to my greatest desire. For once, I wanted to listen to him.

For a moment, I felt my body swaying closer, intent on her parted lips, the flush of her heart-shaped face, the wisps of golden hair haloing her cheeks, her vulnerable sweetness tempting me to taste her at last.

With a rigid snap, I removed my hand and stood, then walked to the window, the thunder having rolled away, the rain a slight drizzle. Because I'd asked her to stop it.

She was grieving for her lost friend, for fuck's sake. I might be the devil incarnate sometimes, but I wasn't about to take advantage of her while she was mourning Mrs. Ferriday. If—*when*—I kissed Clara, there would be no grief or regret involved. And there would be no going back from that.

The rolling clouds reflected my constant melancholic mood. I wondered what it would be like to live in the sunshine of Clara's world.

"I'm very sorry about your friend, Clara."

"Thank you," she said softly. I heard her shift, moving the blanket back around her shoulders. "But there's nothing you can do."

Yes, there is, said the darkness.

No. I couldn't fucking do that.

You did it for Gareth.

And it had nearly put me in a coma.

"I have to go," I said suddenly and marched for the door.

"Henry?" She stopped me as I opened it.

When I looked back, grateful there were no more tears, her cheeks flushed rose but dry. "Will you come to the funeral with me? I know you didn't know her, but it would help me." As she swallowed, I watched her slender throat work with emotion. "It would help me," she said again softly, "if you were there."

"Then I'll be there."

I'd always be there.

"Good night, Clara. Get some rest."

My reward was one of her soft, sweet smiles, the kind that made me want to conquer the world for her, to be everything she would ever need.

As I headed back home at a leisurely pace, the clouds rolled farther away, revealing a sliver of stars and a clear night sky.

CHAPTER 6

~HENRY~

SLATE-GRAY CLOUDS HOVERED LOW, BUT NO RAIN FELL AS THE PRIEST said the final words at the graveside of Miriam Ferriday. The aboveground tombs and headstones decorated with winged angels surrounding her grave seemed like protectors and guardians of all the dead here. My gaze wandered to the sculpture of a weeping angel draped over a nearby grave.

Glancing around, I expected to see a wandering spirit peeking in on the new tenant. But no ghosts appeared. There was no pressure pushing on my shield holding back my own necromancy, which I felt at times when I was near the recently deceased. Only the living here today, mourning in the graveyard.

I stood behind Clara, her sister Violet on one side and Isadora on the other. Livvy and Gareth stood next to Nico with Devraj on Isadora's other side. The only Savoies missing were Mateo and Evie because they had to watch the children. And Jules, who was still in London with Ruben.

Clara's parents had gone to London as well to meet Ruben's parents and help with Jules's recovery, though from what Gareth had said, it was more that their mother needed to see her eldest daughter and be sure she was truly well after what had happened to her in Northumberland last November. They'd return to Switzerland from there.

Devraj was in charge of any Coven business while they were still away, which wouldn't be much longer, I understood. If he should need Enforcer-strength assistance, Gareth was on call as well. Since the secret was out that my cousin could best any supernatural on the planet, Jules and Ruben didn't feel so bad about lingering in England a while longer.

The ladies of the High Tea Book Club each stepped forward to place a rose on the casket after Miriam's niece Rachel placed her own. Clara followed behind them and set a crocheted rose on top of the others. I could imagine her knitting it on her sofa in those pink satin pajamas.

The crowd broke up and meandered back to their cars. Gareth gave me a pointed look and a nod before walking Livvy back to his car. Violet and Nico guided Clara back to their SUV, but then Clara stopped and looked around. She found me. The expression on her face instantly changed from sadness to relief and something sweeter that put a soft smile on her pretty face. Because of me?

I gulped hard at the heady sensation that I could do that to her.

Then she waved me over. I didn't hesitate, my feet moving toward her instantly.

"Thank you for coming." She put her hand on the sleeve of my black dress shirt.

"Of course." I got lost for a second, taking her in.

Her hair had been braided in one of those complicated styles, the tail draping over one shoulder. She looked odd in a black dress, her skin pale against the fabric. She never wore dark colors. She wore no makeup, probably because she'd expected to cry a lot, but her cheeks were dry. Her eyes sparkled with emotion, yet no tears.

She looked small and fragile, and I found myself wondering when she'd eaten last. I hadn't seen her since I'd shown up at her apartment four days ago, and it looked like she'd dropped weight. Too much of it.

"Are you eating?" I blurted out.

"What?" She blinked in confusion.

"Food, Clara." I recognized the anger leaking into my voice, but I couldn't control it. "Are you eating? Because it doesn't look like you are."

Other cars drove away from the gravesite. Violet and Nico were in the front seat of the SUV, waiting on Clara. I ignored Nico's warning glare through the driver's side window since he could obviously hear me speaking roughly to Clara.

"I haven't felt like it."

"You need to eat." I stepped closer and gripped her elbow, giving her a gentle squeeze.

"That's what my sisters keep saying. I—"

"They're right."

"It's not that easy."

"Clara." I squeezed her elbow again. "*Please.*"

I wasn't sure what she saw in my eyes at the moment—most likely the maniacal, desperate plea to feed her body so I didn't stay awake at night wondering if she was unintentionally self-harming by starving herself. The agony was likely clear and apparent. Her gaze softened as if in understanding.

"Okay, Henry. Don't worry."

Don't worry? There was a 100 percent chance I'd obsess over this for the next week. I'd likely drive by her house and peek through windows, possibly seek Gareth's help with some sort of spying equipment, just to make sure she was actually taking care of herself.

"It's just . . ." She heaved a sigh, looking off toward the grave. "I know she's gone, but I didn't really get to say goodbye. To tell her how much she meant to me." She lifted her gaze to mine. "Did you know I first met her in Queen of Tarts? We were both buying the blueberry scones. She had a worn copy of *The Viscount Who Loved Me* sticking out of her purse. So we struck up a conversation, and she told me I should start a book club. She'd be my first member. It was all her idea." Her eyes shimmered with the joyful memory. "I never thanked her for that. Not properly."

You could help her, whispered the darkness.

A flash of screams hit me hard, and I gasped for air. I was smothering. Squeezing my eyes shut, I pushed away the memory.

Yes, I could help her. If I could face my nightmares, but by then, it would likely be too late.

"She knew," I told her. "I'm sure she knew."

Clara nodded, her gaze falling to where I still had a grip on her arm.

I dropped my hand and stepped back. "Promise me you'll eat, that you'll take care of yourself."

She smiled. "I promise. We're having a small reception at the Cauldron. Are you coming?"

I shook my head. "I think that's for your family and close friends."

She opened her mouth to say something else, but I quickly opened the door to the back seat and urged her forward. Once I shut the door, I watched them go before I made my way back home.

I muttered to myself the whole way, knowing there was a possibility I could put Clara at ease, and yet I hadn't done a fucking thing about it.

Slamming the door, I entered the back door from the garage into the kitchen. I unbuttoned the cuffs of my black shirt and rolled up my sleeves as I rounded the island to the Nespresso machine.

"If you weren't such a fucking coward, you'd have offered right then and there." I put a pod of dark roast in the Nespresso and plopped a mug under the brew spout.

"Goddamn coward," I mumbled to myself, punching the start button. I pulled out the creamer and poured a little in the frother, then pressed the button, which whirred it creamy.

"It's likely too late," I told myself, knowing Miriam Ferriday wasn't in distress when she died. "She was perfectly at peace. She won't be there."

I poured the whipped creamer into my coffee and gave it a stir, staring out the kitchen window at the giant oak tree, its branches sprouting with green finger-leaf ferns.

"I'm sure of it. Far too late." I sipped the coffee.

"Did you get into my weed or something?"

I nearly spit out the coffee as I whirled around to find Sean standing there. "What the hell are you doing home?"

"Dude. It's three-thirty."

I checked my watch. So it was. Time had vanished today somehow.

"You okay, man?" Sean asked as he rummaged in the pantry.

"Fine. Everything good at school?"

He scoffed. "Nothing is ever good at school, but no, I didn't break anyone's bones today."

"Good."

"I wanted to," he said with a callous grin, "but I showed quite a bit of restraint."

"Stay away from that asshole, Baylor."

He rolled his eyes and took a bag of Doritos with him toward the living room. I downed my coffee and turned back toward the window, knowing full well what I was going to have to do. My concern for Clara overrode any of my own fears. I'd have to man up for her.

Motherfucker.

Finally giving in, I went upstairs and changed out of the stiff funeral clothes into my jeans and hoodie. Then I watched the clock, waiting till I figured the reception would be over. Finally, I headed out toward the Savoie house.

CHAPTER 7

~CLARA~

I THOUGHT I'D DONE A GOOD JOB OF HIDING MYSELF FROM EVERYONE, specifically Violet. She meant well, but I wanted to be alone at the moment. This wasn't like me. Typically, surrounding myself with my sisters would've been the perfect balm to this pain that wasn't going away.

And yes, I knew it was unhealthy to wallow in grief. I didn't think I was wallowing, but I also knew that I wasn't well. I'd never lost someone so close to me before. No one could prepare you for the gutting loss and surrealism of it. One day, you're bringing baked goods and talking about hot Highlanders who saved their lady, then suddenly she's no longer on this earth and you realize you'll never talk to her again.

The fact that she was elderly and had "lived a good life" as the priest had said at the service didn't make it any better. Nothing did.

My family meant well with all the hovering, but it was getting annoying. Hence, the reason I'd hidden in our secret garden where we did our witch's rounds on the new moon. I tried to stem my aggravation when I heard someone walking closer to the ivy-covered gate. It wasn't fair of me to be angry because they loved me.

I almost blew out the candle I held in my lap to hide, but it wasn't like that would make me invisible. So I braced for more it's-gonna-be-okay sentiments and watched the gate.

When it opened and Henry stepped through, the air completely left my lungs. The instant relief and joy I felt at seeing him hit me hard and true. I wondered if that's what it felt like when Eros shot a love-arrow at someone.

"Henry?"

Those dark eyes met mine, shimmering warmly by the candlelight. He glanced around the garden, then closed the gate.

"I hope you don't mind me disturbing you."

"Mind? I'm so glad you're here." I couldn't help the nervous but happy laugh that bubbled up out of me. "Please. Sit down." I gestured next to me where I sat outside the witch's circle as if this was the most normal place in the world to be and have a chat.

The chalked circle had faded from the recent rain, the rain I'd apparently caused. Funny that I never noticed when that happened. Probably because I was rarely upset, and people didn't tend to remark that it was strange when it was always sunny in our neighborhood. I'd managed to subdue my emotions enough that it was mostly clear tonight, just a few billowy clouds crossing the moon.

Henry walked around the circle and sat on the pavement next to me, extending his legs outward and crossing them at the ankles.

"I won't get hexed or something for planting my legs in your circle, will I?"

"No." I laughed. "It's just habit for me to sit outside of it."

He nodded, tipping his head up to the night sky. The pale moonlight gilded his sharp features in white, caressing all the beautiful edges of his face, the curve of his masculine throat. I could sit and stare at him all night.

"You were looking for me." I stated the obvious. Still, I thought it worthy to say aloud since it was more evidence that Henry cared for me. I'd continue to remind him and myself until he did something about it. Or I couldn't wait any longer and attacked him.

"Yes." His rough voice was lovelier in the dark. It rolled over my skin, raising gooseflesh as it went.

Then he said nothing. Neither did I. I was perfectly content to sit in silence with him until he was ready to explain why he'd come to me now. The candle flame flickered with the passing wind, and he turned his head to look at me.

I hadn't stopped staring since he'd walked in, shamelessly devouring the delicious sight of him.

"I can help you," he stated with hard surety, his black eyes piercing.

The statement and his intense expression seemed to be telling me something monumental. Unfortunately, I didn't know what he was talking about.

"Sorry, but with what exactly?"

His broad chest gusted out a heavy breath. "Your grief. Because you didn't say goodbye."

The realization hit me like a slap to the head. Why hadn't I thought of it sooner?

"You're a necromancer." I stated the obvious again. "I can't believe I didn't think of it. You can bring Mrs. Ferriday back?"

After Henry opened a portal into the netherworld during the trial of Richard Davis, the man who'd attacked my sister Livvy and who'd apparently murdered several young women, I'd pestered Gareth about necromancers every chance I got.

Grims can't help but be secretive. It's in their genes or something, some kind of grim reaper code to keep all information and give none. But Gareth was deeply in love with my sister, and I used it to my advantage. I might seem all sweet and cute on the outside, but I could be manipulative to get what I wanted when I needed to.

What I learned about necromancers wasn't a whole lot, but enough. It was a designation of grim reaper that was rare, but not as rare as grimlocks, which is what Gareth is. That's another story in itself. But he did tell me this.

Necromancers were born when an evil warlock centuries ago cast a blood spell to summon the dead using his vampire wife's child's blood and life to cast·the rite. Unfortunately, when the vampiress came upon the warlock carving witch sign with blood on his sacrificial altar, she attacked and killed him while the hex swirled to fruition. She drank his blood and ingested his dark magic all while an army of dead ghosts was being brought back from the netherworld. Unknowingly, she fed that foul blood to her unborn child. The first grim reaper was born a few months later.

Since then, there have been a special kind of necromancer who can summon the dead at will. Henry is one of these. But according to Gareth, he rejected his gift for reasons he wouldn't tell anyone. However, he did do it for Gareth, for my sister Livvy.

Henry had been staring intently at me as if fighting some demon I couldn't see. Perhaps he was. The trace of fear I caught in his expression dimmed my smile.

"Wait," I said. "Would it hurt you to bring her back?"

For a few seconds, he still didn't answer, then, "I'm not positive I can bring her back. It depends."

"On what?"

"Where she is."

"Sorry?"

He had his knees up now, arms locked around them, one hand holding the wrist of the other arm. He lifted his face back up to the moon. "The netherworld is a layered, complicated place."

I turned my body to face him, my legs crossed, one knee now pressing into his hip. He glanced down at my knee, but I didn't move an inch. He needed to get used to me touching him.

"How so?" I asked.

Those dark eyes were back on me, blacker than they'd seemed a moment ago.

"There's a mid-space where some souls choose to congregate. We call it the Gray Vale."

"The souls choose?"

He dipped his chin once. "The Gray Vale is vast. Some souls are drawn to each other there. Evil ones gravitate together. Good ones the same. Sometimes, souls wander alone, usually those who don't know that they're dead. Some who were wronged, murdered, tend to linger there for a long time before they can move on."

"Why do they gather there? In this place, the Gray Vale." This was fascinating.

"They're waiting for something."

"Like what?"

"Could be anything. The Vale is shallow enough that they can sometimes see into the real world, watch loved ones, even send a message."

"Like when a butterfly lands on you, they say a loved one is trying to send you a message."

His gaze intensified, his mouth slightly parted like he was shocked.

"Did I say something?"

He blinked heavily. "No. Just the reference, it—never mind. But yes, messages can come in various ways from souls in the Vale. But most souls, the ones with nothing left to stick around for, who are ready to say goodbye to this world, they keep going. They move on."

"To where?"

"Whatever is beyond."

"Like heaven or hell?"

"If you believe in that. I don't know what's beyond. Souls don't come back when they leave the Vale."

I finally understood what he was telling me. "So you think Mrs. Ferriday may have moved on to the beyond."

"Yes." He clamped his jaw tightly.

"You didn't answer my question. Will it hurt you to try to summon her?"

His gaze roved my face. "I'll do it for you."

Suddenly angry, I stood up. "No. You won't."

He was up at my side, wrapping his hand around my forearm. "Yes. Let me. Please, Clara."

"How does it hurt you?"

That panicky look was back, but he didn't answer me.

"Does it hurt all necromancers?" I pushed.

"No."

"Why does it hurt you then?"

"It's a little complicated. And embarrassing."

"How can your own personal pain be embarrassing, Henry? We feel what we feel. Your pain, no matter where it comes from or how intense it may be, is valid. And I won't ignore that simply because you're willing to—to what? Help me get over my grief?" I snorted, sounding more like Violet. "It's ridiculous. I'm fine."

"Clara." He had gripped both my forearms, the candlelight dancing on his face, carving grave lines of stark beauty. "You don't understand. I *need* to help you. If I can."

I was right! He did care for me.

"Please let me try," he pleaded. "It doesn't hurt if I don't have to go in."

"Go in where? The netherworld?" My voice raised to a shrieky level.

"Yes. But chances are if she's still there in the Vale, she won't be far. She'll hear me."

I had *so* many questions. How can ghosts hear him? What happens to him when he goes into the netherworld? Why does it hurt? How does it hurt? Who hurt him, and can I hurt them back?

"Okay," I agreed softly. Loving the feel of his hands wrapped around my arms, the pads of his fingers sliding on my bare skin. I didn't want to move from this spot. Ever. Finally, I asked, "What do I need to do?"

The sudden relaxation of his features told me enough. He needed to do this for me. If I let him, that would bring him one step closer to being my boyfriend.

"Nothing," he said softly. "Simply stand right over here." He backed me up behind him to the farthest edge of the ivy-covered fence.

I stood still and watched and waited. He turned his back to me, planting his feet square, his body going rigid. Then I felt it, that familiar sensation I'd sensed in the courtroom—undeniable power and body-shaking energy trembling in the air.

In the courtroom that day, there had been a sudden, gasping punch of power when Henry opened his arms and unlocked a portal into the netherworld. Tonight, he moved his arms slowly up from his sides. The wind stirred in the trees.

Palms up, he continued raising his arms, chanting soft words, a grim spell, the electric energy amplifying in the small garden.

I sucked in a breath of air as darkness shrouded us in a shell, blocking out the moon, the sky, the trees, the garden itself. There was only me and Henry cloaked in dark mist. He stood facing away, slowly opening the roundish door in the ether.

A pale blue light shimmered as the portal emerged and widened in front of him. Again, it was slightly different than the one I'd seen him open before. I could only describe it in emotions since that's how I experienced the world. Rather than hopelessness, fear, and gutting sorrow, I felt a softness, a lightness, like that feeling when you notice the spring flowers have started to bloom.

Henry's whispered words were inaudible, but I felt them, or I felt *him*, igniting me with his magical fire. I bit my lip to keep from making a sound. Then I couldn't help but gasp when his black, smoky wings sprouted from his back and opened wide. Sable and ethereal, they were magnificent, shimmering with magic. He was a dark angel, a necromancer in full control of his power.

"Miriam Ferriday," his voice bellowed loudly, echoing with an otherworldly eeriness.

Rather than frighten me, it only called me closer, attracted me more. What was it about Henry's necromancy magic that lured me in?

My attention shifted from him to movement inside the portal. I couldn't see because Henry was almost fully blocking me— protecting me, I realized. Then he stepped aside, and my dear friend, Miriam Ferriday, stepped from the portal, complete with her favorite green scarf tied around her neck and wearing her favorite pumpkin-orange dress. She'd worn it to Thanksgiving dinner last year.

"Miriam."

"There you are, sweetheart." She opened her arms, and I ran into them.

Strangely, her body felt corporeal even while it was slightly transparent. Her aura was no longer yellow the way it was in life, but pure white.

"I'm sorry I called you, but I needed to see you."

"I was getting a good look around, Clara. No need to apologize."

I pulled back, still half-hugging her. "What does it look like in there?" I whispered.

She shrugged, her eyes glittering unnaturally. "Depends where you go. But I prefer the waterfall area."

"There are waterfalls?" I asked excitedly.

"I think there are waterfalls only for some of us. Different things for different people. I'd been sitting there under an elm tree watching the falls and thinking about my life for quite a while. Not sure how long exactly. I was getting ready to leave when your young man called me."

I didn't look behind me, sensing Henry close, his halo of power cocooning us while the Vale gaped wide. When I peered inside, I saw nothing at all but mist. I had a feeling that's not what Miriam saw.

"Listen," I said seriously, taking her hands, "I'm sorry I never told you, but I appreciated your friendship so much. I love you dearly. Thank you for being in my book club, for being my friend. I wish I'd told you more often."

"Hush now, sweetie." She patted my cheeks with translucent, cool fingers. "I know all of that. I always have."

"I wish I'd known how sick you were." A tear slipped free. "I would've visited you more."

"No need. Don't waste another tear on me, dear. I had a lovely, wonderful life. Now, you go on and live yours." She peeked over my shoulder, then winked at me. "Looks like he'd do the trick in making that happen."

She kissed me on the cheek, which felt like a snowflake touching my face, then she backed away and looked over my shoulder.

"May I go now, grim?"

"You may rest, Miriam Ferriday." Henry's otherworldly voice vibrated in our dark, vaporous shell.

"Farewell." She smiled at him, then me, and then stepped through the gossamer veil and vanished.

Henry muttered words in a language I didn't know. The raven-like wings of black smoke opened wide, then closed as his hands did, palm to palm, fading and disappearing like the portal door into the Gray Vale.

Black veins spread across his face like a spiderweb extending from his full ebony eyes, no whites showing at all. He closed them when the portal was gone, and the world came back into reality— the garden, the wind in the trees, the stars in the night, the bright moon overhead. He lowered his head, shoulders slumped.

"Oh no." I ran the three steps between us and wrapped my arms around him. "Please, Henry, don't tell me you're in pain."

I pushed a giant joy spell outward from my well of magic. It sparked to life the second I touched him, flowing from me to him like a rainstorm bursting free from the clouds.

Hesitantly, his arms came around me, and I smiled, my cheek pressed to his chest. His heart thumped strong and fast beneath my ear.

"I'd say I'm sorry I keep throwing myself into your arms, but I'm not sorry."

His arms held me tighter, drawing me into his warmth. His mouth was at my temple when he whispered, "You can throw yourself into my arms any time you want, Clara."

Laughing, I tilted my head up. "Any time?"

Our faces were much closer than I expected, the laughter dying out of me, replaced by sharp need. The serpentine veins were slowly retracting, but his eyes were still full black.

"You look like a creature from another world."

"A monster."

"Never." My voice was a hoarse whisper, my gaze falling to his lips then rising back to those eerie yet hypnotic eyes. "More like a dark king of the underworld."

His expression was so hard, so unyielding. His arms held me close, our bodies fully aligned. Desire pooled between my legs, and I was certain I had awoken his. The bulge pressing against my abdomen told me loud and clear I was certainly not alone in these feelings.

"Perhaps a dark prince," I amended. "My own prince charming who came to my rescue."

He arched a brow, his face turning adamant. Anyone else would be frightened by such a fearsome expression by a grim vibrating with potent power, his fathomless black eyes still reflecting his gaze into the netherworld. But I wasn't. I wanted to drown in his dark beauty.

"I'm no Prince Charming." He clamped his jaw as if trying not to say something, but he did anyway, his face dropping an inch closer to mine. "But if your Prince Charming ever did come, Clara, I'd have to fucking kill him."

My heart was in my throat, his possessive need simmering in every word, every syllable from his raspy voice. I was completely caught and ready for our first kiss.

The gate creaked. "Oh! So sorry."

I jumped back and spun, finding Isadora in the entrance, looking truly remorseful. "I thought you were alone," she said to me with regret.

It wasn't a secret to any of my family that I was on a mission. And I had been literally seconds away from completing Operation Kiss Henry.

"I should go anyway," he said to my complete disappointment.

When I thought he'd take a wide berth around me and speed out of the gate, he didn't. He moved in front of me, his back to Isadora. Cupping my cheeks with both hands, he tilted my face up, making me look at him. Which was no chore. Trust me.

"Better?" His eyes were almost back to normal.

"So much better. I can't thank you enough."

Then he gave me one of his soft smiles that I knew he gave to no one ever. Or hardly anyone.

"That's all the thanks I need." He brushed his thumb along the crest of my cheek. "Good night."

He quickly left and disappeared from the garden and through the courtyard. I glared at Isadora.

She gave me a pained look. "I am *so* fucking sorry."

"You should be." I walked out of the gate and past her. "But I forgive you."

Mostly.

Sisters were awesome. Except when they were twat-blocking.

"Do you need some healing? That's why I came."

"No need."

Isadora's power was similar to mine. Though she couldn't alter people's emotions the way I could, she could soothe the pain with her healing spells.

"No need?" she asked my retreating back.

"Henry took care of it."

"He did?"

"Yep."

I kept walking, ready to get back to my apartment so I could take care of the one thing Henry hadn't taken care of. Not yet anyway. But one of these days soon, my dark prince would, and it was all going to be worth the wait.

CHAPTER 8

~HENRY~

"I can't believe this shit," complained Mateo. "He's winning with House Greyjoy." He glared at me. And it wasn't even Alpha's voice pushing through, but Mateo's. Unusual since he rarely grumbled about anything. Of course, sleepless nights with triplets could do that to a man, or so I was told.

"Don't get your panties in a bunch," said Nico.

"You're in an alliance with him," accused Mateo, then Alpha's first appearance came out with a deep, feral, "**Traitor.**"

"I'm House Stark," argued Nico. "Of course I'm making an alliance."

"You don't have to follow the alliances of the show." Mateo's less wolfish voice was back.

"Doesn't matter," I told them as Devraj reentered his living room with Gareth, both of them carrying rocks glasses of whiskey or something. "House Greyjoy is going to whip all your asses anyway."

"Just roll, Reek," snapped Alpha.

I laughed at him using the villain Ramsay's nickname for Theon Greyjoy. He was about to lose it all. "Sure thing, Kingslayer."

"Hey, this is a friendly game, gentlemen." Devraj sat down in our circle around the coffee table.

"I want to play Gloomhaven. This is bullshit. I need to kill some monsters. Bash some skulls."

Devraj leaned back, one arm along the sofa back, his whiskey propped on his knee. "Not until Ruben comes home."

Ruben had sent word through Devraj that we couldn't continue our Gloomhaven campaign until he returned home, so we'd been trying a few other board games. Dune was pretty cool. But Game of Thrones was my favorite. Mainly because I apparently had a knack for dominating the shit out of everyone in this game.

"Fighting for world domination of the seven kingdoms of Westeros isn't fun for you?" Nico quirked an arrogant brow at Mateo.

"Those seven kingdoms are more like three now," added Gareth, turning to me. "Would you like one more in your alliance?"

I grinned. "House Greyjoy will happily accept House Baratheon into the fold."

"Motherfucker," growled Alpha. **"You're ganging up on me."**

"You can take it," said Nico. "Let's play. Roll, Henry."

I did and ended up getting another advantage. I swear, the fates were always in my favor when we played this game. I defeated Devraj and knocked his House of Tully out first. He simply raised his glass. "Cheers."

I wiped out Nico and his House of Martell next. Then the rest fell quickly after that, Mateo and Gareth last.

"What is dead may never die, bitches." I smiled, trying not to be too smug, but also enjoying the hell out of winning as Gareth and I started picking up the board pieces.

Maybe it's because I kicked their asses, I wasn't sure, but Devraj was the first to say something about a topic I'd hoped none would bring up.

"Isadora tells me that she caught you and Clara in the back garden together."

Gareth stopped with his hand dangling over the table, cards in hand. "Is that so?" He laughed in surprise.

"I have new respect for you, grim. Fucking outdoors is a good, primal activity with your woman. Back to nature is best."

Gareth's eyes widened. "You and Clara were *fucking* in the garden?"

"No!" I glared at my cousin. He knew more than anyone here that if I was fucking Clara, it wouldn't be in a goddamn garden. "None of y'all's goddamn business what we were doing."

"What did she catch them doing exactly?" Nico asked Devraj, ignoring me and taking a sip of his bottled beer.

I stopped and surveyed the asshats all grinning like fiends.

"She said they were awfully close, a private moment she'd interrupted," added Devraj.

"Shut up," I told Devraj.

"No need to feel shame. You fuck your woman whenever and wherever you want." Alpha was wholeheartedly on my side here, and that was a total mind-fuck. **"It's your job as her man to give her pleasure when she needs it."**

"For fuck's sake," I breathed out. "I don't need any dating advice from you, Alpha."

"**You misunderstand, grim.**" He leaned forward and stared at me intently. "**If you're fucking her in the wild, then you're mating. She's definitely your mate. Do you understand this?**" He turned to Nico. "**Does he not understand this?**"

Nico laughed.

"I'm not fucking her," I protested again.

"Dating?" Gareth sat back and bore a hole into the side of my head with his intense gaze. "You're dating now? And you forgot to tell me?"

"Gareth." I warned him with a look.

"Yeah," Nico interrupted, "Violet said you'd visited her at her carriage house. They're definitely seeing each other."

Gareth heaved a sigh. "You need to come over tomorrow. We need to talk."

"No," I snapped, standing. "I'm heading home, assholes."

"Come on, man. We're just kidding," said Nico.

"Don't be mad." Devraj stood with me. "We're glad you two are finally getting together."

I froze, looking at each of them again. "Finally?"

Nico stood and slapped me on the shoulder. "It's about time, man."

Again, I was surprised his touch didn't make me jerk away. Something was changing inside me.

"That's the fucking truth," added Gareth, still sitting.

Mateo stood and pressed a heavy hand onto my shoulder. It was Alpha's golden eyes that bore into mine. "**These weaklings won't give you good advice, grim. Take it from me. Just pin her down and fuck her hard. She'll know who she belongs to then.**" He gave me another brotherly pat.

With that insanity, I said, "Thanks, Dr. Phil." And turned for the door.

"Same time next week!" shouted Devraj.

"I might skip next week."

I shut the door to a chorus of laughter. Rather than being extremely pissed at that personal attack, I actually found myself smiling. After heading out to the street, I couldn't control my feet, which didn't take me to my car but onto the sidewalk toward the house next door.

Of course, Devraj would have to live right next door to the Savoies. Because there was no way I could simply get in my car and drive home without getting my obsessive fix. I had to at least walk past her apartment.

Standing on the sidewalk, I looked up at the square of yellow light coming from her window, wondering what she was doing, hoping that she was happier now that she'd seen Miriam and said her goodbye. Hands in my pockets, I smiled that I'd been able to do that for her. I honestly wasn't sure I could.

The door I'd sealed shut was easily opened whenever I summoned the magic. I'd thought it would be harder since Aunt Lucille had taught me to bolt it shut so long ago. It was far simpler than it had been summoning the victims of that asshole, Richard Davis. I'd had to step inside to get the dead girls to hear me, to obey my magic and come. I'd only been a single step inside the Gray Vale, and it had put me into a near-death coma.

It wasn't the spirits of the dead girls who'd done that to me. It was the stain of black magic on my soul that had called the malevolent ones. That was the problem. I was broken. A necromancer who couldn't do what others could. Any time I went inside the Vale now, the evil spirits would come. I was sure of it.

Smothering, choking, biting. My own screams echoed through time.

The darkness inside me uncoiled, wanting to fight them back, yearning to be released from his prison. I inhaled a sharp breath, wishing I wasn't afraid to let down my shields and set him free, let my magic fill me once more.

"Henry?"

I jumped, finding Clara standing there in the dark driveway in those goddamn sexy pink pajamas.

Fucking hell.

"Clara. I wasn't—" What? Standing outside her apartment, staring up at her window with deep longing and adoration?

As always, her essence, whatever Clara was made of, soothed me down to my soul, the whispers of darkness vanished and gone.

She smiled and walked over, a small bowl in her hand. "I was just getting a snack. Livvy made brownies today."

There was a brownie in the bowl, barely showing beneath two scoops of vanilla ice cream, whipped cream, and chocolate syrup drizzle.

"Looks good," I remarked because my heart was still pounding at getting caught stalking.

"You want a bite?" She scooped a bite of brownie and ice cream onto her spoon, not even asking why I was here.

"No, that's okay."

"Come on." She held the spoon toward my mouth.

What else could I do? I let her feed me.

"Mmm." I nodded. "Good."

Her gaze dropped to my mouth, and I was instantly hard. That look. Her combination of sweet and sexy was going to slay me. She had to stop looking at my mouth.

With my supernatural hearing, I heard Nico's and Mateo's voices as they left Devraj's house. They'd catch me here any minute.

"I'll see you later," I told her, then traced to my car in two seconds before they came around the corner.

I wasn't going to get caught again and harassed by those bastards. I winced at the thought of leaving Clara so fast and seeming even more like a freak.

As I drove away down the street, I remembered what the guys had said.

Dating?

They'd all thought we were dating. The idea filled me with hope. But we'd have to actually go on a date for that to be true.

Tomorrow, I'd visit her at the shop. I'd behave like a normal person, not like some besotted, crazed psycho. Then, finally, I'd ask Clara Savoie out on a date.

CHAPTER 9

~CLARA~

The new scrying bowls, made of various shades of marbled glass, were beautiful. It was Violet's idea that we might have some serious witches in need of scrying bowls that had me find a sculptor, a Seer warlock from New Mexico, who made these himself.

All of the bowls in shades of blue, green, white, purple, and black had a cool marbling effect that looked like swirls of smoke curling through the glass. I wanted to create a beautiful display for these, something with some dazzle. I'd already filled several balloons of marbled colors with silver and gold glitter and decorated the display with them, placing some in the bowls, others in makeshift stands like they were crystal balls.

Not for the first time, I wished I had my sister's gift. Or at the very least, I wished I could use my own when it came to Henry. Last night, he was so obviously hovering below my window like he wanted to see me. Then after a two-minute conversation, he left so abruptly I didn't even get to say goodbye.

It was pretty rude. Then Mateo and Nico walked up the driveway, and I realized he had been avoiding getting caught.

Was he ashamed of talking to me?

I didn't think so. There had to be a logical explanation. Of course, that had always been the problem with me and Henry. Nothing seemed to go like it should. Not like normal people who were obviously attracted to each other. That was the whole reason behind me coercing him into joining the book club.

As I placed another blue-tinted balloon with silver glitter inside, making it sparkle prettily, I remembered the first time I'd met him. It had been at Ruben's bookstore.

Ruben carried mostly older editions of books that were no longer in print. Some were rare and expensive, but not all. Some were simply pretty hardcovers of classics. I'd been in search of a gift for Evelyn. Her birthday was coming up, and she adored Pride and Prejudice, *having a serious fixation with Darcy.*

I was scrolling through the classic editions in pretty gold-trimmed hardcovers, noting that I also had a not-so-small fascination with the broody, misunderstood hero of Austen's most famous classic. When I found one, I plucked it out and smiled at the embossed lettering, the cover in a deep scarlet.

"There's a better edition over here," came a deep voice from behind me.

I turned to find a tattooed, black-haired man standing several feet away, hands in his jeans pockets.

"Excuse me?"

His dark gaze flickered to the bookshelf beside him, then he pulled a book off the shelf. "This is actually a newer edition than that one, but the binding is better. The cover is more attractive and appropriate for the time period."

He stepped closer, but not too close, and stretched out his hand with the book. I took it, noting the soft matte finish and the Victorian pattern of birds and flowers in the vintage style of Austen's era. It was lovely. Charming, even.

"You're right." I smiled at him. "It's perfect. My friend will love it."

He stared at me with an unreadable expression, but seemed somehow friendly too. Which was even more odd, because he was giving back-the-fuck-off vibes to everyone else in the bookstore.

I stared at the details on the book again, loving the little larks in the branches. When I glanced up, the surly man was stepping away, head down.

"Wait," I called.

He froze, eyes wide like I'd scared him. I'd never seen black eyes, but I swear his were. The magical signature coming off him was potent and read like a grim. But I couldn't feel his emotions. So weird. I could read everyone's emotions.

"You like classic romance books?" I asked.

He pointed around him. "Ruben's my new employer."

I'd heard Ruben mention to Jules that he had hired a grim to help out at the Green Light. This must be him.

"That doesn't really answer my question."

He simply stared, clenching his jaw.

"I've never seen you around the neighborhood," I told him.

Still no response but those otherworldly eyes on me.

"I appreciate your help. My friend Evelyn will love it. It's her birthday."

Again, I was met with silence. It didn't bother me, though. Even though I couldn't sense what he was feeling, I loved being close to this strange, stoic man. It didn't pass me by that his face was carved into beautiful sharp angles, but there was something else that made me like him.

Maybe it was that he was frowning at everyone else in the shop who walked near us, but the frown vanished when he looked at me. Or maybe it was because he tried so hard to portray that sort of cavalier, careless demeanor, yet he stepped out of his way to point out a better edition of Pride and Prejudice. *Whatever it was, I knew that I wanted to get to know this grim more.*

Then Ruben stepped into the bookstore from the hallway leading to his office. "Henry?"

The tattooed Austen expert turned.

"Hi, Clara," said Ruben before heading down the hallway.

My new friend followed.

"Thank you, Henry."

He stopped and looked over his shoulder, that expression still a blank slate, then he'd turned and walked away.

I snapped back to the present, sighing to myself at that first meeting. I knew now that Henry hid his feelings behind that vacant demeanor.

I was on my last balloon, having filled it with air from a pump, when the bell on Mystic Maybelle's entrance tinkled. Tying the knot in the balloon, I called out, "Be right with you."

I was trying to figure out where to place the final balloon when I felt someone beside me, a warmth I recognized. Turning, I wasn't disappointed to find Henry standing there.

Good gracious, he looked so delicious. Nothing really different than the norm. Jeans, check. Dark T-shirt, check. Fine-ass tattoos and finer-ass face, check, check.

"Hi!" I beamed.

One side of his mouth quirked up. "Hi."

He cleared his throat nervously, gaze bouncing around.

"Do you like my display?"

"It's nice."

His thoughts weren't clear, but his smile said he was certainly thinking about something.

"Tell me," I demanded.

"What?"

"Whatever it is that's put that lovely look on your face."

His eyes closed as he made a grunting sort of sound in his throat. "Clara," he whispered.

"What?"

"I don't understand how you do it."

"Do what?"

His expression hardened into something more serious. "Make me feel the way you do."

Now I was speechless, but thrilled to death at the same time.

"I came up here to tell you something. And to ask you something. Then you looked at me and said hi, and all my plans are derailed."

I laughed because I understood this phenomenon of being driven to distraction. It happened whenever Henry appeared. Like now, I was standing there still holding the balloon of glitter and not knowing what to do or say next.

"Tell me what you wanted to tell me first."

Exhaling a deep breath, he seemed to be gathering confidence for whatever it was. Then he spilled it. "I know that I'm not always the most fun guy to have around."

I opened my mouth to protest, but he held up his hand to stop me. "Please. Let me get this out."

I nodded and let him continue.

"I'm a moody son of a bitch. Melancholy, some might say. It all started when I was young. When something happened."

I wanted him to tell me what it was that happened, but I also didn't want to interrupt because it was obviously causing him anxiety just to confess what he was saying now.

"Since that time, I've been"—he glanced away—"not afraid of people, really, but . . . I kind of hate people." He laughed a little. "Sad, but true. Being around them, lots of them. I don't like people close to me. I never have, but it's gotten worse as I've grown older."

Henry was definitely an introvert, but there was way more to the story here.

"So whatever happened to you," I said, "it made you withdraw from people."

He licked his lips. "From almost everyone except Gareth, Sean, and my aunt who helped raise me. And then, one day, I saw you walking out of this shop, and for the first time, I wanted to know someone else. I wanted"—he took a step closer—"to get close to someone else that wasn't family. But I also know that I'm damaged. My magic isn't quite right."

"That's not true." When he opened his mouth, it was me who lifted a hand in protest, my other still holding the balloon. "Give me a second."

I placed a hand over his heart, the strong organ beating hard and true beneath my palm. Closing my eyes, I summoned my magic, whispering a reading spell, begging the Goddess to give me the sight to feel what was happening inside Henry. A spark ignited in my mind, weaving an emotional tale that was rather simple. My psychic eye, the little I had, showed me the truth beneath the gloom inside Henry.

When I opened my eyes, I told him, "I think I know. Depression blankets you because you suppress your magic."

"But if I use it"—he swallowed hard, his Adam's apple bobbing—"bad things could happen."

"What if I were to help you?"

His gaze flitted between my eyes. "You'd do that for me?"

"Henry." I tilted my head, rubbing my palm in a slow circle on his chest. "I'd do anything for you."

His heart beat faster, and his frown deepened. "You shouldn't. If things go wrong, you could get hurt. I couldn't let that happen. I'd never forgive myself if—"

Pop!

We both jumped. The balloon I'd been holding was now a piece of blue rubber in my palm, glitter all over his face and chest and likely on mine. I burst into laughter. Leave it to me to be in the middle of the most intense discussion I'd ever had with Henry and for it to be interrupted by a glitter bomb.

"Omigod, Henry." I reached up and tried to brush some of the glitter off his cheek, but more glitter from my fingers made it worse.

Then I realized he wasn't laughing, but his black eyes were gleaming and intense, his expression near feral with heated desire.

My fingers trailed to his mouth, where I dragged my forefinger across his full lower lip. "For such a hard, serious guy, you shouldn't have a mouth like this."

Lightning fast, he had one hand in my hair, the other wrapped around the nape of my neck, and his mouth on mine. His *glorious* tongue pushed between my lips and swept inside me.

He groaned into my mouth, and my knees buckled. I sank against his chest, clutching his T-shirt at the waist with both hands to keep from falling.

His hand in my hair fisted as he pulled slightly away.

I whimpered. "No, Henry. More, *please* more."

"Fuck, Clara." He bit my bottom lip softly, then trailed his tongue over it, his dark eyes focused on my mouth, his voice raspy and raw. "I want to eat you alive."

"Be my guest."

He came back for me then, softer this time, tilting my head so he could slant his mouth over mine and sweep in with more finesse. Wetness pooled between my legs, and I moaned as I rubbed my whole body against him.

His hands tightened in my hair and at my nape, but his mouth remained gentle and thorough. The hand at my neck slid down my spine and cupped my ass, squeezing softly while his tongue stroked inside my mouth, my entire body lighting on fire.

Good heavens, he was melting me one silken stroke at a time.

"Mmm," he hummed against my mouth, nipping softly with teeth, then coaxing my mouth back open with his own.

Then his mouth coasted down my jaw and throat, leaving little biting stings as he went before trailing back with his tongue.

"You taste so fucking good."

I clutched my hands in his hair, holding his mouth against my throat, blissed out with hot arousal and sharp need.

"Your mouth feels so good," I whispered. "I want it everywhere."

He squeezed my ass again on a groan, then returned to my mouth and kissed me hard. Gentleness gone, he crushed my body against his and swallowed my moans that were escalating to compete with any porn superstar.

I dragged my hands down his broad chest, inching below his belt. He gripped my wrists and planted my hands higher on his chest. Whimpering in protest, I kept them where he put them.

He softened his mouth on mine, cradling my face sweetly. I didn't want this to stop but also, I'd just opened the shop and anyone could walk in. And apparently, my libido was running wild. For a few seconds, I wondered if we could shut ourselves in the inventory closet.

Then he pressed his forehead to mine, both of us panting.

"Clara." His voice was tender but harsh.

"Yes," I agreed. "I know."

The jingle of the bell over the door announced someone walking in. We both jumped apart, facing the front of the store to find Devraj standing there, mouth open, brow raised in surprise. His gaze shifted to confusion as he looked us up and down.

Henry had glitter all over his face, smeared down his chest from my hands to his belt, and a little below. I could only imagine where the trails of glitter marked me.

Glancing at Henry's crotch, I told Devraj, "That's not what—"

"None of my business." He flashed his charming smile. "I can see that Isadora is not here."

I pointed next door. "The Cauldron."

"Right." He flashed a bigger smile at Henry, then turned and marched back outside.

"Great," he muttered.

"Don't worry. He won't say anything."

Henry scoffed. "You have no idea. Devraj and the rest of them talk worse than watercooler gossips after the office Christmas party."

Then he really looked at me, his gaze trailing down my body. He shook his head. "What kind of glitter did you have in that balloon? It's everywhere."

A couple of women looking at the window display from outside caught my attention.

Henry glanced over his shoulder. "I should get going."

"You have to ask me your question," I reminded him.

"What's that?"

"You said you came here to tell me something and to ask me something. So what was the question?"

The door jingled, and the women came inside, browsing the tarot cards on the left wall.

Henry leaned in, his gaze skating all over my face. "I wanted to ask you on a date."

I made an audible sigh. "*Finally.* Yes, yes, yes. I'll go on a date with you."

His pretty mouth tilted up into a wide smile. "Tomorrow at eleven?"

"A daytime date?"

"Is that a problem?"

"Nope. I'll get Isadora to cover for me here at the shop."

He nodded and stepped back. "I'll pick you up then."

When he turned to walk for the door, I scoffed. "Henry?"

He stopped. "Yeah?"

I hurried to him, held his shoulders, and pressed up onto my toes. I placed a soft, quick kiss to his lips.

"We're officially dating, which means you need to kiss me when you say goodbye."

He blinked, looking a little baffled, like I'd knocked him over the head.

"Okay?"

"Yeah." He cleared his throat nervously. "Okay." He planted a hand on my hip and leaned down, giving me another kiss, lingering sweetly. "See you tomorrow."

He hurried out, and I tried not to squeal with delight as I turned to my customers. "Hi. May I help you two ladies with something?"

"We're just looking, thank you."

"Let me know if you need anything."

When I turned and started walking away, one of them said, "Ma'am?"

"Yes?"

She pointed to my skirt and whispered, "You've got glitter on your behind."

"Oh!" I laughed. "Thanks for telling me."

Not that I planned to change clothes or anything. I'd be wearing the proof of my first make-out session with Henry all damn day.

Oh! I had an idea. I ran to my purse behind the counter and pulled out my phone and angled it behind me. After taking a picture, I clicked back to the photo, giggling at the evidence of Henry's hand on my bum, his large glittery print vivid and clear.

"I'm framing this one."

This was amazing! Step two of the make-Henry-my-boyfriend plan was complete even without me needing to seduce him through the book club. We were dating. Well, after tomorrow it would be official anyway.

I spent the rest of the day planning what I'd wear tomorrow and replaying my first kiss with Henry on loop. If kissing him sent me into such a tailspin, I couldn't even imagine what sex with him would do to me. But I sure as hell couldn't wait to find out.

CHAPTER 10

~HENRY~

"I need to talk." I was sprawled on Gareth's sofa in his basement, his dog, Queenie, in my lap.

"I've been waiting." Gareth leaned back in his leather office chair, his wall of computer monitors surrounding him like a NASA control room. He clasped his hands along the waist of his dress pants, his shirtsleeves rolled up after a long day. "Is it true? You're sleeping with Clara?"

"No. For fuck's sake. Don't you think I'd tell you if I were?"

"I don't know. I wasn't aware things between you had progressed till the other night at Dev's house."

Petting Queenie, I admitted, "We're going on our first date tomorrow."

Gareth grinned. "Where are you taking her?"

"None of your business."

He rolled his eyes. "It's me. Your best friend."

"I didn't come for dating advice." I scratched Queenie behind the ear. "Not really."

"Then what did you need to talk about?"

Gareth was my best friend as well as my cousin, but even so, this was a little embarrassing to talk about with anyone. He and Sean were the only ones who knew how badly my affliction, my aversion to people, hindered me. I refused to talk to a therapist about this. It was just too private to me.

Gareth leaned forward, elbows on his desk, concern marking his brow. "Tell me, Henry."

Summoning the courage, I finally did. "I kissed her."

"And?"

"Nothing. No panic. No fear."

"Hot fucking damn." Gareth clapped his hands together, arching a brow. "None at all?"

I shook my head. "I wanted more. So much more."

"That's awesome, man. Seriously. I'm happy for you."

I laughed, a little shocked to admit it aloud. "It's like my phobia doesn't even exist when I'm with her."

"That's because the fear all stems from that one incident. She doesn't intend you any harm, and you know this. Deep down, the darkness does too."

We spoke of our essence, a grim's darkness that we all carried inside, as separate entities. The truth was more complex. It was separate, but also a part of us, sometimes guiding our actions, but we allowed it with our eyes wide open.

Because that darkness was also a direct link to our magic, I'd always felt more separate from my own, and therefore not in control of either—my magic nor the darkness that was a part of me. My necromancer magic wanted me to keep the doors open, to keep communication with the dead so that my gift could do some good.

The problem was, because my father made a wrong calculation and entrusted my care to the wrong person, there was a part of me forever marked by fear. That's what had me bolting the doors to my magic. It was difficult to explain, and even harder to express to people I respected and cared about.

Queenie licked my knuckle, nudging me to keep scratching. "The other women I'd tried stuff with didn't mean me any harm either."

"None of them were Clara."

That's for fucking sure.

He smiled. "Looks like love conquers all, doesn't it?"

I wouldn't pretend I hadn't already thought of her in those terms. My feelings seemed too deep for someone I'd never had an actual date with. I petted Queenie, avoiding eye contact with my cousin, who saw straight through me.

"Something's wrong," he finally said. Always onto me.

I needed to confess my worst fear, so I did. "I'm afraid I'll hurt her. I want her that badly."

"You won't. Trust me. Henry, look at me."

I lifted my head, trying to force the tension from my body.

"Trust yourself."

Wanting to move on from those thoughts, I confessed the rest. "What if I can't control it? What if something happens with my magic?"

"Like what?" He looked genuinely confused.

"Gareth. We both know I'm broken. That's why I keep the door closed." I didn't admit that I'd managed to summon Miriam Ferriday and seal it shut again without a problem. What if that had been a fluke? My fear was that I'd lose control, and something bad would happen again. Except this time, it wouldn't be me they'd attack. It would be her.

"You're not broken," he growled. "You're scarred. And I've told you time and again you can control your magic and use it at will without hurting anyone."

I knew he believed this. He'd been saying the same thing to me all my adult life.

"The problem is," he continued, "you don't trust yourself."

"No," I agreed on a huff. "I don't."

"That's the first step you have to conquer then, cousin. This fear of yours is what's holding you back. It always has."

Queenie licked my hand again when I stopped petting her little head. I rubbed a palm down her back.

"Funny. Clara said something similar."

"Then listen to her if you won't listen to me."

I let that sink in while neither of us spoke for several minutes.

Gareth was the one to finally break the silence. "You should tell her what happened."

My head shot up. "Why? No one wants to hear that shit."

"You're wrong. Clara's magic as an Aura is emotional healing." He held my gaze. "There's a reason the fates sent her into your life. I think the first reason is obvious."

Mate, whispered the darkness.

I cracked my neck at the sudden jarring knowledge that Gareth knew as well as I did.

He went on. "And it's the first reason that leads to the second. She has the power to heal you. To reconnect you with your magic like no one else can. If you don't believe in yourself, believe in her."

I stared, openly stunned at something so obvious that I never realized. Perhaps the universe *had* put her into my life for more reasons than making me her slave—because that's what I felt like in her presence. My need to please her, make her smile, make her happy drove me to the brink of insanity at times. And now that I knew what her moans sounded like, felt like, I was positive that she'd bewitched me for good, whether she knew it or not.

But Gareth had just shown me that she was more than that, more than even my mate. She could be my salvation from living in an eternal purgatory without my magic. The way I'd blocked it off had been like lopping off a limb. Or two. And that's what kept me in this perpetual state of gloom, this living without a part of me that was meant to be a natural extension of myself.

Clara could save me from it.

Nodding, I patted Queenie and stood up. "Okay."

Gareth's brow shot up. "You mean you'll tell her?"

"I'll do more than that. I'll ask her to help me."

Tomorrow, on our first date.

CHAPTER 11

~CLARA~

"I LOVE SURPRISES," I TOLD HENRY AS HE DROVE ME TO THE SECOND destination of our date, sneaking the hundredth peek at him.

He'd worn jeans as usual, but a much nicer dark pair, and a button-down black shirt for our date. The tiny vee of skin his shirt revealed was driving me to distraction.

He'd taken me to eat pho for lunch at Lilly's Café first, which was delicious. He just listened to me babble about my favorite historical romances, not saying much of anything. For him, that was pretty normal. But since we'd gotten to know each other better recently, I could actually detect that this wasn't the usual broody Henry. This was nervous Henry. It had to be about wherever he was taking me next.

"Are you going to give me a hint at all?" I teased.

That was when he turned into a gated driveway leading to a giant mansion set farther from the street.

"Whoa," I whispered.

"This is my father's home," he told me, slowing up the long driveway. "I made sure he's at work so he won't be here."

"So you aren't taking me to meet your dad." I'd already found out from Gareth that his parents were divorced, and his mother lived somewhere in California with a new husband. Henry and Sean rarely saw her.

"No." He scoffed. "If I can help it, you'll never meet my father."

"That bad, huh?"

His dark glance was all the reply he gave me.

"Then what are we doing here?"

"There's a special place I want to show you."

He stopped the car at the head of the circular driveway, the Greek-style home looming high above us.

"Won't he know you're sneaking around his house?" I asked.

"His gardener is an old friend. He'll make sure no one says anything."

Henry stopped the car, hopped out, and rounded the hood to open the door but I was already getting out myself, too eager to wait for the gentlemanly gesture.

"Where to?"

"This way." He pointed to the left where the yard opened up into a giant garden hedged in by thick rows of azalea bushes with white flowers blooming in the warm spring weather.

Henry waited for me to catch up, his body tense as he looked around. He clamped his jaw tight as if he were bracing for something terrible. I reached down and curled my hand around his. He flinched and glanced over, then squeezed my hand tighter and tugged me closer to his side as he guided us farther from the house along a path through box hedges.

"It's beautiful here," I told him quietly.

He nodded, his grip firm around my hand like I might get away. I wasn't going anywhere.

"Mr. John," he suddenly called out.

A big man wearing a cap and a shovel in hand stood next to a row of rosebushes and a wheelbarrow of fertilizer. When he turned, I realized he was older than I'd thought, his face wrinkled from many days in the sun. Not detecting any magical signature, I knew he was human.

"Henry." His smile was wide and affectionate. He left the shovel in the wheelbarrow and removed a glove as we drew closer. "Good to see you, son."

The tenderness in his voice made my heart leap. This man knew him well and loved him. I could feel the genuine affection radiating off him. However, he didn't pull him into a hug as I almost expected. He reached out a hand to shake.

Henry let go of mine and shook his hand, giving the old gardener a pat on the shoulder with his other. "It's good to see you too, Mr. John." He turned and put a hand on my back. "I'd like to introduce you to Clara Savoie."

"Hi." I greeted him cheerily, holding out my hand.

"Hello there." He smiled back, his eyes crinkling at the edges. "It's very nice to meet you." His brow raised in surprise at Henry. "Your father didn't mention you'd gotten a girlfriend."

"He doesn't know." A flush of pink crawled up his neck while my heart soared at my new title. "And she's not really my—"

"Oh yes, I am." I wrapped an arm around Henry's waist and beamed at the sweet older man. "I am absolutely his girlfriend."

Henry made one of those strange grunt noises in his throat when he was surprised about something, then gently wrapped his arm around my shoulders.

Mr. John chuckled. "That's just fine to hear." His smile dimmed a little. "And you're doing well, Henry?"

He cleared his throat, his nervous tic. "Yeah. These days, I am."

"Good. Good to hear."

"We'll let you get back to work. Thank you again for letting us come."

"My lips are sealed." He put his glove back on and tipped his hat to me. "Good to meet you, dear. Take good care of him."

"I intend to," I told him honestly. As Henry guided me farther into the maze of box hedges, I said, "He's awfully sweet."

He kept his arm wrapped around my shoulders. "He is. He's . . . he was very important to me growing up."

"How so?"

"I spent a lot of time in this garden."

"I didn't realize you liked flowers so much."

He let out a little laugh. "It wasn't that actually."

"What was it?"

"I'm going to show you. And it's the perfect time of year."

I didn't know what he meant about the time of year, but I was patient enough to wait and see.

He let go of my shoulders, then took my hand, the look of adoration he shone down on me making me feel like the most special woman in the world.

We wound around a pretty fountain surrounded by benches and more hedges before he guided me onto a white gravel walkway that led out of the box hedges and into an area with tall trees and rows of what looked like wildflowers.

I gasped in delight. "It looks like an English garden."

"That was the intention. Come see."

He pulled me by the hand beneath the shade of trees and out into the sunlight where pink zinnias, yellow black-eyed Susans, orange and white milkweed, and a dozen other flowers bloomed tall and pretty.

"Wow. It's so beautiful," I gushed.

He walked me closer. "It is, but it's what they attract that was always special to me."

When we stopped at the garden, he reached out his free hand and pointed. "Look."

Among the blooming white milkweed there were pretty little monarch butterflies and some larger yellow-and-black swallowtails flitting around.

"Look how pretty," I said softly, admiring their zigzag patterns of flight before landing on another flower. "I've always loved butterflies. I did a study on them in high school once." I pointed to a yellow-and-black one with a splotch of dusky blue at the bottom of her wings. "That's a Tiger Swallowtail with the blue."

He huffed out a low laugh. "Why does that not surprise me?"

Beaming up at him, my heart melting at the sweetness, I asked softly, "You like butterflies, Henry?"

His gaze moved from the garden to me, a serenity there I wasn't sure I'd ever seen before. It was a kind of tranquility I felt down to my bones, and it had nothing to do with my Aura gift. It was pure peace radiating from this so-often troubled man of mine.

For he was mine. I was sure of that. Whether he knew it or not.

He stared a moment, then looked back at the flowers. A black-eyed Susan suddenly snapped from its long stem and levitated upward. It pinwheeled in place, then floated toward me where it hovered in midair, waiting.

Heat flushed my cheeks at Henry using his TK to give me a flower. I took it and held the flower delicately, admiring its gold petals. "Thank you."

"Here." He took it gently from me. "Let me."

He broke away a little more of the stem, then tucked it behind my ear, admiring his handiwork. My belly fluttered with giddiness at his sweet gesture. Catching my obvious gleeful expression, he smiled shyly, then took my hand.

"Let's sit over here." He guided me to a wrought iron bench off to the side of the garden. When we sat, he kept my hand in his lap, cradled between both of his, while watching the butterflies not far away. I knew that whatever he was building up courage to tell me was important, so I didn't push or prattle on like I often did to fill the silence. Finally, he started.

"When necromancers are seven years old, they begin their training to harness and control their magic."

"You knew that you were a necromancer that early?" I asked gently.

"Yes. Unlike grimlocks like Gareth, who don't manifest their full magic until puberty, necromancers know from a very young age what we are. What we can do. Ghosts tend to find us." His thumb brushed a soft pattern over the back of my hand. "For me, I was five when I saw my first ghost. It was my grandmother. She appeared in my bedroom the night after she died. Nearly scared me to death."

"I can only imagine." This didn't seem to distress him, though.

"She'd only shown up to ask me to tell my father a message."

"What was the message?"

"'Power does not equal love.' Then she vanished. I'd told my father the next day at the breakfast table that I'd had a dream of Grandma coming to my bedside. I hadn't even known what necromancers were at the time. But that alerted him to what I was. So the day after I turned seven, we had a visitor."

He squeezed my hand, seemingly on reflex, his focus on the garden.

"Who was the visitor?"

"An old friend of my father's from his younger days at Vanderbilt. His name was Amon. They'd been roommates in college, and though they hadn't kept in touch, my father remembered he'd been a powerful necromancer back in school." He made a disgusted sort of sound. "Apparently, he used to summon the ghosts of former professors for fun when they'd get wasted, just to find out which current professors they hated the most."

"That seems rather dumb," I pointed out. "And cruel."

"It was. I didn't find that out until after."

The way he said the word "after," I realized this necromancer was involved in his traumatic past. I didn't say anything but waited till he was ready to go on.

"It wouldn't have mattered if I'd known what kind of man he was. I was so young, and I'd wanted to please my father, who had never been affectionate toward me. The fact that he'd suddenly seemed excited to spend time with me after my sessions with Amon made me happy. But all he really wanted to know was whether I was doing a good job, how well I was controlling the necromancer magic."

He turned my palm over in his hands, staring down, seeming to find courage for something.

"Were you able to control it?" I asked softly.

"Oh yes. Whatever spirit Amon asked me to summon, they came. I had an inkling he wasn't a good man when he asked me to summon his own sister's ghost. A young woman appeared through the portal I'd made. She was a tall woman wearing an old-fashioned dress. I didn't realize when I started working with Amon that he was over a hundred years old. At seven, I still hadn't grasped the idea of the long life spans of supernaturals. When Amon saw his sister appear, for that's who I learned she was, he made this sinister laugh. Her spirit was timid and seemed shocked to see him. I'll never forget him saying, 'You can deny my summons, but not my pupil's.' He stepped closer to her and said, 'You look plain as ever. Even in death, you're still trying to hide that body behind a dowdy dress.' She'd held her chin high and whispered to him, 'Too bad you can only kill a person once, Amon.' Then he lunged for her, but she vanished back into the portal, and I closed it right after."

"Goddess above, Henry." I swallowed at the sad memory. "He used you to try to get to his dead sister, one he seemed to have killed himself."

"Unfortunately, that's not the worst of it."

I squeezed his hand, not sure I wanted to hear more. But Henry needed me to hear it, so I would. "Go on."

"I'd told my father about the incident after Amon left that day. He said I was just a scared child. Amon didn't kill his sister. She'd died in a boating tragedy at their family's estate. It had been an *accident*. My father had always been a stern man, and I'd been a little afraid of him when I was young. So I didn't argue with him, though I knew the truth. The problem came when Amon returned the following week for lessons. We usually worked in the downstairs parlor where no one went, out of the way of my father's servants, so we could work in private."

Dread sank like a heavy stone in my stomach.

"That day, Amon seemed on edge before we'd even started. He was pacing the room, muttering something, when I appeared in the parlor for lessons. He told me to summon his sister again."

"No, Henry."

"That's what I told him. *No.* I wouldn't do it. I knew that he'd killed her. He realized I'd figured it out. I could see it in the way he looked at me. When he insisted I call her, and I refused again, he said, 'Very well. But remember, bad students are punished. You brought this on yourself.' I thought he was going to whip me or something, but it was far worse. He opened a portal by hissing a spell in Varangian, Old Norse, the language of our maker."

He went silent, looking back at the garden, gulping hard at the memory. I pulled his right hand into my lap and held it in both of mine, trying to comfort him.

"Tell me," I urged softly.

"I still don't know the spell he spat that opened that foul gateway. Then he grabbed me by the collar and threw me inside. It was so dark, and the air, it wasn't just oppressive. It was like it was alive with evil. I'd fallen to my knees when Amon threw me inside, but I instinctively jumped up and turned back around. Only, the monsters in there stopped me from getting away."

I was squeezing Henry's hand now, swallowing the bile that kept crawling up my throat. The fear that coated him was painful to see even without my Aura magic. All I sensed was terror and the rot that had clung to Henry from that incident.

"I don't know how many there were or how long they held me down and . . . hurt me. All I remember was arms sweeping me up and hauling me back through the portal." He scoffed. "It was my father. He'd somehow come into the Gray Vale and snatched me up. I don't remember seeing Amon as Father carried me out of the room, up the stairs, and dumped me on my bed. I only remembered the doctor, a grim who was another friend of father's, tending to me afterward. The doctor asked my father who he should report for this crime, and my father told him there was no need."

He went silent then. I didn't want to pry, but also I needed to know the rest.

"You were badly hurt?" My stomach twisted with nausea.

"I was."

"What happened to Amon?"

He shook his head. "I don't know. When I recovered, I asked my father about him. He simply told me he'd never be coming to the house again and when I was older, he'd find a better teacher for me. But I refused the training every time he mentioned it. And when I was old enough, I left home and took Sean with me."

I wanted to know the extent of his injuries, but I also didn't. The thought of him as a little boy being tossed into a pit of evil spirits who had hurt him badly made me physically sick. I squeezed his hand, pushing my magic into him, giving him a hit of my calming essence.

His smile was instant. "You don't have to do that, Clara." He laced his fingers with mine. "Just being near you soothes my soul." He brought the back of my hand to his mouth. "It has from the moment I met you."

My heart beat wildly in my chest, like the fluttering of the butterflies' wings. I was transfixed by his mouth brushing the back of my hand, his black eyes on me.

"It was the same calm I felt when I used to come here as a child."

"To the butterfly garden?" My voice was low and soft.

"After the incident," he said on a slow exhale, "there were times I'd have unwanted visitations."

"From those evil spirits?" My heart was in my throat.

"No. Not those, thankfully. But others who were lost and angry. Some were even violent. I'd run from the house to this garden where I played as a child, and they never followed me here. I was safe here . . . with the butterflies."

There was a faint hum around this place. A sweet touch of magic. "There's magic here. Or was once."

He nodded. "I think my mother put a spell around this place, knowing it was my favorite play place. She left my father about a year after the incident. As well as me and Sean."

Sorrow twisted my gut. It wasn't his but my own at the thought of this young hurt boy all alone with a seemingly uncaring father.

"I found out later that Amon dabbled in dark spells. Black magic. He'd often summoned demons from Esbos."

"What is that?"

"A foul place in the Vale filled with demons and dark spirits. That's where he'd put me that day."

My stomach twisted tighter into a knot.

"And something about that incident left a stain on me. I was like a magnet, drawing malevolent souls. Fortunately, my aunt Lucille came to the house. I stopped talking for a while after the incident."

"For how long?"

"Three months, they told me. I don't remember it very well."

"Three months?"

"Don't be sad for me, Clara."

"Henry." I cupped his cheek. He leaned his face into my hand. "How can I not be?"

His eyes closed heavily, then opened, tenderness there in those dark depths. "My aunt taught me how to block all spirits when I was ready, and I've kept them sealed away all my life. I'm fine."

I stood and stepped between his legs. Brow pursed in confusion, he opened them wider, then I sat on one thigh.

"I need to hold you, Henry." I wrapped my arms around his shoulders and buried my face in his neck.

His arms came instantly around me, one arm bound around my waist, squeezing me closer, the other hand cradling my skull.

He pressed his lips to the crown of my head. "What on earth did I do to deserve you?"

He wasn't asking *me*, but I answered anyway.

"Everyone deserves another soul who matches them, to walk beside them through this world, to be their best friend and true lover."

His pulse throbbed faster against my palm where I had it pressed to the side of his neck. He heaved a shaky sigh. "Do you mean soul mates?"

"Yes."

Hesitantly, cautiously, he then asked, "Are you my soul mate, Clara?"

"Of course I am, silly." I sat up, meeting an astonished dark-eyed gaze. "I've just been waiting for you to catch up and realize it."

He made a sort of grunting noise in the back of his throat, then pulled my head closer, his hand still cradling it. Without resistance, I leaned forward.

This kiss was different than any other I'd ever had. Not simply because it was given by Henry's mouth, though that in itself made it beyond special. Neither was it the tenderness with which he pressed and brushed and coaxed my lips apart. It was the emotion he poured into the kiss. Yet again, I was astonished that I felt it without the help of magic. That I felt it so clearly.

Adoration. Gratitude. Deep, deep contentment.

"This angel is my soul mate?" he seemed to be asking the universe against my lips.

"Yes," I answered for the Goddess. "I am."

"The fates are too good to me." His black eyes were fixed on my mouth where he pressed the softest of little kisses.

I didn't point out that the fates hadn't always been good to him, that he'd experienced a trauma not everyone would have survived whole. I suppose he was right in the fact that not all soul mates were able to find each other. But we had.

"The Goddess is good to us both," I reminded him.

We sat on that bench for a long time—holding each other, kissing softly, reveling in the fact that we were in the arms of the one person on this earth we belonged to, and neither of us were ever letting go.

CHAPTER 12

~CLARA~

DATE NUMBER TWO. I BOUGHT A NEW DRESS—SKY-BLUE, SHORT, AND frilly.

Everything was waxed and ready. Because as much as I loved kissing Henry, I was ready for the next step. *So* ready. I even had some ideas how this was going to go down.

It seemed he had the same idea since he invited me to his place to cook me dinner. The kitchen couldn't be that far from his bedroom, right? And he did tell me he had something special to show me. *I'll bet it's special.*

He wanted to pick me up, but I insisted I'd drive myself. I actually had to get back in time to watch the triplets. Evie and Violet were working at the Cauldron since Finnie had midterm exams to study for. And Belinda had called in with the stomach flu. Dev had some special date night planned for Isadora, and he didn't want to lose his reservations.

While Mateo could likely handle it on his own, the triplets were a serious handful now that they were mobile. So I agreed to help out as long as I could go on my date with Henry. So here I was, marching up the path to his front door on a Saturday afternoon. This walk wasn't nearly as frightful as my first time.

Before I could even knock on the wooden door, it swung open. There stood my dark prince in all of his goth glory.

"Hi." I smiled brightly, trying not to fidget.

He took a long perusal of my dress and bare legs and arms, making that sexy noise in his throat. I think it was a nervous tic of his, but all I knew is that he did it when he was shocked or really liked something.

"I bought a new dress for you," I told him.

His eyes slipped closed, and he muttered something that sounded like a few foul words strung together. Then he opened the door and stepped aside for me to walk in. When I did, he grabbed me around the waist and hauled me into his chest.

I laughed as he kissed me hello with a soft, lingering welcome. "This dress is for me?"

As well as everything underneath it, I wanted to say. But I decided to keep that surprise for later.

"Of course it is," I murmured sweetly before biting his bottom lip and giving it a good suck before letting go.

"Fuck." His eyes bled blacker into the whites. "I hope you like steak."

"I love *everything* you do." I blinked sweetly at him.

"Stop it."

"Stop what?"

"Teasing me." He pinched my behind.

I squealed, then swatted his hand away. "You stop it."

Grinning like a fiend, he let me loose and closed the door. This was a brand-new side of him. A playful one. My grim could be playful? Who would've thought?

"Is Sean home?" I asked as casually as possible as I followed him into the kitchen. "Oh, wow. That smells delicious."

"He's out with friends tonight." After putting a pot holder on his hand—the sight of which made me giggle—he opened the oven and pulled out a dish that smelled divine.

"What?" he asked, his expression soft and easy even as I laughed at him.

"I don't know." I took a seat on a stool on the far side of the island so I could watch him. "I just never imagined someone who looks like you using a pot holder."

"How do I look exactly?" His brow pinched, but he still wore that cavalier half-smile that made me feel hot and melty.

Like my wettest dream. "You look like a bad boy with fine tattoos and a beautiful face."

He huffed out a nervous laugh and shook his head as he took off the pot holder and opened the fridge to take out a green salad with plastic wrap over the top.

"What?" I asked.

Setting the salad on the island, he braced his hands wide on the top. "I never thought you liked me. I mean, like this."

"I made it pretty obvious, Henry. I invited you to, like, every family event. I talked to you every time I saw you on the street in the neighborhood or hanging at Empress Ink. I couldn't have been more obvious."

"You're nice to everyone, though."

I suppose he was right. "True. But I thought you could tell the difference."

He simply stared. "It never once occurred to me that you looked at me that way. And even if you did . . . I didn't think it right to date you."

"Because you think you're broken?"

He pushed off the counter, turned toward the stove, and flicked on the gas burner. He uncovered two thick, marbled steaks.

"I am, Clara."

"No, you're not. You might be bruised up still from what happened, but your magic is still very strong. Your signature is extremely powerful."

He dropped a quarter block of butter in a skillet, then placed the steaks on with a sizzle. "That may be," he agreed. "But it's useless if I can't actually connect with my magic."

"Why can't you?"

He was quiet, the sizzling steaks the only sound. Then he added, "I can't open that door without the fear of what may come out."

"You did for Gareth. For Livvy."

He flipped the steaks. "I did, but it cost me."

My pulse tripped faster. "You weren't attacked, were you?"

"No. Not that." His back was to me, but I could tell he was tense. "It was me. The fear was . . . overwhelming, and I went into a sort of coma afterward."

Anger welled inside my chest, a rare sensation for me. "Next time, I'll be with you, and I can keep the fear away."

He turned his body to look at me. "You could," he agreed. "You've always made it go away." He cleared his throat nervously. "You always have."

He turned his attention back to dinner. After he forked the steaks onto separate plates, he served us each some potatoes au gratin, green salad, and garlic rolls.

"This way." I followed him not too far to a giant bay window overlooking a small backyard with an English garden very similar to the one he showed me on our first date. The sun was setting, the soft golden light cast across the small round table already set with silverware and a burning votive candle.

There was a window seat and a copy of *When Beauty Tamed the Beast*, our next book club read, sitting on the sill. It showed signs of wear.

"You finished yet?" I gestured to the book.

"Not yet. Working on it."

I needed to call the ladies and set up a new time for our next book club. With Miriam's passing, we'd decided to take a break for a bit.

Sitting at the small table opposite him, I asked, "Do you have a butterfly garden of your own?"

He placed my dinner in front of me, then sat, smiling down at his own plate. "I do."

I had a hot boyfriend who loved books and cooking and butterflies. Someone kill me now. Life couldn't get better than this.

I settled in and ate one of the most delicious meals of my life. It might've had something to do with my view. Henry, not the garden.

He told me about his childhood, which wasn't all bad, and his mother, who he rarely saw anymore. She apparently loved her sons, but not enough to give them the attention they needed growing up. Even before she left their father.

"I don't blame her for leaving him." He picked up our plates. "I ended up doing the same when I was old enough."

I followed him back into the kitchen, where he rinsed the plates and silverware in the sink.

"Yes, I imagine you missed her."

He nodded but didn't answer. When he turned, there was a secretive smirk tilting his pretty mouth. "Come on. I want to show you something."

"My surprise?" I might have bounced a little in my giddiness.

His mouth quirked higher. "Yes." He held out his hand, and I instantly took it, reveling in this lovely feeling of Henry holding my hand. I couldn't imagine this getting any better.

I was wrong. He took me through the living room, the back wall painted black, the fireplace also made of black stone. The surrounding furnishings were lighter, vibrant jewel shades of teal and ruby. It was cozy in a rich, luxurious sort of way.

"I'd like a tour of your house at some point," I told him. "Everything is so beautiful."

"I'll give you a full tour later. I want to show you the room I think you'll like the most."

Please tell me it's your bedroom. I was positive I would love that one the most. But rather than take me upstairs where I was sure the bedrooms were, he strolled past to the other side and another hallway. I didn't have time to feel disappointment before he opened the door and took my breath away.

"Henry!" I gasped and clapped my hands to my chest.

Surrounding me was a giant library, almost twice the size of the living room. The shelves went all the way to the top. With the high ceilings, it looked like one of those fancy libraries on an English estate.

"It's like right out of one of my favorite novels," I told him.

He watched me, dark eyes sparkling. "You like it?"

"Do I like it?" I laughed, my gaze straying back to the rows upon rows of beautiful books. "You even have one of those cute ladders!"

"I do," he said, still watching me with a small smile.

"You know how to impress a girl, don't you? Showing her your *big* library."

My reward for teasing him was a trail of pink flushing his neck and jaw.

Stepping around a lounge area with a comfy looking sofa and club chairs, I trailed a finger along the butter-soft back of the love seat as I passed, staring up at the books. A tall grand-father clock with ticking pendulum stood in one corner, the sound soothing.

"I think you might like that section in particular." He pointed to the far wall next to the grandfather clock.

Following his lead, I walked over and instantly noted many titles I was familiar with. I read them as I trailed a finger along the spine.

"*Lord of Scoundrels, Three Weeks with Lady X, Devil in Spring.*" I looked at him over my shoulder. "Some of my favorites." Then I turned back to the books. "Oh, Henry. You have all of Elisa Braden's Highlander books."

I reached upward, trying to grab hold of one in particular. It slid out of the shelf of its own accord. I peered over my shoulder. Henry stood there, his tilted smile making me all melty.

"Thank you."

Pulling the book from the shelf, I admired it a minute, then pushed it back into place.

My gaze ran up the shelves until I stopped at a particular favorite of mine. The ladder was one shelf over. I pulled it in place and walked up the ladder, telling him, "I've always wanted to use one of these."

"I remember."

"What?" I hadn't ever told him that.

"You wrote that post last year, titled your 'Book Bucket List' of all the book-related things you wanted to do."

"You read that?" I smiled over at him from the third step of the ladder.

"I read all of your posts. I'm your number one fan. Remember?"

He said it jokingly, and yet he suddenly seemed embarrassed. Because it was true. He was my number one fan. Well, I was his too. I intended to show him.

That devil in me reared her horny head, giving me a salacious idea since Henry hadn't yet taken me to his bedroom.

Stepping to the very top of the ladder, I reached for *Marrying Winterborne*, then gasped and feinted as if I were falling backward. Before I could blink, Henry was up the ladder and catching me with his hands on my hips.

"*Careful.*" His rough voice tingled over my skin.

Leaning back against him, I looked over my shoulder, our faces close, his body heat enveloping me. "Thank you."

He must've caught the guilty smile quirking my lips for his stern brow smoothed as he took two steps down the ladder. "You didn't really fall, did you?"

I shook my head as he braced both hands on the wooden handrails of the ladder. He took another step down to let me turn, still bracketing me with arms on the rails. I leaned back onto the step and lifted one knee, propping my foot onto a higher step. My dress slid up my thigh. I helped it along by tugging it higher to show him what I had underneath. Or actually, what I didn't have.

He made that grunting sound, which had some sort of instant connection to my libido. My nipples prickled beneath my thin bralette, showing beneath the clingy fabric of my dress.

He blew out a ragged breath, his gaze laser-focused between my legs. He closed his eyes and clenched his jaw, then opened those dark eyes on mine.

"Are you a damsel in distress, Clara?"

"Yes." I propped my elbows on the step behind me, leaning back farther and widening my bent knee. "See?"

That drew his attention back to my bare pussy and the throbbing distress she was in.

"I saw this movie once," I said softly. The only sound in the room was the grandfather clock ticking, my own voice sounding loud. "*Atonement* with Kiera Knightly and James McAvoy."

Henry hadn't moved. Except for the quick rise and fall of his chest, he'd become a statue.

"There was a scene in the library."

Pools of obsidian drifted up my body to meet my gaze, leaving a trail of heat in its wake.

"Similar to this one."

Suddenly seeming to snap out of his stupor, he heaved himself above me, bracing one hand on the step beside my head, and leaned close without touching.

"I saw it. Great movie." His breath coasted across my mouth. "And that was a great scene."

He took my mouth in a devouring kiss. I whimpered, clutching my hands into his shirt. Then I felt his free hand grip my outer thigh with strong fingers.

I moaned into his mouth, stroking my tongue alongside his, squirming when his thumb brushed against my skin.

"Oh, Goddess," I murmured when he coasted his hand higher and then maneuvered it between my open thighs. "Yes, *please*, Henry."

I didn't think I'd ever wanted a man to touch me so badly. When his fingers slid along my wet slit, I flinched. He froze.

"No, no," I panted, "keep going."

He nipped a line down my throat while softly circling my clit. I tilted my head back onto the step, arching my neck. He groaned against my skin as he continued to slide his fingers, but too gently.

"More," I begged, "please, more."

He pulled off me and stepped down to the floor. I whimpered at the loss, but then I realized he was at the perfect height for something delightful. So did he, apparently. He flipped up my skirt and scooped my ass into his hands, his legs straddling the base of the ladder. Then he leaned forward and put that beautiful mouth on my pussy, his eyes riveted to mine.

"Oh!" I cried out at the stunning intensity.

Pure pleasure shot through me as I rocked against his mouth, chasing my first orgasm with Henry Blackwater like it was my last breath.

I wanted his fingers inside me, I wanted all of him inside me, but it was impossible in this position on the ladder and him needing two hands to hold me. I was about to suggest we move to the sofa, but I didn't want him to stop. It felt so damn good. Then he flicked my clit back and forth with the tip of his tongue, and I forgot my own name.

My head fell back again to the step as I circled my hips against his mouth, my moans increasing. When he opened his mouth on my clitoris and sucked, I nearly lost my mind. His deep groan vibrated against my sensitive nub, and I came on a scream, reaching up to clench a fist in his hair.

Moaning, I rocked my hips while he sucked and licked me clean. I was expecting sex, but I wasn't going to complain about getting licked into oblivion.

I was still panting and trying to remember where I was when Henry set my hips back on the step and slid my skirt back into place, a feral grin on his beautiful face. And a sizable bulge in his jeans.

If he thought this was over, he was sadly mistaken.

Standing, I stepped down the ladder toward him. "That wasn't what I was expecting."

"Disappointed?"

Strangely, he seemed serious.

I stepped onto the floor close in front of him, planting my hands on his chest. "The screaming orgasm might've given me away, but I'm not disappointed."

His lips tilted up on one side, then I slid down his body to the floor. His smile vanished. I reached for the buckle of his belt, but he grabbed my hands.

"You don't have to do that."

"Henry, I've imagined sucking your cock over a hundred times. Probably a thousand." I pulled my hands gently from his, working on the buckle. "Let me find out what it's really like."

He clenched his jaw as well as his fists at his sides. He stared with primal intensity, the black of his eyes seeping into the white. I wasn't sure what that meant, but I wasn't going to ask right now. I sensed no danger. Not from my Henry.

"You've imagined this?" he asked as I finally worked open his zipper.

"Many times."

I pulled his jeans and boxer briefs down his hips. I froze, not expecting *this*. His size, yes—because Henry always projected a ton of BDE—but not the silver stud piercing at the head. A Prince Albert.

"Oh my."

Gripping him at the thick base, I was instantly rewarded with one of those guttural sexy noises he liked to make. I whispered, "What a lovely surprise."

Leaning forward, I swirled my tongue around the silver ball and then the head of his dick.

"*Fucking hell*," he grated violently, then his hands were in my hair, fisting tightly. The sting turned me on.

I moaned as I swallowed him down as far as I could, relishing the sensation of him tapping the back of my throat. I'd worked on reducing my gag reflex this past year, preparing for Henry. I had a feeling he would have a big dick, and boy, was I right. My slight psychic abilities had been correct in that category. I'd used the toothbrush massage method until I could slide it to the very back of my mouth without gagging at all. It had paid off.

Bobbing slowly while pumping the base, I kept taking more, relaxing my throat so he could go even deeper. My eyes only watered a little. He made those animalistic sounds of pleasure, grunting and slowly pumping his hips forward. I let go of the base and gripped his bare hips, pressing forward till my mouth hit the hilt.

"Goddamn," he hissed, eyes completely black, glittering with ferocity. "You want to swallow me whole, don't you, angel?"

I made a grunt of assent of my own, sliding backward and sucking him to the tip. His dick swelled even bigger. He cupped my face with one hand, the other still tightly fisted at the base of my skull. Sliding his thumb to the underside of his dick, he caressed my bottom lip, feeling himself slide in and out of my mouth.

"You can take my whole fucking soul if you want." His voice was that otherworldly eerie, prickling with pleasure along my skin. "You've wanted this dick in your pretty mouth for a while?"

I nodded, sucking the crown like a lollipop.

"Keep those eyes on me and take me deep again."

Trailing my hands to his firm, round ass, I grabbed hold and showed him what I could do.

"So beautiful," he murmured, his thumb brushing my bottom lip again. "Deeper, angel. Like you did before."

Focusing on breathing through and relaxing, I swallowed him to the back of my throat and then some.

"So fucking beautiful," he murmured before pulling out to the tip and grabbing the base of his dick.

I opened my mouth to suck in a deep breath, but he kept the crown on my tongue, his fierce gaze never leaving me.

"I'm about to come," he groaned while pumping himself harder.

Eagerly, I slid my mouth forward and sucked hard, tonguing the underside and his stud as I went.

"You're going to be the death of me." He fisted my hair harder, his eyes glittering black pools. "You want my soul?"

I never broke from his dark gaze. His hard expression contorted with sweet agony, tortured pleasure.

"It's already yours," he ground out before he held my head still, hissing as he came.

Warm spurts coated my tongue and throat. I hummed in pleasure as I swallowed everything he gave me.

"Fucking Christ, Clara," he whispered, pumping gently.

He pulled out, panting, a few spurts still spilling. Some hit the top of my dress, but it didn't bother me at all. I wiped my mouth with the back of my hand, sitting back on my heels with satisfaction.

"Shit." He glared at the spot on my dress, tucking himself back into his pants quickly and hurrying out of the room.

"It's okay," I called, but he was already gone.

I hopped to my feet and grabbed a tissue out of the box on one of the side tables and wiped it clean. Henry reappeared at reaper-speed, nearly knocking me over with the rush of wind.

"Whoa!" I laughed.

He caught me before I tipped backward since he was already standing in front of me with a warm washcloth and dabbing at my breast. Or rather, the stain on my breast, but it made me smile cheerily regardless.

"You're so sweet."

He scoffed. "For wiping my come off your dress? Yeah, I'm a real romantic."

I cupped his face and forced him to look at me. "Wow. Your eyes are back to normal already. Why'd they turn black like that?"

His frown deepened as he folded the washcloth and said, "Let's go to the living room."

I followed him into the bathroom where he dropped the cloth in a bin and washed his hands. I maneuvered next to him, hip to hip, and washed mine too.

"Not that I mind having your come on my hands," I told him.

He barked out a deep laugh. "The things you say. It shocks me a little."

"Why? Because I'm the sweet sister?"

He shrugged. "Maybe it's just unexpected."

"Good unexpected? Or bad?"

We were standing side by side, soaping our hands, and staring at each other's reflections in the mirror over the sink.

"Good," he finally answered. "Very good."

We dried our hands in mutual silence and smiled at each other, then he took one of my hands and led me back to the ornate living room where I wanted to curl up in a ball on the teal velvet sofa and never leave. It was opulent and dark but also cozy and comforting. I could only imagine what it would look like in winter with the fire crackling.

"What are you thinking?" he asked, taking a seat on the sofa.

"Just that I love this room."

He swallowed and averted his gaze for a moment. "I'm glad you do. Really glad."

I took a seat next to him, sideways, and swung my legs across his lap. "You mean like Mr. Darcy-glad that I approve of your estate?"

And all that Darcy's pleasure at seeing Lizzy's pleasure implied. I could see myself living happily here. Henry was here, after all.

He fell back against the sofa, huffing out another laugh, his hands on my shins, then he dropped his head to the sofa back.

"I know, I know," I admitted, sighing. "I'm too forward. Going too fast. My mother would kill me if she'd heard me, but seriously, we've been dancing around each other for too long. Now that I know you like me, and I know that I like you, no reason to play any sort of games, right?"

He watched me with open fascination and then lifted a hand to cup my face. I leaned into the warmth of him.

"Like you?" he seemed to whisper to himself rather than to me. "God, Clara. It's so far beyond that now."

I cupped my hand over the back of his. "Yes. I suppose it is."

We stared at each other for a moment, both of us seemingly content in the quiet of one another's company. Finally, he spoke up first.

"The eyes." He gestured toward his own. "It's a sign of my magic. I didn't realize it was making itself known until you told me."

"You mean it's never happened before when you were with another woman?"

Bringing up other women wasn't usually my thing, but I wanted to understand everything about the grim gripping the back of my calf and tucking my legs close to him.

"I don't know."

Now it was my turn to frown. "No one ever mentioned it? That your magic responded to arousal?"

Again, a pang twisted my stomach into a knot, thinking of Henry and other women, but I couldn't help myself. I was curious about his magic's reaction to me.

"There's something I wanted to tell you."

Oh dear. This sounded serious.

"What is it?" I asked, unable to even guess what grave tragedy he was about to tell me.

He turned his head away, cursing under his breath, his grip tightening on my leg.

"You can tell me anything," I assured him, pumping my joy spell into him since his mood had taken a sudden irritated turn.

Clearing his throat, he blew out a heavy breath, his expression hard with resolve. "I've never done that before."

I blinked, trying to narrow in on what he was referring to. "You mean in a library?"

He shook his head.

He couldn't mean he'd never had a blow job. It wasn't possible. Was it?

"You've never had oral sex?" I asked gently in case I was right. I knew how fragile the male ego was.

"I've never given it either. Until today."

My mouth gaped open as I tried to absorb what he was telling me. "How is that even possible?"

"I might as well confess it all," he said almost boyishly. "I've never had sex either, Clara. And you are the first girl I've ever kissed."

Shock would not begin to define my current state at the words spilling out of Henry's mouth. At the stunning, unfathomable reality that no woman had ever had this beautiful man in any way.

"Me?" I pressed a hand to my chest. "I was your first kiss?" I whispered like it was a secret.

He looked downright predatory when he said, "You're going to be my first everything, angel." His head angled in a way that screamed confidence. "And you'll be my last."

I blinked quickly, my brain racing to catch up with the atomic bomb he'd just dropped on me.

"But"—I licked my lips—"you were so, *so* good at it. How can it be even possible?"

He laughed, a blush creeping up his neck. "Porn. Lots and lots of porn."

There was a moment when he seemed unsure, that's true. I had chalked that up to jitters. His technique had been downright sinful.

"Good instructional porn, I take it."

"Apparently," he admitted almost shyly, squeezing my calf, "if you were satisfied."

I burst out laughing. "Satisfied, he says." I stared at him, shaking my head.

His expression softened into sadness. "It's not a turn-off, is it?"

"No way!"

I pulled my legs up and got onto my knees to crawl over to him. Up on my knees, I was a tiny bit taller than his seated position. Clasping my hands behind his neck, I smiled big and wide. "I am more than happy to be your firsts. It's just kind of incredible that you haven't. I mean, look at you."

He gripped my waist. "It was the incident when I was a child. I haven't been able to . . . let anyone close. The anxiety was too much. It isn't crowds that bother me, but to have anyone close to me." He shook his head. "I can't stand it. Except for you, obviously." He tried to laugh it off.

My happiness evaporated. For a few seconds, I was on cloud nine that I was the only woman who'd ever know Henry intimately. Then the reason behind it hit me, and my joy turned to ash.

"I'm so sorry, Henry." He'd never experienced the bliss of intimacy because his father had put him in the hands of a psychotic necromancer when he was a child. "That's not fair."

"Doesn't matter." He tucked a long strand of my hair behind my ear, the pad of his forefinger trailing the outer shell before he dropped it away. "You're here now."

"I am," I promised with every molecule inside me. "And I'm not going anywhere."

He pulled me into his lap, and we kissed with long, lingering, soft kisses until I had to go home to the triplets. He then scooped me up bridal-style and carried and kissed me through the house, down the hall, and all the way to my car where he belted me in and kissed me goodbye.

Blissed out beyond reason, I looked in my rearview mirror. He stood on the front walk, hands in his jeans, and watched me go, never leaving that spot until I disappeared around the corner.

Yeah, Henry. You are a romantic.

CHAPTER 13

~HENRY~

I COMBED FINGERS THROUGH MY SHOWER-DAMP HAIR AS I WALKED toward the entrance to the Cauldron. It was Sunday, and Clara had invited me to her family's Sunday dinner. This was a traditional gathering I knew all about. Hell, I knew everything about her.

My mind drifted to the library scene yesterday. Well, apparently not everything. I had no idea that she could steal the last ounce of my self-control and apparently my very soul by falling to her knees in front of me and sucking my dick.

She'd thought I was surprised because she was the sweet sister, a label I'd never actually given her, but perhaps she'd given herself. True, she was all pink princess and pretty smiles for everyone, but that wasn't what surprised me yesterday.

It was that Clara never seemed to waver. She said how she felt and did whatever she wanted, when she wanted, no thoughts to any consequences, emotional or otherwise. No fears ever kept her from marching steadily onward.

Meanwhile, I'd felt paralyzed by my own anxiety and fear my entire life. I hadn't stayed a virgin by choice. I'd tried to get close to other women in my twenties. A few times anyway. But every single time one would get close or try to kiss me, that clawing, smothering sensation of suffocation wrapped itself around me with alarming intensity. It never went away. So I eventually gave up and satisfied myself with my right hand. All was well.

Then I saw Clara. And then I met her. Rather than choking fear, a wave of relief and contentment stole over me. A rightness I'd never felt with anyone else. One hit of her soothing essence, and I was addicted. Enthralled. Wholly and absolutely enraptured.

If I hadn't met other Auras, I might think it was simply her magic that had me tied in knots. It wasn't just that she held the power to make others feel calm, peace, and joy. It was that she was Clara who held that power—the one person in the world meant for me alone.

Our ancestry and relations to vampires had given us the same possessive gene that vampires had. While werewolves' mates were chosen in a more animalistic manner, something their inner wolves determined for them, it was different for vampires and grims. For vampires, their mate's blood called to them. For grims, our mate's souls called to ours. It was a bone-deep knowing, sealed with our own magic and dark essence.

Mine wanted Clara. And no one else. It was the only concession I'd give the darkness since I kept it caged so well behind locked doors.

Stepping up to the entrance, I read the *Closed* sign, smiling at the fact that I'd read it from afar for too many Sundays to count, wondering what it was like on the other side of this door with the

Savoie family. Today, I'd find out. Not because I was an intruder, but because I belonged.

Clara had asked me to Thanksgiving dinner once, and I'd said no. It gutted me to refuse her then, but I hadn't felt like I'd belong. Today, I felt differently.

Still, my stomach flipped when I stepped inside, the murmur of voices overlapping filling the pub. Tables had been shoved together at the center of the restaurant area to make one long table. It was set with plates and silverware. But no one was sitting yet.

The entire clan hovered near the bar where three baby swings had been set up perpendicular to it. The Cruz triplets swung gleefully in the swings, Mateo standing near them with Nico, the two talking about something.

Everyone else sat or stood at the bar itself, except for JJ who was behind it. JJ and his boyfriend, Charlie, were the brother-figures and best friends of the Savoie sisters. Clara caught sight of me and literally ran across the room, launching herself into my arms. Chuckling, I held her against me and hugged her.

She squeezed me tight and then pulled back. "I'm so happy you're here."

And she was. I could feel it radiating from her like a physical touch.

"I am too," I told her honestly.

She took my hand and led me toward the watching crowd. Clamping my jaw tight, I stared right back, daring anyone to offer any kind of resistance to me being there. Then I noticed the smirks on Devraj and my cousin Gareth who sat on stools facing us.

"Everybody," announced Clara, "I think you all know Henry, but here he is."

She seemed nervous too.

Then Devraj started a slow clap that took about five seconds to catch on and for the entire bar to erupt in hoots and cheers and applause.

"About fucking time, grim," Violet shouted over the cheers and tilted back her drink.

Clara's face turned a deep shade of pink as they continued harassing us with applause and catcalls.

"You embarrassed? I can knock them on their asses for you." I could and would with my TK if she wanted.

"No." She laughed in that bubbly, bright way that sent my heart racing. "I'm just happy."

"That's enough," yelled Livvy. "Leave the two lovebirds alone."

The clapping died down but the laughter didn't as Clara pulled me closer to the bar.

"The look on your face," said Gareth as I stood next to him.

"I'm a little shocked at this sort of welcome," I admitted.

"You shouldn't be. They've all been taking bets on how long it would take for you two to finally get together."

"And I won," Livvy added, winking at me and then grinning at Clara, who hadn't let go of my hand yet.

"You had the benefit of Violet," added Gareth, curling an arm around her waist.

"Exactly. If you've got a good psychic for a sister, then you use that."

"She didn't tell me," argued Clara. "And I'm her twin."

"You know how she is." Livvy put her hand on Gareth's knee, the leg propped on the rung of the stool. "She's all superstitious and careful about her magic."

"Was she afraid it might not come true if she told me?" Clara snorted. "As if there was any chance of that happening."

I stood there and absorbed the scene, feeling like Alice falling down the rabbit hole. This was so surreal. I'd imagined myself at Clara's side a thousand times and the fighting I'd have to do to stay there. Grims weren't always welcome. Especially misfit ones.

Sure, I'd seen how easily they welcomed Gareth into the fold, but he was a respected businessman, accustomed to being sociable and likable. I was the opposite, preferring to be alone and brooding in a corner. This was not at all how I pictured my first family event with the Savoies and their men would be. I suppose it was the Savoies, the Kumars, and the Cruzes now that Isadora had married Devraj and Evie married Mateo.

I glanced down at the beauty at my side, my hand squeezing tighter of its own volition. My heart beat erratically at another thought—a distant dream and deep desire I couldn't even voice.

Clara Blackwater. Could that be possible?

"All right, all right," called JJ with his deep-barrel voice. "Enough harassment of the new guy. What would you like to drink, Henry?"

Grateful to step out of the maelstrom of emotion threatening to overwhelm me, I leaned on the end of the bar. "Any beer will do. I'm not picky."

"Coming right up."

Clara let go of my hand and turned to Charlie on her other side, sitting on a stool. She wrapped an arm around his shoulders. "Hi there, handsome. How's work?"

"All good," he said, looking across her at me, "but I want to officially meet the man that has you all moony-eyed."

Again. Surreal. I'd been blindly obsessed with her for so long that I took all of her casual conversations on the street, or wherever, as nothing more than Clara's embedded kindness. The way she was with everyone. But apparently, she'd been nurturing a crush as well. Though I could never call what had been growing inside of me something as small as a crush.

"Charlie, this is Henry Blackwater. Henry, this is Charlie."

He held out his hand, and I shook it. "Nice to meet you."

"Same," I told him as JJ delivered my bottled beer.

JJ crossed his arms and gave me a once-over. "I'd threaten you and give you the don't-hurt-her-or-I'll-kill-you warning, but I have a feeling that's unnecessary."

"Very," I confirmed, the darkness hissing in his cage at the mere thought of someone hurting Clara.

"Good to know. Welcome, grim."

"Dinner's ready," called Mitchell from the open door to the kitchen. He was the Cauldron's second chef to Jules but currently the only chef until she and Ruben returned from England.

Finnie, a waiter, and Sam, one of the line cooks, carried out bowls of something. Isadora was right behind them with a giant mixed-green salad.

"Come grab your plate," said Clara, leading me to the table. "You'll sit here by my regular spot."

She handed me a bowl and salad plate, then we filed into the line at the buffet table where the food was set out.

Mateo ambled up beside me and Clara. "What was this glitter incident I heard about?"

Devraj chuckled behind me. I glared over my shoulder. "It was an accident."

"Glitter-covered crotch doesn't sound like an accident," Mateo added cheerily.

"Who's got a glitter-covered crotch?" asked Violet, turning around from in front of Devraj.

"Nobody!" shouted Clara. "It was my fault. I was doing that glitter in the balloon display, and one popped."

"All over Henry's crotch?" Violet grinned.

"And his chest and mouth apparently," added Dev.

"A glitter grim." Violet arched a brow seriously at Dev. "I thought only vampires were supposed to be glittery."

"Fuck y'all," I grumbled, which had them all laughing at my expense.

Somehow, it didn't make me mad at all.

"Sorry," Clara whispered. "They're just joking around."

"They don't bother me," I told her honestly.

Somehow, their harassment made me feel like I belonged here. Besides, that memory was permanently embedded in my brain as one of the best moments of my life. My first kiss with Clara Savoie.

Mitch had made shrimp and corn chowder with corn bread and salad. Once everyone was settled and eating, Clara on my left, Gareth on my right, the conversation centered around the triplets. Now asleep in their swings, Evie dove into her bowl across from me.

"Oh my God, this is so good. I almost forgot what a hot meal tastes like."

"I second that, babe." Mateo devoured his meal at her side, both of them eating like they were starving.

"Just call me from my apartment when y'all are ready to eat." Clara wiped her mouth with a napkin, drawing my gaze to the perfect pink bow. "I'll watch them while y'all eat dinner."

"Thanks, Clara, but I don't want to bother you." Evie never looked up as she shoveled a big bite into her mouth.

"It's no bother."

"Well, you have been preoccupied lately," noted Violet from farther down the table.

Several pairs of eyes looked at me, but I ignored them and gripped Clara's knee under the table. Her hand rested over it.

"Is it not to your liking, Isadora?" asked Mitch at the other end of the table.

Isadora, who was dragging her spoon through the chowder, jumped, her smile weak, and said, "No, Mitch. It's fine."

Devraj wrapped an arm across her shoulders and leaned in to whisper something. He was telling her they could leave if she wanted. She shook her head.

Before I went back to my own meal, wanting to give them some privacy even though I could hear the conversation no matter how low they whispered, I caught Mateo and Nico giving each other a knowing look before they, too, went back to eating.

The werewolves knew something, but it seemed the sisters didn't. I hoped it wasn't bad news from England. Apparently, Jules had been well when they all went to visit her several months ago, as well as could be expected after what she had gone through, nearly sacrificed on a blood altar. The black magic that had been used on her that night had done some damage, putting her in a coma for days. I knew more than anyone the lingering effects of black magic.

Isadora had been the one most in contact with Jules and Ruben since she was checking in with the healer still watching over Jules. As far as I knew, Jules had made a full recovery. I hoped whatever seemed to be bothering her and Devraj wasn't a setback of some kind. Surely, their parents would send word to all of the sisters if that were the case.

"Clara, where are you planning to do for Jules and Ruben's welcome home party?" Violet asked from across the table.

"I'm not planning the party."

Livvy, Isadora, and Violet all swiveled their heads to Clara.

"I'm not," she declared emphatically.

"But you're our party planner," argued Violet.

"Usually, yes. But I think it's time someone else took over. I have other things to do with my time." She squeezed my thigh under the table.

Gritting my teeth, I refrained from jumping and dug into my meal.

"Oh, I see how it is. You finally get a piece of—"

Nico clamped his hand over Violet's mouth and looked at Clara. "Violet and I will take care of the party."

Violet muffled a surprised *what* under his hand, but he flashed her his wolf eyes with a growled, "Behave."

When she rolled her eyes, he let go of her and went back to eating.

"Fine. We'll give sis a break. Nobody blame me if it's a lame party, though."

Clara appeared pleased, sliding me a sneaky smile. I was finishing up my meal when Gareth pulled out his cell phone and checked a text. My attention immediately went to him when he stiffened at whatever he was reading. Then his gaze shifted to me, his expression hard as stone.

"What?"

"It's Sean." He nodded his head for me to follow, then said to the table, "Excuse us for a minute."

I was on my feet and following. Worried expressions watched us head toward the kitchen.

As soon as we pushed through the swinging door, I demanded, "Tell me." My heart was already pounding like mad.

Clara came in behind me, concern etched on her brow, but my focus was on Gareth.

"He's been arrested," he told me.

"*Arrested?*"

I felt Clara's hand on my back. Rather than try to wash away the sudden fear rippling through me with a joy spell, she simply gave me her calm presence.

"What the fuck for?"

"Peony didn't know exactly, but the charge was assault on another juvenile."

"Motherfucker. It's that same kid. I can fucking guarantee it. Wait. Human police or super?"

While supernaturals were often thrown into human jails after being caught by the local police, they could always get themselves out using any number of magical abilities. The supernatural jails and hospitals only got involved when it was a major crime. And while Jules presided over and dealt judgment for serious supernatural crimes, grims had always handled their own.

"Human." Gareth was already texting. "Peony is sending me the address. I'll get it to you."

Peony was our personal contact at Obsidian Corp, my father's company that dabbled in marketing but was really a front for its true business—intel. Grims could buy whatever they needed to know from my father. Ranging from what fights were fixed and who would fall in what round to which politician would win in a race to corporate espionage to whether or not a man's wife was cheating on him. Anything you needed to know—big or small—could be bought at a price at Obsidian Corp. It was private investigation on steroids.

"That's not all." Gareth wore that mask of stoicism, but there was a simmering anger I recognized behind his black eyes. "They called your father since he's his legal guardian."

"Fucking hell." I turned and stormed for the door. "Send me the address."

"I'm coming with you," said Clara, right on my heels.

I didn't protest, but acid churned at the thought of her seeing the shit show that was about to take place at the police station. Selfishness overrode any embarrassment because I needed her near me.

My father had wanted nothing to do with us since we'd left home. Except for birthdays when his secretary sent a card with a check, we never heard from him. But I knew for a fact that if he discovered what Gareth and I suspected of Sean, he wouldn't leave this alone. He wouldn't leave Sean alone, that's for damn sure.

Clara made some apologies to her family as she grabbed her purse and followed me out. My eyes were on the door, but I was trying to imagine what the fuck Sean had done to that bully at school this time. Pretty soon, the grim police weren't going to keep turning a blind eye.

We hopped into my car. Once her seatbelt was on, I tore off toward the downtown police station.

"Sean has been in trouble with a kid at school?" Clara had her palm on my leg, pouring her calming essence into me. It was the only thing keeping me sane at the moment.

"Yeah." I combed a hand through my hair before taking another turn. "Some football player's had a beef with him for a while. Sean lost his temper a few times."

"And?"

I didn't want to tell her because it made Sean sound like a psycho. He wasn't. But since his true grim magic was manifesting a little late, it seemed, his darkness guided his will.

"He pushed him down a stairwell with his TK, broke some bones in his arm. And fractured his hand on another occasion." I glanced over, her expression concerned. "He's not a bad kid, though. I promise. He might be a smartass, but he's never hurt anyone before. Well, not before this whole thing started with this kid, Baylor."

"I believe you. But breaking bones is worse than a school-yard fight."

"I know." I heaved a sigh. "Fuck, I know."

"It's more than that, isn't it?"

With a jerk of my head, I took another turn. "Gareth and I believe he's a grimlock. Like Gareth."

Clara was there during Richard Davis's trial, the one who'd targeted her sister Livvy and who'd been convicted in front of a supernatural jury, including Jules as final judge. She'd seen Gareth's beast execute Richard in the courtroom that day. She knew the deadly power of a grimlock.

"You're afraid of your father using him?"

I nodded. "Grimlocks are the most powerful of all supernaturals, and my father loves power. More than anything."

After pulling into a parking spot in front of the police building, I turned to her. "Are you sure you want to go inside? You can wait here."

"I'm going with you." Her brow pursed like she was angry with me for asking. "That's what partners do for each other."

I didn't know my heart could love her more. It was unbelievable how much.

"Let's go."

Taking her hand on the sidewalk, I led her into the police station. An officer at the reception desk looked up as we entered.

"I'm here to see Sean Blackwater. He's my brother."

The policeman eyed me for a second, then picked up the phone and called someone. "Status of Blackwater, Sean."

He listened to whatever the person on the other side said, then hung up. "He'll be out shortly with your father."

"Can't I see him now?"

The policeman laughed with a sneer. "This isn't a country club. You're lucky he's being released at all. The charges are being dropped."

"Come on," urged Clara, both her hands wrapped around my forearm, pulling me toward the waiting room.

The charges weren't simply dropped out of the kindness of their hearts. My father was powerful in the supernatural world, but he had influence in the human world as well. Because of his information highway at Obsidian Corp, he had politicians in his pocket. I was sure he'd made a quick call to someone important, who then made another call to the police station.

I didn't want to admit it, but he likely got Sean out of this mess when I couldn't have. One look at me, and people usually thought I was a thug.

Fortunately, I didn't have to stew long with the manic thoughts spinning through my head. Sean exited through a door to the right, followed by my father. Sean's gaze dropped when he saw me. Then another teenager with a blackened eye and his two parents, very well off by the looks of them, exited right after.

With Clara beside me, I walked to the exit in front of them and then held the door for Clara and my brother. When we made it to the sidewalk, I turned to him, ignoring my father, who trailed casually behind us. But before I could get one word in, the other teenager, obviously Baylor, stopped beside Sean.

"You better stay the fuck away from me, you freak."

With his usual cocky assurance, Sean replied, "You better stay the fuck away from Alicia."

"Come on, Baylor," called his father. "You've caused enough trouble for one day."

Baylor muttered, "Fucking freak," and then stomped away to join his parents.

"Good to see you, son," my father said to me with perfect poise, looking completely unruffled in his expensive suit. He looked healthy and fit as always, a bit more gray in his black hair at the temples.

I always marveled at how a man who was estranged from both of his children always talked to us as if we'd moved out of his giant mansion on friendly terms and still actually associated with one another. He was the king of denial.

"You didn't have to come," I told him.

He scoffed with arrogance, reminding me of Sean, which had me clenching my jaw. "If I hadn't come, my youngest son would be in jail."

I didn't argue that point because I knew it was true. Instead, I turned to Sean. "What did I fucking tell you about staying away from him?"

"I did," he argued. "I haven't gone near that asshole."

"Except today."

Sean's brown eyes darkened to black in a millisecond. "I caught him harassing Alicia, a nice girl in my math class. They were beside her car in the parking lot when I left late after my make-up test." The black bled into the whites of his eyes as he recounted the rest. "He had his hands all over her, up her dress even, and she was crying, trying to push him off. I wasn't going to turn my back and just go to my fucking car."

Of course not. As cocky as Sean was, he had a heart of gold. He'd defend anyone, but especially a poor girl caught by his greatest enemy. And I would've done the same, so I couldn't yell at him about that.

"So what happened then?" I asked.

His eyes widened and fell to the ground. Then my father stepped forward.

"That's when his grimlock essence manifested. His beast grabbed hold of Baylor's head and smashed it against the top of the girl's car." He smiled at me.

Shit. He knew.

"Yeah." Sean sighed. "Alicia was crying and covering her face, so she didn't really see my . . . monster. But Baylor saw it. Told the police I had used some kind of mind trick to make him see black snakes. Said I was a devil worshipper or some shit."

"So I," Father interjected, "then told the police that the poor boy must've hit his head so badly he was hallucinating. Once I explained that my son was only defending an innocent girl who might want to bring her own assault charges against Baylor, the parents agreed we should probably let this go. Then, of course, there was the call from the mayor's office that helped it along. So all is well. Come along, Sean."

Father turned and started walking away, his expensive shoes clicking on the pavement. Sean followed.

"Wait a fucking minute," I called to Sean. "Where the hell are you going?"

They both turned. Father's face no longer wore the amiable smile and now looked more like the stern asshole I grew up with. "You should've told me he was a grimlock, Henry. He should've been in training and learning to control it."

"What? Like you trained me?"

He flinched. "That was a mistake. You know I regret that."

"Do you?" Rage seethed through my veins, and I could feel the darkness swelling inside me. "If I recall, you were ready to start the training as soon as I came out of a catatonic state."

"I was only doing what was best for you. You *still* needed training."

"Which I got from Aunt Lucille."

He scoffed in disgust. "From my addle-minded sister. Right. Who only taught you to fear your gift, to cage it, not control it."

"I don't want to control it. I don't want it *at all*." Fury shook me from the inside as a shadowy darkness billowed around me.

"I only want to help you, son." He stepped forward, some new emotion I'd never seen flickering in his eyes before. "You'd know that if you'd answer my calls and texts, but you're so goddamn stubborn—"

"Like father, like son," I snapped.

"For Christ's sake, Henry, when are you going to forgive me and let us move the hell on?" His own anger rose in his voice.

"When hell freezes over, *Father*." My voice also rose with his.

"Stop it," hissed Sean, looking back at the police station.

Suddenly, Clara's hand was on the small of my back, and she poured calm through me. I breathed it in and swallowed the anger, the shadows receding instantly.

My father, stoic and cool as always, simply said, "Just because you refuse the help I can give you doesn't mean Sean wants to do the same."

When I looked at Sean, my heart sank. I could see it in his face. He did want to go with him. It gutted me.

He stepped closer and whispered, "Don't worry. I'll be home tonight. I'm not moving out or anything." He looked at Clara. "Take care of him, Blondie." Then he turned and left with my father, the one person I'd tried to protect him from his whole life.

Clara wrapped both her arms around my waist, hugging me from the side. "Come on, Henry. Let's get out of here."

Inhaling a deep breath, I watched Sean get in my father's car, trying to rid myself of the desolation coursing through me. Clara nudged me into motion, so we went to the car.

Once back on the street heading toward Magazine, I finally spoke to her. "I'm sorry you had to see all that."

"Why are you sorry? I want to be with you through the hard times too."

Swallowing hard because of the heavy emotions those words made me feel, I told her, "Thank you."

"You don't have to thank me. This is what we do for each other."

Reaching over, I grabbed her hand and kissed the back of it. "You have some questions for me? I'm sure you want to know more about my manipulative father."

"I do, but not right now. Will you drive to my house?"

Squeezing her hand I held in my lap, I murmured, "Sure."

Of course she'd want to go home. As kindhearted as she was, she likely wanted to get far away from the shit that was my life. I didn't blame her at all. We remained silent as I drove the rest of the way to her house and pulled up into the driveway, putting my car in park.

"Thank you for coming with me. I know it wasn't exactly pleasant. Will I see you tomorrow?" Likely, she needed a break from me.

"Henry?"

She smiled in that way that made me want to conquer the world for her. Like Helen of Troy, she could launch a thousand ships with that smile, she could command me to do anything and I'd do it. Even leave her alone for a while if she needed a break from me already. I'd do anything for her.

"Yeah?"

"I want you to come inside with me. And stay the night."

Swallowing hard, I let that sultry look she was giving me sink in. "Are you sure?"

"I'm positive. And we won't be sleeping until we're completely exhausted from having sex three or four times." With those words, she blew my mind and stepped out of the car.

CHAPTER 14

~CLARA~

I DIDN'T WAIT TO SEE IF HENRY WAS FOLLOWING ME. I HEARD HIS CAR door open and close by the time I was halfway up the drive. It was dark now so Evie didn't see me from the kitchen as I passed toward the carriage house.

Not looking back, I continued up the stairs, hearing Henry climb them behind me. When I unlocked the door, I kept walking, dropping my keys and purse on the counter before I made my way down the dark hallway to my bedroom. I turned on the small lamp that gave off the soft, cozy light I liked. My pulse raced, knowing I was going to see Henry's naked body under that light very soon.

Standing beside the bed, I kicked off my flats, pulled my top over my head, and then dropped it on the chair next to my vanity dresser. When I put my hands on the button of my skirt and unsnapped, Henry commanded sharply, "Stop."

"Why?" He wasn't about to put me off, was he?

He walked toward me, primal heat searing me in place. "Because I want to do it."

Oh my.

When he reached me, he lifted both hands to the straps of my white, lacy, transparent bra. "This is pretty."

His voice rolled over me, pebbling my exposed flesh. He eased the straps down, but my full breasts kept the cups in place. With his index fingers, he trailed over the curve of the cups, tingling my skin. My nipples responded instantly. He circled them through the lace.

"But this is prettier." His voice was husky as he lowered the cups, unsnapped my bra, and scooped my breasts in his palms, thumbing my erect nipples.

Breathing faster, I held on to his waist as he lowered his head and sucked one tip into his warm mouth.

"Heaven above," I whispered.

He tongued the tip, then sucked it again before giving the other one the same attention. Panting, I combed my fingers into his black hair. He lowered to his knees, staring up at me as he unsnapped and unzipped my skirt. I watched him, my curtain of blonde hair falling forward and caressing my sensitive nipples now that he'd tortured them with a short *hello*.

"I could probably come with you sucking my nipples alone," I told him frankly.

His mouth quirked on one side. Confident, self-assured Henry was alive and well and pulling my skirt and panties down my legs. "We'll try that sometime." He coasted his palms up the outside of my thighs, then to the front of my hips. He brushed one thumb along my tiny runway strip of hair. "But you said we need to have several rounds of sex before we can sleep, so I think we should get started."

"I think that's a wonderful idea."

He slid one thumb between the folds of my slit, my swollen nub already coated in arousal. "I love how wet you get for me."

I might've been embarrassed otherwise, because my pussy adored Henry Blackwater. All he had to do was walk in a room, and she was salivating. And when he put his hands or mouth on me, she was downright ridiculous with her enthusiastic response.

"Glad to hear it," I said breathily as he continued to explore, using his middle digit, palm up, to stroke through the slickness, "because she is quite a fan of you as well."

He laughed, flicking me a black-eyed glance before he angled his head and opened his mouth on me. He was French kissing my pussy, long tongue strokes and all. I sucked in a breath and clenched my fists in his hair, but that didn't stop him. Not that I wanted him to. I'd never experienced this level of pleasure from oral sex.

"Spread your legs wider," he whispered before going back at it.

When I did, he slid his middle finger to my entrance and then pushed inside me.

I cried out as his tongue went to work on my clit while he thrust a finger in and out of me. When he added a second finger, I came with a powerful jolt. He hummed through it. But when my legs trembled like I was going to fall, he pulled out his fingers and scooped me into his arms.

Two steps later, I was lying on top of my white comforter and Henry was shoving off his socks and shoes. He pulled off his T-shirt and dropped it. My heart dropped as well.

Still buzzing from my orgasm, I pushed myself into a sitting position and then pulled him closer. He came easily, letting me look my fill.

The tattoo I'd always wondered about was a stunning raven in flight, so huge it covered the upper left half of his chest, its wing tips draping down his abdomen and up to his neck. It was the edge of one wing I always had obsessed over that stuck out of his T-shirts.

There was another large tattoo covering the left half of his body. Melding from one tip of the raven wing was the upper edge of a butterfly wing. An absolutely beautiful butterfly was connected to the raven, all of it in shades of black ink.

"Your sister did this one." He tapped the butterfly.

"She did?" I scowled at him. "She never told me."

Now he was frowning. "Should she have told you?"

"She's known I've had a thing for you for a long time."

He went silent as I continued to explore with the fingertips of my right hand. My forefinger brushed over a ridge. I was so stunned by the beauty of his ink I didn't notice the scars protruding all over his chest and up to his neck. There was even a small one at the top of his neck that the wing tip covered.

My heart hammered for a different reason now. Not excitement, but dread. "What are these from?" I whispered.

He flinched as I roved my fingers over a nasty one near the raven's beak.

"That was from the incident with Amon."

"Spirits can actually harm you?" I nearly shouted.

He grasped my hand, lifted it to his mouth, and pressed a kiss there. "We can talk about that later."

He was right. Mood kill. I pulled my hand free and went for his belt buckle.

"Nope."

Suddenly, a force pushed me back onto the bed. I fell onto the pillow, and then my hands were pinned to the mattress beside my head. Henry was using TK to bind me. He already had his clothes completely off by the time I'd realized what he'd done.

"I can't touch you?" My eyes dropped to his erection, his hand giving it a stroke.

"Clara, I want this to be longer than fifteen seconds. You putting your hands on me is only going to speed up the process."

I spread my legs and bent them, giving him full view and access. His gaze dropped between my legs. I grinned, noting the piercing again.

"Why'd you get the Prince Albert?"

"It's supposed to increase a woman's pleasure during sex."

"But you've never had sex."

"I knew I would one day." His eyes blackened more as intense emotions swept through him. Even though I couldn't feel them with magic, I felt them wrapping around me in the natural way— from the way he devoured me with that dark gaze and the way he licked his lips as he stroked himself. "Was hoping anyway."

"When did you get that piercing?"

"Three days after I met you at Ruben's bookstore."

My heart melted into a bowl of mush. Yes, I was swooning and giving him heart-eyes over a penis piercing. "Let's try it out and see."

He crawled up the mattress and knelt between my legs. He wrapped a hand around my ankle and lifted it, turning his head to kiss the inside. He then proceeded to trail kisses upward.

"For someone who's never done this, you're really good at it." My breath quickened, chest rising and falling faster.

"Am I?" He'd reached my inner thigh. He bit with teeth but not enough to sting.

"Uh-huh."

He kissed a line up my belly, coasting over the globe of one breast until he was hovering inches above me. His eyes were full black now, his pensive frown and tightened features revealing a maelstrom of emotion coursing through him.

Since he wouldn't let me have my hands, I trailed a foot up the back of his calf. "Fuck me, Henry." Finally, I said the words aloud I'd said a thousand times in my fantasies.

He slanted his mouth over mine, maneuvering a hand between us to take hold of himself. He stroked his tongue deep as he slid the crown of his dick over my slit before pushing into my core. He groaned as he sank deeper and deeper. I rocked up and gasped at the tight, full sensation of him filling me.

"Too much?" he asked, his entire body flexed and tense.

"Perfect." I bit his bottom lip and sucked it before letting it go.

It was like I'd flipped a switch. He slid out to the tip and plunged back in. Pure ecstasy. Then he did it again and again, harder, and my toes curled. His piercing was hitting my G-spot on every deep thrust.

"Goddamn," he hissed, thrusting faster and harder. "You feel so fucking good."

I could no longer form words, fully focused on the insane pleasure tightening my body and catapulting me toward a second orgasm.

He nuzzled into my hair and sucked the tender spot below my ear. I arched my neck so he could get to whatever skin he wanted.

"I could do this forever, angel." He nipped my earlobe with teeth. "Could fuck you forever."

"I'm coming again."

He pushed up onto his forearms and stared down. "I want to see you when you come."

He rolled his hips and slowed his pace, still thrusting deep so that his lovely piercing worked a magic all its own.

A deep rumble vibrated in his chest as he watched me. "Goddamn. So fucking beautiful. Squeeze me tight just like that."

I cried out as I came, my sex clenching around him.

"Yes, like that." He pounded me harder, reaching his hand between us to pinch my nipple softly. Then I was lost in orgasmland, coming so hard my thighs started trembling.

"No, don't close your eyes, angel. Give them to me."

I'd squeezed my eyes shut when the peak hit me. It was impossible to keep my eyes open in that moment.

I pulled at my arms. He glanced at the movement and then set them free. I curled one hand around his nape, the other on his back, letting my claws dig in a little.

He groaned. "Love that. *Harder.*"

I dug my nails in a little deeper. "You like seeing how crazy you make me?"

He was still pumping inside me nice and steady. "If it means it'll make you forget any other man but me. Then fuck yes."

"Oh, Henry." Clenching my fingers in his hair, I pulled his head down to mine so I could whisper against his mouth. "There will never be another man inside me but you." Winding my legs around him, I rested my heels on his thighs while he rocked inside of me. "No one will lick my pussy or make me come or kiss my lips. No one but you."

He kissed me on a deep groan, throbbing and pulsing inside me. I whimpered as his body jerked roughly, losing a little control as he came. He thrusted a few more times, his chest rumbling with pleasure and vibrating against mine.

Finally, he pushed up onto his forearms, sweeping my hair away from my face with one hand. "That was"—he shook his head—"amazing."

"Understatement of the century."

His brow pinched with concern.

"What is it?"

"I was just wondering." He blew out a gusty breath, avoiding my eyes.

"Wondering what?"

"How long do you need before we go again?"

I burst out laughing, admiring the devilish glint in his coal-black eyes, the whites showing again.

"Whenever you are," I told him.

"Let's do it in the shower," he suggested, grinning with uncharacteristic glee.

"Fabulous idea."

So we did.

Once we were dry and burrowed under my covers together, skin to skin, I found myself drifting toward sleep, my head on his chest and one hand coasting up and down his chest. His hand was doing the same, trailing circular paths over my buttocks and hip.

When my fingers grazed yet another bumpy scar, it reminded me of something.

"You know," I told him, the room now completely dark, "Kinstugi is a cool Japanese art form. They take broken pieces of pottery and mend it together with gold to emphasize the brokenness of it becoming whole again. They believe there is beauty in that."

He remained quiet, breathing softly, his fingers still trailing sweeping circles over my bare hip.

I continued to explain. "The philosophy is that it is true that all things fall apart. Kinstugi teaches us about true strength and resilience through adversity. To accept our imperfections that make up the perfect whole that we are."

"Is that what I am?" he asked. "Broken pieces made whole again?"

"I don't know. Only you can answer that." I sighed, wrapping my arm around his waist and hugging. "But I always thought it was a beautiful idea. To mend the broken parts of us with gold, to be more beautiful because of our brokenness."

"There is nothing broken about you."

"Not broken perhaps, but I'm far from perfect."

"Name one imperfection of yours. I'd love to hear it."

"All right. I love to sing, but I sound absolutely horrible when I do. My sisters think I don't know, but I'm not an idiot. I just love to sing."

He chuckled below my ear. "Nothing wrong with that."

"But I get jealous that my twin sister can. And she doesn't even care. She's also crazy talented. Her artistic ability is absolutely beautiful. And Evie is even better. They got the artistic gene for sure. Then there's Isadora who is like the Goddess herself, growing plants and flowers and herbs with such ease, it's ridiculous.

Every time I try, I kill the damn plant. Livvy is not only more beautiful than anyone should be, she's smart and professional and everyone wants to be around her all the time. I know she's an Influencer, but she still has that charismatic charm that simply attracts everyone. Then there's Jules, who is this creative genius of a chef on top of being a badass Enforcer." I huffed in frustration. "The only thing I can do is make a mean cupcake."

He'd stopped laughing and seemed to be listening intently. He rolled over onto me, pushing me back onto the pillow, half laying over me. He looked angry. Furious even.

"What?"

"Clara. You are literally the kindest human being I've ever met in my entire life."

"So I'm nice. So what?"

"You seem to think that because you're not crafty or creative—"

"I am crafty actually, but it's not the same as what my sisters can do."

He shook his head, staring down with such intensity, it was a little unnerving. "You don't understand what I'm saying."

"Sure I do. I'm a nice person. I know that, but—"

"How many people do you know take food down to tent city—a dangerous part of town—to give food to the homeless? Most people lock their doors or speed on by when they hit that part of town. How many people do you know visit elderly ladies when they're sick? Bring them baked goods and not just deliver something, but sit down and give them their time."

I blinked swiftly, tears pricking a little.

"Do your sisters do any of that?"

"My sisters are nice too," I argued.

"I know they are. Yes, they've got their own talents, but Clara, the kind of good, giving heart that you have that speaks with actions and not words, it *is* a talent. It's a gift beyond compare, and only you have this. You walk into a room, and people instantly smile. You bring joy wherever you go. I know this because I've been watching you for over a year now, watching how people literally light up when you are around."

I blinked and sniffed, a tear rolling down the side of my cheek into the pillow. He wasn't done apparently.

"I've met other Auras. Nice witches and warlocks, all of them. Comes with the territory. But none of them have the innate gift of spreading love with nothing more than their presence, making others feel seen and important and loved, like they matter." He cupped my face and brushed his thumb along my cheekbone. "You do this, Clara. Every day. And you are the only one I—" He licked his lips. "I could ever have fallen in love with."

My heart stopped beating. I was sure of it. "Oh, Henry."

I pulled him down into a hug and buried my face in his neck. "I love you too."

He clenched me tighter and rolled sideways. We stayed like that for a long time, still holding on to each other as we both fell asleep.

CHAPTER 15

~HENRY~

I HONESTLY HAD NO IDEA I COULD EVER FEEL THIS WAY. SURELY, I DID once when I was a child before the tragic experience that damaged me beyond the scars left on my skin.

This feeling wasn't something as simple as joy or happiness. It wasn't just contentment or satisfaction either. It was something in between and above all of them, an emotion that calmed my heart and lifted my soul and made me feel whole again.

Clara. My beautiful Clara. The gold that was mending all of my imperfect, broken pieces.

I smiled as I gazed at her. She lay face down, her cheek burrowed into a pillow, long blonde hair spilling around her. I trailed a finger along her cheek and tucked a lock of hair back so I could look at her.

She made a little, soft sound of protest in her sleep, sounding like a puppy. I couldn't help but smile. She was so sweet and adorable and achingly beautiful and goddamn sexy at the same time. How did I ever land here? I'm not sure, but I wasn't going to protest my good fortune.

After sliding out of bed, I dressed quietly, then found a pen and a blue memo pad with puffy clouds all over it in her dresser. I scribbled a note, tore it off, and put it on the pillow next to her. Leaning over, I pressed a lingering kiss to her temple, inhaling the scent of her I was already addicted to. She didn't even move, completely knocked out. I worried I'd pushed her too hard last night.

That was another thing I knew for a fact I was addicted to. I needed to take it easy, but holy fuck. Finally being able to be intimate with a woman without wanting to claw my skin off with fear was one thing. But being able to be inside the woman I was profoundly, ardently, hopelessly in love with was like being handed the keys to heaven. Only, I felt like the devil in the playground of paradise.

What I *didn't* feel was what surprised me the most. I'd always looked at Clara and thought her too good for me, too benevolent to entangle herself with someone as fucked up as I was. But the truth was different. We matched. We fit together so completely that I knew the Goddess or Creator, or whoever the hell dabbled in our fates, had put her on my path for a reason.

When I met her, I had been in a state of denial that I'd ever be able to have a normal relationship with a woman. I was convinced I'd been cursed by the world, cast out because I'd rejected my magic, the gift I was given. So I'd been content watching her from afar, marveling at her beauty and unwavering kindness. Until I wasn't.

Until she bestowed that kindness on me. Little by little, my heart opened and my soul began to believe that maybe, just maybe, it could come out of its own cage. Just knowing her, talking to her briefly on the street or being invited to their family gatherings—something I wasn't ready for—slowly eroded away the shell of cynicism and defensiveness I wore wherever I went.

By the time we were speaking on a regular basis, the coldness I wore like a cloak had vanished altogether. And when I held her in my arms at Devraj and Isadora's wedding, I knew she would be it for me. If I couldn't have her, then I'd live out life alone.

Brushing my lips one last time to the crown of her head, I walked through her apartment and locked the outside door as I left. When I made it down the stairwell, I sensed a vampire.

To my left, in his backyard, Devraj stood in one of those yoga poses on one leg, completely balanced, his eyes closed. Moving more quietly, I thought I'd made it, but then . . .

"Good morning, Henry."

He remained perfectly still, eyes closed, but was grinning with obvious knowledge of where I'd been.

"Morning," I mumbled, stuffing my hands in my pockets and heading for the driveway.

I cringed when I heard voices on the porch. Evie and Mateo had been drinking coffee and whispering quietly till they saw me.

"Good morning, Henry!" Mateo yelled.

Evie laughed and raised her coffee in a cheers gesture. "Have a good time last night?"

I waved, feeling rather awkward and not knowing at all what to say. I tried to get to my car without running like I was guilty of something. Right as I reached my Mustang on the street, Violet pulled up in her SUV behind me. Before I could get into my car, she was out of hers.

"Hey there, Blackwater. The walk of shame looks good on you."

Fucking hell.

Gritting my teeth, I managed to say coolly, "Nothing to be ashamed about."

She carried a box of pastries with the Queen of Tarts logo on it. "That's right, grim. I'm sure you gave it to her good."

Surprised by the vulgarity, I frowned at her as she walked up to me on the driver's side of my car, where I was apparently frozen.

"She's your sister," was all I managed to shoot back.

"That's how I know she gave it right back to you. Didn't she?"

She clapped a hand on my shoulder. Strangely, I didn't react with my usual nausea or panic as she was well within my personal space. She was Clara's identical twin, but no one would ever mistake them. Violet not only dyed her hair frequently, though now it was more blonde than normal with faded lavender at the tips, she carried and expressed herself so differently. Violet was more swagger and sarcasm. Clara was . . . Clara.

"I've been waiting for you two to get together for a long time," she told me.

"You have?" Pure shock.

"Yeah, I saw it a long time ago." She patted my shoulder again and started walking away. "Took you fucking long enough to take the hint."

"I suppose so," I agreed.

"Bet some fireworks went off in the old carriage house apartment last night."

I had no words for that.

She grinned wide over her shoulder and kept walking. "Good thing I got donuts. She'll be hungry this morning."

Shaking my head, I finally got into my car and drove away, wondering at them all. They were so open with each other, and now with me. Like I was part of their inner circle. If I intended to keep Clara, then I suppose I was.

It was just strange to have lived such a guarded life—first, as a grim, and second, as someone who'd experienced childhood trauma—to now be thrust into a family where there seemed to be no boundaries. No hiding behind walls or pretending.

I wasn't sure how I felt about that. It was uncomfortable, but also welcome. How weird.

That's what was on my mind when I parked my car in the garage next to Sean's car in his spot, then went inside. It was still early, so I was surprised to find him in the kitchen at the breakfast table, shoveling some sugary cereal down his throat.

"Morning," I said, going to the coffeepot where he'd already made some. I poured myself a cup and took a deep sip of it, black.

"Hey."

Now this felt a little awkward, which was not the norm for Sean and me. I'd taken Sean with me when I left my father's house years ago. Sean had been in elementary school at the time, but Father didn't protest. Nor had our mother, who lived a world away and didn't care much about us anyway. Since then, I'd raised him and we'd become as close as any brothers could be.

Sitting across from him, I noticed he was beginning to fill out more. He resembled me in all ways, just less tattoos and more gangly. That was beginning to change, the hint of manhood cutting his jaw harder and broadening his shoulders.

"Look." I sat back in the chair as he shoveled and chewed. He was always hungry. "I get it. You want to learn more about

162

who you are, about your magic, but you can learn all of that from Gareth. You know that, right?"

He nodded and sat up, no longer hunching over his bowl like a caveman. "I know."

"Our father is just not trustworthy, Sean."

He looked at me a moment, and for the first time, I saw the man he would become looking back at me.

"I know how you feel about him. And you know I've never been a big fan either. But I want to get to know him." He clenched his jaw and looked away out the bay window.

"You can tell me." Because there was definitely something else he wanted to say but was holding back.

"I feel like I never had the chance to get to know him. I don't regret moving out with you, please don't think that. That's not what I'm saying. I just . . ." He shrugged and stared down at the table, tapping a finger next to his milk-filled bowl. "I know what he did to you was wrong. He told me he regrets it."

My abdomen clenched, my core tightening. As I opened my mouth to say I didn't give a fuck if he regretted it, he cut me off.

"I'm not saying you have to forgive him or that I even do. It's just that he is our father. He's the only one I have, and I want to get to know him."

These were words I never thought I'd ever hear. They were gutting and surprising but also told me a great deal about my baby brother.

He was growing up in more ways than one. This was the first moment I didn't look at him like a kid.

"You're right," I admitted reluctantly. "You deserve to get to know him if you want to."

God knows I'd wanted my father's love and approval at one time too. But I'd cut that fruitless desire away like a rotting limb long ago.

"Just be careful," I told him.

"Don't worry. I am. I actually told him that Gareth can teach me all I need to know as a grimlock, but I'd like to learn more about his business."

An unexpected flare of jealousy hit me. Not because I ever wanted to work for my father's company as he'd practically begged me to, but because Sean seemed to be beginning to have the relationship with Father I'd always wanted. And never could have.

"He's a selfish prick," I warned him.

"I know that." He snorted a laugh. "I'm not moving back to his house or anything." His smirk dropped. "This is my home."

It was the closest declaration of loyalty or love I'd ever heard from Sean. We weren't the touchy-feely types to express our emotions easily.

Swallowing hard, I held his dark gaze. "I'm glad to hear it."

For us, that was equivalent to *I love you, brother.*

"So you want to work at Obsidian Corp?" I asked lightly, wanting to shed the heaviness of the morning.

"I can't be a receptionist at Empress Ink forever."

"You could become an artist," I suggested.

He shrugged again, reminding me of the kid he still was. "Maybe. But I want options."

"I get that."

"So"—his smirk reappeared—"how was last night?"

"What are you talking about?"

He scoffed. "I know you stayed the night with Blondie."

"Who told you?" I'd just left her house.

"Where else would you stay overnight? Violet told me she needed a lot of comforting after her friend died." He ate his last bite of cereal. "It was just a lady in her book club, right? Not related or anything?"

"You don't know Clara. When she feels for someone, she feels deeply. Profoundly. Even grief. She can't help it. It's in her nature."

He plopped his spoon in the bowl of milk and sat back, grinning. "I'm sure she's feeling just fine today. After you *comforted* her all night long."

"Don't fucking talk about her like that."

"Ouch." He laughed. "Got it."

"And pick up your mess when you're done." I shoved his bowl toward him with my TK, which sloshed a little on the table.

He laughed as I stood and walked away.

"And stay away from that motherfucker, Baylor."

"I plan to," he called, then, "I was actually thinking of dropping out."

"*What?*" I rounded on him with anger.

"Wait, wait. Not quit school. I mean, Dad said there were homeschool programs at Obsidian for grims who didn't want to go to the human schools. I thought"—he cleared his throat, nervous—"maybe it would be better for me to get away from that school. From Baylor."

To hear him call our father "Dad" punched me right in the sternum. It wasn't that he shouldn't. My father wasn't really an evil man. He was a selfish, arrogant, power-hungry asshole, but I'd never thought him evil. Not truly.

I also didn't like to hear him make an educational decision without me and to be taking our father's advice. But still, I couldn't argue against it.

"You're right." I gave him a nod. "That might be best."

Then I headed upstairs to take a shower, my mind wandering back to Clara. That was all I needed to wipe away the negative feelings of this morning's conversation about my father. I smiled, hoping she liked the note I'd left her.

CHAPTER 16

~CLARA~

STRETCHING MY NAKED LIMBS, I YAWNED, MY BODY SORE. BUT IN THE best way. Smiling, I looked to my left, expecting Henry to be there. I sat up quickly, sad that I was alone. Then I noticed a note Henry wrote on my cloud stationery. Giggling, I picked it up and read.

Dear Clara,

There are moments in everyone's life where they think, 'after this day, I will never be the same.' It's those life-changing moments that are followed by either profound grief or extreme joy. So far, I've experienced both kind. One of acute despair— the day that Amon summoned demons and pushed me into the Gray Vale. And one of deepest happiness—last night.

I don't know what life has in store for us. I'd like to say I don't care, but I do. I want to be the one to bring only joy into your life. The way you have for me. I hope for this with all my heart. The one thing I do know is that I want to spend all of the rest of my moments—good or bad—with you.

Love, H

I reread it thirteen times. Tears of pure bliss rolled down my cheeks, one fat droplet falling to the paper. I quickly wiped it off with the edge of the sheet, noticing my skin.

"Oh my." I lifted my arm and stared at the length of it to my fingertips. Then looked at the other arm, both of them glowing with an opalescent light under the skin. "That's new."

Filled with utter contentment, I dressed quickly in gray joggers and a blue tank top. After brushing my teeth and tying my hair into a messy bun, I headed to my kitchenette. My tummy growled, which I didn't blame it. We'd worked up quite the appetite last night. That thought had me grinning even more.

After rummaging a few minutes, I realized that in my absent-mindedness this past week, I hadn't gone to the grocery. So I toed on my pink slippers and went downstairs.

Devraj was doing his cool garden yoga. "Good morning, Dev!" I waved.

He wobbled in whatever position that was, staring at me like I'd grown a horn or something. I looked at my skin. It was definitely *something*, but I had no idea what.

"Clara! Are you okay?"

I turned around to find him staring at me with concern. I laughed. "Never been better in my entire life." Then I waltzed into the kitchen.

Violet and Evie were talking in the living room. A baby babbled. One of the triplets was up. A pastry box from Queen of Tarts sat on the counter, so I bypassed saying hello first. I flipped open the top. Apple fritters!

My mouth was full when Violet walked in. "Holy hell!" She stood there all wide-eyed while I chewed. "What the fuck happened to you?"

"I don't know." Stretching out my arm, I admired my glowing skin. "It's pretty, though, isn't it?"

"You look like a fucking firefly."

Evie walked in, Joaquin on her hip, eyes bugging out when she saw me. "Omigod. Clara, sweetie. What happened?"

Giggling at their concern, because whatever was making my skin glow wasn't malevolent, I shrugged. "I don't know."

"Are you okay?" Evie hustled over and put a hand to my forehead. "Do you feel feverish?"

Joaquin reached out and petted my cheek. I laughed again, the joy bubbling up from inside me, as I kissed his tiny palm. He smiled, which was rare. He was such a serious baby. Old soul, that one.

"I feel absolutely *amazing*." Then I took another giant bite of the fritter. "This is so good. I may need another one."

Violet walked up to me and lifted a strand of my hair. "Your hair is glowing too. What the hell is this?"

I shrugged and bit another chunk of the fritter. "You know?" I said with a mouthful. "I do sort of feel something."

"What?" they asked in unison, concern written all over their faces.

"High." I laughed. "I feel totally high. Vi, you remember that time that Tia brought Isadora that batch of magic-infused weed, and the four of us smoked it in the garden? That's kind of how I feel."

Violet snorted. "Damn. That was a good high. I actually thought I could fly that night. Remember that? I almost jumped off the roof with a broom. Thank Goddess Tia wasn't as fucked up as we were."

"I remember." I laughed and then shoved the last bit of fritter into my mouth while skirting around them to the pastry box. "I thought I was a real fairy princess."

"Did you eat or drink anything odd or unusual last night?" Evie asked, still frowning.

Leaning against the counter, I held a chocolate glazed donut and grinned, remembering how I deep-throated Henry in the shower.

"For fuck's sake," said Vi, "not your grim's dick. She means actual food or drink."

"Nope."

"I think she's getting brighter," said Evie with concern. "Here, take Joaquin." She passed the cutie pie with strawberry-blond curls over to Violet, then went into the living room and returned with her phone, looking for a number or something.

"Y'all are getting worried for nothing," I told them. Setting the half-eaten donut down on a paper towel so I could get some milk, I poured a glass. "Whatever this is, it isn't bad. I feel wonderful."

"Look, Miss Aura," snapped Vi, hiking Joaquin higher on her hip. "You don't know. This could be some kind of weird curse."

"Is it a curse?" I asked Evie because she would know.

She stepped forward, the cell phone to her ear now, and pressed a palm to my chest. Closing her eyes, she searched for a hex with her magic. It tingled through me, making me giggle again. I couldn't help it. Everything seemed so funny and delightful this morning.

"No. It's not," she replied before talking into the phone. "Hey. Are you busy?"

Another pause as she stared at me while I continued eating. Joaquin was simply his quiet self, observing all that was going on. Then Isadora and Devraj walked through the patio door that led into the kitchen, Dev frowning and Isadora with the same wide-eyed look of shock Evie and Violet had a few minutes ago.

"What happened?" Isadora rushed over and pressed her palm to my forehead, pushing her healing magic into me.

"I'm not sick, y'all."

"Clara is glowing," Evie told the person on the phone. "I mean, head-to-toe, hair and all, glowing like a light bulb."

"Is it a curse?" asked Isadora.

Evie shook her head while Devraj crossed his arms and leaned back against the counter, frowning at me.

"I'm fine," I assured them.

"Yeah," said Evie. "Hang on. I'll video back." She hung up the phone and started a video call.

"Jules?" Violet asked.

Evie nodded. I rolled my eyes and licked my fingers from the last bite of donut.

"Look," said Evie, turning the phone to face me.

"Hey, Jules." I waved and took a sip of my milk.

"Hey, Clara. Are you feeling okay?"

"Good heavens. How many times do I have to say it? I feel *incredible*. Better than I ever have."

Jules's expression shifted, then she bit her lip, trying not to laugh. "Clara, did you take my advice about that issue you were having? The one we talked about when y'all video called me in London?"

"Yes!" I took the phone from Evie. "You were so right. I should've done it ages ago."

Jules was the one who told me to take the reins in dating Henry.

"And"—she lowered her voice—"have you guys been—Are the others still close by?"

"No need to whisper," shouted Violet, "we all know they had sex last night in her apartment."

"All night," Dev added with a sly grin.

"Shh." Isadora shoved him on the shoulder.

"What? I'm a vampire."

"Turn off your hearing."

He chuckled. "It's kind of impossible, love."

Jules smiled. She looked healthy and wonderful. Love looked good on her. "I think I know what this is."

"Yes?" I asked. The others shut up and listened in, but I didn't care. Nothing bothered me today.

"I've heard of this happening with some Auras. It's a sort of side effect after consummation with your soul mate. A manifestation of their deep joy through an aura everyone can see. It's called a soul-halo."

I beamed brighter. Literally.

"Whoa there, Tinkerbell," said Violet, taking the phone from me. "Dial it down. Jules, witches and warlocks don't believe in soul mates."

"Just because your race doesn't believe in it," added Devraj, "doesn't mean it isn't real." Then he pulled Isadora in front of him, wrapping his arms around her middle. She placed her arms over his and leaned back into him.

"You better not say that where Nico can hear you," advised Evie to Violet. "Werewolves are sensitive about the mate stuff."

She scoffed. "I didn't say *I* didn't believe it. I just meant that most witches and warlocks don't believe that one-mate-for-every-person thing."

"Like I said"—Devraj pressed a kiss to Isadora's temple—"witches and warlocks don't know everything."

"So . . ." I turned back to Jules on Evie's screen. "This is my magic telling me I've found my person. My *one* person."

Jules smiled. "Yes, Clara."

"I knew it anyway, but it's good to have magical confirmation."

Violet eased into view beside me. "Yeah, but what can we do about it? How long does it last? Is she going to explode into sparkles or something if she keeps having sex with Henry? Which is most definitely going to happen."

"She's going to be fine." Jules laughed. "I have no idea how long it lasts. But I can check with Clarissa and see if she does."

Clarissa was the head witch over all covens of our southern region.

Jules glanced over her shoulder, then turned back to us. "So I've got a little news I was waiting to tell all of you together. Well, kind of procrastinating."

"What's that?" snapped Violet, frowning.

"Um, Ruben and I got married last week."

"What?!" shrieked Violet and then Isadora, stepping away from Devraj and into view.

"We were going to have a giant wedding when you got back home," said Isadora. "That was the plan."

"I know, I know! But our mothers were driving us crazy about the wedding plans. And one day we decided, Gretna Green isn't so far away. We have some werewolf friends in Scotland who were happy to help out and attend. So we told our parents to pack their bags, and we all headed to the Famous Blacksmiths Shop in Gretna Green and got married over an anvil." She laughed, her cheeks turning pink. "It was *amazing*. My only regret was not having y'all there."

"Oh, Jules," I said into the phone, "that's the most romantic thing I've ever heard. Gretna Green! Just like Sebastian St. Vincent and Evie in *Devil in Winter*."

"Thank you, Clara. I knew you'd appreciate it more than anyone else."

"We're happy you're happy," Isadora added with a smile.

"I'm not. I'm pissed. That would've been a cool wedding to see."

"Sorry, Violet." She shrugged. "Ruben and I just didn't want to waste any more time."

"I get it," huffed Violet. "We can't wait to have you home soon. We're planning a big party to welcome you both back."

"Thanks, you guys. I can't wait either." She glanced off screen. "I've gotta run. Ruben is taking me to lunch. We're actually in Bath on our honeymoon." She giggled. Jules never giggled, and it was such a sweet sound. "But I'll see you all in two weeks. I miss you!"

There was a chorus of miss-yous and love-yous, then we disconnected with her.

"That reminds me," I told Evie as I handed back her phone. "Y'all need to finish planning their welcome home party."

"Why can't you do it?" Violet was still staring at me like I was a weird bug or something. "You love planning parties."

"I do. But I have lots of things to do these days."

"You mean your grim?" Violet arched her brow. "You might not want to do him anytime soon until this is all fixed." She waved to my body.

Ignoring Violet as I often did, because there was no way I was going to keep my hands and other parts off Henry, I finished the last of my milk and set the glass in the sink. After washing my hands quickly, I headed for the door.

"Where are you going?" asked Evie.

I turned to a full audience staring at me. "To get dressed for work. I have to open the shop."

"Pfft. As if. Make this stop first." Violet pointed up and down my body.

"I can't." I laughed again.

"Then you're quarantined, sis. You can't go in public looking like that."

I stared down at my glowing skin, smiling at how pretty and sparkly it was.

"I'll work Maybelle's today," said Isadora.

"You sure?" asked Devraj.

Isadora worked at the shop plenty of times by herself. She mostly handled inventory and bookkeeping, but she could manage customers for a day without me even if she didn't like it. Isadora was extremely introverted and preferred not dealing with people, and Dev was super protective.

Mateo then walked in wearing nothing but boxers, a sleepy-eyed Celine on his hip.

He took in the scene on a yawn. "What did I miss?"

"Clara fucked the grim all night and is now glowing like a goddamn firefly. And she can't stop it because apparently this happens when Auras have sex with their soul mates."

Mateo grinned, but it was the deep rumbly voice of Alpha that said, "**Sweet. All night? Gotta give that grim some respect.**"

I laughed, then headed toward the back door.

"You better not be planning to leave your apartment today," fussed Violet. "Not until you dim the lights."

"I can find something else to do."

"**Or someone to do,**" added Alpha, eyes flashing bright gold.

Actually, I had no problem spending the day in my apartment, playing last night in my head on loop. Of course, that might not make my skin stop glowing. A day off, crafting at home, would be nice, though.

And I had the perfect idea for what I wanted to make Henry.

CHAPTER 17

~HENRY~

I'D BEEN WORKING IN MY OFFICE AT HOME MOST OF THE DAY, GOING through the Super-tracer app on my Mac. This was an app Gareth had created to assist grims in tracking supernatural movements. By tapping into government satellites and using high-tech drones, he was able to create a monitoring system of supernatural movements using their heat signatures. All supernaturals looked different than humans in infrared.

Vampires were the most predatory of supernaturals. Grims should know since we were related. We could be the same, but we didn't crave blood the way vampires did. Their desire for blood could sometimes push them to do nasty things to other people.

When Ruben discovered we had the Super-tracer app, he wanted to use it himself to track his people in the city, to make sure no one was stepping out of line. Especially after that last blood-trafficking ring he'd discovered where some young vampires under his jurisdiction hurt quite a few girls and almost hurt

Isadora. That's when he partnered with Gareth to get the app to all those in charge of our kind.

The app showed up like a bird's-eye view of the city, tracking vampires through heat signature, zeroing in on anyone tracing. Vampires traced for a number of reasons. To get somewhere fast or to get away from somewhere fast.

Ruben and I usually split the monitoring duties, but I didn't mind taking over while he was gone. Devraj was handling the Green Light, and I was covering the app. It kept me busy.

I'd been at it for a few hours, finishing up last night's videos when Sean walked in. "Hey. You left your phone downstairs. It's buzzed a few times." He set it on my desk, then turned back for the door. "Headed to work."

Yeah, I'd left it downstairs, but not on accident. I'd done it on purpose, wanting at least one floor between me and my temptation to text Clara. I was well aware that I'd confessed quite a lot of personal feelings last night. And while she'd reciprocated, we were both riding high on post-orgasm endorphins.

It's not that I didn't think Clara would lie to me or exaggerate her feelings even. It's only that I wasn't comfortable sharing my feelings so openly. And then I went ahead and left my heart on her pillow in the form of a love letter expressing I wanted to be with her forever. I'd all but proposed the night after I lost my virginity to her.

Maybe she was thinking I was moving too fast or my admitted feelings were only because I'd lost myself between her legs, a heat-of-the-moment kind of confession. But that wasn't the case.

I'd been having these thoughts about her for a while now. Every time I saw her, learned more about her, talked to her, got close to her without sinking into a panic, I was aware that I wanted her. For a lifetime.

After leaving her apartment above their garage this morning, I'd started to get this itchy, nasty feeling in my gut. It wasn't regret exactly. I didn't regret my feelings. But I was starting to wish I'd waited just a little longer before I opened myself up to the kind of rejection that would slay me if it came.

I stared at my phone, my foot tapping, knee jumping under my desk. It buzzed again. Devraj's name with a text popped up on the home screen: **I just thought you should know.**

Shit. Something had happened. I swiped it open to find three missed texts from Devraj. None from Clara.

Devraj: You should probably check in on
Clara today.

Devraj: She's not hurt or anything, but
something's happened to her.

Devraj: I just thought you should know.

What the fuck did that mean?

Me: Is she home? Is she okay?
What happened?

Devraj: You should come and see for yourself.
She's in her apartment.

"Mother fuck, Devraj!"
What was this cryptic bullshit?

It didn't fucking matter. I just needed to get my ass to her house and find out. It didn't sound like she was hurt, or he would've said so. Unless he was just trying to keep me calm and she was really bleeding out on her sofa under a mound of pink fuzzy blankets.

Heart racing, I traced to my car and sped all the way to the Savoie house. Parking, I practically tore my driver's side door off getting out. I raced up the stairs of the carriage house and burst in without knocking.

"Clara!"

"Down here."

There was a light coming from the floor, her big club chair blocking the view of her.

"What's going on?" I hurried closer to the little living area. "Devraj said—" I froze, trying to understand what I was seeing. "What happened?"

Clara sat cross-legged, with a bunch of spools of craft string spread out on the floor. But it was the fact that her skin glowed with some sort of magical light from the inside that had stopped me in my tracks.

She smiled wide when she saw me and popped off the floor from her sitting position, some little stringy craft in her hand. "Isn't it awesome?" She glanced down at her arms and legs bared by that torture device of a pink pajama set.

"Who did this to you?" I growled, closing the distance and grabbing her arms. Expecting to be struck by whatever magic this was, I felt nothing but her soothing essence.

She laughed. "You did."

"Me?" What the hell? "Because I'm a necromancer or something? Is this some sort of ghost thing? I don't sense anything."

All I sensed was my own heart trying to beat out of my chest. I'd done this to her? How? "Is it permanent?" I practically shouted in her face.

Calmly, she looped her arms around my neck. "I have a present for you."

"Clara, what do you mean I did this to you? What is this from? Does it cause fever?" I felt her forehead.

"I'm not sick. This is perfectly normal. Rare, but normal. Come sit down." She took my hand and tugged me to her sofa and then shoved me down.

I dropped onto the sofa because it was obvious that whatever the hell was happening to her, it wasn't hurting her. And that was all that had concerned me in the first place. Still, she couldn't walk around like this.

"What is it then? Tell me," I demanded.

"Hold your horses." She straddled me on her knees, then settled down on my lap, scooting close.

I grunted, my dick instantly awake, but I wasn't giving him any chance on taking over this situation.

"Do you need medical attention? Can your sister Isadora help?"

She put two fingers over my mouth, so I would shut up, apparently.

"First, I have a gift for you."

She took my hand with the butterfly tattooed on the back of it and started tying the crafted thing—a bracelet in woven black threads, I could see now—around my wrist.

"I tried to keep it subtle." After tying it, she flipped my hand over, showing me the front of the bracelet and trailing her finger over the word I didn't know.

"Is this French or something? I don't know it."

She belted out a throaty laugh. "It's not French. It's us!" She trailed a finger along the letters woven in pink thread, reading, "*Clarenry*. It's our couple name."

"Couple name?"

"I thought of some others, but Henlara and Clenry sounded kind of weird. But Clarenry sounds so pretty. Sort of lyrical, don't you think?"

I stared at the black bracelet with hot-pink lettering, the girl of my dreams straddling my lap, wondering how I'd gotten here.

"Oh no. You hate it."

I jerked my head up, realizing I'd drifted off in thought. "No." I cupped her face—her sparkly, glowing face—and pressed a gentle kiss to her soft lips. "It's perfect."

"I know it isn't classy or very masculine. I was halfway through making it when I realized you might not want to wear pink. You'll really wear it?"

"I'll never take it off."

Her face lit up, literally, then she kissed me hard, angling to the side and stroking her tongue inside my mouth. On a groan, I kissed her back, my fingers edging into her hair. Automatically, my hips thrust up into her as she squirmed and made those sweet, sexy sounds.

Not yet. Breaking the kiss, I pushed her back a little. "Tell me what's going on with you."

There was no way I could relax until I understood her condition.

"I did some research today and made a phone call to my grandmother."

"The crazy one that was at Devraj and Isadora's wedding?" I rested my hands on the top of her spread thighs.

"I only have one living grandparent, and yes, that's the one. My shop, Mystic Maybelle's, is named after her. She gave us the investment money to open it up. She's a really sweet grandmother, even though she comes across a bit salty."

"Clara. Please tell me what you discovered today because I've never heard of"—I slid my palms up her thighs to the hem of her pajama shorts, marveling at the glow highlighting my fingers— "whatever this is."

"Let me tell you then. This happens only to Auras, but not to all of them. Apparently, it only happens to Auras who are so in sync with their magic that when there's a manifestation of emotion through this"—she pointed to her body—"light glows from within our magical core."

"Why is it happening, though?"

"Stop talking and listen, Henry."

Clenching my jaw, I forced myself to be patient, tightening my fingers on her thighs.

"This condition is called Aura Essence Reverberation, or more simply, it's a soul-halo. It happens when an Aura witch or warlock consummates their relationship with their soul mate. Actually, Maw Maybelle said it doesn't always have to be after sex. She'd had a friend, like two hundred years ago, and it had happened on the first day she met hers. Anyway, it's all very normal and expected actually, considering you're mine."

While she'd been rambling about Aura Essence Reverberation and soul-halos, I'd gone totally still, swept away with a potent concoction of emotion. Frankly, I was surprised I wasn't glowing too.

While fingering the bracelet on my wrist with one hand, she wrapped her other one around the side of my neck. "I loved my letter this morning," she whispered shyly.

There was not an ounce of regret simmering inside me. Not now. "I meant every word."

She leaned forward, pressed her breasts to my chest, combed both hands into my hair, and kissed me hard. She rolled her hips, stroking her pussy on top of my dick, making those little mewling sounds.

Fuck, I wanted her so bad.

Clenching her bare thighs, I rocked up, and we started a perfect rhythm, kissing and grinding and getting more aroused by the minute.

After coasting my mouth along her jaw to the silken skin of her throat, I licked and nipped down the slender column. "Sorry I did this to you."

"I'm not," she replied in a breathy voice.

"But you can't leave." Slowly, I slid the strap of her tank top and bra down until one pink-tipped breast popped free.

"Then I guess you have to stay with me."

Groaning, I opened my mouth on her nipple, tonguing and scraping gently with my teeth.

"Oh God!" she cried, rubbing her hot pussy harder against me.

Licking a circle around her hard nipple, I murmured, "Bet you could come with me sucking on these pretty tits."

"Yes." She trembled, trying to rock faster.

I yanked the other side of her top down her shoulders, pulling the bra strap with it, admiring her. Pressing her elbows back a little so that her breasts lifted toward me, I pinned her arms in place with TK.

She was panting, her cheeks flushing pink.

"Good?" I leaned forward and licked a circle around her other breast.

Her eyes glazed with arousal, her pupils nearly full blown, eyes dark, she nodded with a whining moan.

Gripping her hips, I helped her grind on my upward strokes. "Feel that?"

She kept making those insanely intoxicating sounds. Could a person get addicted to the sounds someone else made? I was afraid I'd need a hit every single day from here till eternity.

"Yes," she hissed, watching me tongue and suck one nipple, then coast to the other and do the same.

"That's how hard you get me." I thrust up, ready to come in my jeans for her.

She whimpered and moaned, her perfect tits jutting out for my pleasure. And hers.

"I could lick and suck these all fucking day." Another little stinging nip with teeth, then a suckle. "But what I really want is to feel you soaking these pretty pajamas for me."

She rocked faster, moaned louder.

"That's it, angel. Rub that sweet pussy on me. Mmm." I suckled noisily, her nipples hardening even more. "Come all over me, Clara."

Her moans intensified. She was close. Banding one arm around her waist, I shifted her up off me.

"No," she whined.

"Just a minute, baby."

"Please, Henry. Please. I need it so bad."

She was trembling as I went back to sucking one reddened tip. Using TK and my free hand, I pulled my dick out, slid her loose pajama shorts and panties to the side and thrust deep inside her.

"Ahh!"

I released the TK holding her arms. She gripped my shoulders, nails digging in, and started fucking me fast.

"Mmm. There you go. Ride me hard, angel. Take what you want."

She leaned forward, her mouth close to my ear, the slick slide of fucking and her panting breaths the only sounds in the room.

"All I want is you," she whispered. "I want you inside me all the time."

It was my turn to groan, my dick thickening even more as I stroked up inside her at a faster pace. I fisted a hand in her hair at her nape, whispering against her neck. "Does it feel good?"

"So good, Henry. I want it all the time. So bad."

"It's yours. Whenever you want it, I'll fuck you just how you need me to."

"Unh." She pulled back on her little grunt, her hands in my hair as she stared into my eyes. "So dark . . . so beautiful," she murmured as she slowed, tiring out.

I took over, holding her waist tight and pumping up inside her with quickening speed. She reached down and stroked her clit while I fucked her hard from the bottom.

"Goddamn. Yes." I watched her. "Let me see how you like that pretty clit to be rubbed."

She arched back, thrusting her tits out, letting me have a better view.

"Nice and wet, aren't you?"

"So wet," she panted. "So wet for you, Henry."

"Fuuuuck." I rumbled a growl, unable to stop my own orgasm. She felt too fucking good.

She circled her clit faster. I leaned forward and opened my mouth on her nipple as my dick pulsed inside her. Thank Christ, she came right on top of mine, screaming as her nails scraped into my scalp. I tongued and sucked her tip to keep her orgasm rolling with mine.

"Yes," she breathed as she continued to writhe gently on top of me. "So good."

A growl rumbled in my chest as I swept my mouth down her throat, kissing her as she came down from her climax, her pussy still throbbing where I was buried deep inside her. It was the most satisfying feeling I could imagine. To have this woman I loved experiencing pleasure that I gave her.

"Oh my," she said, still breathing hard. "What's that look for, Henry Blackwater?"

I looked up, meeting her gaze, her soul-halo glowing even brighter than it was before. "I really enjoy fucking you."

She burst into laughter, which had her sex squeezing around my dick.

"Hey! Careful." I laughed with her.

"So glad to hear it, because for someone who hadn't done it before, you sure know what the hell you're doing."

"There's not much to it," I told her.

She rolled her eyes. "That's what you think." She ghosted a kiss across my lips. "I love the way you fuck me, Henry."

My dick jerked inside her.

"He likes to hear that, doesn't he?" she teased.

"He likes everything you do or say."

"So compliant. I like that." Then she hugged me, arms wrapped tight around my neck, letting out a satisfied sigh.

I hugged her back. "You're mine, Clara. Just like I'm yours. And I'm never letting you go," I promised her.

"That's wonderful to hear. I'm not either." She squirmed. "But you might have to let me get up before we make a mess on my sofa."

"Oh shit. Right."

Hands on her waist, I lifted her off and stood at the same time. Tucking myself back into my jeans, I noticed my come dripping down her inner thigh.

She was looking down at it. "Uhhh. Could you help me out and get—?"

"Fuck. Of course. Stay right there."

I traced to the bathroom and grabbed a towel, wetting it with warm water before tracing back to the living room. I started to dab her clean.

She smiled. "I've got it."

Then it hit me. My pulse pounding even harder than it had during sex. "What the fuck have I done, Clara?"

She glanced up, puzzled as she righted her panties and pajama shorts, her top already back in place. "What's wrong?"

"We didn't use condoms or anything." I clasped my hands on the back of my neck. "Shit. I'm so sorry."

"It's okay," she said easily. "I'm on the pill."

I clasped a hand to my chest. "Thank God."

She slipped past me to head to the bathroom with the towel. My pulse still pounded from the dizzying sex and then the scare that I might've knocked her up because of my stupidity. I hadn't once thought about pregnancy. Since the second she brought me up to her apartment, the only thing I was thinking about was getting my dick inside her.

Hell, I had to do better than this, think about her more than being a selfish prick. I doubt she'd take kindly to getting knocked up because I'm such a self-centered asshole. Thankfully, she had already been thinking with her brain, not her libido. Or maybe both.

When she returned, she had on some joggers and a T-shirt, looking adorably rumpled. "I got dressed earlier, but then once I realized I couldn't leave the house right now, I redressed in my pajamas."

"Until I ruined them."

She grinned as she finally made it over to me. "Delightfully ruined."

I pulled her into my arms and pressed my face into her neck, inhaling that delicious scent of hers. "Thank you."

"For what?" she asked, all sweetness and Clara-like.

"For being mine."

She giggled and kissed me on the jaw. "I love this."

"What's that?"

"The sweet, adorable boyfriend Henry. I've been waiting to see this side of you."

Feeling oddly comfortable in her apartment after I'd only been here twice, I sat down in her club chair and pulled her to sit sideways on my lap.

"So what now?"

"Looks like I'm quarantined, so I'll be staying here for the time being."

"Any idea when this will go away?"

"Maw Maybelle said it might linger only for a few hours or even a day or two."

"Is this going to happen every time we have sex?"

She stroked a finger over my raven tattoo's wing tips that crossed one collarbone. "I don't know, but I don't think so."

"Maybe we should abstain for a bit so your skin can go back to normal." I wanted to cut my own tongue out for suggesting such a thing, but she was definitely a brighter wattage since I'd walked in.

"Will you watch *The Great British Bake Off* with me?" She blinked those gorgeous blue eyes at me, ensuring I'd do anything she wanted.

"Sure. Will you bake me something afterward?"

"Of course." She beamed. "I love baking. I still have the ingredients for cupcakes."

Instantly, I was hard again. Huffing out a breath, I dropped my head to the back of the chair. "Dammit, Clara. Now you've got me thinking of strawberries and cream cupcakes again."

"So? What's wrong with that?"

I lifted my head, gaze back on her. She blinked innocently, but there was a devilish sparkle to her eyes.

"Don't even fucking play. You know what." I pinched her ass.

She squealed and squirmed closer, then pressed her forehead to mine. "You liked my cupcakes?"

"I love your cupcakes." I cupped her ass and squeezed. "All of them. I'm not sure I'll ever be able to walk into a bakery again without getting a hard-on."

She giggled. "What if I need you to go get me something at Queen of Tarts?"

"I'll wear a long jacket."

"Then people will think you're weird or a robber for wearing a long coat in this weather."

"I am weird, and I don't care what people think. If my baby needs pastries, then I'm gonna get pastries. Erection be damned."

Smiling wide, she nuzzled her nose along mine. "I love you."

She said it so easily. Like it was nothing at all when, in fact, it was everything. Those three words from her were now synonymous with breathing. I needed them to survive. I needed her.

"I love you," I rasped against her mouth, then kissed her slowly, all lips and no tongue.

Before she tempted me further, I gave her rump a gentle slap. "Grab that remote. Let's watch some *Bake Off*."

"Yay!" She did a little dance in my lap, then quickly bent over to grab the remote on the side table.

That was how I spent the next twelve hours. Curled up on her sofa, wrapped around my girl, watching British people bake puddings and breads and cakes. In between, she baked a vanilla cake herself with strawberries-and-cream icing. We ate it on the sofa with milk and with our clothes on.

It was the best day of my life.

CHAPTER 18

~CLARA~

"Piers was just too stubborn." Evelyn sipped her Earl Grey with mint from the pink English Chippendale china teacup.

I loved this china pattern. I'd bought it from an estate sale on eBay and had it specially shipped from the family in Maine running the sale. Apparently, it had been in the family for decades from when they lived in England. But none of the grandchildren wanted it, the seller had told me. I didn't understand how anyone could throw away something so beautiful just because it was old and had a few chips here and there.

"Of course he was stubborn," snapped Martha. "He's the beast character. What did you expect him to be? Friendly and charming?"

"Settle down, Martha." Deborah passed her a plate. "Here, eat a brownie. That'll make you feel better."

"I don't feel bad at all." Martha gave Deborah one of her looks. "I'm just confused why Evelyn didn't like the stubborn hero who happens to be based on the beast from the fairy tale."

"I didn't say I didn't like him. I'm just saying he could've been less ornery."

"Hmph." Martha stuffed her mouth with the brownie. "Mm. These are good, Clara."

"Thank you. I did a lot of baking this week." I glanced at Henry.

His dark gaze was laser-focused on me. I don't think he'd moved from that position since we'd sat down. My tummy fluttered.

"Martha's right," I said to the group, feeling Henry's nearness on my right like a warm caress. "The main characters definitely follow what we'd expect for Belle and the Beast. I think that's what made the tragic, climactic incident with Linnet so devastating."

"I'm not afraid to admit that I cried at that part," said Fran. "When she fell sick and she was wishing he'd find her, and he was tearing up the countryside to save her."

I blinked back tears, Fran's emotions bleeding heavily into the room and onto me. Clearing my throat, I added, "That part always gets me, too, Fran. I get emotional every single time, but more at the end at the swimming hole. When he's trying to convince her she's worthy of love, of his love, no matter what she looks like."

"Oh yes. I cried at that part too," added Deborah, picking up an oatmeal raisin cookie.

"Me too," added Fran.

Martha turned a sardonic look toward Henry. "What about you, Mr. Blackwater? Did you cry too?"

As usual, he took her goading easily. He looked so handsome, sitting there with one ankle crossing the knee of his other leg. I loved that he appeared so much more confident in the book club than he had the first time.

"I think the ending scene between Piers and Linnet perfectly exemplifies one of the main themes of the novel." He sidestepped Martha like a champ. "Like Piers had to deal with his own injury, Linnet is faced with bodily imperfection from the sickness that changes her perception of herself. Makes her bitter and angry, self-loathing. And like she did for Piers, he is the only one who can make her see the reality."

"Which is?" asked Martha.

All of the ladies were riveted by Henry. How could they not be? So was I.

"That her beauty doesn't matter. Only their love. That's what saved him from a life of embittered despair, and that's what will save her too."

Yet again, Henry had entranced the room into silence. His insight was always so deep. Perhaps because he felt things deeply as well.

The clock on the wall showed it was nearing the hour.

"I suppose that's the perfect way to wrap up today's meeting."

"Well, nobody can top that," added Martha as the ladies started picking up napkins and plates.

Evelyn stood from her seat next to Henry. "You're such a joy to have with us," she told him with a pat on his tattooed arm.

For some reason, her gesture and the sight of her wrinkled hand patting him with affection brought tears to my eyes. I blinked them away and helped Fran with her purse and then quickly stowed the remaining sandwiches and sweets in the boxes I'd set out on the table near the doorway.

"Don't forget your to-go boxes," I told them.

"Thank you." Deborah beamed, taking her box.

"What's our next read?" asked Fran as she took hers.

"*Lord of Scoundrels* by Loretta Chase," I replied.

"Ooh." She waggled her brows. "That one sounds delicious."

By the time they'd all left, Henry had carried the dishes to the kitchen. The house was quiet since Evie and Mateo had taken the kids to the park today while I held my book club meeting.

I met Henry in the living room, coming out of the kitchen.

"You ready?" I asked him.

"For what?"

"I'm taking you somewhere."

"A surprise?"

"Yep."

He smiled one of those rare bright ones that sent my pulse racing as I grabbed my bag and we headed to his car.

"Okay, where am I going?" he asked as he pulled up to the intersection of Magazine and our street.

"If I told you, then it wouldn't be a surprise. Just take a left."

He followed my directions all the way to the New Orleans Botanical Garden in City Park. "Have you ever been here?" I asked him.

"No." He looked around at the gardens at the entrance area.

"Come on."

I paid for the tickets, shoving his wallet away when he tried to pay. "My surprise," I told him.

It was a weekday so not as many visitors, which is what I'd hoped. I pulled him along through the giant garden, only slowing down when he seemed to be admiring something. Eventually, I wound him around to the back where I'd wanted to bring him.

I'd never been here either until last week after talking to Isadora. She'd told me about this place. I'd checked it out and found exactly what I was looking for.

"Okay, it's not like a big surprise." Suddenly, I was doubting he'd see anything special in it. "I mean, I'm not sure it's as beautiful as the one you grew up loving."

Finally, we arrived in a secluded spot with an array of flowers that attracted the butterflies he seemed to love. Little orange and black ones flitted around them.

He stared at the garden, giving zero reaction. This was always the hard part for me—when Henry went blank-faced—because that was the only way I knew what he was feeling and thinking.

"I thought maybe you could come here when you need to. It's not the same as the other one, but there's a little privacy back here. And you wouldn't have to sneak around your father."

He squeezed my hand, still looking at the butterfly garden.

"I was thinking we could relax under that tree and watch them. I brought a book in my bag."

Maybe this was a silly idea. Then he turned to me and scooped me into his arms, pressing a kiss to the side of my neck.

"No one has ever been so good to me."

I hugged him back, cherishing the feel of his strong arms and warm body surrounding me.

"I don't deserve you." He pulled back to meet my gaze.

"Of course you do. Don't be ridiculous. Do you think the Goddess made a mistake tying us together? If so, you're wrong. We were meant to find each other."

Rather than respond with words, he lowered his head and brushed his lips along mine, coaxing them apart with gentle sweeps. He sealed his mouth to mine and kissed me deeply. Pressing my body against his, I suddenly wished we weren't in public.

He broke the kiss, grinning down at me. "Don't even think about it."

"What?"

"You know what." He took my hand and headed toward the tree I'd gestured to just a minute ago. "The last thing we need is for you to start glowing like a light bulb."

"We don't know that's going to happen every time." I frowned as we settled onto the grass. I leaned back against the tree. "And I'm getting kind of, you know . . ."

Rather than sit next to me, he lay down with his head in my lap. He tugged on a lock of my long hair, twirling it in his fingers. "No, what's that?"

"Horny," I said flatly.

He chuckled, dark eyes full of mischief. "I know the feeling, beautiful. I just don't want to quarantine you to the house again."

"Next time, let's do it at your house. I wouldn't mind being quarantined there." I played with the longer locks of his hair on top, pushing them aside. "I'll stay there forever if you want. You can chain me to your bed and do whatever you want with me."

His eyes darkened in a millisecond. "Fuck, Clara." Then he adjusted his cock in his jeans. "Don't say things like that. I'm getting all sorts of images."

"Are they of me in a see-through lace teddy, my arms and eyes tied with silk cloth? Because I could go for that. I already have the teddy." His black eyes were already bleeding into the white.

"You wouldn't technically need the silk ties, though, since you can use your TK, but I like the imagery of it. Don't you?"

"I'd sell my soul to make that fantasy a reality." His voice was deep and rough.

"No, sir. You will not. Besides, you already said your soul was mine. And I'm not giving it back."

He started twirling the lock of my hair again. "My heart too."

"Not giving that back either. Now." I reached over and pulled the paperback from my bag. "Let's read a little Lisa Kleypas, shall we? I'll read Helen's dialogue and the narration, but I want you to read the part of Rhys."

"Why's that?"

"Because hearing you read Rhys is perfect foreplay before we go back to your house. I also have my teddy in my bag."

He shot up and scowled at my bag. "You do not."

Arching a brow at him, I dropped the book into my lap and reached over and opened my bag. Pulling out the black lace teddy that was less material than the bottoms of my bikini, I held it up for him. I could see his stricken face through the material.

"See?"

"Goddamn, Clara." He snatched it from me and shoved it back in my bag. "You literally are trying to kill me, aren't you?"

"That's not my intention, no. Quite the opposite."

"Let's go now."

Laughing, I shook my head. "No, sir. Come put your head in my lap and let's read and enjoy this beautiful day."

It was one of those perfect spring days where the temperature didn't get above seventy-two and puffy white clouds floated across the blue sky.

Groaning, he lay back down in my lap, adjusting himself again. Smiling, I opened the book. Before I could even start, his big hand was on the pages, pushing the book out of the way.

"I'm not going to be able to concentrate now."

"Sure you will. And now we have something to look forward to."

He stretched his hand higher, cupped my cheek, and brushed his thumb on the underside of my cheekbone. "I always have something to look forward to when you're with me."

My eyes misted instantly. I blinked the tears away, feeling so emotional today for some reason. Leaning into his hand, I then turned and placed a kiss on his palm.

"Let's read."

So we did. We settled in for an hour at least, soaking in the beautiful day and the blissful company of one another.

I was a happy person pretty much all of the time. Even in moments of sadness and grief, I never lost myself to negativity. I'd been lucky with a loving family and a wonderful life. It wasn't perfect, but even as an Aura, who were always optimistic people, I'd experienced a life of joy.

Yet still, nothing compared to this, my current state of pure, unbroken contentment and pleasure simply basking in the presence of my beloved. I had no idea it could feel this way. I thought my fascination for him from afar was what it would always feel like. I was so wrong.

This reciprocated love, this growing friendship, this soul-deep bond with my now best friend in the world set all the other joys in my life apart.

I was admiring the way his gorgeous mouth moved as he read the passage when Rhys gets Helen at the train station. My skin tingled at the way he read the aggressive, possessive hero of the story. Then he stopped, his phone buzzing in his pocket.

He pulled it out and looked at the number, frowning.

"What is it?" I asked him.

He sat up and answered. "Hello."

His expression darkened the longer he listened.

"Are you fucking kidding me?" he asked the person on the other end.

I placed a hand on his shoulder.

"Did you do it?" he asked angrily. "You better tell me the truth."

He listened more, then finally hung up, staring into the distance.

"What happened? Is it Sean?"

He looked at me. "No, it's my father. He's been arrested for murder."

CHAPTER 19

~CLARA~

The guard in the front reception area stared at us. The lobby contained only a sleek modern desk and black well-stitched leather sofas. Glasgow, the grim jail in NOLA, was named after its founder, who had established the first prison network and offices entitled the GOA, Grim Office of Authority. It looked like a posh billionaire's penthouse rather than a prison.

"Why did you bring a witch here?" asked the glaring guard, a beefy, hulking guy.

"Because I fucking wanted to. I'm on your list. Grant me entrance," demanded Henry, his voice vibrating with power. "Now."

Beefy Guy glared at him another minute, his eyes turning blacker, but he ended up punching a button. The soft beep of the door being unlocked gave us the go-ahead. Henry opened the door for me, still giving the guard a murderous look.

"Why are you being so mean to him?" I asked as the door shut behind us. "He's just doing his job."

"No, he's not. He's being a bigoted, witch-hating prick."

"What?"

He had his arm around my waist, one hand resting on my opposite hip as we walked down a white hallway with abstract paintings on the walls. Apparently, we'd exited the penthouse pad and entered the high-end art gallery.

"Look, grims are, in general, rather superior bastards as a whole. Most of them see themselves above everyone else because many of them think they're more powerful."

"According to Livvy, you are more powerful. I saw what you and Gareth did in that courtroom. And from what Livvy told me, you guys have an awful lot of TK power you don't let others know you have."

"Just because someone has that kind of power doesn't mean they're better than other people."

"I know that." I wrapped my arm around his waist and squeezed him. "But treating them with disdain isn't going to change their contempt or attitude toward us."

Henry looked down at me as we approached a guard at an elevator. "You're too kind, Clara. Guys like that don't deserve it."

"Who does? Just because someone is an asshole doesn't mean they aren't deserving of kindness."

Then we were at the next guard.

"Henry Blackwater to see Silas Blackwater. His attorney put me on his list."

The grim world was interesting. They had their own prisons and their own rules. Their jail had no bars, no scary, high-security locks on doors, but there were lots and lots of video cameras. Everything was high-tech.

The new guard tapped on a thin laptop at his station. He wasn't big and muscly like the front receptionist guy. His power came from within. When he turned his cold gaze on Henry, then me, there was a near-menacing pressure filling the air. Lots of power, this one. Subtly, Henry eased his body in front of me.

The grim never stood from his station. He simply looked at us with glacier-cold eyes. "You've been approved, but there is no . . . *witch* on the list."

He didn't make the mistake of referring to me with condescension. However, there was still a subtle dismissive tone in his voice.

"Call his attorney if you need to, but she's coming with me."

He clicked on the computer, then picked up his cell phone and furiously typed something.

"You're clear. Room 1013. Exit to your left."

Henry ushered me into the elevator ahead of him.

"Why haven't they taken our IDs for verification of who we are?"

"There are scanners everywhere. This place is fully wired with biometric security."

There was a camera in the upper corner of the elevator, a small, inconspicuous one.

"What's biometric security?"

"Grims have developed the top biometric software in the world. It identifies people by face recognition, voice, fingerprint, retina. Glasgow was fully loaded to observe exactly who everyone is the second they walk in the door, scanned for multiple biometric recognitions." He took my hand as the elevator approached the tenth floor. "They're watching our every move. They control our entrance and exit of the building."

"But your TK is strong. So is Gareth's. What if y'all wanted to just come up here and break your father out of jail?"

He laced our fingers, his thumb rubbing little circles. "First of all, I don't want to get him out of jail. We'll likely discover he is guilty, and it'll be good riddance of him."

Lie. I detected it instantly. Perhaps he wanted to *want* to leave his father rotting in jail, but deep down, Henry wanted him out. Probably the young boy inside him who still wished his father had been a good one also wished his father was innocent of this crime.

I didn't say anything as the elevator dinged open and we stepped out onto the tenth floor of the prison facility.

I was expecting something ghastly, even after being marshalled through this extremely clean and stylish place. After all, we were now being admitted into the prison cell area.

It was another long hall, at least double the one we walked down from the reception area. There were doors on both sides of the hallway, and I could see that it turned a sharp corner to the right about ten rooms down. Apparently, each floor was a square block of prisoners, seeming to house about fifty or sixty of them on each floor.

Henry tugged me behind him until we reached room 1013. He looked up at the camera in front of the door. There was one in front of every door.

A clear voice—the one belonging to the Laptop Guard—resonated through a small speaker. "You have twenty minutes for visitation. The doors will lock at exactly six-thirty. If you're not out of his room, you'll be on lockdown with him until tomorrow morning."

"We'll be out in ten," snapped Henry to the camera, then he pushed the steel door open.

His father sat at a clear, plexiglass desk bolted to the floor. He was no longer wearing the expensive suit I saw him in at the human police station. He now wore something akin to high-quality black pajamas.

Across the room, there was a window with a view of the Mississippi River. Beneath the window was a double bed covered with a soft down comforter and fluffy pillows. The bed frame also seemed to be made of plexiglass, not steel or wood. Other than the odd transparent furniture, this place was freaking nice.

Was grim prison a luxury resort?

Henry's father looked up, seemingly shocked that we were both standing there. His demeanor was no less regal and confident than before, but I could sense the anxiety beating off him. That could be because he was guilty and had been caught or because he was innocent and had been framed. It was too early to tell.

"Father."

"Thank you for coming. Both of you." He stood and nodded.

"Clara isn't here out of the kindness of her heart. She's here to determine if you tell me a lie."

I pinched the back of Henry's biceps. "Don't be so mean," I whispered.

Silas Blackwater's foul expression softened. "Don't fret, Miss Savoie. I'm accustomed to my son's harsh treatment."

"You're going to chastise me about harsh treatment?" snarked Henry.

"Not at all. You take your shots, son. If it makes you feel better."

Henry was vibrating with rage. I placed a hand at the center of his back, and the tension instantly receded. He blew out a breath and glanced down at me, his eyes not as black as I'd expected.

"Have a seat." His father gestured toward the small set of leather chairs and love seat beside the desk.

"Grims sure know how to treat their prisoners well," I couldn't help but comment.

Henry's father looked at me and smiled. It was genuine. Even the emotion rolling off him felt real. He was relieved I was here. Thankful even. Interesting.

"Grims are a hard race." He sat in the chair perpendicular to the love seat. "But they do believe in innocent until proven guilty. If there's a chance they have an innocent man on trial, they want to be sure he's afforded a comfortable place to live and build his defense."

"Does that mean all of the prisoners here are waiting for trials?" I sat closest to him on the love seat, knowing what my role would be once the real inquisition began.

"No." He rolled up his sleeve. "Some are waiting out their sentence. Not all convicted are put to death or even stripped of their magic."

"Though that's usually the final sentence," added Henry.

I didn't need to have my Aura connection with him to know that he was angry. It was written in every hard line and angle of his face, not to mention the hard tone of his voice.

"True enough," said Silas, holding out his arm for me. "Are we ready to get started?"

"You don't mind?" I asked, hovering my hand over his forearm.

"Not at all. I have nothing to hide."

Henry kept quiet, but the tight set of his mouth and his stiff posture said enough.

On the way over, Henry had called his father's attorney and gotten a brief explanation of the charges. After he hung up, he'd merely told me that Silas was accused of killing his lover. He'd seemed to want to say more but then we'd arrived and he ushered me into Glasgow. So here we were, interrogating his father.

"Let's get started then." I looked at Henry. "Go ahead."

Henry didn't hesitate. "Did you kill Beatrice Plath?"

"No," he said emphatically but not with anger or defiance. "I did not murder Beatrice. I found her in a pool of blood one minute before the authorities arrived."

I waited to be sure. Sometimes detecting truth required waiting for a delay in response. Sometimes lies lingered behind the speaker's stalwart belief that they were innocent. Either way, I'd know it if he lied. There would be an ugly rippling effect of the speaker's magic, stinging me with their falsehood.

Hesitating a moment longer than was necessary to be absolutely sure, I detected no lie at all. The steady thrum of his magic, cool and strong, pulsed through him and vibrated under my palm and fingertips, vindicating him.

I turned to Henry and held his sad, hopeful, furious, desperate gaze. "He's telling the truth."

His eyes widened slightly, his jaw clamped, and he stared at me as if waiting for me to change my mind. There was no changing an Aura's mind. Our magic was clear and true.

"I am certain," I told him anyway since he seemed to need me to say it a second time.

Turning back to his father, he asked, "Did you in any way plan or hire someone to murder Beatrice Plath?"

"No."

Henry waited. So did I. Then I said, "Truth."

"Do you know who would want to murder her? Or why?" he asked.

"No," Silas answered emphatically.

"Again, truth," I said.

Henry was leaned forward, his elbows on his knees, hands clasped between them, one knee bouncing. "You can let him go, Clara."

Removing my hand, I then sat back.

Silas did the same, pushing his sleeve back down. "I was framed."

"So you said on the phone. You have theories who did it and why?"

"Son. I am head of a multibillion-dollar company that tracks the sins and crimes and depraved activity of thousands upon thousands of people, most of which is used against them by a former lover, political opponent, or business rival. My enemies are innumerable."

"Tell me in complete detail what happened. How you found her."

He exhaled a heavy breath, radiating not only frustration and anger but also sadness. "We were meeting on Friday night as we always did on the weekend."

"At your home?" asked Henry, seemingly shaken.

"No. I have a rooftop condo in the warehouse district for the two of us."

Henry's posture relaxed. He obviously didn't like the thought of someone being murdered in his childhood home, which meant he still had some fondness for it.

"I'd picked up takeout. Bea likes the ceviche and shrimp tacos from Lucy's on Tchoupitoulas. It was right around the corner from the condo."

He coasted a hand through his hair, looking so much like Henry it was startling. It was also a nervous tic of Henry's when he was anxious. Reaching out with my Aura senses, not to be invasive, but to seek more understanding, I brushed along his emotional psyche.

"So I'd left her at the apartment. She had just arrived from work at the gallery where she's curator. She said she planned to get a shower while I picked up dinner." He cleared his throat, staring at the carpet now. "I returned to find the door slightly open. I didn't think. I rushed in. There was a magical signature in the room. Definitely a grim. Bea was—" He cleared his throat. "She was on the floor in her bathrobe. It had been partly torn off. There were red marks around her throat, already bruising."

"But you said she was in a pool of blood."

"She was. A bottle of wine had been broken, the one I'd brought home with me and set on the counter. The killer had broken it and used the jagged handle to stab her in the heart."

He stood and paced away to the window. I pressed a hand to my chest, overcome with the mixture of rage and deep sadness emanating from Henry's father.

"You loved her," I said softly.

Henry's gaze jerked to me, but I was watching the proud man with his hands clasped behind his back, looking out at the river.

"I did," he finally admitted. "After being without a partner or any family around at all for so long, I'd finally found someone." The sadness spilled into the room, pooling much like the blood of his beloved, I imagine. "Bea was so smart. Bright and beautiful. She had a great sense of humor too. Terrible at remembering things. I'd bought her a grim-made smartwatch to help remind her of things so that I could add dates I planned to her calendar."

An awful silence filled the room. Henry stared at his father like he didn't even know him. Perhaps he didn't. Perhaps he wasn't the man Henry had known as a child anymore.

"Bea was the only person in this world who gave a damn about me. And some fucking bastard murdered her."

Another brief silence. Henry had become a stiff statue next to me. But he finally asked in a much more even tone than he'd been using when we walked in here. "She was human, wasn't she?"

He turned around, the afternoon sky silhouetting his tall figure against the light. "Yes."

Henry visibly flinched next to me. Unsure why that would cause him to react, I put my hand on his knee, which was no longer tapping a mile a minute.

"And so you were there with her, then the police came in minutes behind you?"

"Yes. They'd received an anonymous call of someone screaming in my apartment."

Of course. The killer wanted them to arrive as soon as Silas returned. He continued.

"I'd pulled her into my arms and was—" He swallowed hard. "They entered the open door, a group of grim officers from here. Though I was obviously grieving over her, they thought it a sign that I regretted my 'act of passion,' they'd called it."

"What about your own security surveillance?" Henry's brow furrowed deeper. "It would've caught everything on video."

"The surveillance footage was completely fried when it was viewed. The grim officers claimed I'd obviously tampered with the surveillance video myself to keep the authorities from seeing my crime." He scoffed disgustedly and returned to the chair, sitting down with another weary sigh. "The stupidity of it is ridiculous. How can you call it a crime of passion if I'd planned it so well I'd tampered with the surveillance?"

"Did you tell them that?" Henry asked eagerly.

"I did. They said any grim who'd committed that sort of crime, even in the middle of a rage, could've taken two seconds to fry the circuits. Especially a tech-charmed grim."

"Tech-charmed?" I asked.

"Someone whose magic is supernaturally attuned to tech. Like Gareth. And my father."

"Why don't they just use an Aura?" I asked. "They could verify if he was telling the truth."

"It's not enough proof for grims." Henry looked at his father. "It's like a lie detector test that humans use. It can't serve as evidence. Some people can beat a lie-detector test."

"What about psychics?" I urged.

"They tried," Silas added bitterly, now slumped back in the chair, looking defeated. "The killer used her blood to perform a black magic rite. A deceiver spell."

I must've looked confused because Silas explained further.

"A deceiver spell can disguise a scene and the events that took place there. Sealing it with blood assures there's no breaking it. No psychic will be able to penetrate the cloak and discover what happened there through their Sight. Not through a blood hex."

"And the GOA thought you'd cast the spell, right?" I asked gently.

"Yes. Because I've killed someone before, they thought it easy enough for me to lose my control in another act of passion."

Henry stiffened. "What are you talking about? Who else did you kill?"

Silas stared at his son steadily. "Amon, of course. After what he did to you, I murdered him. Once you were upstairs in your bedroom, I called the authorities. They brought their psychics, who saw what had happened. Because of his crime against an innocent child, which is punishable by death, they let me go. I was never charged, but they keep records, of course. And now, they see that as evidence I'm the most likely perpetrator here. They believe I'm a powerful grim who'd do 'anything to escape justice,' they said. Even use the blood of the woman I loved to do it." He paused, a burst of anger rolling off him. "The bastard used my Beatrice's blood to cast a curse."

I couldn't help but walk to him, put a hand on top of his arm, and push a calming spell into him. He was in so much pain. "I'm sorry."

Silas looked at my hand, then at me. For the first time since I'd heard about this cold-hearted father who'd raised Henry, I saw a soft vulnerability in him. His dark eyes, just like Henry's, sparkled with bitter sorrow.

"I was going to marry her," he whispered.

"I'm truly sorry," I said again, pushing more of my emotional healing into him.

It seemed to soothe him. He closed his eyes and inhaled sharply. I stepped back, not wanting to gauge Henry's reaction to me feeling sympathy for the man he'd grown to hate so much over his adult life.

"What is it you want from me, Father?" He wasn't angry anymore but resigned, it seemed.

"Henry." His voice cracked. "I need you to go into the Gray Vale and find her."

"No," snapped Henry, standing and pacing away.

Silas stood from the chair and walked closer to him. "You're the only one."

"What are you fucking talking about?" Henry spun around. "There are literally hundreds of necromancers you can get to do the job."

"They can't." He shook his head. "They've already used three, all top-tier necromancers. She's nowhere to be found."

"Then she's gone. She's moved out of the Vale, and there's nothing we can do."

"She hasn't," Silas stated with hard conviction. "She wouldn't go on. Her spirit would've lingered and seen what happened afterward. You know more than anyone that newly severed spirits, especially those cut from the physical plane in violence, linger a few minutes before they go into the Vale. You *know* that. And those who die in violence never move beyond the Vale right away. Never."

I wanted to ask how he knew all these things, but Henry didn't argue. So it must be basic knowledge of necromancy.

"She would've seen her murderer, and she would've seen me come in after, only minutes before the GOA showed up and arrested me. She wouldn't want me to be falsely persecuted."

"What makes you think I can find her if the others can't?" Henry faced his father with very little defiance and anger, but still seemed cold to him, his body stiff and rigid.

"Because you're my son. Our blood is the same. She'll answer to it."

They stared at each other, Henry clamping his jaw and Silas seeming to beg his son with a soft, sad expression.

"I can't do it," Henry finally answered, stepping around him to return to my side. "I'm sorry. But I can't go back in there, especially not where you want me to go." Henry held out his hand to me. "Come on. Let's go."

"Henry," I said softly, "I think you should at least—"

"They'll kill me." Silas's words were followed by a deadly silence.

Henry dropped his head and closed his eyes, muttering something to himself.

"Whoever did this, they planned it well. They knew all the ways to ensure I'd be convicted. I believe the killer placed two hexes that night. One to cover the evidence with a deceiver hex. But before that, he cast a spell on Beatrice's spirit, to banish her into the darkest depths of the Vale. To Esbos. No necromancer would look for her there."

"Because no sane necromancer would go there willingly," snapped Henry.

"I know that. But son, her soul could be trapped in Esbos. I can't sleep, thinking about it."

"You could be wrong. She might not be there."

Silas didn't respond at first. It was obvious Henry was denying all possibilities of finding her. Then finally Silas broke the tension-filled silence.

"She was a good woman. She had no enemies. She was murdered because of me and is likely now trapped in a hellish place with no way out. I can't go on knowing my sins put her there."

Henry spun, his voice vibrating with fury. "You realize what you're *asking* me. Where you're asking me to go."

"I know. Please, son. I wouldn't ask if I knew any other way. No one can prove my innocence but you. My penalty will most definitely be death."

"Un-fucking-believable," Henry muttered. He turned away, his body visibly trembling. "I can't. I can't fucking go back there." He pressed a hand to his chest, his breathing quickening as he paced farther away.

Silas dropped his head, a look of defeat folding his shoulders inward. I walked to stand beside Henry and placed a hand on his rigid back.

"I can't fucking do it," he muttered, his face bleached of any color. Fear had wrapped its sharp tentacles around him, panic etched in his expression as he stared at nothing, remembering what had happened to him as a child.

I rubbed my hand along his spine, pushing my calming essence into him. "It's okay, Henry. You *can* do it. I know you can. You're a strong, powerful grim. You brought Miriam back in a blink."

He finally snapped back from the panic, turning to look at me. "You can do this. I believe in you."

For a moment, he simply stared, his face full of the anxiety riding him. Then slowly, it melted away, the confident Henry I knew returning from his ghostly past.

"Fine," he finally said, never turning to his father. "I'll try."

"Thank you, son," said Silas in a low voice.

"I'll need to see what she looks like. She may not come to me when I call her."

Silas walked quickly to the desk and opened a folder. "My lawyer can send you any information you need from the crime scene. For some reason, they let me keep this photo of us at an exhibition of her favorite artist."

He handed over the photo. I peered down at Silas, looking sharp as always, but smiling abnormally wide next to a stunningly beautiful woman. She wore her hair in a short, pretty pixie cut which accentuated her smooth sandy-brown complexion, high cheekbones, and full lips. She seemed to be laughing in the photo, not simply smiling. They were happy and in love. Again, grief wafted over me from Silas.

Henry's eyes widened in shock as he looked down at the picture.

"My attorney can get you anything you need," added Silas. "Peony has the number."

"How is Obsidian Corp managing without you?" Henry's voice had softened as he looked down at the photo.

"Harold and Priscilla are managing it. They'll be fine without me."

Henry stared at the photo for a long minute before finally saying, "We have to go." He ushered me toward the door with a hand at my back. "I'll send updates as I have them."

Henry didn't look back as we left, but I couldn't help myself. Silas Blackwater stood in the middle of his bougie prison cell, looking heartbroken and crushed but somehow hopeful too. Henry opened the door for me to walk through, but I stopped and smiled at Silas.

"It'll be all right. I'll help him find her."

His disheartened expression softened with relief and gratefulness, his voice full of nothing but the utmost respect. "Thank you, Miss Savoie."

Once we were down the hall and to the elevator, I turned to him. "What is it?"

"I knew her." Then he frowned. "Well, not really. She came looking for me a while back to talk to me about my father. But I didn't bother calling her back when I had time."

"Why didn't you?"

He wouldn't look at me, seeming a little ashamed. "I thought it was work-related, my father wanting a favor or—no—what I really thought was that my father didn't deserve my time. So I ignored her." He clamped his jaw. "And now she's dead."

"That has nothing to do with you. It's not your fault. And you're perfectly within your rights to still be angry with your father. Right now, it's about saving his life. Because he is innocent of his crime, Henry. That, I am absolutely sure of. And it's about saving her soul if she is actually in that place."

He gave me a tight nod, then reached for my hand and laced his fingers with mine. "Then I'll do all I can."

"Of course you will." I leaned my body close to his, giving him the emotional support I could, reveling in the absolute goodness of him.

The fear was bright and true in his eyes at returning to the place that had left deep scars—both physical and mental—on him. Yet, he would face his old demons anyway to save his father who'd helped put them there and the soul of a woman he didn't even know. I loved him more than ever in that moment.

CHAPTER 20

~HENRY~

"I FEEL LIKE I'M IN A JAMES BOND MOVIE," CLARA WHISPERED AS WE walked away from the reception area of Obsidian Corporation and down the long hall toward my father's office.

We'd come straight here from seeing my father at Glasgow.

There was a sleek, secretive vibe to the entire building of Obsidian, including everyone in it. I'd gotten the side-eye from the girl at reception, but she knew who I was on sight. When I confirmed that I was the CEO's son, she didn't bat an eye that I had a witch at my side and was parading her around my father's business that rarely, if ever, had a supernatural other than a grim in its hallways.

"My father's business is based on confidential information, so everyone here is a bit, I don't know—"

"Cloak and dagger? Spy-like?"

"Yeah." With a hand on her back, I guided her to the right toward the CEO and top executive offices. "My father's right-hand man is Harold Stansbury. He's the Chief Operating Officer and handles the day-to-day operations. He's also been my father's best friend since their college days. Priscilla is the CFO and manages the financial end of the company. She's been with Obsidian for over a decade."

Clara nodded. "And Peony is your father's assistant?"

"Mm-hmm. She's also been Gareth's secret contact for ages," I whispered low, even though all of the office doors we passed were closed.

Surprise lit up her face as she whispered, "Gareth's got a spy in the spy company?"

"Yep."

She grinned and arched a brow at me. "You grims are so cool."

Smiling, I finally guided her into the large reception area that was Peony's office, the gateway to my father's. Peony sat at the wide, glass-top desk, tapping away on her computer, an AirPod in one ear. She looked the same the last time I'd seen her—straight black hair to her shoulders, professional, colorless blouse and skirt, and no-nonsense demeanor.

Standing behind her was Priscilla, watching what she was typing. She wore an equally boring business suit, but it fit her slim figure to perfection. Her gray hair was twisted into a tight knot on her head, her cat-eye glasses in place.

Peony looked our way first and then smiled. She knew that I knew she worked for Gareth on the sly, but of course neither of us ever addressed it. Still, it seemed to make her friendlier to me than most people. She was a snarky woman. Reminded me a little of Violet.

"Hi, Henry." She stood and walked around her desk and shook my hand. "And you must be Clara." She shook hers cordially as well. "Your father's attorney told me you'd be coming."

Priscilla was then there, shaking my hand next. "Good to see you, Henry." Though her monotone voice didn't say so. "How's your father holding up?"

"As well as expected for someone accused of murdering his mistress."

"His fiancée," Priscilla corrected.

I glanced at Peony, who gave a tight nod. "She was."

Strange that the sadness I felt was split in half—one for the loss of a woman who meant a great deal to my father and second for the fact he'd never even thought to introduce her to me or Sean. As well as the fact that I'd had the chance to meet her and threw it away.

This whole situation felt so strange. That I even gave a damn about a man I'd basically cut off from my life. Maybe it was the child's hope that still lived inside me for a father who cared about his sons more than his company. Apparently, he had. His fiancée, Beatrice, was trying to tell me so.

My mind drifted back to the day she showed up at Ruben's Books & Brew. The day I'd refused to even meet her. A stinging pain pinched inside my chest. I was so adamant to reject my father, I hadn't even met with or listened to her. I figured he'd sent her to try to bridge the wide gap between us, and I suppose she had. I'd gotten so used to my own stubborn willfulness to deny my father any sort of truce that I couldn't soften a little bit that day. I could've met her, this lovely woman my father loved.

The fact that my father had loved a human was even more mind-boggling. He'd never stoop so low to even date anyone but a grim before. Perhaps people can change.

"I won't keep you," said Priscilla, as if she had, her gaze flicking to Clara. "I would like to—" Then she paused and frowned.

"Excuse me?" I urged. "You'd like to?"

Priscilla glanced at Clara, then Peony. "Nothing." Then she turned sharply to Peony. "Send the report as soon as you finish."

Then she left the office at a brisk pace.

"Don't mind her," Peony told Clara. "She's rude to everyone."

"Does she always stand over your shoulder while you work?" I asked.

"Only when she's in a hurry for something. Which is basically always. But she's been keeping everything in line, including the board members calm, since your father's arrest." She rose from her chair, strode toward his office door, and opened it, letting us walk in first.

"I hadn't thought of that."

Father's office certainly reflected the man—cold and minimalist except for a picture frame on his desk.

"I keep his extra apartment key in his safe," Peony explained. "He sometimes asks me to drop confidential files by the apartment after hours rather than to send digitally. The apartment is much closer to Obsidian and to my own place, so I always leave them on his foyer table."

"Does anyone else know the combination to the safe?" I asked, wondering if someone here had used that key to get into my father's apartment. Perhaps someone had gotten the combination from Peony and then took the key but replaced it before anyone noticed. Or maybe it was even Peony herself. It was no secret that she and my father argued over company finances all the time.

Father said there had been no forced entry. There were some grim telekinetics who had extremely sophisticated skills like Gareth who could open a complex lock system, but they were rare. And as far as I knew, he was the only grimlock living in the area. My father would have installed a supernatural-proof lock on the condo as he did on the home I grew up in. It wasn't an exaggeration that he had many enemies. Some of whom would want to kill him—or frame him for murder apparently.

"Priscilla has access since there are financial records stored here as well." She gave me a knowing look over her shoulder as she went to the far wall. "It isn't a combination, though."

She pressed her hand to the pad on the outside of the safe and then peered into the biometric detector above it.

"It's double-protected. Not to mention the lock to his office door and mine and the building itself. As well as the video surveillance. Someone would've had to lop off my hand and taken an eyeball or Priscilla's in order to get into this safe."

There was a tiny click, and she opened it. She took out a thick manila envelope and a key on a ring with a fob.

"The fob opens the door to the building. And this is a copy of crime scene photos and notes from his attorney. Your father instructed him to give it to you."

I scoffed. "Father was confident I'd come here, wasn't he? That I'd help him."

"Your father is always confident, Henry. You know that."

I took the keys and then the envelope, staring down at it. I wasn't sure I wanted to see those photos.

"He loved her," Peony said quietly.

When I looked up at her, she was staring at the photo on his desk. It was a different photo of my father and Beatrice from the one he had in his cell at Glasgow, perhaps another gala or something. They were both smiling and looking at each other, her arms around his neck as if they were dancing.

"They did love each other," Clara added softly.

Peony walked to his desk and picked up the photo. "This was at the annual fundraiser Obsidian hosts."

"He took her to the company fundraiser? So she knew what he was?"

"He told her everything about our world."

"Maybe that's what got her killed," I suggested. "Maybe it wasn't an enemy of Father's but someone who didn't think a human should be privy to my father's world."

"Perhaps. Whoever did it . . ." Peony looked pointedly at the envelope that I held in my hands. "They did it with hatred in their hearts for someone. Either your father or her."

"Knock, knock." A man rapped on the open door followed by the familiar figure of my father's best friend and business partner.

"Harold." I gave him a warm smile as he'd always been kind to me, even when my father wasn't.

We crossed the room and shook hands.

"So good to see you, Henry." He clasped my shoulder as he shook my hand, giving me a sympathetic look. "I'm so sorry about this whole business with your father. They'll discover he's innocent, don't you worry. He has the best supernatural attorney in town."

"Thank you. We know he's innocent." I glanced back at Clara, who was watching us quietly, her expression blank, which was unusual for her. "And I plan to prove it."

"Indeed. Hopefully you've found some evidence that the GOA hasn't. They seem to be clueless, accusing Silas of some sort of crime of passion."

"True," I admitted. "But I have my own ways to prove he's innocent."

He observed me keenly. "Good, good. Using your necromancy skills, I hope?"

I nodded. He grunted, then his gaze wandered past me. "And who is this lovely young woman?" He walked toward Clara.

"This is my girlfriend, Clara Savoie."

Harold's eyes widened. "Not one of *the* Savoie sisters, is she?"

"Yes. Her sister Jules is head of the New Orleans coven."

"Nice to meet you, dear." He didn't reach out to shake Clara's hand. Harold had always been a bit of a grim snob. Then he turned back to me. "Clever of you to snag one of the top witches in town." He clapped me on the back like I'd done something amazing. "Just like your father, eh?"

He glanced toward Peony and my father's desk, then around the room, suddenly looking sad. "I'd better get back to work. Just wanted to say hello when I heard you were in the building."

"Good to see you, Harold."

"You too, son. If you need anything, please let me know." Then he disappeared.

"We'd best get going too," I told Peony. "Thank you for this."

"Of course."

She walked us back to the door of her office. "I hope you find this asshole. Beatrice didn't deserve that. And though you likely believe otherwise, neither does your father."

"Whatever my father's done to earn my anger, he doesn't deserve to be falsely convicted of murder."

"Or to be executed for it," Peony added.

She didn't have to reiterate that the penalty for murder in our world was death. That fact had been on my mind since the moment my father called me.

"I'll be in touch," I told her as I took Clara's hand and led her out of there.

"Nice meeting you," she told Peony, but her voice wasn't the usual upbeat tone.

When we entered the elevator, she turned to me but then noticed the small surveillance camera in the corner. Once we exited into the parking garage, I told her, "Wait till we're in my car."

"Okay."

The second we were, I turned to her. "What did you sense?"

"Something is off about Priscilla and Harold."

"Priscilla seemed even stiffer than normal," I agreed. "It could be she's just uncomfortable, seeing as my father's been accused of a violent murder."

"It could be." Her brow pursed in pensive thought. "I'm not sure what it was, but my Aura senses didn't like it."

"Priscilla has been with the company for over ten years. And Harold loves my father dearly. They've been friends going back decades, not to mention they built Obsidian Corporation together."

Turning on the engine, I drove us out of the parking garage and back toward the lower garden district.

"I agree that Priscilla acted a little unusual, though."

"Perhaps she's frustrated she's running the business on her own," offered Clara.

"But Harold is there. That's actually *his* job. Unless there are financial issues."

At the next light, I texted Gareth, asking him to see what he could discover about Priscilla's movements the past few days since my father's arrest. To see if her behavior was strange in any way. He texted back immediately that he was on it.

"Now what do we do?" Clara asked.

"I'd like to read through that file." I'd put the envelope in the back seat. "Then I'd like to take you home so I can go to my father's condo. And before you ask to go, I'd rather you didn't." Her sad eyes instantly gutted me. "Clara, a blood spell was cast there, and there's going to be a terrible residue of emotions there. I don't want you to feel what Beatrice felt. Or the rage of the murderer. It hurts me just thinking about you feeling what they did."

She reached over and placed her hand on my forearm. "Okay. I'll wait until you get home."

"In My Veins" by Andrew Belle played from the playlist on my phone.

"I'll come and pick you up right after," I assured her.

"No. I meant, I'll be waiting at your home. I want to be there in case you need me."

We sat at a red light. I turned to look at her, soaking in her loveliness, her kindness, her unwavering beauty.

"I don't know what I did to deserve you." I licked my lips. "But I'm forever grateful to the universe or whoever's in charge for giving you to me."

She laughed and leaned across the console to press a kiss against my lips. "Then you can be grateful to me, silly. I gave myself to you. Just like you gave yourself to me." She pressed her forehead to mine, whispering softly, "And now we are in one another's keeping."

"I'll take extra good care of you," I promised.

"I know you will. That's what soul mates do."

Then the light turned green, so she popped back into her seat, pulling my hand into her lap and clasping it with both hands, channeling her own spell for me.

I'd experienced her joy spells and her calming spells before, but this one was different. It was altogether more intense, wrapped in her own essence. It wasn't simple happiness she sent but a bone-deep euphoric sensation that felt like warm sunshine on my soul. There was only one name I could give this spell she poured into me now. *Clara's love.*

CHAPTER 21

~HENRY~

I STOOD OUTSIDE MY FATHER'S CONDO DOOR WITH DEVRAJ, GARETH, Nico, and Violet behind me. Mateo would've come, but he didn't like when he and Devraj were both away from the triplets. No matter how many times we explained they were perfectly safe in the hands of the ladies, his wolf wouldn't let him leave unless there was a protective family male within hearing distance of danger.

I was glad Clara had agreed so easily not to come. But I was also glad to have her twin sister here. Violet's psychic ability could detect more than an Aura could.

When I turned the key in the lock and opened the door, I was relieved I'd made Clara stay behind. The others followed except for Gareth, who acted as guard at the door in case some officers from GOA decided they'd missed something.

A stain of dark blood still remained on the wooden floor of the kitchen area. Nico instantly growled as I expected.

"This place is tainted with dark magic," he rumbled from close to Violet.

"You tell no lies, babe," she said softly, not the usual snark in her voice I was used to. She sounded more like Clara. "Why'd they leave the bloodstain?"

I shrugged. "No one to clean it."

Guilt hit me at that. There were no family members to take care of his place after his fiancée was murdered here and he was jailed for it. The scene had only been cleared of any objects that might give evidence to the killer.

I'd told Sean last night when I'd gotten home after dropping Clara off at her apartment. As expected, he was distraught. He didn't believe our father was guilty. Amazingly, I found myself believing it as well. I couldn't deny what I'd seen at Glasgow. Clara had seen the truth of his innocence using her magic, and it was obvious he'd loved the woman, Beatrice.

It shocked me that he'd fallen in love at all, but especially with a human woman. In the grim world, humans were considered lesser because they didn't have magic of any kind. She was obviously a beautiful, intelligent, and successful businesswoman—certainly, traits my father would find attractive. She seemed so different from my own mother who'd been pampered her whole life and taken care of by wealthy parents, then passed on to a wealthy husband. Even after the divorce, she had enough money to live her life in extreme comfort without ever finding a goal to strive toward.

Father respected goals and hard work. I suppose that's why I liked to appear like the vagabond, aimless son in his presence. Or I did for a while until Gareth told him I was employed and doing important work for Ruben Dubois. I'd been angry at Gareth because I didn't want my father to know about my life.

But what was all that anger for? How did it make my life any better?

I stared down at the dried pool of blood and then at the lamp that had been knocked over and broken in an obvious struggle. Even a few shards of the dark green bottle of wine were left scattered. No one was here to set things right when my father was in crisis because I'd made sure Sean and I were cut off from him completely.

Nico knelt down and sniffed audibly, leaning forward farther.

"Do you smell two people?" asked Violet.

"No." He shook his head. "Just one."

Violet sat on the wooden floor, cross-legged, facing the dark stain where Beatrice had died. She touched one palm to the stain and sucked in a breath, her eyes brightening with the Sight. Nico stood at her back in a typical protective stance. Not that Devraj and I were a threat, but werewolves couldn't help themselves. Their wolves drove them to be over-the-top in their possessive nature.

Devraj stepped into the bedroom. Devraj was a Stygorn, an elite vampire warrior with rare abilities. One of these was called memory echo. He could hold an object that was important to a person and psychically see flashbacks of memories. He wasn't a true Seer like Violet, but his ability might help us see who the killer was.

We were hoping to find the robe she was wearing when she died. The chances were slim since the grim coroner likely took her away in it. Still, we hoped.

Since Father had described it to me, I followed Devraj to help search for it. We both moved around the room and then into the bathroom.

"Nothing." He sighed.

I scanned the bathroom. "She'd been in her robe, readying for bed. Or a relaxing night with my father." He'd gone to get dinner so she wouldn't have brushed her teeth yet. "Look."

Next to one of the sinks on the vanity, a washcloth was crumpled. Beside that sink stood several cosmetic bottles and lotions. My father's shaving lotion was on the right.

Devraj walked toward the sink. "She might've washed her face."

"Yes," I agreed.

He picked up the washcloth and closed his eyes. After several minutes of agonizing silence, he opened his eyes, now glowing silver. "Nothing."

"Damn."

"It has to be something important to her for the memories to attach. I can't say she deemed a washcloth very important to her."

"Jewelry?" I asked.

"Yes." His brows rose with excitement. "Good idea."

We both searched the bedroom. He went for the dresser, and I went to the end tables. There was my father's watch but nothing else.

"Here," Dev said. "Diamond earrings."

She'd been wearing them in that picture of her and my father at the gallery exhibition.

"They might've been a gift from my father." Looking at the karat size of them from here, it was certainly something he could afford.

Devraj held them in his hand and closed his eyes. Then a whisper, "Yes."

Marching to where he stood, I waited impatiently, my anxiety mounting that he might actually have some insight into what happened. He grunted but kept his eyes closed for several more minutes.

The second he opened them, I snapped, "What did you see?"

"Yes, she wore them the day she was killed. I saw her standing here and looking in the dresser mirror. She was smiling as she took off the diamond earrings. It was when she was removing the second one that she heard the front door open and close. She called out your father's name. 'Silas. Did you forget your wallet?' She frowned into the mirror when there was no answer. Then she set the diamond earring on the nightstand. That's where it ends."

"Fuck." I paced away. "I'd hoped she might've seen him."

"Not before she left this room. The only thing that could help us is the robe. And that's only if the robe was important enough to her for the memory to attach itself."

"Would its importance escalate if it was what she was wearing when she died?"

"It could."

Nico stepped into the doorway. "Violet's finished."

We left and joined her. Violet was leaning over the island in the kitchen, her head in her hands.

"What is it? Did you see him?" I asked anxiously.

She stood, distress all over her face. "Well, you were right," she told me. "Or your father was. A blood spell was cast in this room."

"So you saw nothing?"

"Nothing worth mentioning. Except that she died in agony and terror, hoping her lover would return and save her."

Bile rose up my throat. I didn't even know her, but it was obvious they loved each other. She'd longed for my father to save her, but he was too late. It was absolutely gutting.

"What I can tell you that might be useful is that the grim who cast this spell was no amateur or dabbler in the dark arts. He or she was calculating and efficient and knew what they were doing. So much so that they entered, killed her cruelly, cast two blood spells after stabbing her, wiped the surveillance video, and left all within minutes of your father returning and the authorities right behind him. The killer planned to do this right and had the magical ability to pull it off. In your father's list of enemies, I can't imagine there are that many who could do what the murderer did."

"This was personal too," added Devraj. "He wanted to hurt your father, not just get him executed."

My heart plummeted. I didn't want my father to be executed. I didn't want him to die.

Combing a hand through my hair, I nodded. "I'll have my father make a list of the top-tier grims in his circle. Anyone who might be an enemy of Obsidian Corp or a personal enemy. Someone who also would have this level of skill and magical power."

They were heading for the door, but I walked over to the kitchen and opened the cabinets beneath the sink.

"What are you doing?" asked Violet.

"Looking for cleaning supplies."

We all split up to find what we needed. There was a plastic bucket under the sink that I filled with warm water and soap.

"I've got it," said Devraj, taking the bucket from me, a dish-rag in hand.

"I found some Mr. Clean pads in the bathroom." Violet waved a packet in her hand, pulling one out and handing it to Nico.

Rather than protest, because they didn't have to do this, I knelt on the floor, and the four of us went to work and cleaned my father's lover's blood away until it was sparkling clean. When he returned here to clear out the condo of their things, because I was determined that he would be set free eventually, there would be no tragic reminder of what had happened here.

Nico swept up the small fragments of bottle, while Devraj and I cleaned up the broken lamp, dumping all of it and the soiled rags from cleaning the floor into a trash bag. I looked back at the apartment from the doorway, crushed that my father had found happiness and lost it here.

"All good?" Devraj clapped me on the shoulder in his brotherly way.

"Yeah." Clearing my throat, I hefted the trash bag. "Thank you all for doing this."

"What are friends for?" said Nico, patting me on the other shoulder as we exited.

Gareth nodded and led the way toward the elevator.

Violet followed right behind him, calling over her shoulder, "I'd like to not make it a habit of helping each other clean up murder crime scenes, though, if it's all okay with y'all."

I smiled, noting how different she was than her sister. She was somehow endearing in her own prickly way, but looking at her just made me miss Clara.

I needed to get to her and prepare for going into the Vale. Because there was no way I could put this off. Somewhere in the darkest realm of the Gray Vale, an innocent soul was trapped and waiting for rescue. My father couldn't save her from being killed, but maybe I could save her soul and set it free. That was, after all, what my magic was all about.

Perhaps my father had been right all those times he'd urged me to get training. I'd assumed it was solely to increase his power at Obsidian Corp. Maybe it had been more than that. Maybe it was so that I could do what only necromancers could—set the wrongs done in death back to rights.

CHAPTER 22

~HENRY~

"People do change, Henry." Clara set the camping lantern on the grass between us. "It often comes after a cataclysmic event. What could be more tragic than causing severe mental and emotional damage to your own son? So much so that he hated his father and tore his other son from him as well when they moved out of the family home."

We were currently sitting in the small backyard of my own home at night. It had high fences and tall shrubs to keep the neighbors from spying. Old Mrs. Webster always seemed overly curious about what was going on over here. Not that anything happened beyond Sean getting into trouble. Still, I liked my privacy.

I thought this would be the best place to open the portal. I needed an open, dark space so no one would see the portal. Mrs. Webster was asleep by seven-thirty. The bachelor who lived on my other side, Brody, was out for the night. I'd gotten Gareth to use one of his surveillance apps to listen in. That's how I discovered Brody was headed to an all-night rager on the Westbank.

Another reason I wanted to do this outside was if a demonic spirit got out, I didn't want them in my house. Their darkness would stain the place with bad mojo.

I wasn't going to let any of them out anyway. Not with Clara standing right there.

Sean was working at Empress Ink and wouldn't be home till late. After the visit with my father two days ago, I'd dropped Clara off at her house. She'd wanted to stay the night with me, but I needed to sort through my feelings alone.

I needed to simply think and find the courage to do what I had to do for my father. The one I was still angry at for making the tragic mistake of trusting his young son with an evil man.

Rather than get upset or angsty about me needing alone time, she hugged me and kissed me gently, then told me to try to get some sleep. And after going to his apartment yesterday, I'd talked to her on the phone but she didn't come over. She didn't complain then either. It wasn't that I didn't want to see or be with her. I just knew I'd be bad company and wanted some time to wrap my head around going back into the Vale.

She was amazing. I'd kind of expected her to tell me I didn't need to be alone, that I needed to talk through my feelings or some other emo shit. Not Clara. She understood how I worked, how I processed things, and gave me the space I needed.

"You disagree?" she asked.

"What?" I'd zoned out again.

"About your father changing."

"Oh no. He's definitely changed. I honestly had no idea my father had loved anyone."

"You were certainly wrong about that," she pointed out without any menace at all, simply speaking the truth. "He loved Beatrice. I'd likely say he loved your mother before their marriage fell apart. And he loves you and Sean. He loved you then and still does now."

I swallowed hard at that. I could've gotten defensive and pointed out all of the years he never tried to mend our relationship or reach out or even apologize for what had happened to me. No, he simply killed the man and never told me about it, even though he'd nearly gone to prison for that too. Then again, we come from a long line of non-communicators and emotionally stunted grims.

Maybe he'd been planning to tell me. If I hadn't ignored all those texts and phone calls, maybe he would've explained a lot of things.

"Why didn't he tell me, do you think? About killing Amon."

Clara plucked at a blade of grass. "Maybe he thought it wouldn't have made a difference. You already hated him for being an irresponsible parent."

"He was an irresponsible parent," I pointed out.

"Maybe he knew that too. He blamed himself for what happened to you. And because you'd sealed off your magic, he knew that was all his fault. That what he'd done was unforgivable."

Fucking hell. I gulped against the emotion welling inside of me. She was right. That was exactly why my father so easily let us leave his house. He didn't deserve his sons.

But he made sure I'd gotten my inheritance early so that I could use it to get my own home, to raise Sean well.

"Gareth's here. And Livvy's with him," said Clara, standing to walk toward her dark-haired sister.

Gareth followed behind her in his dress pants and shirt, looking like they both just left the office. They'd opened one together where he could run his app software businesses and she could run her small public relations business side by side. And also where he could guard her like a dragon.

Most of her work was done remotely, but she needed a space for meeting and presenting to new clients. So Gareth simply bought an entire building in the Lower Garden District so they could work in the same building. I thought nothing would ever get him out of his bunker at his own home, but he'd quickly leveled the building up with sleek, modern renovations and top-of-the-line security and technology. They'd recently hired their fellow contestant, Willard, from that PR contest they were all in.

"Why are you here?" Clara asked her sister as they walked side by side toward me.

"I'm here for moral support." Livvy grinned at me. "Besides, Gareth said I could see some badass necromancer action."

Suddenly stressed that there was more than one vulnerable woman about to be on the other side of a portal that would open into Esbos, the darkest level of the Vale, I stepped over to Gareth. "I'm not so sure this is a good idea."

"I'll be here," he assured me. Already, I could see a sliver of dark essence trying to emerge from his forearm, his eyes growing blacker by the second, bleeding into the whites. "I can handle anything that tries to escape the portal."

"I don't plan on letting anything escape," I said emphatically before glancing over at Livvy and Clara.

"Are you ready?" asked Gareth.

I'd never be ready, but I wasn't going to tell him that. Ever since I'd sealed the door years ago, I'd only unlocked it once to let my dark beast out. When Gareth and Livvy had needed me to discover evidence of Richard Davis's murderous crimes, I'd gone into the darker part of the Vale where souls who were victims of violence roamed. I'd found them all there, never having to go too deep into Esbos.

Even so, I'd spent too long inside, trying to find all of them. I'd managed to escape without coming in contact with demonic entities somehow. Still, by being there too long, my mind and body suffered. To save me from the emotional overload, I slipped into a coma for a few days.

Fortunately, I was able to show up at Richard Davis's trial and summon the souls I needed. After that, I'd put the animal back in his cage. He didn't like it.

What I never admitted to anyone, not even myself, was that I didn't like it either. Those moments I let him loose had sent a jolt of power through my veins. The sensation was almost like being high, a euphoric kind of feeling. I'd enjoyed the powerful sensation of letting my magic free.

Gareth had always said I was so damn broody because I was suppressing my magic. He was right. I knew that he was right. Still, the thought of letting it go free 24-7 was terrifying.

I didn't want what other necromancers described as the *midnight visitors*, spirits showing up in your bedroom at night. That was creepy as fuck. Besides, I was an introvert by nature. People were needy. Dead people were needier. I didn't want to become a ghost psychologist or some shit like a lot of necromancers did. Some even got themselves business cards for it. Fucking nuts.

The other problem was that I wasn't simply a necromancer. I was a necromancer descended from the Blackwater line. In grim history, we'd had a number of powerful ancestors.

Our great-great-grandfather was an extremely strong telekinetic, one of the strongest ever recorded. He was also a mean drunk, apparently. One night, on one of his binges, he got into a fight at a pub. He was kicked out, which only angered him more. He used his TK to topple the pub, but it ended up causing an avalanche that decimated the entire village.

There was another Blackwater, a great-great-aunt who was a grimlock like Gareth, who had lived during the Ottoman Empire. She became angry with her lover, who happened to be the sultan, and used her grimlock monster to strangle him and his entire house, including his harem. That might not seem too amazing, except she did it from outside the palace gates, her tentacled beast seeking out every living thing inside the palace and murdering them in their sleep.

These were the ancestors that Blackwater parents used as warnings to their children when they came into their power. That's one reason I always hesitated when my monster prodded me to let him out. I was sometimes afraid of what he might do in the netherworld. And in our own.

"Nice day for some soul searching," Livvy said, then nudged Clara. "See what I did there."

It was a cheesy joke, but Clara laughed anyway, the sound like an arrow to my heart. In the best sort of way.

"Might as well get started," I said, walking over to Clara. I pressed a swift, hard kiss to her lips. "Stay near Gareth."

I ignored Livvy and Gareth's quiet discussion about me kissing Clara so openly. They had a telepathic link and could literally talk to each other without saying a word. I didn't care what anyone thought, or even if they teased me anymore. They might as well get used to it because I wasn't ever going to hide how I felt about the love of my life.

She lifted onto her tiptoes before I could walk away and kissed me again. "Be careful."

"I will be. Don't worry."

But I was worried. I'd never been to Esbos except for the time Amon had opened the portal and thrown me inside. I waited until they were a safe distance away. Not that Gareth would let anything get near the girls. His monster could handle anything, from any dimension.

Turning toward the other direction, I closed my eyes and went through the process of mentally unlocking the door to my beast's cell. Already, he rumbled an approval that I was letting him out.

He didn't hate me or try to fight against me, not like what happened to Mateo and his wolf when Alpha tried to take over. Mine never did that. He just wanted to be a part of me.

It made me sad to think I couldn't keep him out. I was too afraid he'd cause me problems like other necromancers had, summoning spirits all hours of the day. Even summoning evil spirits so the beast could battle and destroy them.

That was something I learned in my own research not long after I left home. Curious about what I was, I discovered that one power we had was in evaporating evil spirits. I'd never done it myself, but I wished I'd had the ability when I was seven years old.

A humming sensation vibrated my body. I sensed the dark essence pulsing through my veins, filling me up with powerful energy. When I opened my eyes, the entire yard was cocooned in a black, smoky shroud. The sensation was one of extreme ecstasy to feel my magic surging in the air around me.

Black, ethereal wings spread wide from my back. No one knew exactly why necromancers sprouted sable-black wings when opening a gate into the Vale. History had no answers. Some said it was because we were some sort of dark angels of the Vale and protected the living from demonic forces on the other side. Some said it was an embodiment of the black raven, the messenger between the living world and the land of the dead.

I always favored the latter. Some believed a person with the raven spirit animal preferred quiet to noise, stillness to constant movement. They also preferred one person to many. That felt truer to me than me being some sort of angel.

Channeling the magic to my core, I bellowed inside the smoky dome, *"Opna."*

Using Old Norse, the language of our Varangian forefathers, it seemed to work better in opening the door to the Vale than English, as if our bone-deep magic only heard the calling of the old tongue.

A heavy boom echoed within the magical chamber I'd created, and the swirling portal opened, the space inside darker than out here.

There was no remote-control dial to set, or even special words, to open a portal in one part of the Vale versus another. I simply told my essence where we needed to go, and he did the rest.

Sure enough, the portal he'd opened reeked of the same foulness I distinctly remembered from long ago. Sibilant whispers carried on the wind.

I stepped up to the portal, squaring my shoulders, my hands fisted at my side. Fear caught me around the throat, the phantom pain of being bitten stopping me at the door. Then my dark beast swelled, his voice, usually silent and content to be so, spoke up.

You could destroy them all. None will hurt us.

I didn't simply hear it. I felt it, the power rippling through me.

With that, I cracked my neck and stepped into the Gray Vale, into Esbos.

CHAPTER 23

~HENRY~

I DIDN'T REMEMBER THE OPPRESSIVE PRESSURE OF THIS PLACE FROM when I'd been here as a child. My mind likely blocked all of it anyway. Esbos was cold with rocky formations, an otherworldly hell. Something shrieked in the distance.

Walking forward, I whispered quietly, "Beatrice Plath, I summon you."

A tug of my magic led me to the right, away from the doorway I'd created. Something with red eyes blinked to my left, then disappeared beyond a craggy rock. It was so dark that the farther I stepped from the portal opening, the less I could see. I could barely see three feet in front of me.

I needed light.

Instantly, my magic flared, burning along my fingertips, lighting beneath my skin. I raised my hands, the sizzling sensation pooling in my palms until a ball of purple light appeared between them. Clara had told me once that my aura was purple.

Apparently, my magic manifested in the same color. The ball hovered as if waiting for my direction.

With the purple glow lighting my path, I walked on, following my instincts. For a supernatural, our instinct was simply our magic guiding us. The Goddess knew best, so I followed where she was taking me.

"Beatrice Plath," I spoke into the darkness.

A menacing presence crept from behind another rock, its body malformed. Only about four feet tall, it hobbled closer, sniffing the air to see what I was.

"Be gone!" I shouted.

The creature yelped and vanished into the mist to my left. I wasn't sure how the evil spirits would react to me. That alone had my pulse beating wildly behind my rib cage. What if they all didn't scatter in fear like that little creature? I needed to find Beatrice's spirit fast.

"Where is she?" I whispered.

This way.

Following his lead, I continued farther until I was marching through a tunnel-like path, the rock formations of this place high as mountains. I couldn't see where it ended since the glow from my small, floating ball of light didn't extend that far.

When I came out the other side of the tunnel, a powerful punch of evil slapped against my chest.

"Fuck."

I braced myself. In the gloaming, there were several pairs of eyes watching me. Some red, some yellow, some silver—all extremely unnatural hues. The menacing whispers increased.

My beast rumbled a growl that seemed to scare the demons away.

She's there.

Feeling a tug on my right, I looked. There was yet another jagged, rocky hilltop. But it was silhouetted by a pale blue light. A beautiful aura of something good. It didn't belong here.

Striding quickly toward the boulder that was hiding who I was sure would be Beatrice, I wasn't disappointed when I rounded the corner. I was horrified, however.

Standing in an ethereal dome of blue light was the soul of Beatrice. She wore a red silk kimono-style bathrobe as she had been when she was killed. I'd looked at the crime scene photos my father's attorney sent this morning.

The dome surrounding her reminded me of the ones collectors might use to protect their porcelain doll. That wasn't the most terrifying part of it.

Dancing around her, gnashing their sharp teeth and making vulgar gestures with their disgusting genitals, was a band of about twenty demons. Rage welled inside me that this was what her murderer had condemned her to.

She was bound here by the blood spell that kept her in place, but also a prisoner of terror as the demons seemed to be enjoying tormenting her. One of them, a one-horned, pot-bellied beast whipped out some sort of jagged knife and scraped it on the dome as he circled.

Sparks spit up into the air where his blade dragged across the spelled dome. Whatever black magic this was, it was beyond torture. The only thing saving her soul from assault and suffering by demons was this ethereal dome. Her murderer couldn't take a chance of her escaping, so he'd kept her caged by the dome. She would spend her eternity right here, being threatened and tortured by demonic spirits.

"Move, you motherfuckers!" I yelled right as I opened my wings wide.

With the sharp upthrust of my wings, a ripple of power leveled them to the ground. A few of them shrieked and fled into the darkness. Most of them looked back at me with fury and malice.

"Come on, assholes. Bring what you've got."

Beatrice stared with wide eyes at me. She must've known who I was from pictures my father had shown her. For I could see her lips move behind the soundless dome, mouthing, *Henry*.

Three small, yellow-eyed demons hissed and stalked toward me on all fours. On instinct, I manifested a long whip made of my grim magic. Hauling my arm back, I cracked it at the crouching demons, hitting one square in the face. Instantly, it exploded into cinders and smoke. The other two skittered away and circled back behind the others.

That had never happened before. Of course, I'd never been wholly in sync with my magic either. I'd never encountered demonic entities like this except when I was a helpless child. Another surge of power filled me. Not simply with magic but with the newfound realization that I could destroy these beings.

"Begone," I called, flapping my raven wings, sending another electric sizzle into them.

They burst wide, scattering back behind the dome and an outcropping of rough rock. Beatrice turned in her cell, watching the creatures slink into the darkness.

I wasn't sure how to break the spell exactly. I hadn't thought her spirit would be in some sort of hexed prison. I thought she might be wandering here on her own, simply lost. I was almost thankful that wasn't the case because it was clear that the demonic spirits who'd bitten and clawed me as a child could do the same harm to her.

She was as corporeal here as any person on the living plane. When I approached, she spun again, fear shining brightly in her eyes. She pressed a palm to the glass-like dome.

"I'm going to get you out," I told her, mouthing the words slowly so she could understand.

She nodded and smiled, a tear slipping down her pale cheek. She mouthed, *thank you.*

Nearly to the edge of the dome, I lifted my hand only to be jarred by the ground shaking beneath my feet. It knocked me off-balance, and I fell to the side.

Then an unearthly, deep growl accompanied the shaking earth. The demons I'd scared off a minute ago suddenly reappeared from around a giant boulder, chittering and hissing. Leaping to my feet, I then stepped forward and manifested my whip again.

From around the boulder came a monster like I'd never seen before. Not even in my worst nightmares. It was easily twenty feet tall, packed with thick arms and legs, long black claws, three horns sprouting out of his bald skull, serrated teeth, and black-as-pitch eyes—three of them—that glinted silver in the dark.

"What in the hell—"

I wondered for a moment if Esbos *was* Hell, for this place was completely forsaken of light. Oppressive malice blanketed this dark realm. The only light here was that of my purple orb and the dome hovering around Beatrice's spirit.

The giant monster stalked closer, and so did the creatures. There weren't just twenty now but many more slinking out of the blackness toward me. I cracked my whip, which made a few jump back and circle behind their leader.

Suddenly, ten of them attacked, jumping at me with frightening speed. I beat my wings and summoned my magic, whipping it out of me in sharp bursts. It incinerated two of the creatures but several more escaped with a charred arm or face, still coming at me with those razor-sharp teeth.

"*No.*"

The old fear wrapped around me, reminding me of the pain. The sensation of suffocation closed off my throat as panic began to pump through me.

This couldn't be happening. But it was.

I was having a panic attack, the kind that always paralyzed me with fear. The horde of demons lurked closer, making horrific, menacing sounds. And there was still their leader coming closer and closer.

Three demons leaped on me, biting and clawing, knocking me to the ground. I couldn't do anything, couldn't even call my magic because the panic had stricken me so completely.

Was I to die here in this hell in the exact way I'd always feared I would, unable to get free of these evil spirits who still haunted me in my nightmares?

No!

My beast answered for me, even while I felt rows of teeth sinking through my clothes into my skin. My magic pumped wildly through my veins and filled the space around me. The creatures flew off me a few feet. As they rallied to come back at me a second time, the purple orb spun in a circle around me, faster and faster, glowing brighter and brighter.

The giant beast huffed and roared but stopped moving forward. Its minions skittered farther away, shielding their eyes from the glowing light. I was completely enveloped in my own aura, the purple orb now surrounding me. Suddenly, it lifted my body and began flying me back toward the way I'd come.

I reached out to Beatrice where she cried and screamed in her soundless chamber, beating her palms on the cage. To my utter shame and despair, I understood the words she repeated over and over in her prison as I drifted farther and farther away.

Please don't leave me.

CHAPTER 24

~CLARA~

It seemed like hours had passed while we waited for Henry, but it had only been forty minutes when a purple beam of light shot through the open portal and spat Henry out onto the lawn. In the dim lantern-light, I could see those regal raven wings dissipate into the air as the portal snapped shut. Then my heart jolted because his shirt was torn and there was blood.

"Oh no!" Rushing to him, I then fell onto my knees and helped him sit up. "Are you hurt? Henry, you're bleeding!"

"I'm okay." His voice was raspy, and he seemed sluggish. "It looks worse than it is."

Lifting up his shirt, there was a nasty, jagged gash on his abdomen. "You're not okay. Livvy, we need to get him to Isadora."

Lightning flashed in the near distance. Henry looked up at the sky, then at me, cupping my cheek. "Calm down, angel. I'm okay."

Gareth muttered spells around the place where the portal had been, incantations of protection. He'd told us he would once Henry was out, just to be on the safe side that the portal was completely sealed so that no demonic spirits could escape into this world.

"Calling her now," said Livvy, pulling out her cell phone.

Staring into his full-black eyes, I noted the sadness there but reassurance, too, that he was indeed okay. I pushed my frightened feelings away. The rolling thunder overhead quieted as my temper calmed.

"Come on." I helped him up.

He grunted but there didn't seem to be any broken bones or serious injuries. Gareth joined me on the other side.

"I can walk," Henry griped.

"I'm sure you can, but let us help you anyway. For our sakes, not yours."

Gareth was a perceptive guy. I needed to be able to help Henry more than he likely actually needed mine. This feeling of helplessness, not knowing what he'd experienced on the other side of the portal to send him flying out with rips in his clothes and more teeth marks, had me in tears.

"Don't cry." Henry moved his arm from around my shoulders to my waist and tugged me closer.

"I can't help it." I sniffed. "What happened in there?"

"Get in." Gareth opened the door to the back seat of his Audi, and Henry slid in. I ran around the other side while Livvy slipped into the front passenger seat.

"What happened?" Gareth repeated once we were on our way.

I held one of Henry's hands in both of mine, squeezing it frantically. Henry's gaze was on our hands.

"I saw her."

"You did?" I squeaked. "Beatrice?"

As if there was anyone else "her" would be in reference to. He lifted his gaze to mine, regret etching the strained lines.

"Yes. She's been spelled into some sort of cage, so she can't escape. My father was right. There were two spells put on her at her death."

"You couldn't break her out?" Gareth asked, glancing back in the rearview as he drove toward Devraj and Isadora's house.

"I didn't get a chance to. There was a horde there."

"Horde?" Livvy had twisted around, her concerned expression fixed on Henry.

"Demon horde," he clarified. "Twenty or more. Then there was a giant beast."

"Goddess above," breathed Livvy, her blue eyes wide with horror.

I trembled in fear at the thought of what he'd seen, what he'd faced in that place.

Henry swallowed and licked his lips. "At first, I was able to beat them back, but there were too many of them."

"Beat them back how? Like punch them?" Livvy asked.

"Not exactly. My necromancy magic took control. I produced a sort of whip."

"Produced?" I asked, having never heard of something like this.

"Necromancy is malleable," stated Gareth, taking another turn. "It adjusts to the grim's needs."

"So does yours," Livvy added with suggested innuendo.

He glanced at her, his expression never changing. "Mine acts as an extension of me, manifesting with lots of"—he waved a hand in the air—"arms."

Livvy had told me they were more like tentacles.

I looked at Henry. "Is that what your grim magic did?"

"Not exactly. It manifested into a whip that was laced with potent magic. When I hit one of the creatures, it evaporated into thin air."

We were all silent, looking a little surprised. And impressed.

Then he went on, despair apparent in his voice. "There were just too many. I couldn't fight them off fast enough or get back to Beatrice." He stared out the window, his features sad under the streetlights. "God, I'm sorry," he whispered.

"It's not your fault," I told him.

"But it is." He scoffed, seemingly disgusted with himself. "I panicked. Before I knew it, they were on me, and then my magic took me out of there."

"What do you mean took you out of there?" asked Livvy.

"It's hard to explain."

"Please try," she urged.

I glared at her, but she simply shrugged.

"When I needed light, an orb of my aura light appeared and guided me. When I was being attacked, it surrounded me, defended me against them. Then it lifted and carried me back to the gateway and pushed me out."

Again, silence.

"I've never heard of magic being so corporeal," said Livvy. "Witch and warlock magic is more ethereal, taking form only in our abilities as a Seer, hex-breaker, Healer, and so on. Grim magic can actually become a living appendage." She looked at Gareth. "It's remarkable."

"Just noticing that now, darling?"

"Of course not. It's not like I can ignore *your* monster."

He arched a brow at her.

I turned back to Henry. "How badly are you bitten?"

"Just a few. Not too deep."

Then Gareth pulled into Devraj and Isadora's driveway, the house right next to ours. Dev pulled open Henry's door before Gareth had even turned off the engine.

"Let me help you."

"I can walk," Henry said, hissing in pain as he eased out.

Devraj didn't argue. He simply grabbed hold of him and traced into the house, the door already open. We followed quickly behind them to find Isadora already sitting on the sofa next to Henry reclined on a sheet. They'd prepared for the blood.

Archie, their little dog, whined from somewhere in the kitchen. They must've put him in his kennel, knowing we were coming.

"Don't push yourself," warned Devraj, hovering over Isadora.

"I'm fine, Dev. Let me do my work."

He clamped his jaw, seeming more agitated than normal.

Gareth let out a near-silent, "Oh."

"Oh, what?" demanded Livvy next to him.

Then Gareth got suddenly quiet, Devraj glaring at him.

Dev and Isadora had been acting awfully secretive for a while. Instinctively, my gaze trailed down her body. Her aura had always been a green glow, but there it was. Low in her abdomen, right about where her womb would be, was a tiny flickering orange light.

My heart lodged in my throat. "You're pregnant."

Everyone's gaze twisted to me. Isadora smiled, her eyes misty. "I am."

"Oh, Is." Livvy gave her an awkward side hug since she was sitting on the sofa, one hand on Henry's chest.

She patted Livvy's shoulder and laughed. "We were waiting to tell anyone since it's still early."

Dev smiled wide, seemingly glad the cat was out of the bag. "It's been hard to keep it a secret. The wolves have known for weeks."

"How did you know?" she asked me.

"I don't know. I can just see a separate, tiny aura inside you."

"But you didn't see that with Evie," Livvy added.

"I did actually. I just didn't know what I was seeing. Evie's children all have blue auras like her, just different shades of blue. I didn't recognize what it was until she told us she was pregnant. I think you have to be a little farther along for me to see it."

"We can talk about this later," snapped Isadora. "Let me tend to Henry. Why don't y'all go into the kitchen?"

Devraj instantly started herding us away, tending to his wife's sharp demands. Isadora had always been a direct person, but these days she seemed to have less patience.

"I'm staying," I told Devraj, skirting around him to kneel on the floor.

He didn't argue but followed the others into the kitchen where I heard a cabinet door open and glasses clinking.

Henry had been silent and withdrawn, his eyes now back to normal but tired and sad.

"Clara, help me get his shirt off," said Isadora in her calm, steady tone.

I knelt at his head, and we eased his T-shirt over his head. He grunted a little but was mostly quiet.

"Goddess save me," I murmured, seeing at least ten shallow bite marks on his chest, abdomen, and arms.

"Are there any below the belt?" asked Isadora.

He shook his head.

"These aren't too deep. I believe I can make them heal completely. Relax, Henry."

His stomach muscles eased. Without looking at me, he lifted a hand, palm up. Instantly, I grabbed it and pressed the back of his hand to my chest. Then he closed his eyes as Isadora whispered her healing spells in French, a halo of green light brightening above her hands on his abdomen.

At first, Henry winced, but the longer Isadora worked and whispered, her magic a warm hum in the air, he drifted off, his face going slack.

"Go get me a washcloth," she whispered to me.

He didn't wake when I set his hand back on the sofa and fetched a washrag, wetting it with warm water first. I started to clean the dried patches of blood, finding small indentations of teeth as I cleaned.

Isadora nodded and continued to whisper her charm, a bright light glowing from her hands and fingertips as she brushed them to each mark again and again. I cleaned his chest completely of any blood. When Isadora finally stopped whispering her spell, his body looked as good as new. Well, as good as it was before.

"These scars look the same as the ones I just healed. But worse." Isadora trailed her finger over one of the old, ridged bite marks, camouflaged as part of the raven's claws.

"He was attacked as a child by spirits."

Her brow pursed. "They must've not gotten to a good healer in time, though these look deeper than the ones I just healed. They were, likely."

I swallowed hard, blinking away the tears that started welling.

"How is he?" Gareth asked softly from behind.

"Fully healed." Isadora gave a weak smile and stood from the sofa.

Devraj was there, helping her. "You need to lie down now."

She smiled and nodded, but then turned to me. "He should be fine. The healing spell often puts people to sleep, but he needs it anyway."

"If you want to leave him here, that would be fine," said Devraj.

"No." I stood from the floor finally and brushed a lock of black hair away from his forehead. "Gareth, can you carry him to my apartment for me?"

"Of course."

We said our goodbyes, and Gareth carried Henry over his shoulder like a sack of potatoes, tracing to my apartment. Livvy and I walked along the sidewalk, the full moon almost here, lighting our way.

Livvy wrapped an arm around my waist and gave me a squeeze. "He'll be all right."

"I know." I wrapped my arm around hers, basking in the sweet comfort of my sister.

"I wish I was an Aura so I could send you some of that happy juice you always give to us."

"You're giving it to me right now," I assured her.

She squeezed me again. "Another Savoie baby on the way."

"A Kumar baby," I corrected. "Half Savoie."

"I think Devraj is going to lose his mind. The way he dotes on Isadora. Now he's going to have someone else to pamper and adore."

"It'll be lovely," I added.

"It absolutely will be."

I stared up at the almost full moon, realizing Nico, Violet, Evie, and Mateo would be leaving town tomorrow. Isadora, Livvy, and I had baby duty while Evie and Mateo were gone a few days. When they returned, we'd be welcoming Jules and Ruben back home.

"So you and me with grims," I wondered aloud. "I suppose that means our kids are going to be all Goth and emo, wear black all the time and listen to The Cure in the dark."

"God, I hope so," snarked Livvy.

I laughed because she was totally serious. By the time we made it upstairs, Gareth had Henry undressed down to his boxer briefs and tucked in my bed.

"Thank you, Gareth."

"Of course." He smiled and looked at me in the most curious way. "Thank you as well."

"Why?"

"He's happier than I've ever seen him in his entire life." Then he corrected. "Today aside, you give him the happiness and contentment I believe he's always longed for."

I smiled, again having to beat back the well of emotions. *What was wrong with me these days?* I suppose so much was happening, both good and bad, that my psyche couldn't keep up.

Showing them to the door, I said good night and locked up. I changed into one of my pajama short sets and climbed in bed next to him. He slept on so soundly. I brushed my palm gently over his chest, reassuring myself that none of those new injuries were there. They were all gone.

Sending a thankful prayer to the heavens, I curled up next to him and fell asleep.

CHAPTER 25

~HENRY~

A NIGHTMARE WOKE ME. A MEMORY, ACTUALLY. AND NOT THE ONE I'd dreamed a thousand times since I was seven. No. This time, I dreamed of magical glass shattering, of demons grabbing hold of Beatrice's spirit and carrying her away, all while she looked back at me, her arms outstretched, screaming, *Please don't leave me.*

This nightmare was worse than any I'd ever had. Because it was about someone else, not myself. And because it could actually happen if they found a way to break the blood spell holding her captive. And if they didn't, if I couldn't find a way to save her, then she'd be living out her own personal hell for eternity.

For once, I wished I'd listened to my father and gotten the lessons on necromancy. I didn't have to use one of his goons. I could've sought my own teacher. Hell, I could've asked Aunt Lucille to teach me more than wards and caging my magic.

Sitting there in Clara's bed, I stared down at my abdomen, amazed that there wasn't one mark from those things. Not even a thin line broke into my tattoo designs. Not only that, but I felt amazing. The only thing I was missing was my beautiful girl.

My jeans were folded on a chair next to her dresser. A pink sticky note was stuck on top of a folded T-shirt.

Dear Henry,

You're so lovely to look at when you're sleeping. You're lovely to look at when you're awake too. But since you needed to rest, I let you sleep. Come to the main house when you get up. Here's one of Mateo's T-shirts. Yours was too far gone to salvage.

Love you!

XOXO, Angel

P.S. I bought you your own toothbrush for my bathroom for when you sleep over.

P.P.S. You should bring some clothes over too. I've emptied the second drawer of my dresser for you already.

P.P.P.S. Hurry over when you wake up. I miss you!

Grinning like the lovesick dog I was, I hurried into the bathroom, took a two-minute shower, brushed my teeth with the new purple toothbrush on the counter. Purple. Of course. Then I dressed and headed next door.

Tapping lightly on the back door leading into the kitchen, I heard Clara shout, "Come in!"

She was putting Celine in one of those bouncy things where she could spin in place and play with the attachments. Joaquin was already in a second bouncer.

"No, Diego!" She ran over to him and pulled a phone charger cord out of his mouth. "Where did you get that?" Once she delicately pulled it out, he blinked at her, then giggled and started swatting at her long locks of hair hanging near his face.

"Let me have him," I told her.

Round-eyed with surprise, she whirled and beamed at me with one of her wide smiles. "Henry! Good morning." She marched over and kissed me on the lips, trying to hold Diego far enough away since his little chubby hands were still swiping at her hair.

"Morning. Give him to me."

"Gladly." She handed him over. "I need to get their bottles heated for naptime. This should be fun trying to get all three down."

"I'll help you." Diego blinked his big brown eyes at me, then leaned forward and sniffed the T-shirt I was wearing. He grunted, staring at me with a tiny baby frown.

Clara giggled. "He's wondering why you smell like Daddy."

"I guess I don't look like his daddy," I said, following her into the kitchen.

"Not *his* daddy." She waggled her eyebrows before turning to the fridge, giving me a nice view of her from behind.

"How long do you have to babysit?"

"Livvy and Gareth have night duty, so I'll be free by this afternoon. Isadora is handling the shop today. Tomorrow I'm off from babysitting but need to work at the shop."

She set three bottles in three electric bottle warmers at the same time and started the timer.

"They don't use just one warmer?" I asked.

Clara smirked at me. Actually smirked. "Oh, sweet summer child. When three babies need bottles in the middle of the night all at the same time, there is no waiting for them to heat individually."

Diego grabbed my nose. I pulled his little paw off. "Guess I don't know much about babies. Sean had nannies and was a grown kid when we moved out."

"Don't worry," she assured me. "You'll be a great daddy."

I flinched, hoping I'd be better than my own. What a huge loss our entire relationship was. If my father was convicted of Beatrice's murder, he would be executed. The thought had acid churning in my stomach. I was still waiting for his attorney to send me the trial date.

"You do want children, don't you? You seem upset."

Snapping out of my reverie, I found Clara watching me, near tears.

"Oh shit. Yes, of course I want kids. One day. Yeah."

She smiled. "Good. That wouldn't be good if you didn't."

Diego pulled my hair. "Why's that?"

"Something our cousin's buddy Travis told me."

"What did he tell you?"

She froze for a second, then—

Ding.

"Bottle one is ready." She plucked it out of the warmer. "Could you please handle the wild man, and I can take care of the other two?"

"Sure."

Diego was already trying to climb me like a fucking tree to get to the bottle in my left hand.

"Dude. Calm down."

I wrestled him, literally, until I plopped down on the sofa and surrendered the bottle. He snatched it, his tiny claws scraping on the plastic bottle. There were scratch marks all over the thing. He sounded like a pig suckling on its momma as he worked on that bottle.

"Damn, dude. You need to slow down." I tilted him back in the crook of my arm, his legs dangling off my lap onto the sofa. He was a big boy, bigger than his siblings. "I bet you hogged all the food in your mother's tummy, too, didn't you?"

Another ding for bottle two sounded in the kitchen.

Observing his mop of dark curls and brown eyes, I told him, "You look like your father, that's for damn sure." He was halfway finished, his eyelids growing heavier. I bounced my knee gently to rock him a little. "Don't fight it. Just go on to sleep."

He cooed at me around the nipple, never letting it out of his mouth. A tiny stream of milk slipped out one side.

The third ding went off for the last bottle.

"Don't talk with your mouth full either. They've got a lot of manners to teach you."

He grunted, his eyes falling closed completely, his mouth still working hard on sucking the milk down.

"That's right. No one's gonna take your bottle, Diego. Just finish it off and go to sleep."

I had no idea what I was saying or why, only that it seemed natural to whisper softly to a baby as they went to sleep.

When the bottle was empty and he was sucking on air, I slowly removed the nipple. He was already making little baby snore sounds. I smiled. He was really fucking cute. When I looked up, Clara was staring at me with hearts in her eyes.

Celine fussed and banged on the bouncer. She jumped in place and held out a hand, flexing her fingers in the gimme sign.

Clara set the two bottles on the end table and hurried to get Celine out.

"Do I put him upstairs?" I whispered.

"Yeah," she whispered back, putting the bottle in Celine's mouth before she could wake up her brother. "Doesn't matter which crib."

Heading upstairs, I stared down at the crib before I laid him on his back. Just as I turned, I stepped on some squeaky toy that made a loud-ass sound.

"Fuck," I whisper-yelled.

Peering into the crib, Diego hadn't even twitched. I tossed the toy into a basket by the door and headed downstairs. Celine was still working on her bottle. Joaquin was watching patiently from his bouncer where he wasn't bouncing. Simply watching.

"I've got him," I told her, picking up the third bottle.

"Thank you," she whispered. "I thought I could feed these two together, but they're getting so big."

I settled on the sofa with Joaquin in the same position as Diego. Rather opposite than his brother, he drank his bottle down like a normal, tiny, civilized human being.

"Only a month ago, I could hold both of these two on my lap and feed them at the same time," Clara said. "They grow so fast."

Scanning Joaquin's features, the mop of curls was similar to his siblings, but his was strawberry blond like Celine's. His eyes were bright green, his round face starting to take on familiar features.

"Now, you look like your mother," I told him.

One side of his mouth quirked, revealing a cute dimple, before he went back to drinking his bottle. He examined me the same way I examined him.

"He's a curious one, isn't he?"

"You have no idea." She shifted and pulled a baby blanket tightly around Celine. "She likes to be snuggled." Then she smiled over at Joaquin. "He's the genius of the bunch. He's already identifying shapes, and I swear to you, I think he's figuring out what letters are used for too. He won't play with the blocks we got them, stacking them like normal kids."

"Really?"

"He lines them up with the letters and stares at them, then flips them over to stare at more of them."

We were both still whispering.

I looked down at him. "You're a little genius, aren't you?"

He blinked at me, still wide-eyed and sucking down his bottle.

"You should go to sleep, little man," I told him. "Then you'll have energy to look around and learn about the world some more."

He blinked at me softly, then closed his eyes. Sure enough, by the time his bottle was done, he was asleep. So was Celine. I followed Clara up the stairs and into the nursery where we lay them both down.

Clara pulled the curtains closed, which brought my attention to the mural on the far wall I hadn't noticed when carrying that first sack of potatoes and putting him to bed.

It was a fairyland scene with wild wolves running across a creek and fairies flying in the trees, some dancing in the meadow, and a picturesque castle in the distance. Standing on top of the castle wall were two little boys, one with dark hair and one with red, and a girl in a princess dress with long reddish-blonde hair.

"Evie did the mural for them. Isn't it beautiful?"

"Pretty awesome."

After turning on the monitor, she gestured for us to leave. She pulled the door quietly shut. "Whew. That'll give me about an hour and a half break."

I followed her back downstairs where she turned on the other monitor that had a video screen.

"I bet Gareth could come up with a better one that doesn't have that grainy black-and-white picture."

"I bet he could. And he'd make a fortune."

"I'll mention it to him."

We were standing there in the living room, facing each other awkwardly. Perhaps it was just me that felt awkward because Clara easily looped her arms around my neck.

"What's wrong?"

Holding her at the waist, I let the comfort of having her nearby fill me up. Still, it didn't make the pain go away.

"I left her there," I finally said. "Beatrice."

"You couldn't help it, though. You said so yourself. There were too many."

"Maybe I could've if I hadn't had one of my panic attacks right at that moment."

"Henry, you were surrounded by—what—twenty demons, you said? And some kind of freaky giant?" She shivered. "Just the idea of it terrifies me."

"If I'd trained myself and gotten over my fears before this, I could've saved her." I looked away out the window because I didn't want to see the disappointment in her eyes, but I also wanted to be totally honest. "She begged me not to leave her. She was terrified, and I left her anyway. An innocent soul trapped there. I can't live with myself if I don't get her out. Not even for my father's sake, but for her sake. For my own."

Small, warm hands cupped my face and turned my head to look down. Her pretty face with a kind, soft expression held me.

"Of course you're going to get her out."

"Of course?" I chuckled. Clara was always so sure of everything. Her confidence was staggering. And inspiring.

"I've been thinking for a while this morning about it. I know what you need."

"What's that?"

"One of my sister's spelled tattoos. You know what they've done for the werewolves. The charmed ink in the skin helps the supernatural tap into their magic on another level. There's a harmony I've never felt before. Every super who gets one says the same. It may give you the extra control you need."

My heart sank. "I've already gotten one from your sister."

I hated seeing the light in her eyes dim. "The butterfly?"

Nodding, I added, "I thought the same thing, but it didn't work. The nightmares and the fear are still here. Obviously."

Her blank expression brightened again. She beamed up at me, filling me with her warmth, her undying affection. "Don't worry. We'll figure it out."

I slid my hands to her back and held her closer. "Yeah," I agreed, even though I didn't believe it.

"I can't believe she never told me she gave you that tattoo." Her brow pinched into a line.

"Is there something wrong with that?"

"Yes." Her lower lip jutted out into a little pout when she was upset. Her mouth kept distracting me. "She saw you shirtless before me. So not fair."

"I'd asked her not to mention it to anyone. That I'd gotten a charmed tattoo."

"Why?"

"We grims are secretive. I wanted to see if it would work first anyway." I brushed my mouth along her soft cheek and whispered at her temple, "The butterfly is you."

She flinched in my arms, but didn't pull away. "Really?" came her sweet, soft voice.

"It's always been you, Clara. Before I even knew you, the universe was preparing me for you. You soothe my soul in so many ways." I brushed another kiss at her silky hairline. "You're my one and only."

"And you're mine." Her voice broke with emotion.

"Stay with me tonight. I want to show you something."

"I want to show you something too." She rubbed her breasts against my chest.

I laughed and groaned at the same time. Dipping my head lower, I nipped the spot below her ear with my teeth. She jumped, then moaned. Pressing my lips to that tender spot, I told her, "I can't wait to see your something."

I kissed her for a long time, standing there in the Savoie living room. No telling how much time had passed, but her pretty mouth was swollen when I finally headed for the door.

CHAPTER 26

~CLARA~

I STARED AT THE CARVED RAVEN ON THE FRONT DOOR AS I WAITED.
Three seconds after I rang the doorbell, the giant door swung
open.

"Hi!"

Henry grinned and pulled me into the house, kicking the front
door shut.

"Turn around." He made the twirling gesture with his finger.

Immediately, I obeyed. A black silky scarf was tied around
my eyes.

"Ooh. Are we doing something kinky?"

He chuckled, then scooped me up into his arms like a baby.

Squealing, I didn't have time to even ask what this was about
because he traced somewhere in the house. When he set me
down, dizzy and laughing, I was in front of him, his hands on
my shoulders.

"Ready?"

"I'm not sure. I think so."

"You can take it off."

I lowered the scarf to loop my neck and stared up at an incredible metal sculpture hanging on the wall beneath two recessed lights.

His hands remained on my shoulders. "I commissioned it from Mateo last year."

It was a giant metal butterfly, but the wing on the right looked as if it had broken into pieces. Each piece was a small butterfly taking flight and going free.

"Mateo is an exceptional artist." He'd made the wires connecting the tiny butterflies to the mother of them so fine you could barely see them. Mounted on the gray wall with the perfect lighting, the effect was stunning.

"This is how you make me feel."

The sculpture screamed one emotion brighter than any other—hope.

He swept my hair away from my neck and pressed a sweeping kiss there.

"Henry."

"Hmm?"

"I'm ready to show you my something."

He let go of me, so I turned around, realizing for the first time that I was in his bedroom. Like the rest of the house, it was draped in rich fabrics and dark walls; the lightest wall was where the sculpture hung opposite the bed where Henry now sat, his hands pressed to the mattress.

In jeans and a T-shirt, barefoot, he looked absolutely delicious. I hoped he felt the same about me. I slipped off the straps of my spring dress and let it fall to the floor, revealing the black lace teddy I wore underneath. The only thing I wore underneath.

Angling his head in that sexy way of his, he devoured every inch of me, my skin pebbling at his perusal.

Licking his lips, he ordered, "Put the scarf back on."

As I lifted it back into place, I sensed him moving behind me. He tightened it and whispered low, "Feel okay?"

"Yeah." My pulse skyrocketed the second I couldn't see anything, arousal warming between my thighs with anticipation of his touch.

Holding my waist, he urged me forward until my knees hit the bed. He turned me around to face him, though I could see nothing.

"Sit down."

I did.

"Don't move."

A belt buckle, zipper, and the rasping of clothes coming off were the only sounds besides my breathing.

Then his fingertips were on my jaw, trailing down to my chin where he tipped it up. "Open your mouth."

I knew what was coming and eagerly opened for him, licking my lips before I did. I felt the swollen crown of his cock pressing into my mouth so I flicked my tongue over the metal piercing.

He made that sexy noise in his throat and hissed when I sucked him deeper. "Such a good fucking girl."

He cupped my nape, holding me still, and thrust a little deeper. I took him eagerly, reaching up to grab hold of his thick thighs.

"Fucking this pretty mouth is as close to heaven as I'll probably ever get."

I wanted to argue that he was definitely going to heaven one day because I was going to be there and I wanted him with me, but at the moment, my mouth was full.

Gripping the base of his cock, I pulled out until I could tongue that piercing I was becoming obsessed with.

"You like that, angel?"

"Uh-huh." I tongued it some more.

"You want to feel it in your pretty pussy?"

"Yes, please."

"Stand up."

Sucking the crown one more time, I let him go and stood. He gripped my waist and twisted me around toward the bed.

"Lean forward."

I caught myself with my hands.

"All the way down. Rest your face on the mattress."

He still held onto my waist as I pressed my cheek into the mattress, arms curled by my head, breathing quicker with anticipation.

"Mmm. Yeah, just like that." His big hands on my waist coasted over my hips, down my outer thighs. "Spread your legs wider."

I did, finding strangely, that I enjoyed hearing him give me commands while I could see nothing. Even more, I enjoyed obeying him.

He coasted one hand over my ass and down the back of my upper thigh, fingers close but not close enough to where I wanted them. "Did Livvy ever tell you that grims are descended from a vampire?"

"Yes."

"Then you know I can smell you. I could smell your arousal the minute I opened the door."

He teased, trailing one hand along my inner thigh but not higher, the other gripping my hip.

"Like right now. I know you're dripping for me, Clara. I know that sucking my dick turned you on."

I whimpered but didn't respond.

"You have any idea what that does to me?"

Finally, one finger slid over my lace-covered slit.

He groaned. "Just like I thought. Soaking wet."

Then I heard him lower to his knees. I panted softly, fisting my fingers into his gray coverlet. Then I felt his hot mouth over the lace.

"Ahh," I cried out.

He sucked me through the fabric, pressing his tongue against my clit, the sensation of the lace barrier driving me crazy. I moaned and rocked my hips.

"More," he growled. I felt the fabric rip between my legs and then his tongue was inside me.

"Yes, yes!"

His fingers curled into the flesh at my hips, holding me tight as he groaned against my clit. Suddenly he was standing behind me, his palm on the small of my back. I arched my spine at his touch, tilting my ass higher.

"I'm gonna have to fuck you hard, angel. Need to feel you deep."

"Yes," I breathed into the mattress and the curtain of hair that had fallen over my face.

The head of his dick slid through my folds, then lined up at my entrance. He gripped both my hips and pumped into me three times till he was seated completely.

"Ah!" I clenched my fists into the covers.

He felt so big, and the sensation without seeing somehow made it more intense.

He rumbled a groan, sliding his palm to the back of my throat where he pressed me down harder. "Yes, Clara. Take my fucking cock. It's yours."

My sex fluttered at his dominance, liking the sound of his possessive words.

"You ready to come already?"

I moaned louder. He pulled out to the tip and thrust in so deep I jolted on the bed and cried out with pleasure.

"Hold on, angel."

I did, but it didn't really matter. Henry fucked me senseless. Long and hard and deep. He groaned and then fucked me even harder. The sound of flesh slapping and slick sex filling the room carried me to another plane of existence. It was decadent and dirty and lovely.

"Henry," I called to him.

He fell forward, pressing his chest to my back, sweeping my hair to the side and brushing his mouth against my neck. He slowed his tempo.

"I'm so fucking deep in love with you."

For some reason that had me crying, and the blindfold was too much. "I need to see you."

He pulled out of me, untied the scarf, and gently rolled me over. I blinked up at him. He closed his black eyes, the black veins already prominent around the edges.

Reaching up, I cupped his jaw. "I love you, Henry."

When he opened his eyes, there was a pinpoint of gold light in each of them. His raven wings stretched from his back, cocooning us in a protective shell. The room went dark as he rolled his pelvis and sank inside me slowly.

"You don't know what those words do to me." His voice resonated with magic. His dark essence had joined with him, but not to summon a spirit or portal. It had simply *joined* him.

Reaching past his shoulder, I brushed my fingers along the feathered arch of his wing. I expected them to disappear or something, unsure if they were made of anything corporeal. But I felt the silky texture of feathers.

Henry groaned deep in his chest, still fucking me nice and slow as I petted him. Or maybe that was his monster growling his pleasure. It seemed they were one and the same, which I'd never sensed before now.

"I'd do anything for you," he said in that otherworldly voice. "I'd die for you."

"The feeling is mutual," I told him, pulling his face to mine so he'd kiss me.

As soon as his mouth touched mine, my sex fluttered with my orgasm. I moaned into his mouth as he stroked his tongue in tempo with his thrusts inside me. I came, digging my heels into the backs of his thighs and kissing him deeply.

He picked up the pace, driving into me with a little more force, his cock swelling inside me until I felt it throbbing with release. He buried his face in my neck, kissing me everywhere his lips touched as he climaxed.

I closed my eyes and basked in the post-orgasm bliss of sex with Henry, of being loved by Henry. It was overwhelmingly wonderful.

"What are you thinking?" he whispered against my neck, still pressing light, sweeping kisses on the underside of my jaw.

"That this is better than anything in the world." I opened my eyes to find his raven wings gone. "And I love you."

He lifted his head, his eyes returning to normal, though he was frowning. "Then why are you crying?"

I smiled, reaching up to wipe a tear away. "I cry for happy things as well as sad."

His expression softened as he wiped my cheek with the backs of his fingers. "Let's take a bath together, then get some sleep."

He kissed my lips, then pulled out of me before walking into his bathroom. I heard the sound of water filling a tub and soft music playing. While I waited, I looked around his room to get acquainted with a space I'd be spending lots and lots of time in from here on out.

Rather than call me, he walked back. I admired the view of him completely, unashamedly naked, stalking toward me with that intense expression that always made my skin tingle with pleasure.

I didn't say a word of protest when he scooped me out of bed and carried me. I rather liked it.

"I could get used to this." I looped my arms around his neck.

"What's that? Sex in my bedroom? Good. Because we'll be doing a lot of it."

"No, silly. Being carried by you."

He lowered me to my feet next to a giant soaking tub, easily big enough for two. A lavender scent from the bubble bath filled the room. But my gaze drifted to the rest of the bathroom. He'd lit a few candles, the black-and-gold wallpaper accented by baroque gold fixtures. Like the rest of the house, it looked old-world but also new.

"Good gracious, Henry. I had no idea you were such a romantic."

"Romantic?" He chuckled and helped me into the tub. "How do you mean?"

He stepped in behind me and sat first, pulling me gently down to sit between his legs in front of him. I leaned back, draping my arms on his thighs, sighing at the lovely heat of the water and him. It was the most luxurious throne a lady could have.

"Look at this room. And this house, for that matter. It's draped in elegant and opulent furnishings, ornate light fixtures, dark walls, and luxurious wallpapers. Candles and candelabras. Did you choose the decor of your home?"

"Yes. With a designer." He wrapped an arm just under my breasts, pressing a kiss to my temple. "That makes me romantic?"

"It tells me you have a romantic heart. Good for you that I appreciate such things. I'll enjoy being surrounded by all your lovely rooms and furniture."

"Good thing is right." He coasted a hand up one of my arms, rubbing soapy bubbles on my skin. "Could you . . ." He paused, dipping his hand into the water and pouring it over the bubbles on my arm. "Could you see yourself living here?"

"And leave my carriage house loft?"

He stiffened. "Yeah."

Hesitating, only to torture him, I tipped my head back to see his expression. "In a heartbeat."

He laughed and pulled me closer, angling his mouth over mine and kissing me deeply. What seemed like a short kiss morphed into a long, lingering one. His hands coasted over my breasts, then my arms, legs, stomach. He mapped me slowly. I dropped my head back to his shoulder and closed my eyes, enjoying his petting.

"The soapy water makes your skin feel like silk," he murmured, sliding a finger lightly through my folds, "especially here. So soft."

His gentle, cursory, gliding hands put me in a sort of hypnotic trance. It was arousing and relaxing at the same time.

"I need to schedule spa days like this once a week."

"I could do this for you every night," he whispered against the crown of my head, now playing with the long strands falling into the water.

"That would be too luxurious. You'd spoil me."

"I want to spoil you."

Smiling, I watched his hand play with my hair in the water, then glide over my skin. "At least I'm not glowing this time."

"Does that mean I didn't fuck you good enough?"

I giggled. "You know better than that."

"Mmm." His chest rumbled as he swept his big hands over my body.

We grew silent again, the music catching my attention. It was the song "Perfect" by Ed Sheeran, the version with Beyoncé.

"I love this song," I gushed.

"I know," he rumbled.

"See." I trailed an arm down his thigh. "Romantic."

After a few minutes of soaking in the steamy water and being caressed like a mermaid queen, I told him what I'd been thinking most of the afternoon since he left our house. "I have an idea."

"What's that?"

"I think I know of a way to help you with the panic attacks."

His hand paused, then started moving again. "Like when I was in the Vale?"

"You said you were forced back out because of the panic attack, right?"

"Carried, actually."

"Yes, your magic was protecting you by taking you out of there. But what if you were strong enough, more in sync with your magic, so you trusted yourself more? If you were able to use your magic to its full potential, that wouldn't have happened."

His hand paused again, resting on my knee. I sat up and twisted around to face him, then wrapped my arms around his neck and lay against his torso. His pensive expression, a slight pinch between his brow, reminded me of Gareth.

"What are you thinking?"

Smiling, I hauled myself closer. "I want to try another spelled tattoo from Violet."

His mouth quirked as he tucked a wet lock of hair behind one ear. "I've already tried that, remember?" He added with resignation, not bitterness, "It didn't work."

Sitting up onto my knees, I gripped the side of the tub and repositioned myself on the other end where I could look at him. Besides, I couldn't think clearly when I was pressed against his glorious, naked, and slippery wet body. I tucked my feet on either side of his torso.

Violet was exceedingly talented at the charmed tattoos. It was actually the ink that was charmed, not the tattoo itself so much. When the spell was right, it helped the supernatural— witch, warlock, vampire, or werewolf—tap into their magic on a superior level.

"It took Violet a while to figure out what spell would work on the werewolves."

He merely looked at me and didn't respond, lifting my ankle and beginning to massage the arch of my foot.

Good heavens. That was lovely. And distracting, but I forced myself to focus. I was onto an idea. I could feel Spirit nudging me toward something important.

"I think the main issue for you is that you've been severed from your magic for so long. You've shielded yourself from it and haven't properly reconnected. You might not have ever properly connected since you were so young when you stopped using it altogether."

"Could be." His big hands held my foot, his thumb pressing semicircles along my instep.

"This time, it won't be Violet spelling the ink for the tattoo. It will be me. I think I could spell the right charm. No, I *know* I could."

He stopped massaging, his gaze meeting mine over the steamy water. "Why do you say that?"

"Because Goddess is guiding me. I can feel it, Henry. I'm supposed to do this for you."

He paused and just stared, that pensive look more intense. "It would make total sense."

"I think so too."

After all, I knew him better than any witch out there. I could summon the right spell just by following where the Goddess guided me. She always told me the right thing to do. Always.

"You're an Aura. Your magic exists solely to heal emotional wounds. From the first second I met you, your nearness soothed me like no one else ever had, and I knew your magic was special."

Gulping hard at the adoration in his words and voice, I rubbed a hand up his shin. "You've never felt that way with other Auras?"

"No. Not like it is with you. Then, of course, I fell in love with you. With your kindness, your beauty, your generous, caring heart."

Tears threatened to sting, but I laughed instead. "Because I'm your person, Henry. And you're mine."

"So maybe you're right. You're the one to spell the ink with your magic, not your sister."

"And then Violet can do the tattoo . . ." I frowned.

"What's wrong?"

"Usually, the new moon is the best time for spells."

He smiled and threatened to make my heart stop when he lifted my foot and pressed a kiss to the inside of my ankle.

"You don't need the new moon, angel. You've got all the power in the world at the tips of your fingers."

"I do?" I watched his mouth coast around the arch of my foot.

"You vibrate with magic." He set my foot on his chest. "Let's see if your sister can do it tomorrow."

"She's usually got a long wait list for clients, but seeing as I'm her favorite sister, I suppose I can twist her arm." Pulling my hair to one side, I twisted it into a long rope. "What tattoo do you want for it?"

"You'll see." He watched me arranging my hair as I sat up, trying to squeeze the water out of it.

"Well, what color ink do you want? I'll need to know that at least."

He held my gaze. "Pink."

I burst into laughter. "Oh, dear, sweet Henry. You are *such* a romantic."

He grinned with devilish glee. "Let's go to bed."

"Yes, *sir.*" I rubbed my foot down to his lower abdomen.

His gaze sharpened. "Do you want to use the scarf this time?"

"Yes." I coasted my foot back to the middle of his chest and pressed a little. "On you."

He groaned and closed his eyes. "Out of the tub."

I obeyed, hopping out quickly. When I reached for the towel, he pulled it from my hands and proceeded to dry me everywhere.

"No one would've ever guessed it," I told him as he stood in front of me, wrapping the towel under my arms, candlelight casting his face in shadows.

"What's that?"

"That you're a nurturer. Just what I always dreamed of having one day all to myself. A man who loved loving. That's you, Henry. You love loving."

Wrapping an arm around my towel-wrapped waist and coasting a hand under my fall of hair, he tugged me into his naked body. "It's so easy to do with you, Clara."

There he went again, wooing my heart with little words and dizzying kisses. It goes without saying, we didn't sleep much our first night in his bed together.

CHAPTER 27

~HENRY~

"ALL I'M SAYING IS DON'T SHOOT OUT ONE OF THOSE TENTACLES AT me or anything if the tattoo hurts." Violet popped her second glove on and picked up the cordless tattoo machine loaded with the ink Clara had spelled this morning.

"What are you talking about?" asked Clara from the stool on my left.

She'd woken me before the sun was up this morning, fully dressed and fresh-faced as always.

"Come on," she whispered. "We have to go now to meet the Goddess before the world wakes."

I didn't know why that was important, and I wasn't going to ask her.

She told me anyway as I drove us both to the Savoie house. "I can hear her more clearly when the world is still," she said.

It wasn't even five yet, the streets still empty, so it seemed the world was quiet enough.

We crept into the backyard where she took my hand and guided me to their secret garden, a place where she and her sisters did their witches rounds, she'd told me, to align with the Goddess once a month and reenergize their magic.

Then she'd produced a vial of pink ink. When I'd asked her when she'd gotten it, she told me from Violet before she woke me. It was almost terrifying how solid I'd slept through her coming and going. We did wear ourselves out quite a bit last night.

It was humbling to sit there and watch her wield her magic. She sat cross-legged with the vial in her hands, murmuring a spell in French. Her magic felt like beauty personified. If it could breathe air, that would be Clara's magic. Just because it was beautiful didn't mean it wasn't powerful. Just like Clara.

It hummed with electric energy, raising the hairs on my arms. Not only that, but I felt him stirring behind his door, yearning to be set free, to speak to her. For the first time, I wondered what would happen if I unlocked him for good. He'd gone right back where I'd put him after he'd gotten me out of the Vale. He wasn't a misbehaving beast like Gareth's monster. He wanted to obey. Or perhaps he knew I wasn't willing to accept him, considering what might happen if he were truly a part of me.

Would I be flooded with unwanted spirits stalking and harassing me all hours of the night and day? It was strange, necromancy. It was a magic that gave us the power to summon souls and open portals into the netherworld, but it also attracted spirits who'd escaped the Vale on their own, or for some reason had never even made it there when they died. I didn't want to be that kind of necromancer.

But for the first time, after seeing Beatrice caged in that horrific nightmare where she was still a captive, I wanted to use my magic. The way I always was supposed to.

Clara had murmured softly for nearly an hour, her skin beginning to glow. I'd sat there, mesmerized by her unearthly magnificence. If anyone could help me, it would be her. My Clara.

Just as birds began to chirp in the wide-branched oak tree above us and gray light filtered into the garden, she stopped muttering her chant and opened her eyes. "We're good to go," she assured me with all the lightness that was completely and totally her.

"Puh-lease, Clara," said Violet in her usual sassy way. "Don't tell me you're not into the tentacle kink like Livvy is. I heard all about what grims have got under the hood."

"Tentacle kink?" Clara didn't look horrified. She looked interested. Excited even. Then she looked at me. "You don't have tentacles. Do you?"

"Not that I'm aware of."

But that didn't mean I couldn't. Or wouldn't. Once I'd freed my monster from his cell. I knew Gareth's monster was like something out of a horror movie when it made its presence known—vicious, cruel, and bloodthirsty. I was also aware that his monster adored Clara's sister, Livvy. Gareth didn't talk to me about his sex life, but it didn't surprise me the beast had made himself known when they were intimate. I'd sensed my own pushing forward last night. Heightened emotion always got a grim's monster's attention.

"Wait a fucking second." Sean was standing in the doorway of Violet's workspace. "I'm going to grow fucking tentacles during sex?"

Since the partitions didn't exactly block sound, especially for a grim with supernatural hearing, Sean had obviously overheard.

"You?" Violet snorted and leaned over me, the buzz of the tattoo needle humming as she began to fill in the lines of the butterfly wings as I'd asked her. "You'll be the worst of them all. Like the fucking kraken or something."

Then Sean grinned like a fiend and bobbed his head in that dopey teen way of his. "Sweet." Then he returned to the reception desk, chuckling to himself.

"You know, Blackwater," Violet continued in a hushed tone, likely not wanting Sean to eavesdrop, "they say little kids, little problems, big kids, big problems."

"I've heard the expression." I watched her fill in the lines of the left wing. Clara watched, too, seemingly mesmerized.

"I think you're in a hell of a ride with that kid."

"Well aware," I told her.

"Does it hurt?" Clara asked as Violet's needle worked close to my breastbone.

"Nah. I'm used to it."

"I could hold your hand if you needed me to."

Staring at her sweet face, I said, "I always need you to hold my hand."

She popped off her stool, moved it closer, took my hand into her lap, and gave me those lovey eyes.

"Ewww," Violet huffed under her breath. "Can y'all keep that googly-eyed shit down to a minimum?"

"No," said Clara with a bit of fire. "We will look at each other and touch each other any way we want."

Sean's voice rose over the partition from the reception desk. "You can use the supply closet for privacy if you need."

"What?" I asked.

Violet's face suddenly turned a shade darker, but she never lifted her head from working on the tattoo. "Shut the hell up, Sean! Get back to the inventory."

He cackled loudly. "Yes, ma'am!"

"That little shit," she muttered. "Sorry." She glanced at me.

"No, you're right. He's a little shit."

"But also kind of adorable and endearing," added Clara.

Violet sighed and then added reluctantly, "He is." She leaned back and swiped the excess ink with a cloth. "There's a lot of power in this ink, sis. Good job."

"Thanks." She squeezed my hand in her lap.

"I'm going to settle in and spell a while if y'all can keep quiet."

Clara and I had no problem simply keeping quiet and staring at each other. It was one of our favorite pastimes. Or it was one of mine, at least.

Violet wove a spell with her chanting, her fingers glowing as she continued to embed the ink into my skin, lining the butterfly with pink. With every line she completed, there was a definite change slowly taking place inside of me. It felt like stitches being pulled free, or like coming out from under a suffocating blanket.

The longer Violet's needle moved along my skin, the more I felt Clara's magic being woven into me. It was what I felt when she touched me—whole and happy—but amplified. This wasn't a simple touch. This was her magic being literally stitched under my skin. Seemed rather appropriate since she'd been there for years now.

I grunted my approval at the sensation, at the feeling of Clara becoming a part of me in a new way. My dark friend didn't simply stir in his cell; he stretched and unwound himself like a dragon waking from a long slumber, one who'd been hiding in a dark cave for decades, finally ready to awaken and fly.

Clara's expression changed, her eyes widening with surprise as she watched. But she didn't say a word. Before Violet was finished, the other two artists she employed, Tom who was a warlock and Lindsey who was a witch, showed up in the doorway, watching quietly. Like something had drawn them in here.

After what seemed like forever, Violet straightened in her rolling chair and turned off her cordless machine. Her hands glowed brightly from using her magic. "All done."

When Violet's gaze connected to mine, she jumped. "Holy fuck, Blackwater. What happened to your eyes?"

I frowned, but Clara hopped off the stool and drew closer, smiling down. When she cupped my face, I felt her emotion of overwhelming joy. I don't think it was an intended joy spell. It was simply her own happiness bubbling over.

"I'm pretty sure this is a sign that you're clear of the past."

Pushing out of the chair, I then marched over to the full-length mirror. There was a residual glow from the magic infused into my skin, emanating from my chest, the hum of power rippling through me. But it was the amber-gold color of my eyes that nearly knocked me on the floor.

"They'd turn this color when I was a kid. When my magic was dialed up."

Clara stood partly behind me, staring into the mirror. "Before the incident?" she whispered.

Swallowing hard, I nodded, staring into eyes I hadn't seen since my heart and soul had been clouded with dark nightmares and black magic.

"I don't know if it was Violet's intention," said Lindsey from the doorway, a pretty, petite witch. She was a Conduit like Isadora. "But I sensed healing magic taking place here. That's what drew me in."

"I'm not a healer," said Violet emphatically. "My magic just connects supernaturals to their magic."

If she only knew how valuable that was, especially to someone like me. I couldn't express it in words. Not to them. Except with Clara or Gareth or Sean, I'd never been good at expressing myself. Clara did it for me.

"That's exactly what he was hoping for. That was the healing he needed." Clara leaned closer and asked, "How do you feel?"

"Fucking fantastic."

She placed a hand on my back and hummed. "You feel stronger to me. You're free of it, Henry."

Holding her gaze in the mirror, I said, "Only one way to find out."

CHAPTER 28

~HENRY~

HERE WE WERE AGAIN, STANDING AT THE PORTAL IN MY BACKYARD around midnight. Gareth, Lavinia, and Clara were there. But Devraj was, too, just in case something nasty crawled out of the portal when I brought Beatrice back. *When*, not if.

The confidence that Clara had always worn like a cloak seemed to be wrapped around me now. I wasn't sure if that was because her essence was now embedded in my skin, or if it was simply an effect of the bindings finally being torn free between me and my magic.

Turning to look at them, I gave Clara a wink. "Be right back."

She smiled wide, her face glowing by the camping lantern sitting on the grass.

"We'll be waiting," she told me.

Then I slipped into the Gray Vale, back into Esbos.

The same malevolent pressure pushed down at me, but this time I pushed back. My monster growled, vibrating the air with its power. Necromancy pulsed through me like a living organism, drawing me forward, empowering me with the will and knowledge of exactly what to do. I stalked through the darkness like I owned this place, my kingdom beyond the real world.

A yellow-eyed demon crept from behind a rock, got one look at me, and then tittered and skulked away. The giant raven wings at my back stretched and fluttered, scaring off another creature. Something hissed as I stormed back through the tunnel, but I ignored all of the demons lurking here. They had no effect on me this time. Nothing made me hesitate as I strode closer to Beatrice's domed prison cell.

Up ahead, there it was, as expected. The glowing blue light and the distinct, guttural sound of demonic spirits echoed as I drew closer.

It wasn't as shocking a sight when I rounded the craggy rock to find them still circling and harassing her, one of them rubbing himself against her dome. She was sitting on the floor of her cell, curled into a ball, her head tucked low so she wouldn't have to see them.

Behind the dome of her ethereal prison was the giant demon reclining in a rocklike throne. His hand was between his legs, stroking his disgusting genitals. While I sensed that his lackeys were all former human or supernatural souls, malformed by their sins and their damned existence in Esbos, the giant was something else entirely. He'd never lived in the real world. He was something other—a demon born of some rot deep in the recesses of the netherworld.

His red eyes caught sight of me. Instantly, he was on his feet and circling around Beatrice. His attachment to her presence told me that he considered her his own toy down here. There would be no getting her without going through him.

She lifted her head, sensing some change in the air. When she saw me, she leaped to her feet and pressed her palms against the domed glass, relief and hope bright in her features. But my attention was on the demon giant as he stomped closer.

"Begone," it rumbled darkly, his demonic friends spreading out behind him and then around me, forming a tight circle.

With a flourish of my arm, I summoned a sword made of black steel, a deadly weapon made of my magic. My beast hummed approval.

"*No*," was all I told the foul creature narrowing his eyes on me, his three horns jutting asymmetrically out of his head.

He charged, shaking the ground as he stomped his way closer, hauling back an arm to swipe down at me. I leaped upward on instinct, flapping my giant wings to launch myself higher. Flipping in the air, I swung the sword, cleanly slicing through the creature's arm at the elbow.

It roared and staggered backward, clinging to its half-chopped limb, dripping some sort of black ooze onto the ground. It wasn't streaming blood, but more a gelatinous substance, seeping slowly in oozing globs. Apparently shocked at its injury, as I was sure it was the first time it had come into contact with a necromancer intending harm, it roared in anger, all the while backing away.

"Yeah. *You* fucking begone," I told him with another wave of my black-steel sword, which made a whirring sound as I swung it, my magic pulsing in the air.

The giant growled one last time, baring serrated teeth and then charged away, its followers scuddling behind him, yipping and hissing back at me. As if I gave a fuck.

Beatrice was crying with a bright smile on her face as I stormed closer, the sword disappearing into smoke. I had no idea how to break her out of the dome. Before I could even think about it, I found myself using the same Old Norse word to open the portal.

"*Opna*," I bellowed as I smashed my fist against the invisible field.

Like shards of glass, the spell shattered beneath my fist and my magic, the blue light evaporating into flickers that sputtered out in the darkness.

"Thank you," she cried as she fell into my arms.

Her spirit felt light. Of course, I'd never held a spirit in my arms.

"They're gone now. But they may come back."

Instantly, she drew back and looked around. "Yes. You're right. Let's go."

Quickly, I took her hand and led her back the way I'd come, back down the dark tunnel, no creatures at all hiding in the rocky crags as we passed. Then I saw it, the soft gold light of the lantern coming from the portal opening.

"This way," I told her. "Right through there."

She tugged me to a stop as we approached the portal. "I can't go through there."

Stopping just a few feet from the opening, I frowned down at her. "What do you mean?"

"That's the mortal realm."

"It's okay. I've brought other souls into the mortal world. You can come with me, and then I'll open a new portal to send you on."

She shook her head. "It won't let me."

"It?"

"The blood spell he put on me. I can't pass back over there."

My heart thumped hard. "You know your killer?"

"Of course." Her eyes glistened with sadness. "It was your father's business partner, Harold Stansbury."

My gut tightened at the realization my father had been betrayed by someone who pretended to be his friend. It would crush him to find out.

"Why?" I asked. "Why did he do it?"

"Jealousy." She shrugged. "I met your father and Harold at the opening gala of our new gallery. Harold had shown interest in me and tried to coerce me into a date several times, but I wasn't interested."

"You were interested in my father."

Her eyes filled with joy. "I was. I knew that Harold resented the fact that I chose Silas over him."

"But enough to commit murder against your best friend?" I was baffled.

"I think it was more." She looked worried. "Silas had begun to complain about Harold changing things at the company without his permission. Harold wanted more control."

I'd never bothered to get the entire story of how my father and Harold had started the business. I'd never given a damn. But when I asked once how they'd decided who'd be CEO and who the COO, he'd simply said, *The better man always wins, son.*

It seemed Harold was tired of losing.

I had to get this information to my father's attorney and the GOA. And my father.

"Here. Hold my hand. Let's see if I can guide you through."

Though I'd never been trained, I'd read enough books on necromancy and grims to know that they could cross into any realm in the netherworld, and they also could summon any portal openings. But I wasn't sure about souls who'd been blood-spelled upon their deaths.

I held her hand and pulled her closer, seeing Clara and the others on the other side. When I tried to pull her through the gateway, her hand was snatched from mine. I sensed the essence of dark magic circling her. She wasn't entirely free of it.

She breathed faster, fear returning to her expression. "Am I doomed to stay here?" She looked over her shoulder as if expecting the demons to be right behind her.

Of course, Harold would've spelled her in a way that she could never go back into the mortal realm where she could bear witness to his crime and condemn him.

"No," I told her. "I'll open another from here."

I'd wanted to bring her through and have witnesses to what she told me. Even a video could be manipulated into a deep-fake by savvy techs. That's why grims rarely used video evidence as truth. However, several credible supernatural witnesses like Devraj, Gareth, and the others would definitely force the GOA to listen.

But there was no way I was leaving her spirit here in this hell for demons to find and tear her apart. I knew that if I opened another portal into the lighter realm of the Vale, it was likely she would continue on into the afterworld. I might have to prove my father's innocence without her.

"Stand back."

She stepped away. I whispered an old chant, a spell I remembered from my early lessons with Amon, one that would open all portals. The old Norse poured from my lips easily iike I used this spell all the time, when in fact I'd only tried it once as a small boy.

"Opnað til ljóanrealmr."

There was a tearing in the air, the earth of this realm shaking beneath our feet. I was ripping open a portal that didn't belong here, but I didn't give a fuck. I wasn't leaving Beatrice in this place. No innocent deserved this damnation.

Distant screeches of alarm echoed as I bellowed louder, the cracking sound emanating from the sliver of yellow light that appeared in front of me. Raising my wings, I reached out and slid my hands inside the fissure of light and stretched it apart, all the while whispering for it to obey me.

It fought against me but finally yielded, opening a small window into a higher layer of the Vale, a lighter world of the in-between.

"Beatrice!" I called back to her, straining against the walls trying to close in on me. "You'll have to squeeze through."

She was suddenly there, crawling beneath my arms. My muscles bulged and threatened to fail, but I held it open as she stepped through. Her face full of light and joy, she turned at the last moment and put a palm to my cheek.

"Thank you, Henry. You are the son your father always told me about. Please tell him I love him." She let go and backed away, her spirit becoming more ethereal, more transparent. "Tell him I'll be all right now."

"Please wait in the Vale a little longer. If you can," I begged her for my father.

She nodded and then vanished. I let go of the walls. They slammed together with a resounding crash and a spittle of sparks, quaking the netherworld around me. More shrieks in the night echoed from the darkness, closer this time.

Without hesitation, I sprinted toward the portal and the gold lamplight. I leaped through with a rush of relief and a furious determination to find Harold Stansbury.

CHAPTER 29

~HENRY~

I KICKED THE DOOR OF HAROLD'S BEDROOM IN FRUSTRATION. IT CRACKED against the wall behind it.

"Yes," said the GOA agent, Fowler. He stood cool and calm in the bedroom of the man who'd condemned my father to execution. "He's gone."

Devraj and Gareth searched the front of the house when we realized that Harold had already known we'd discovered he was the one.

I wanted to punch myself for not recognizing his behavior as a little off when we met in Father's office. He had said all the right things, but there were subtleties to his expression that should've set me off. I'd fallen into the trap of never thinking someone you trust could be the guilty party. Because of it, I'd admitted to him I'd be using necromancy to find the murderer.

He knew my entire history. It was probably why he'd never seen me as a threat, knowing I'd never go into Esbos to try to save a father who was never there for me. He'd underestimated me and now was on the run.

Fowler stepped up to me, cool and grave. He was a no-nonsense grim who worked solely on logic. "If there is no evidence here linking Stansbury to Miss Plath's murder, then we'll need more evidence. You're a necromancer. You'll have to summon her in your father's court hearing."

I scoffed, disgusted by the entire turn of events. "I don't know if she'll still be in the Vale. She may have gone on already. But I'll try."

Fowler's expression finally showed the slightest emotion. Concern. "You'd better hope she hasn't. Because the only evidence we have so far points to Silas. There is no video surveillance or evidence from our psychics that can corroborate what you're telling me." He stormed toward the exit. "Court hearing is next Thursday. Be there."

I returned to the living room where Gareth and Devraj were scouring the place. Dev looked up from a desk in the living area. "Nothing. Just random business documents."

"This fucking sucks," I muttered in exasperation.

"Are you sure she's left the Vale?" asked Gareth.

"No."

"Then there's a chance," added Devraj.

Gareth met me near the front door. "I think we should go talk to Priscilla."

"Why?"

"Peony sent me word this morning. I'd asked her to check the history of openings on the safe. The biometric system they use keeps track. I wanted to know if there was any unusual usage."

"And?" I urged.

"It seems the night before and after Beatrice was killed, Priscilla had visited the safe after hours. After Peony had left for the day."

"She doesn't work late often?" asked Devraj.

"She does, but rarely does she go into Silas's office without Peony being there."

My phone buzzed in my pocket. When I saw who was calling, I frowned and blew out a breath.

"Who is it?" asked Gareth.

"It's Priscilla." I looked up at them. "She said she needs to talk to me immediately."

"How fortuitous," said Gareth. "We were just about to visit her anyway."

As we rode the elevator to the top floor of Obsidian Corporation, I wondered what had Priscilla summoning me to the office like it was an emergency. It didn't make sense for her to be working with Harold, to help him kill an innocent woman.

Turns out, I was right. When we marched into Priscilla's office, found her alone, and demanded to know why she'd gone into the CEO's safe the night before and the night after his fiancée was murdered, she asked, "How did you know?"

"The biometric system doesn't lie," I told her. "The data for Father's safe clearly shows you opening it at 9:33 p.m. two nights before Beatrice's death and 10:13 p.m. the night after. We have the records."

She blinked, her expression pensive and determined as she tapped on a digital calendar on her desk. "That was the twenty-third and the twenty-sixth, correct?"

"Yes." I shared a questioning glance with Dev and Gareth.

Then she added quickly, "I have something I need to show you. And tell you."

She waved us over to her large computer monitor facing the wall, away from the door, and sat down before tapping at the keyboard.

"I was suspicious about something, so I'd asked security to send me video footage inside the building the week Beatrice Plath was murdered. But security said the days I wanted were missing."

"Missing?" Gareth stepped around the desk, as did Devraj, to watch her screen. "It's digital. Someone would have to hack into the system and delete it."

"This is Obsidian Corp, Mr. Blackwater," she responded snappily. "There are plenty of tech wizards who could handle it."

"Which two days were you looking for?" I asked as video footage popped on screen. But it wasn't my father's office. It looked like a break room with a kitchenette and fridge.

"Two days before Beatrice was murdered and one day after. Just like you said." She fast-forwarded, people coming in and out of the room, then the lights went out.

"Where did this come from?" asked Gareth.

"My assistant, Felix, was furious about someone stealing his organic yogurt and diet sodas he'd stocked in the fridge. We don't have surveillance in the break room, so he'd set a hidden camera in there last month to catch the culprit. He did, eventually, but he'd forgotten about the camera." She turned her head to give me a pointed look. "Something had been bothering me, but I kept pushing it out of my mind until Harold failed to show up for work yesterday. Then this morning, the GOA walked in with a search warrant and raided his office. That's when I couldn't ignore my suspicions anymore. I was relieved Felix had forgotten about this camera."

She slowed the video when the footage got to a certain number she must've noted, the light in the break room coming on on-screen. Harold walked across the room and set a bag of Chinese takeout on the counter. He pulled a tray from the cabinet and then used the hot water dispenser to make two cups of tea. He looked over his shoulder at the door, then pulled a vial from his jacket pocket and poured a liquid into one of the teacups. He put both on the tray along with the Chinese food containers and left the room, the light blinking out.

Priscilla hit the pause button and swiveled to face us, crossing her arms. "Harold spelled me."

"Explain," I demanded.

"He came in here unexpectedly and asked me to work late on a European contract he needed help with. He said Silas was too busy. So I did, of course. He got some takeout for a late dinner and made me my favorite chai."

Her shoulders stiffened, her voice vibrating with fury. "I remember getting a migraine toward midnight and woke up the next morning on my sofa with the throw draped over me." She waved to the gray sofa, a cream blanket folded over the arm of one end.

"Harold told me the next day he didn't want to wake me since I'd seemed exhausted. It wasn't unusual for me to sleep over in my office."

She stood and stared out of her corner window overlooking the Mississippi River.

"I thought nothing of it. I'd just overextended myself like normal. I get migraines when I work too long. Sometimes, if it's bad enough, I have to sleep it off. I agreed to stay late again with Harold three nights later. The same thing happened. I got a migraine, then fell asleep on the sofa, but I don't remember falling asleep. It wouldn't be so unusual if it wasn't on those two specific days, the ones you're now telling me were when my biometrics showed up on the data for the safe."

"Why didn't you tell the GOA as soon as my father was arrested?"

She turned back to us, chin lifted. "Because I didn't think anything of it. I didn't know I'd been hexed and forced to open Silas's safe. I didn't backtrack and look at the dates till later. Honestly, the arrest of your father turned this whole corporation upside down. I was running around, putting out fires with high-end clients and the board. I'd forgotten all about it."

"When I came the other day, you wanted to tell me something. What was it?"

"Harold was acting strange around the office, and it bothered me."

"Strange, how?" asked Devraj.

"He'd called a board meeting without my consent. It's in the board policy that we must have two-thirds consent for unscheduled board meetings. He didn't tell me about any meeting, nor would I have known about it, except that I ran into Carol Feathers in the coffee shop downstairs as I returned from a meeting across town. She'd just left a board meeting with Harold."

"What was the meeting about?"

"Interim control of Obsidian."

I scoffed. "And that didn't make you suspicious enough?"

"Truthfully? No. Harold has always been somewhat pushy about being in charge. He's a vain peacock. I thought he simply wanted to assure the board that he was the man in charge while Silas was away. I never thought he'd actually murder the fiancée of his best friend of five decades for control of the company. That seemed ludicrous."

"Something changed your mind, though, didn't it?" urged Gareth.

She gave a stiff nod. "The afternoon you came by the office, I walked past Scott's office, one of our lead tech guys, and I overheard Harold talking to him. All I heard was Scott saying, 'I thought you were hot for that art chick last year but Silas beat you to it.' When I glanced into the office, they both got quiet, then Harold followed me down the hall, rambling about some nonsense totally unrelated." She bit her lip thoughtfully and added, "He was acting guilty of something. That's when I looked up those dates on my calendar and started thinking."

And Harold knew she was onto him, and likely I would be, too, soon enough. So he vanished. "We'll need you to testify at the GOA hearing next Thursday."

"Of course. What about Harold? Do you have evidence to keep him in custody?"

"He's gone," said Gareth. "He's in hiding, likely trying to flee. The GOA will suspend his passport so he can't get out of the country. Not legally anyway, but he may have illegal means."

"They'll find him," I told Gareth. "The GOA is ruthless."

Gareth nodded, clamping his jaw. What he didn't say was that he hoped it was by next Thursday. Or that I was able to summon Beatrice. Or that the GOA jury decided to postpone sentencing my father until we found Harold.

Priscilla leaned forward, planting both hands on the desk, exhaling heavily with emotion. "I just can't believe it was Harold."

Gareth looked at Dev. "We'll wait outside." They quietly left the office.

"Have you ever," I started, quietly, "noticed Harold being envious of my father?"

"No. Not in any substantial way. Although you and your father are estranged, he is a very well-respected man in the wide grim community with powerful friends. Harold has always been second-best to Silas, but I never thought Harold might be so jealous as to murder an innocent woman and frame him for it."

"No one did, apparently. Not even my father."

I reached out a hand for her to shake. "Thank you for your time."

She shook my hand. "Send me the details of the court hearing. I'll be there."

Leaving, the three of us waited until we were out of the building and back in Gareth's car before saying a word.

Gareth tore out of the parking lot into afternoon New Orleans traffic. "Her account of what happened with Harold, even with the biometric data to support her claim, is circumstantial at best."

"I know." I stared out the passenger window.

A group of laughing women walked into a pub. A couple looked in a shop window together, the girl pointing at something she liked. An older man held a little boy's hand, his grandson most likely, as they stepped into an ice cream shop. The world seemed so normal when mine was turning upside down.

I'd cut my father off for obvious reasons long ago. I'd determined that I'd never bother with him again, having the most minimal contact possible for mine and Sean's sake. I'd never thought I'd be hurled back into his world like this, where failing him could mean his life. It was too much to bear.

My phone buzzed in my pocket. Pulling it out, my heart tripped with aching need.

Clara: I'm waiting for you at your house.
Come home.

"Drop me first, please."

Gareth glanced at me, catching the urgency in my voice. He took the next turn toward the upper Garden District to my house.

When he pulled up in front, I thanked them both, then hurried up the front walkway. The door opened before I reached it, Clara standing there in a pretty floral dress, waiting for me.

I crossed the threshold, shut the door, and fell to my knees, wrapping my arms around her waist. Pressing my cheek to her abdomen, I whispered, "Thank you."

She didn't ask for what. It was clear enough how desperately I needed her comfort. Rather than question my dramatic behavior, she combed her fingers through my hair and let me hold her there in the foyer.

"I'm here," she whispered down to me, emanating her soothing essence. "Always here."

CHAPTER 30

~CLARA~

"I'M JUST SO EXCITED," I PRACTICALLY SQUEALED AS VIOLET DROVE me and Livvy to the party location. "And why is it such a secret where the party is?"

"It's not a secret." Violet headed across the bridge to the Westbank. "And I'd totally tell you, but Shane wanted it to be a surprise."

"Shane? We're having the party at his place?"

"Sort of."

Shane was the head of the Blood Moon pack who'd moved into town a while ago. They'd caused trouble for Nico and Violet, but they'd all settled their differences. The real problem had been that they needed Violet's skills with spelled tattoos. Since then, they'd decided to stay.

Livvy called from the back seat. "I already know."

Spinning around, I scowled at her. "How do you know, but I don't know?"

"They're my new client. They needed promotion."

"They? Like the whole pack? So they've opened a new business?"

Violet turned onto another street that led to the outskirts of town. "Fine. I'll tell you," said Violet.

I smiled. She never was great at keeping surprises to herself.

"They bought that abandoned workshop where they'd taken me that one time."

"You mean when they kidnapped you and dragged you across New Orleans and gave Nico a heart attack?"

"Yeah. That time."

"Okay," I said on a laugh.

"They've renovated the whole thing. Made it into a body shop for cars and bikes."

"They opened a mechanic shop?"

"No. A body shop," explained Livvy. "They do custom paint jobs on remodeled cars and high-end motorcycles and stuff."

I knew nothing about cars. Didn't know the difference between a mechanic and a body shop. Well, now I did.

"Sounds cool." I looked out the window as we turned onto a gravel road into some woods. "So they've definitely decided to put down some roots in New Orleans."

"Looks that way," said Violet. "Besides, since neither Nico nor Mateo wanted the first official werewolf seat on the High Guild Coven in New Orleans, Jules offered it to Shane."

"I didn't realize that."

Livvy unbuckled her seatbelt and leaned forward between our seats. "You've been a little busy with your sexy grim to notice the world around you. It's okay. We forgive you."

Ignoring her, I added, "I'm glad for Shane and the pack. They're good guys."

"They are," agreed Violet. "And I thought since they just finished renovations and it's a big space, it would be a perfect place for the party."

I was about to protest that a body shop doesn't exactly scream fun and party, but then we rounded the bend and the shop was in full view. I'd expected a small, ramshackle sort of place, but it wasn't at all.

The garage had four large bay doors open, the siding a pristine white with Blood Moon Body Shop painted on the side with their logo of a wolf howling at the moon. They had fairy lights strung up in one of the bays with tiki torches lining the outside garage. Tables with food and kegs were set up. I even saw JJ and Finnie working behind a makeshift bar near the first bay opening.

"Wowza," I said.

"Damn straight." Violet grinned over at me. "I knew they'd do a good job."

"You made them do the whole thing, didn't you?" I accused as she parked the SUV.

"Yep. Those fuckers owed me after all the trouble I went through for them."

I laughed as we got out. Leave it to Violet to wiggle out of actually doing anything for the first party she had to plan on her own. Nico stood with a group of them, watching us walk up. I recognized Shane, Rhett, and Ty right away. Rhett was a sweet, auburn-haired hottie who liked to flirt with me a lot.

As we drew closer, Nico's attention zeroed in on my sister, as was natural. Glancing around, I saw that Henry and Gareth weren't here yet.

"You told Gareth how to get here, right?" I asked Livvy, suddenly nervous they didn't know where the party was.

"Yeah. They've been here before."

"Henry and Gareth?"

"The night Violet was kidnapped. They know where it is."

Devraj and Isadora were picking up Ruben and Jules from the airport and coming straight here. When they'd informed me yesterday, I'd worried about jet lag for them coming directly to the party, but Isadora said they'd actually left London a few days ago and had spent a couple days in Salem first. *Putting some issues in order*, Ruben had told them.

I felt a little out of sync with my family. Usually, I was the one who had all of the information and was making sure everything and everyone was taken care of. It was the nurturer in me. Henry was right about me. I was definitely that person for everyone I loved.

But I'd been preoccupied lately, which was expected. I'd fallen madly in love with my soul mate. Being with him had been my only priority, especially with this sudden tragedy with his father. I suppose it was normal that I'd been feeling so off lately, but also blithely, unquestionably happy at the same time.

"Welcome, ladies," said Shane proudly, arms spread at the shop. "What do you think of her? Isn't she beautiful?"

"Amazing," I agreed.

"I have to give it to you, wolfman," said Violet as Nico pulled her into his side. "Y'all did a fantastic job. When do you open?"

"Next week. The shop is ready. Still setting up the paint shed for full body jobs, but we're ready to get started."

"You'll have clients lining up soon enough," said Livvy. "I've launched your social media pages, but I need to get some video footage for reels and ad videos."

"Not a problem." Shane arched an eyebrow. "Would you like shirts on or off for this campaign video? We raised a good bit of money at your last gig without them."

"Damn straight, you did," added Violet. "That was a fine show."

Nico pinched her butt. "Ouch!" She jumped. "Of course, I was only watching my own werewolf take his clothes off, so I'm only going off rumor."

Rhett and Ty laughed before Shane added, "Yeah, we saw you got the best show in the house that night."

"Actually that would've been me," Livvy added cryptically.

"What was that?" asked Violet.

"Nothing." Livvy smiled. "I think I'll go say hello to the DJ I hired for this shindig."

"Hey, sweetheart," said Rhett, sidling up next to me and greeting me with his flirty smile. "How about a drink?"

"Sure." I looked over at the bar where Finnie was working. JJ had disappeared. "I saw JJ a minute ago."

JJ made my favorite cocktail, the Grave Digger. I loved drinking tequila at parties. Music suddenly started pumping loudly from giant speakers set up on either side of the drive. The DJ Gareth and Livvy had hired for the Werewolf Wet T-shirt Contest last year was set up in the second bay, colored lights adding to the mood as the sun slipped lower behind the garage.

"Yeah. He's probably unloading ice or something. Come on."

Rhett took my arm, which was fine. He knew I was with Henry. At least, I hoped he did.

"So how's that grim treating you?" he asked as "Ghost Town" blared from the bay.

Whew. He knew.

"Great actually."

We leaned against the bar where Finnie was setting up a second keg behind him.

"Hey, Finnie," I called.

He smiled wide. "Hey, Clara. JJ will be back in a minute. I know you don't want a beer."

"You know me so well."

"Damn," sighed Rhett as he peered down at me, obviously liking the hot-pink dress I was wearing, a little tighter than my usual style. "Wish I'd had a chance with you, beautiful."

He'd kept a respectful distance so far, not touching me inappropriately or anything. That's what I loved about these werewolves. They looked like bad boys—and according to Nico, most of them had been very bad in the past—but most of them were true gentlemen.

The music pumped loud, so I put my hand on his forearm and leaned up on tiptoes to yell, "You're an amazing catch for some lucky lady."

He laughed, his amber eyes flashing, his hand on my shoulder to steady me as I'd leaned up. Then his smile dropped with dread. "Holy fuck, Clara."

Letting go of his arm, I stepped back. "What?"

His gaze lowered to my abdomen, and then he glanced around nervously. "It might be better if your grim didn't catch me talking

314

to you all alone." He looked at his own hand on my shoulder and dropped it like something had bitten him. "Or touching you."

I laughed. "He's protective, but he won't kill you or anything."

"I know grims can behave erratically when their mate is in your condition."

I stared at him and blinked. "What?"

He laughed again, nervously this time. "Um, Clara. You do know you're pregnant, don't you?"

A shot of adrenaline suddenly knocked my knees out from under me. "What?" was all I could say again.

He grabbed me around the arms as I tottered. "You didn't know. Oh shit." He looked around nervously again. "Hope I'm not overstepping. I say stupid shit when I shouldn't."

"Does that mean you're wrong? You're mistaken?"

"Oh no." He stared down at my belly.

I looked down. It was no more rounded than normal. Werewolves had super senses, though. Nico and Mateo knew about Isadora before any of us, I'm sure.

"Are you sure?" My heart was in my throat, my mouth gone dry.

"Positive. One hundred percent."

How did this happen? I was on the pill. Of course, I'd forgotten to take it one day last month, but I took it the day after when I remembered. And I did it again the day after Henry ate me out on his library ladder. I'd been a little forgetful, my mind in the clouds and totally obsessed with my grim whose cunnilingus skills scattered my brain cells. Apparently.

"Omigod," I whispered, breathing faster.

"It's okay." He squeezed my shoulders. "Do you want me to get someone? I could grab Violet."

"No!" I shook my head, trying to regain control of my breathing.

He looked up, then instantly dropped his hands from me. "Oh fuck. Gotta go, Clara. Good luck, sweetie."

Looking in the direction he had been before he vanished into thin air, I saw Henry stalking through the party. Wearing black jeans and an all-black Henley, his eyes dark as midnight, he looked like the grim reaper he was. The angry set of his jaw and flickering gaze, as if looking for someone—undoubtedly Rhett who'd just performed a magic trick and disappeared—had my heart hammering even faster.

When he reached me, his arms wound around my back and waist. He leaned in to brush a kiss on my cheek and then coasted his mouth to my ear. "What's wrong?"

"Nothing." I gripped his waist, leaning into him, not wanting him to be angry with me. That thought only made my pulse race even faster.

"Your heart is beating out of your chest. What did the fucking werewolf say to you?"

"He didn't say anything."

Lies, lies, lies. Thank the Goddess he wasn't an Aura.

"I'm going to rip his head off for upsetting you. Where'd that bastard go?"

"It's not Rhett," I told him honestly, pulling back to look up at him.

Concern etched deep groves in his forehead, his mouth a hard line. "What is it? What happened?"

"I'm not sure." *More lies.* "I think it's just everything that's happened lately with your father. I'm afraid we won't be able to help him."

His hard expression softened. "Don't worry about that. That's for me to get anxiety over. Not you."

He pulled me back into his arms and rocked me. "Trampoline" by SHAED pumped a steady beat. Henry coasted a hand up and down my back, his mouth pressed against my temple.

"Please don't stress about that, angel. I'm taking care of it."

"I know you are."

I did. He'd already summoned Beatrice again, asking her to stay close in the Vale, not to cross into the afterworld yet, as he'd called it. She said she could wait a little longer, but she wanted to keep going.

My mind was on that morning after we'd had sex and he'd freaked out because he hadn't used condoms. I'd assured him that it was okay. He'd looked horrified when he thought he might've gotten me pregnant. He didn't want kids right now. He'd all but said so.

While Henry held and rocked me in his arms, others had meandered to the makeshift dance floor in the garage. Violet and Nico danced together. Evie and Mateo were right next to them, Evie smiling and whispering up to him. Aunt Beryl had offered to watch the triplets tonight so we could all be here for Jules's and Ruben's arrival.

Our family friend Tia was here with her giant Italian boyfriend. He scowled at her for dragging him to dance, but he was going anyway.

Belinda, the only waitress who'd been working at the Cauldron as long as Jules, was now flirting with a couple of the werewolves. Mitchell, Sam, and Elsie were also here, too, milling around together near the food table. We'd all decided to close down the

Cauldron tonight so everyone could welcome Jules home properly and congratulate her and Ruben on their marriage.

Ruben's men Sal and Roland were here too. They were at the center of a group of werewolves closer to the bar where we were. I could hear Sal regaling them with a story about how they'd killed a bunch of evil assholes in the north of England near a place called Wulfric Tower.

"If it wasn't for that Scottish wolf Magnus, we'd have been toast," he was telling them. "Right, Roland?"

Roland tipped his glass. "To badass warrior werewolves."

They all cheered and clapped them on the back. All the while I was in a daze, trying to come to terms with what Rhett had just told me. Maybe he was wrong. But probably not. I couldn't wait to get home so I could run to the drugstore and get a pregnancy test. I needed to see that positive pink line on the test kit to be sure.

"Here you go, Clara." I lifted my head to find JJ at the bar to my right.

He set a Grave Digger on the bar for me with a wink. "A double for my girl. That'll fix you up."

"Thanks, man." Henry took it and passed it to me. "Here you go. This will calm your nerves a bit."

I took the drink and stared at it. No way in hell was I going to ingest tequila and get my baby drunk.

My baby. Our baby. Omigod, I was going to throw up.

There was a rush of noise toward the parking lot as Devraj's Lamborghini pulled up. Cheers erupted as Devraj helped Isadora out, and then Jules appeared, Ruben at her side two seconds later. Livvy and Violet launched themselves at Jules. Ruben stepped aside and spoke to Gareth and Shane.

"Come on." Henry took my hand. "Let's go see your sister."

I set my drink on the bar right as he pulled me through the crowd to greet them. Everyone was laughing and shouting *welcome back* and similar things. Livvy let go of Jules, who was beaming up at her, then she turned and looked at me, giving me that sweet big sister smile as she tilted her head. She looked like Mom.

Without hesitation, I ran the last few steps and wrapped her in my arms, bursting into hot tears.

"Clara, honey." She patted my back, laughing. "I didn't know you missed me that much."

"Mm-hmm," was all I could manage, hugging her tight.

I wished Mom and Dad had come back with them. They'd returned to their home in Switzerland and would come back to New Orleans for Christmas. I wanted to curl up in Mom's lap and have her tell me it was all right.

"It's okay," said Jules, running a hand down my hair, as if she sensed what I needed and that perhaps this wasn't just me missing her terribly but something bigger. "We're all back together again. I'm all healed now. Everything's going to be fine, Clara."

I nodded and finally let her go, then went to give my new brother-in-law Ruben a hug.

Oh, hell. I glanced toward Henry, who was in conversation with Devraj though his gaze was steady on me. Would he be mad?

One way or another, I'd have to tell him the truth.

We were going to have a baby.

CHAPTER 31

~HENRY~

SOMETHING WAS WRONG WITH CLARA. SHE WAS OFF LAST NIGHT. NOT her normal joyful self at all. She'd said it was about this thing with my father, but instinct told me otherwise. Had someone done something to upset her? I'd thought that flirty fucking werewolf Rhett had done something and was prepared to rip his throat out if he had, but he'd made himself scarce the whole damn night.

Then Clara wanted to leave early with Jules, who was exhausted from traveling and a long day. Ruben had said he'd take them home. I wanted to protest, but Clara had thanked him and seemed genuinely happy to leave the party.

I was afraid she might be having second thoughts about us or something, which seemed impossible, but she hugged me tight before she left and told me she loved me like always. She just didn't look me in the eye before she climbed into Ruben's car.

I'd gone home and told myself it was nothing. Then I slept like shit without her in the bed with me. This morning, I woke up with a bad feeling in my gut. I was determined to get some answers.

That's why I was pulling up to Mystic Maybelle's. After parking on the street, I hopped out and went into the shop, the bell tinkling over the door. My gaze went straight to the glitter balloon display Clara had made, remembering our first kiss here.

"Hi, Henry." Isadora walked out from behind the cashier counter, a list of some kind in her hand. Inventory, it looked like.

"Morning. Is Clara in yet?"

Isadora avoided eye contact and looked down at her list. She was an introvert, but I got the feeling she wasn't being shy or simply people-avoidant at the moment.

"Um, yeah. She decided to take the day off. I'm filling in."

"Take the day off?"

Something was definitely fucking wrong. The only reason she'd taken a day off since we'd started dating was to spend the day with me.

What the hell was going on?

"Where is she? At home?"

"No." She lifted her head from the inventory sheet. "She's visiting Violet at Empress Ink."

Violet lived with Nico now so it made sense she'd go there to visit her twin sister. But what on earth would make her need an in-person visit with her closest sister? Eyeing Isadora, who was steadily avoiding looking at me, I realized she knew what was going on.

"What is it, Isadora? What's going on with Clara?"

I'd expected her to pretend she didn't know what I was talking about. Instead, she lifted her gaze to mine. "You should go to Empress Ink and talk to her."

Fucking hell.

Something *was* wrong.

I was gone in a heartbeat, forcing myself not to speed or run any red lights. By the time I got there, parked my car, yanked open the door, and marched inside, my mind was running wild with possible scenarios. The worst of which was that she'd decided being with a grim with so much baggage was too much for her. My heart was going to literally crack in half if that's what was about to happen here.

After I'd swung open the door to the tattoo shop, which wasn't even officially open yet, I found Sean at the reception counter. He looked up from the Mac desktop in front of him. He sat back in his chair and crossed his arms, grinning at me like the devil himself.

"*What?*" I snapped.

"Not saying a fucking word. Though I've heard everything those two have said this morning. Man, are you in for a surprise."

Storming past my brother, I walked into Violet's workspace to find them sitting on stools, facing each other, and Clara crying. Violet had a comforting hand on her shoulder.

Clara gasped and jumped to her feet when she saw me standing there. "Henry."

Then Violet stood next to her, folding her arms and shooting an accusatory look at me. "You've done it now, grim. Like literally."

Planting my hands low on my hips, I demanded, "Tell me what's going on, Clara."

If she was breaking up with me, I wish she would have told me first instead of her whole damn family. I deserved that.

She wiped her cheeks with the back of her hand and walked up to me, fear in her eyes. It nearly killed me. Didn't she know she never had to be afraid of me? Not even if it was to tell me to fuck off for the rest of my life. I'd do anything to make her happy. Even walk away and leave her alone.

"We need privacy." She took my hand and guided me out of Violet's cubicle.

She peered down the hall where Lindsey was just walking into the break room. Then she turned and marched in the other direction. She opened a closet door, the supply closet from the looks of it.

"Sean," she called over her shoulder. "Turn up the music."

"I know the drill," he said in his snarky manner, turning up the house music they always had playing. Currently, SYML crooned "Where's My Love" on the playlist.

Once inside and she'd closed the door, she let my hand go.

I turned to face her. "Tell me."

She nodded, staring down at the floor. "This is hard."

"Just say it. That's always the best way."

Let's get this over with before I cut my own heart out.

"Okay." She nodded nervously, finally lifting her gaze to mine. "I'm pregnant."

Freezing in place, I tried to absorb the words she'd just said to me. But it wasn't sinking in. I was prepared for *I'm breaking up with you.* I wasn't prepared for that.

"And before you get mad . . . ," she snapped when I hadn't made any response whatsoever. I was still frozen in place, blinking down at her. "It's your responsibility too. I mean, yes, I know I told you I was on the pill, and that wasn't a lie. But I'm also not always good about taking them. Mostly, I am, but I forgot once or twice in the past month or so. I was distracted. You were distracting. *Very* distracting. Still, even if I hadn't forgotten, they're not one hundred percent effective. Look at Evie."

She gasped, her blue eyes rounding with fear. "Oh no. Evie! Triplets." She squeezed her pretty eyes shut. "Dear Goddess, don't let it be triplets. We can't handle another set so soon. But even if it is, I'm not doing this alone."

She bounced between angry and sad so fast I couldn't keep up. "But also, please don't be mad at me," she begged, tears spilling again. "I didn't mean for it to happen, Henry. But it's true. I'm going to have a baby."

Then she burst into tears.

Without hesitation, I snatched her into my arms and pressed her against me, thankful this wasn't the nightmare of a day I thought it might turn out to be. Quite the opposite. It might be the best day of my life.

I burst into laughter. My poor angel had been spinning out of control with worry. And so had I. All for nothing.

"You're laughing?" She pulled back to look up at me.

Cupping her face, I slid my fingertips into her hair and dipped my head low. "This is a happy day, my love. Don't cry." I wiped her tears away with my thumbs.

She gripped my wrists and peered up with those angel eyes that held me in their thrall. "I thought you might be mad." Her voice cracked, which broke my heart a little. "You might think I was trying to trap you or something."

"Please trap me." Brushing my mouth against hers, I whispered low, "I'm already your slave, Clara. I'd do anything to be tied to you forever. But I didn't do this on purpose."

"I know you didn't." She frowned, her gaze on my mouth. "So you're okay with having a baby?"

"Okay?" I kissed her again, backing her up to the wall. "I'm ecstatic." Another kiss. "I'm going to have a baby with the love of my life." I pressed her into the wall. "I'm the happiest man alive."

Then I slanted my mouth over hers for a soft kiss. That wasn't going to happen, though. The kiss became frenzied, heated, and desperate. She clenched one hand in my hair, the other in my shirt. But then she broke away and sniffed.

"Shhh," I whispered against her temple, noting she was working herself into tears again. "I'm here." I pressed my forehead to hers. "What were you scared of, love? That I'd be mad at you?"

"Mm-hmm." She sniffed again. "That you'd be *really* mad. That you'd break up with me."

I pulled back to look at her, stunned that she could think such a thing.

"Look at me, Clara," I whispered. Ocean-blue eyes met mine. "I'm never leaving you." I cupped her face. "I'll never let you go."

She buried her face in my neck and whispered against my throat, "I love you, Henry."

Instantly, my world was right again. I held her for several minutes until her breathing evened and her sniffling stopped, her fingers playing in my hair.

There was a stack of paper towels on a shelf. I took one out of the package and handed a sheet to her. She wiped her pink nose and swollen eyes, mascara smearing. She still was the most beautiful woman in the world to me.

"You better now?"

She nodded on a little laugh, dabbing under one eye. "Much."

I kissed her on the forehead and then opened the door.

Sean looked up from his computer, the music still blaring. "She's crying?" He looked pained before shaking his head at me. "Bro, you're doing it all wrong."

"Fuck off."

I grabbed Clara's hand and took my girl out to lunch. Had to make sure she was eating enough for two now.

CHAPTER 32

~CLARA~

"So this is where everyone is." Violet walked into Jules's library. "I've been wandering around the house like an idiot."

I'd sought out Jules as soon as I'd gotten home from a wonderful day with Henry, the two of us more moony-eyed than usual now that the idea of being parents together was sinking in.

I'd found my oldest sister in her library with Isadora, the two of them tucked together on her window seat, Z curled in a ball between them. One of Isadora's candles made with a dose of healing magic for stress was burning on the coffee table. I'd settled on the sofa right as Livvy and Evie had walked in, the triplets down for the night. Then Violet entered and plopped in the last spot on the sofa next to Livvy. Evie took the wing chair facing the coffee table across from the window seat.

We'd all missed Jules terribly and had gravitated to her like planets around their sun. She'd always been our grounding force.

Without her, an important part of our world had been missing. Now, everything felt right.

Since I'd spilled the news to Henry, I figured I'd better tell the few sisters who didn't know yet. Isadora and Violet already did. But before I could say a word, Jules looked at me intently and asked, "Is Henry okay? Devraj and Gareth told us everything going on with his father."

Swallowing the sudden lump in my throat, I tried to sound hopeful, "He's okay. Better now that we have proof his father is innocent. I think he'll be relieved after the trial this Thursday."

"He's going to do that spooky ghost-show again like he did last time?" asked Violet, purposely avoiding saying Richard Davis's name. We'd stricken him from all conversation since Livvy's incident.

"Yeah. But I think he's pretty down about having to talk to his dad about Harold's betrayal. He was his father's best friend."

They didn't have to say anything. A wave of sympathy washed through me from my sisters, comforting me with their compassion for Henry.

"I reached out to the GOA last night," said Jules.

"What's the GOA?" asked Violet.

Isadora and Evie looked confused, too, but Livvy didn't. I'm sure Gareth had filled her in.

"The Grim Office of Authority. Even though any supernatural occurrence that involved humans or other supernaturals other than grims is under my jurisdiction, I informed them I'd be sitting on the jury at the trial. I let them know they were lucky that I wasn't taking the suspect into my custody from Glasgow and holding my own trial as it should be."

"And what did they say to that?" I asked.

"They very begrudgingly acquiesced. Gareth happened to be standing beside me. With him on my side, they couldn't disagree with my demands."

"The Grim Office of Authority?" Violet scoffed. "Those grims are some shady fuckers."

I slapped her on the arm from my side, and Livvy slapped her from the other.

"Ouch!" shouted Violet. "Damn, I'm just kidding. Jeesh."

"Jules, you knew about these Grim Reaper police?" asked Evie.

"Actually, not until rather recently. When we started delving deeper into the werewolf issue, Gareth told me there was more I needed to know about the grims' own law enforcement."

"Didn't the grims get angry with him for telling you?" asked Isadora.

"If so, it doesn't matter. He could level their entire building if he wanted. Hell, he could level New Orleans for that matter."

"Damn right, my baby could." Livvy looked pleased as pie.

"Anyway, we are trying to open more lines of communication with the grims." Jules took another sip of her tea. "At least when it comes to crime and punishment. While they've always had a seat at the table of the High Guild, they rarely, if ever, have anyone actually occupying it. Gareth is working on improving the situation."

"That's so awesome," said Evie. "All the strides you and Ruben have made for the werewolves. And now this."

Jules looked a little sad. "We're just opening the doors. It doesn't mean everything will remain equal or fair because people are inherently flawed." She shrugged. "But we'll keep trying to make it better. That's all we can do."

"It's amazing," I told her. "If we model here what all covens should look like, the others may eventually fall in line."

"That's what we're hoping. That was one reason we stopped in Salem. Ruben wanted to ensure the coven there was on board and would add a seat for the werewolves in the region."

"I'm sure that went over well." Violet picked at the black nail polish flaking off her thumb.

"Ruben has a way of getting what he wants." Jules grinned.

Violet snickered. "I'll bet he does."

"Clara, if you need anything," said Jules, "we're here for you. For both of you."

Smiling at that, I inhaled a deep breath, readying myself to spill the news but was cut off before I started.

"Well, I have something to say." Evie sat cross-legged in the wing chair in the corner facing us. She was wearing her new T-shirt that read *Mama Bear: Cuddly & Lovable with Razor-Sharp Claws.* But my favorite was the matching shirt Mateo wore—*Papa Wolf: Beware... All Claws.*

"Uh-oh," said Violet. "This sounds serious."

Evie smiled. "No. I've just been thinking a lot lately about how much all of you have pitched in since the triplets were born." She had a throw pillow in her lap and was picking at the fringed tassels. "It's been hard, like really hard sometimes."

She laughed, but it sounded a little watery. Not sadness, but simply heavy happy emotions. I knew something about that.

"We know," said Isadora. "That's why we're here."

Evie smiled at us. "I wanted to thank all of you. Mateo and I both did. And for letting us move our family into the house. I couldn't imagine a better home to raise them in."

"Please don't start crying," said Isadora. "I've been weepy about everything lately. These baby hormones make me cry over every little thing. Yesterday, Devraj fussed at Archie for chewing on a charger cord, and I burst into tears because he hurt Archie's feelings. Then Archie ran over to lick me to try and make me feel better."

"What did Devraj do?" asked Livvy.

Isadora laughed. "He apologized and looked horrified, asking if he could get me a blanket or a cup of chai." She tucked a lock of her long blonde hair behind her ear. "He's so sweet, but also a little terrified of anything stressing me out."

"When is Devraj not sweet?" snorted Violet.

"True," agreed Isadora.

"Well . . ." Jules straightened from the window seat where she usually had her evening glass of wine. She had only a cup of warm tea on the windowsill, probably one Isadora brewed up. "Evie, this might make you cry even more but hopefully all happy tears."

"What?" asked Evie. "What's happening now?"

Livvy and Jules shared a look. But it was Jules who spoke. "Livvy and I are moving out so that you can have all the space you need. Now that the babies are sleeping through the night, you and Mateo deserve your own home without a bunch of sisters on top of you."

"No, y'all." Evie really was about to cry. I already was. "You don't have to leave."

"Stop that," Livvy added sweetly. "And it's not like we aren't going to be popping over all the time to see our sweet niece and nephews."

"And Clara will be in the carriage house," added Jules.

"Doubt that," muttered Violet.

"Why's that?" asked Jules.

But then Livvy butted in. "Evie, seriously. I'm already practically living at Gareth's place. We're just going to make it official."

Evie looked at Jules. "And of course you'll move into Ruben's mansion now that you're married."

Jules sipped her tea and set it back on the windowsill. "There's something I need to tell y'all too."

Violet leaned forward on the sofa next to me, her eyes going glassy for a few seconds as her Seer magic sent her a psychic vision. It happened out of the blue like that sometimes, not just when she was tapping into it intentionally. "Oh shit, Jules. You're pregnant, aren't you?"

She smiled, looking suddenly very young. "I am. Ruben and I decided we'd waited long enough to start our lives. To start our family."

Isadora reached over and took her hand, giving it a squeeze.

"What the fuck, y'all?" Violet turned and stared at me. "Are you going to tell them?"

"Um." I cleared my throat. "I'm pregnant too."

Livvy burst out laughing. Evie gasped and clamped her hands over her mouth, then she was up and across the room sitting next to me and hugging me. "My baby sister's going to be a mommy?"

I hugged her back, joy zinging out of me like sparkly rainbows.

"What is this?" snapped Violet. "The pregnancy edition of Oprah? *You* get a baby, and *you* get a baby, and *you* get a baby."

We were all laughing then, some of us crying too.

"Lavinia?" Violet addressed her sharply. "Are you fucking pregnant?"

"Hell no!" She shook her head on a giggle. "I am absolutely not. Though Gareth and I do love practicing."

"Good, keep it that way. I don't want any undue pressure on me and Nico. We're waiting awhile."

"How are you feeling?" asked Evie, still hugging me. "How does Henry feel?"

"We're excited," I said almost shyly. "Obviously, we did not plan this like Is and Jules."

"Well, you should move into the main house now. Unless you think Henry will want you to move to his place."

"He will definitely demand that I move into his house."

The thought of living in that beautiful Gothic house with him wrapped me in warmth. "Do y'all know he has a giant library with shelves that reach the ceiling?"

"Of course he does," snarked Violet. "Bitches love libraries. Especially bitches like you."

I shoved my twin on the shoulder, who quickly leaned in and hugged me from the other side.

"Well, make room. Now I feel left out." Isadora hopped up from the window seat and sat on Evie's lap so she could hug us too.

We looked over at Jules, still the demure, mature one of the group.

"Come on," I urged her.

She rolled her eyes and stood anyway. "You all act like a bunch of children, not grown-ass women."

"You better sit your ass on my lap before you're too fat to fit," snapped Violet.

Jules sat heavily onto Violet's lap.

"Ugh. Too heavy already."

We had the biggest group hug. I poured out my love to them through my magic, filtering it through the bodies and hearts of my sweet sisters.

"I love y'all so much," I told them.

A chorus of *love you toos* and joy came back to me.

"This hug has to end soon because Jules is breaking my damn leg," said Violet.

"Shut up, Vi." Livvy laughed.

The group hug didn't last long because it actually was pretty uncomfortable with six women on a smallish sofa, but the happiness of the afternoon lingered much longer.

It wasn't until Thursday drew closer, the day of Silas Blackwater's trial, when my mood finally dropped. The trial was a day away, and if I was getting stressed, then I knew my sweet Henry would be way worse. I had to do something to change that.

CHAPTER 33

~CLARA~

As expected, Henry was brooding. Sean had let me in the front door when I arrived mid-morning on Wednesday and snapped, "Please get him off the couch. He hasn't moved since yesterday. It's getting gross."

"I'm on it."

I frowned as I headed down the long hall to the living room, feeling a little guilty for leaving him a whole day. I'd wanted to catch up with Jules, so I'd stayed at home the past two nights. It was rather painful only talking to him via text and phone, but he seemed okay. Maybe he wasn't all that okay.

As I drew closer to the arched doorway of the living room, I smiled at hearing Mary Berry's voice from *The Great British Bake Off*. "Your sponge is rather higgledy-piggledy."

He was prone on the sofa like Sean had said, lounging in sweats under a gray plush blanket.

"Hi there."

He turned his head, taking me in, fresh as a daisy in my pastel-pink, low-cut summer dress.

Giving him my brightest smile, I added, "I got you addicted to this show, didn't I?"

He sat up and pushed the blanket off. I sat next to him.

He looked terrible. His hair stuck up everywhere from being slept on and not washed recently. His jaw was unshaven and scruffy. His sweatpants were a little tight. Okay, maybe he didn't look all that terrible.

"It's my comfort show now," he said, running a hand through his messy hair. "This is probably my tenth rewatch."

"What have you needed comfort for before?"

He looked sideways, gaze dropping down my body. "There was this girl I wanted for a long time. She didn't know I existed."

"She most certainly did," I argued. "She talked to him all the time, but he wouldn't take the hint and ask her out."

"He was scared she'd say no. Then he'd have nothing to hope for."

I maneuvered my bum onto his lap and brushed his mussed locks out of his face. "He doesn't have to worry about that anymore. She's desperately in love with him."

For the first time since I'd walked in, his lip quirked up. "Is she?"

"Mm-hmm. It's so bad she can't even sleep well anymore without him beside her."

His arms tightened around my waist, and he tucked his head against my neck and chest beneath my chin. "Then she needs to stay with him every night."

"I think that's a good idea." I rubbed a hand down his back and let his love sink into me. We sat in silence and held each other for a while before I finally asked, "Did you talk to your father?"

"No. But I sent a message through his attorney about Beatrice. She's no longer in Esbos. And he knows about Harold. The GOA sent word that he's emptied his bank accounts, obviously to avoid being tracked through credit cards. But they've sent information to all of their offices nationwide. They'll catch him."

"Of course they will." We hugged for a little longer, then I said, "As good as you look in these sweatpants, you've got a spaghetti stain or something on your T-shirt and you can't go to the book festival looking like that." I eyed the unfashionable pants that hugged his lovely physique, while he glanced down at the stain.

"It was manicotti, actually."

"You got takeout last night?"

"No, I cooked."

"Without me?"

That got me my first real smile since I'd walked in. "You were spending the night with your sisters. I still eat meals when you're not with me, Clara."

"I know. But manicotti? That's a fancy dinner, and I love manicotti."

"I saved you some." He brushed a kiss on my cheek.

"Good. I'll eat it when we get back."

"What book festival?"

"The Tulane Book Festival. I go every year. Usually, I drag Violet or Isadora, but this year, I have the delight of dragging you."

"Woman, you could drag me to hell, and I'd go happily."

Laughing, I hopped off his lap and lugged him to his feet. "Go get dressed. I'm taking you somewhere I think you'll love."

"Yes, ma'am." He flashed his most devilish, handsome grin before hurrying upstairs.

I busied myself wandering around the living room, making note of a few pieces of furniture we might have to move somewhere for a while when the baby came. That end table had supersharp edges. It would probably take a while to babyproof this house.

Baby gates. That's what we'd need. Or the baby would just get lost in this big old place. I was trying to count how many we would need to keep the baby penned in downstairs when Henry reappeared in a fresh T-shirt and jeans, his hair shower-damp.

"Ready."

As usual, he drove. He plugged his phone into his car charger, down to ten percent, and headed toward Tulane. I pointed to the best parking spot. The tables and tents were always set up in an open quad in the middle of the main buildings of campus.

"This is good. It's a short walk that way."

Putting my purse strap over my shoulder, I led him in the right direction, knowing exactly where the book festival was always held.

The tall tannish-gray buildings with a Colonial style, as well as Romanesque arches, gave them an old-world vibe when they were built in the 1800s. Not quite as old as the architecture hinted at. Still, it was a beautiful campus, and today was a lovely day to walk its grounds and shop for books with my adoring boyfriend.

Henry laced his fingers with my own, and we followed the small crowd, grinning at each other like the lovestruck fools we were. Just as always, the tents were lined neatly over tables and racks of books from local publishers, as well as regional authors signing their own works.

We slowed down by one author who had a small crowd, checking out his displays. He had a new murder thriller out, apparently. I raised my brows at Henry to see if he wanted to get in line. He caught my gaze and shook his head with a semi-sneer.

I laughed and tugged him away.

"What?" He hauled me closer.

"My badass, tattooed boyfriend doesn't like murder books. He likes pretty romances." Then I batted my eyelashes teasingly.

He didn't seem embarrassed at all. He simply shrugged. "As they say, don't judge a book by its cover."

"Ooh. Except that one." I pointed to a booth with some pretty gold-embossed editions of classics.

Henry sighed dramatically. "I can see our future now. You're not going to break our bank with clothes and shoes. It's going to be books, isn't it?"

"You know me so well." I wrapped my free hand around his forearm while I looked at the pretty covers. "I might spend a small fortune on clothes, too, though." I peered up at him. "Baby clothes."

His smile tilted in a sexy, secretive way. "That's fine by me, love."

My heart fluttered with giddy happiness when he called me that. He waited patiently while I flipped through the books in dark jewel tones with gold lettering.

"See any you want?" he asked over my shoulder.

"All of them."

He laughed. "I'll get all of them if you want them."

"No, Henry. I have all of these." I was being greedy as I flipped through. "Wait. This one, I need." I showed Henry the book in dark sapphire with an embossed raven above the title.

"*The Complete Collection of Edgar Allan Poe,*" he read with a smirk. "That's a little dark for your tastes, isn't it? Not many HEAs in his works."

"Yeah, but look at the cool bird on the front." I winked.

He laughed, then bought it for me.

We wandered on, both of us slowing at a tent full of brightly colored children's books. With a knowing glance at each other, we immediately wandered under it.

"Oh, look, Henry!" I let go of his hand for the first time and jumped at a table stacked with a familiar orange board book. "It's *Goodnight Moon!*"

I picked one up and flipped through the bedtime story with sparse words and pretty rhymes. "My mom used to read this one to us." Henry stood over my shoulder as I paged through it.

"*Goodnight light and the red balloon. Goodnight bears, goodnight chairs,*" I read in the singsong way my mother used to do as I flipped through it, remembering the familiar words with bone-deep joy. "I loved this book so much."

Henry plucked the book from my hands and stepped toward the attendant, removing his wallet. "How much for *Goodnight Moon?*" he asked her.

I watched him buy our baby's first book, feeling misty and lovely and mushy inside. He took the pretty paper bag with my copy of the beloved bedtime book that I knew I'd read to all of my children and then handed it over to me. I tucked the Edgar Allan Poe collection into the bag with it.

"Thank you," I said almost shyly.

He stood directly in front of me, smiling. "You're very welcome."

"Claraaa!"

The spine-tingling shriek of my name across the courtyard jerked our attention toward the person screaming. It was Violet, red-faced and tears streaming, looking near hysteria, running in our direction and pushing through the thin crowd.

Then a blurry streak swept past her and toward us. Nico. Werewolves couldn't move as fast as vampires or grims, but they ran a hell of a lot faster than humans. They also weren't supposed to do it in front of humans, especially in crowds like this one.

I frowned, my pulse tripping at my sister's panic. "What in the—?"

Before I could even complete my thought, my magic ignited like wildfire, the Goddess turning my head toward the danger. On the rooftop of the building to our right stood a man pointing a gun, aimed at us. Not us.

Henry, the Goddess whispered in my ear.

"No." Spirit moved with me as I stepped in front of Henry, holding up my hand like I could stop a bullet. I didn't. It hit me with supernatural force before the echo of the gunshot had even ricocheted off the quadrangle of buildings.

Screams and movement. Henry bellowed and caught me, but I couldn't make sense of anything as I fell back into his arms. I tried to touch my upper chest where the bullet had gone in, but I couldn't lift my arm. I was fading so fast, and it hurt. It burned.

The entire incident happened in a matter of seconds, but everything felt so slow. I was on the ground in Henry's lap. He was screaming at me, but for some reason, I could barely hear him.

"Why did you do that! *Christ,* Clara! Why'd you do that!"

"Goddess told me to," I said faintly.

"Hang on, baby! *Please* hang on." He cradled and rocked me against his chest, his gaze going to mine. "No, please don't take her. Please." Tears sprang to his eyes, and that broke my heart.

I wanted to lift a hand and touch his face, reassure him, but my body was slipping into some sort of paralysis. It felt like sickness. Like death, I suppose, but so wrong.

"Goddammit, Clara. Don't you fucking dare." His voice shook with fury and fear, his gaze lifting as he screamed, "Get Isadora!"

"She's coming," my twin sister cried out over the screaming crowd.

But there wasn't going to be enough time. There was so much I wanted to say, so much I wanted to tell him. And so much I'd wanted to do.

Oh. My poor sweet baby never even had a chance.

I never heard my baby's heartbeat, saw their first steps, or held them close and sung them lullabies.

Goddess whispered something I couldn't hear over the yells and frantic voices, my eyes growing heavy.

"No!" Henry shook me. "Don't close your eyes." He pressed his forehead to mine, one of his tears falling hotly on my cheek. "Don't you *fucking* leave me here, Clara."

"Don't worry, sweet Henry." I smiled, a tear slipping into my hair. "Goddess always knows best."

Then I died.

CHAPTER 34

~HENRY~

A DROP OF BLOOD SLIPPED FROM CLARA'S MOUTH AS HER EYES WENT glassy and her heart stopped beating. For several seconds, I was frozen in horror, just staring. Mindless. Numb. Unable to face the reality of what just happened, my entire soul going ice-cold.

A trickle of blood seeped from the bullet hole on the left side of her chest. I pushed over the material of her dress, stained dark red, to see spiderlike black veins spreading under her skin. A fucking black magic blood spell. It had to have been embedded in the bullet.

What the fuck had he done to her?

Violet finally made it to us from across the courtyard and fell to her knees on the other side of me, screaming, "No, no, no, no!" Falling into a puddle of tears, she experienced what I'd felt a few seconds ago. I settled Clara in her arms.

Now I was in some sort of out-of-body state, my darkness rising from my blood, my bones, and outside of my flesh. The shadow essence of my beast lifted me to my feet. I'd managed to observe that Nico had shifted at the sound of the gunshot, his monster bursting from his body as he raced into the building to get our attacker. It was Harold.

My gaze shot up, expecting him to be gone. He wasn't. He stood there, staring down, gloating. Without even whispering a command, my TK shot out of me and exploded the upper corner of the building into dust. A monster tentacle shot from my body and caught Harold around the throat as he plummeted toward the earth.

No. He would not be going gentle into that good night. He was going to experience excruciating pain first.

My wings stretched and expanded, then beat, causing more chaos among the humans. Many had already fled the scene, thinking an active shooter was there to kill them all. He wasn't there to kill and take out bystanders in a random crowd. He'd come here to kill me, but my beautiful mate stepped in front of me and died instead.

The seething rage that coursed through my veins blackened my vision and the world around me, likely my very soul. For the things I wanted to do to Harold were beyond any kind of salvation.

A giant cloud of impenetrable darkness extended farther than I'd ever reached. My monster growled deep in my belly, furious at me for letting something happen to Clara, but angrier with the soon-to-be dead man who took her from us.

We were one and the same, my beast. No separation anymore. No doors or bars between us.

Flapping my raven wings and floating in midair near the height of the building I'd just destroyed, I stared into the face of my father's best friend and betrayer that was turning purple. Another thick tentacle shot from my chest and encircled his entire arm. I let go of his throat so he could breathe, his body's weight suddenly dropping and pulling his arm out of the socket.

He screamed in pain. The sound sent a satisfying thrill through me. But not enough. Not nearly enough. The tentacle that had had him around the throat wrapped his other arm and snapped a bone.

"What did you do to her?" I growled into his contorted face while he screamed again.

He panted and whimpered, my focus so intent on him, I barely registered that Isadora and Devraj had arrived. The vampire was spelling into unconsciousness the people who hadn't fled, still cowering under tables. My smoky shield surrounded us all, blocking the rest of the world out. There were likely cops on the way, but they wouldn't be able to cross my warded boundary.

Isadora had her hand over Clara's heart, glowing green, but her heart wasn't beating anymore. He'd done something to her that there was no coming back from.

"*What*," I began, my voice reverberating with ethereal power, booming inside my domed shield, "did you do to her?"

His eyes widened with fear for a split second but then settled into a kind of fatal resignation. "It was meant for you."

"What did I ever do to you? Or my father?"

"You'd never understand." He shook his head. "Do you know I dated your mother first?" he rasped. "Just one date, but then she met Silas." He grunted disgustedly. "And that was it. Then our business, our brainchild, where I've been forced to play second. Then I met Beatrice, and he stole her from me too. Always getting *everything* he wanted and never deserved."

He sneered, revealing the evil man he was in the glint of his vacant eyes. Grims were so good at hiding emotions. It's no wonder my father, nor anyone else, ever suspected what evil lay beneath Harold's false facade.

"Then he was getting his sons back. After all he'd done to you, you were helping him, forgiving him. Revolting. But I put Beatrice in a hellish place. To punish him."

"I set her free," I informed him, my voice still resonating with dark power.

"I know." He must have his own spies in the GOA. "I'd planned to keep you from making it to the trial tomorrow."

To keep me from convicting him of his crime and freeing my father.

He winced as I twisted one of his arms. "It doesn't matter now. At least I'm the one who wins. You and your father may both be alive and free after you kill me, but you'll never have your heart's desire."

He cried out in agony when my tentacle wrapped his chest and began to squeeze.

"What did you do to her?" I loosened my hold so he could breathe and speak.

"I spelled the bullet so you'd be lost to any necromancer in the Vale. It would've done the trick if the bullet had killed you instead."

But the bullet *hadn't* hit me. Harold seemed to gain some satisfaction in that, his mouth splitting into a gruesome smile.

"I suppose it's your girl who is lost to you forever. How fitting. A necromancer who can't summon the one ghost he wants the most."

My tentacles tightened, crushing bones as they slithered tighter around his arms and his body.

"You don't know me, dead man." I stabbed a tentacle into his belly, needing a taste of his blood. "No hell in this world or the next can keep me from her."

Then I threw his body, barely noting the gory crunch of it hitting the side of the building before it fell lifeless to the ground.

Lowering myself swiftly, I stalked back to Clara. A man stared at me in horror. He scrambled backward and fell over a display of books. Two women cowered beneath a table. I didn't care who or how many humans saw me now. Putting myself in jeopardy for exposing our kind meant nothing. The only thing that mattered was *her*.

Isadora looked up at me, eyes widening. No telling what terrifying sight she saw before her. I felt the pitch blackness in my eyes. I felt it everywhere.

Violet still held Clara in her lap, my love's eyes closed now. "Bring her back, grim," said her sister, unable to even turn her face up to me.

With a punch of my hands into the air, a portal appeared with a deafening quake of the earth. Isadora and Violet braced against the unseen force pushing out of the gateway. Devraj and Nico were suddenly there, shielding their women and Clara's body.

Without a word, I stepped into the Vale, back into Esbos. The familiar pressure and sinister darkness of this place wrapped around me like an old friend. I didn't walk back into the gloomy lair. I beat my wings and flew. Soaring over the rocky caverns, demon eyes watching me pass above, I searched for my love.

There was no blue light like I'd seen with Beatrice, no guiding force beckoning me toward my Clara. All I saw were hordes of demons and malformed spirits skulking from one place to another, torturing and beating their own kind, cackling and hissing as I soared over them.

Where was she?

What had Harold done to separate her from me? To hide her even in this place, which was my realm to reign?

Harold had no idea the extent I'd go to find her. I'd remain here as king of the dead forever if needed, only to see her and hold her one last time before I sent her spirit to the upper realm where she belonged.

The thought of sending her on as I did Beatrice was like severing my own soul from my body. I wouldn't survive in the mortal world without her. I couldn't walk past her house, knowing she wasn't there, or see her shop, Mystic Maybelle's, without grieving, or even sleep in my bed with the smell of her on my sheets. There was no living without Clara—my true heart, my only love.

I soared on, deeper and deeper into the darkness.

It was my monster who finally hummed in my chest, raised the tentacle that had stabbed Harold, and whispered to me the solution.

Blood for blood.

What a fucking fool I was. I lowered myself to the cavern floor and drew a circle with the bloodied tentacle. On instinct, I stood within the circle and spoke the old Norse commands to reverse the spell.

"*Blóð fyrir blóð.*" My voice boomed across the emptiness, screeches of ghoulish creatures in the dark echoing back to me.

A ripping sensation opened up that third eye of psychic guidance inside my mind. Or perhaps I actually developed a third eye, I wasn't sure. Everything felt other and surreal yet right.

At first, I felt nothing. Then all at once, a rush of scent—sunshine and spring flowers and . . . butterflies.

"I'm coming, my love."

Turning toward the scent of her, I ran, tracing supernaturally through the dark purgatory, winding through twisting caverns and rocky crevices, deeper and deeper into the abyss. Until finally, a current of air pushed back against me. I slowed, confused at the whirling dust in the air. This place had no weather system at all. Only the cold, stale air of nothingness.

Yelps and cackles of demons drew me closer. Then I saw it. A towering twister reaching up into the black void. Surrounding it were the hellish creatures who lived in this place, trying to find a way in.

"Clara."

She'd shielded herself from them. My heart sank with dizzying relief and overwhelming pride.

The malformed creatures suddenly turned toward me, gibbering and buzzing in sibilant whispers as they crept closer. From behind the twister stepped the one-armed giant I'd mutilated when I freed Beatrice. He carried a spiked club, his sinister glare on me lit with malice.

He snorted, steam rising out of his giant snout, then he charged, shaking the ground as he came. He was the embodiment of rot and wickedness in a giant beast of a monster. But all I saw was a barrier between me and my love. An evil that I must vanquish.

I swiped my hand through the air and bellowed, *"No."*

My single word cracked in the air, pulverizing the giant into dust. He was bounding toward me with hell in his eyes when suddenly he was ash and sparks, carried away by Clara's winds spinning behind him.

Yes, whispered my inner beast.

With a flick of my hand, I struck the other creatures with my tentacles, my magic exploding them into cinders on impact. When I'd evaporated them all, I pushed toward the tornado Clara had erected.

Somehow, I was able to surge through it, though I floated in its winds for a few seconds before I came through to the other side, landing lightly on solid ground. My heart raced so hard it pulsed in my throat. I expected to find her like Beatrice, cowering on the cold ground, terrified and hopeless. That is not what I found. Tears sprang to my eyes at the sight before me.

In the middle of an imaginary patch of grass full of an unnatural sunlight was Clara, chasing butterflies and laughing. Several golden butterflies emitting a magical light flitted and fluttered, dancing around her, turning her in a circle. Her laughter—the sound of pure joy—echoed in the round, eviscerating me with astonishing relief. No darkness here at all. Only happiness and Clara, my sweet angel.

Then she turned to me, smiling brightly, no surprise on her face as I expected. "Henry," she crooned softly. "We've been waiting for you."

The butterflies gleamed with an effervescent glow as they floated closer together and merged into one. Clara held out her hand, where it landed on her palm, opening and closing its delicate wings. Nothing but bright, golden light.

Clara held the butterfly up to her face, casting her lovely features in the radiant glimmer, and then she looked at me.

"She's just like you, Henry. A little moody, but she has the biggest heart in the whole world. We've been waiting," she said with calm and poise, not like she was trapped in the middle of this hell. "We knew you'd come."

Then she moved her palm and the butterfly toward her belly and pressed it there. The butterfly melded into nothing but light, sinking back into her body, into her womb.

Frozen in disbelief and a touch of fear that this was a dream or hallucination created to torture me, I didn't move or say a word.

Clara walked lightly toward me, her spirit emitting a pinkish, golden glow. When she stood before me in all her perfection—no blackened gunshot wound in her chest—and cupped my face, I shuddered, making some unnatural sound of shock in my throat.

"I told you it would be all right. Goddess knows best. And the heavens are on our side, my darling."

"You died," I explained to her because obviously she wasn't aware. "You're dead."

"Temporarily, yes. But if you'd taken that bullet, you'd be lost forever. My future husband and father of my children would be bound to this place. No necromancer would have the power to find you and get you out. Nor would they have the blood of the spellcaster to reverse the black magic hex. We'd be separated for eternity."

She stepped even closer, pressing her spiritual body against mine. I held on to her waist, afraid she'd slip away or vanish.

"Don't you see?" she asked. "Spirit guided me in front of the bullet because she knew that you'd come for me, that you'd have the strength and power to find me here." She brushed her thumb lightly over my cheek. "And bring me home."

"You're right."

Without another word, I lifted her spirit into my arms and cradled her against my chest. She was too light, not the substantial weight of her in human form. She tucked her head beneath my chin, her arms wrapped around my neck, her touch warm, not cold, filling me with the knowing I needed. Flapping my wings, I lifted us high above the black-rock earth of this realm and flew over the craggy hills toward the way I'd come.

Clara hummed a familiar melody, "Perfect," her soft voice filling our path ahead and behind with joy, her essence streaming outward. Foul creatures stopped in their tracks, staring up in wonder as we passed, a longing filling their empty eyes and vacant souls for what they missed when they were human or what they never had and never would know.

Love. True, deep, soul-stirring, world-changing love.

As we crossed the dark planes, Spirit guided me farther, leading me on.

Centuries ago, my original forefather—a powerful warlock—once spoke a spell of his own making in Old Norse. It was the night he attempted to raise the dead using black magic and a powerful blood spell. If it weren't for his vampire wife who'd ripped out his throat for using her own son's life to cast the blood spell in summoning his army of ghosts, legend told us he would've been successful.

It was also the night, upon his death and his vampire wife ingesting his blood, that the first grim was formed in her womb.

As far as I knew, the words he'd spoken that night had never been written anywhere, yet they came to me unbidden, filtering into my mind and traveling out of my mouth with no effort at all. I knew they were the powerful words he once spoke as if I'd known them all along, like they were stitched into the magic he'd passed on to me.

As we flew through Esbos, I poured them into the ether, smoke billowing and thickening around me while Clara hummed on as if nothing were wrong.

That was her way. Full of confidence and knowing. It gave me the strength to believe she was right, that no barrier would hold me back when I carried her into the mortal realm and placed her into her body.

Finally, a light in the darkness up ahead revealed the gateway I'd punched into the world from the scene of her death. My voice boomed louder as I spoke the spell faster and beat my wings harder as I soared toward the opening. Without resistance, I burst through to the other side, back into the mortal realm with Clara's spirit still in my arms.

A group of shocked faces jerked toward me as I slowly lowered us to the earth. All of her sisters were there, huddled around her body, Violet still holding her half in her lap. So was Devraj, Mateo, Ruben, and Nico, back in human form, having found some jeans somewhere. Likely Mateo had brought them. Gareth was there, too, a look of relief washing over his face.

Everything was silent now. No screams of the crowd or frightened humans. Devraj must've handled it.

Walking toward them, still chanting in the old tongue, I carried Clara, who hadn't even lifted her head from my chest, still humming softly. Finally, Violet moved, hope shining on her tear-streaked face. She laid Clara down on the ground in front of her and shuffled back as I knelt.

On instinct—and with difficulty because I was afraid to let her go from my arms—I placed her spirit inside her body. Her soul vanished within her body, but nothing happened. Holding out my palm, I wiped the blood from the tentacle, which had reappeared for a second. After it absorbed back inside me, I held that palm to her wound.

I commanded her to rise in the old tongue. *"Heyr mik! Komtilr mik! Clara. Andla. Komaptrr til mik."*

Come back to me. Come back to me. Come back to me.

I repeated the last words of the mantra over and over, my magic brightening my skin until a deep purple glow surrounded all of us.

Suddenly, Clara gasped, sucking in a deep breath. Her sisters cried out at once but didn't move. Then she opened those beautiful blue eyes. I scooped her torso into my arms and pressed my cheek to hers, then pulled back to look at her again, afraid I was dreaming.

She gave me that sunlit smile that made my whole world right again. "I knew you could do it."

I laughed, clutching her tighter, still staring, making sure she was breathing all right. "Don't ever do that again. Not fucking ever."

"Okay, Henry," she agreed lightly and in a way that told me she'd do it again and again if necessary.

"I love you," I whispered against her lips.

"I love you too."

"Okay, you guys," butted in Gareth, "we need to get her out of here so Isadora can heal her. I've called the GOA and they're en route. They'll clean up the rest of the mess, including handling the humans."

"You don't mean like *handle* handle, do you?" asked Violet, doing the slit-your-throat gesture.

"*No.*" Gareth grimaced. "They'll have their connections in local law enforcement to block the perimeter, devise a logical reason for the building being half-blown apart, and take away the body of Harold Stansbury, and Ruben and I will wipe everyone's memories."

I was only sort of listening, my gaze sweeping Clara with feral intensity. The wound was still there, but the black veins were gone. I lifted her in my arms, loving the substantial weight of her in her human form. Before I could take another step, her sisters were around me, all giving Clara kisses and half-hugs in my arms.

"Love you, sis," said Violet. "Thanks for not staying dead. I'd have never forgiven myself."

"Why?" she asked lightly as we walked back toward my car, my cocoon of black smoke slowly dissipating from the quad.

"I had a vision and saw you die. Nico and I were in his Jeep, and I knew where you were so we hurried to the scene. You wouldn't answer your phone, and I texted everyone else. But I was too late."

"No, you weren't. I was supposed to die. So Henry wouldn't. But it's okay. My baby girl and I are all fine."

Violet said something else, and so did Livvy and Evie, but I'd already blocked them out, holding her smiling gaze.

355

"A girl, huh? You're sure?"

"Positive." Her fingers played with the short hair at my nape. "She's going to look just like you too. Are you okay with a girl?"

"Clara, baby. I'd be happy if you had a unicorn."

She laughed, the sound filling my soul. "Don't worry. We'll have six boys down the line."

"Six?" I didn't ask how she knew.

"I hope that's okay."

"As long as I'm with you, everything is okay. Everything is perfect."

"Mmm." She pressed her head beneath my chin and her cheek to my neck. "It certainly is."

CHAPTER 35

~CLARA~

"THANK YOU FOR LETTING ME OUT OF BED," I TOLD HENRY AS WE SAT on the bench in the butterfly garden of his father's house around midnight.

It had taken all week to process Silas Blackwater out of Glasgow. Even though there was proof of his innocence, it had to be completely sorted and presented in full detail before a special council that included my sister Jules. By the time they'd voted and finally released Silas tonight, it was after dark. All he wanted was to see Beatrice. Of course, Henry obliged him.

During this last week, Henry had barely let me leave the bedroom. And not because he was lavishing my body in sexual pleasure. Nope. I'd gotten platonic foot rubs and back rubs and was fed homemade soups and praline ice cream.

Every time I'd kicked off the covers, trying to seduce him in my panties and tank top, he'd quickly cover me back up and warn me against getting a chill. It didn't matter that a GOA surgeon had personally come to the house, removed the bullet, and stitched me up. Or that Isadora was there twice a day, giving me healing treatments and medicinal teas for me and the baby. He was still treating me like a feverish flu patient. He was being awfully sweet and nurturing but also ridiculous.

Though I have to admit that the butternut squash soup he'd made had been absolutely divine. I had no idea Henry was such an amazing cook. I imagine he'd want to make our baby's own food. I could see him now, frowning at our baby and force-feeding her whatever super healthy, mashed food he'd doctored up.

Though he'd let me come with him tonight because I'd begged, he still made me wear a cardigan and a lap blanket while we sat in the garden, giving his father and Beatrice's spirit some privacy.

They were in the far corner near the bed of wildflowers, standing beneath an elm tree, moonlight shining on them through the leaves. Silas held both of Beatrice's hands in his as he spoke softly, the portal open nearby, radiating a soft blue light.

"You do know I'm not ninety years old, right?" I asked Henry.

He was tucking the blanket around my thighs.

"Also, it's like seventy-five degrees."

"During the daytime. Tonight, it's"—he looked at his smartwatch—"sixty-eight. And there's a slight breeze." He glanced around for the offending wind.

"In your own imagination."

He clenched his jaw before he finally looked at me. I simply smiled back at him. Sighing heavily, he straightened and wrapped an arm around my shoulders, pulling me tight against him. Most likely to ensure I was receiving his body heat, not necessarily to snuggle up sweetly.

"I just want to be cautious, Clara."

"I'm perfectly fine now. You can ease up. I promise."

He scoffed. "You threw up three times this week."

"It's called morning sickness. See, when women get pregnant, they get nauseated and tend to throw up a lot." I sounded rather sassy like my twin sister.

"But two times it was in the afternoon, not in the morning."

"It's still morning sickness." I wiggled my arms out from the covers and pulled his opposite hand into mine, fingering his *Clarenry* bracelet he never took off.

"That makes no sense."

"I expect I'll be nonsensically sensitive and weepy for at least a couple more months. All the books say your hormones level out the farther along you get."

"Did you make the doctor's appointment like I told you to?" He was so snippy today.

"I'm still deciding."

"What are you talking about? I vetted Dr. Sorrel, Isadora's doctor. She's the one to go with."

She was a Conduit like Isadora. But, of course, nearly every warlock and witch doctor was.

"Vetted? This isn't a business transaction, Henry. This is a baby."

"I'm well aware. My vote is for Dr. Sorrel. She's got the longest track record. I don't want you in the care of one of these young quacks who don't know what they're doing."

"You mean Dr. Bienvenu?" I blinked innocently up at him.

His frown deepened. "I don't like him."

"Is it because he's young and less experienced? Or is it because he's drop-dead gorgeous and could double for Henry Cavill?"

He inched away so he could look at me better. "You think he's drop-dead gorgeous?" His gaze wandered over my face, always drifting to my chest where the bullet had gone in. There was no sign of it at all anymore.

"Pfft. I have eyes, don't I?"

That drew his gaze back to mine, which was what I wanted. I didn't like it when his mind wandered back to that day and the trauma of it all. He still flinched in his sleep sometimes. I'd asked Isadora to spell some tea leaves to ease his worries and stress.

"Better looking than me?" He arched a brow.

Finally! Playful Henry was with me now.

"As if that were possible," I teased. "Although . . ." I traced a finger along his jaw, his unshaved jaw rough under my finger. "I haven't seen much of you lately, so how could I really know for sure?"

"What are you talking about? I barely leave your side."

"True. But you're always fully clothed."

His gaze darkened and became downright primal. A shiver of need trembled through me.

"How about I give you your massage tonight"—he tilted his head and caught my finger in his mouth, nipping gently at the tip with teeth—"in the bathtub."

I watched his mouth as he nibbled teasingly on my finger. "That would be lovely."

"I think my girl has other needs besides food and rest."

"She so does," I agreed, leaning forward and pressing a kiss to his pretty mouth. "*Lots* of needs."

"I'll take care of you, beautiful." His hand cradled the back of my head as he kissed me a brief moment longer before breaking apart to turn his attention back to his father and the spirit of Beatrice.

"It was kind of you to let them say goodbye." I couldn't help the wave of sadness that came over me.

Henry went silent as we watched and waited, giving them as much time as they needed. My gaze wandered to the open portal emitting the soft light and swirling gray of the Vale. Beatrice had told us she'd been waiting to see Silas, but was ready to move on.

Henry and I had talked about the possibility of putting her back in her body the way he'd done for me. But her physical body had already been autopsied and was in the process of decomposing. There was no possible way she would return as herself, he warned. And he was afraid to dabble in that part of his necromancy, the part that came directly from his forefather who'd committed a terrible, sinful murder to produce the spell Henry had used to bring me back from the netherworld.

He believed that it wasn't just his spell that had brought me back either. He thought it was also me, that my magic as an Aura and my bone-deep belief that I was meant to die so he could bring me back was the main reason it worked. Basically, I manifested myself back to life.

I didn't think that was entirely true. Partly true, maybe. But it was Henry's strength of will and commune with his magical essence that allowed me to return. The aftereffects of that day were still present in his eyes.

Rather than near-black eyes, they now shone a deep hazelgold. Gareth had said his eyes were that color when he was a young boy, before the incident with Amon. It seemed he was truly healed from his trauma, his body and soul one and whole again.

"I will say this," I said, not wanting him to get sad over the two still whispering their love and goodbyes to each other not far away. "Your eyes are way prettier than Henry Cavill's."

That got his attention. "Yeah?"

His irises darkened at the edges. They still flooded black when he was in high emotional states. Like arousal.

"Tell me more about this massage in the bubble bath."

"Did I say anything about bubbles?"

"No. But I'm adding them to the list. And candlelight please."

He finally smiled and tugged me up against him, tucking the blanket back around my legs. He was a little obsessive about me catching a chill in April.

Then Silas stood from the bench, as did the spirit of Beatrice. It was time. I stayed on the bench as Henry walked over to them. I couldn't hear what was being said between the three of them, but I recognized the gratitude on Beatrice's face and on his father's before she walked through the portal and into the Vale for the last time. She would be moving on to the next world this time and never coming back.

Henry spoke quietly to his father, whose head was bowed as he said a few words of his own.

Henry hadn't yet completely forgiven him for Amon and for his childhood, or lack of one. There was still much healing that needed to take place before they had a genuine relationship. But Henry was trying to forgive. Not just for his sake, but for Sean's as well.

Silas was a self-serving man, but his relationship with Beatrice proved that he did indeed have a heart. It was enough to show Henry that they might salvage some sort of relationship in the future.

Once Beatrice had slipped through the portal with a last wave goodbye, Henry closed the gateway. His father said something else to him, tucked his hands in his pockets, and turned to walk deeper into his gardens, his expression grim and pensive.

I stood and met Henry halfway, both of us watching his father disappear around the corner.

"He'll be all right," I assured him. "In time."

Instead of commenting, his gaze went to the bed of tall flowers. The pink zinnias, black-eyed Susans, and orange and white milkweed swayed in the breeze. Henry wrapped himself around me from behind as we watched two monarch butterflies flutter and land on the milkweed.

He pressed a kiss to my temple. "I can't wait for December," he whispered.

I leaned back into his arms. "We're getting the best Christmas present ever."

"We are." He skated a palm to my belly that still wasn't showing much. I couldn't wait for that mommy bump. And I couldn't wait to meet our baby girl.

CHAPTER 36

December

~HENRY~

"Let me hold her." Clara reached out her arms to Isadora.

My wife's heart-shaped face was rounder, as was the rest of her. But I'd never seen her look more beautiful than she was at nine months pregnant.

Thankfully, she'd agreed to a small double wedding with her twin sister this past October—close family and friends only. She'd told me she'd always wanted a simple, small wedding, but I was fairly sure she'd planned it mostly for me—her introverted husband.

Violet and Nico loved the idea, mainly because Violet just didn't want to have to plan another event. Clara took over, and that made Violet happy as hell. It made Nico even happier because he'd been trying to get her to agree to a wedding date. They had been leaning toward the Vegas option like Evie and Mateo did when Clara suggested her idea.

It was a small affair in my father's backyard, the butterfly garden to be more specific. I couldn't imagine a better place to bind myself to the woman I loved. And who was now holding Isadora's newborn baby girl, cooing sweetly to her.

"Hello, Samara, my little angel. It's your favorite aunt, Aunt Clara," she whispered.

The soft little bundle with a cap of black hair and creamy bronzed skin cooed in response, as if she knew the most loving aunt in the world held her tightly to her breast, sitting atop her large, rounded belly.

The entire family was gathered in the Savoie house, spread out in the living room and the kitchen. Their parents had returned last month right before the birth of Isadora's baby. Jules's baby came not long after.

Ruben walked in from the kitchen holding his newborn son, Morgan, in the crook of one arm, one of JJ's glasses of bourbon eggnog in the other.

"Can I hold him?" asked Charlie, walking in behind him from the kitchen where Evie, Jules, and her mother were setting the table for the seafood gumbo and where JJ was doctoring his famous eggnog in a punch bowl.

"Of course." Ruben handed the sleeping Morgan off to Charlie, who then settled on the sofa next to Clara, the two of them grinning at each other and whispering over the babies. Morgan was mostly bald with a sprinkling of fair hair and easily five pounds bigger than his cousin, little Samara.

"Are you two going to sneak off and do a private thing like Jules and Evie did?" Violet asked her sister Livvy, where they sat near the crackling fireplace.

"Hell no," snapped Livvy. "We're going to have the biggest fucking party New Orleans has ever seen. It's going to be obscenely grand." She grinned up at Gareth, who wore his typical enigmatic smile. "We decided on a date, though. It'll be this spring in May. I picked out the most gorgeous bridesmaid dresses."

"Let me see," said Isadora, sitting on an ottoman stool beside Livvy, who scrolled through her phone to show her.

"Hey, Clara," Devraj called from next to the twinkling Christmas tree, looking at the stack of wrapped presents for the White Elephant game, concern etched on his face. "There are only regular, normal gifts in this pile, right?"

My wife laughed. "Yes. None of my spells on anything this time."

Clara had told me about the time they played White Elephant for Christmas and Devraj and Isadora had gotten an ornament she'd spelled with a love potion, which was really a lust potion. It had been intended for Violet so she'd make her move on Nico, but the present went home with Isadora and Devraj instead.

"Good to know," said Devraj. He turned back to where Nico, Mateo, and Sean were sitting on the floor with the triplets and then took a seat in the club chair behind them.

The living room furniture had all been pushed back and lined along the walls to open up the room for the party and games later. We were celebrating early since Clara was due next week.

Diego and Celine were playing with some baby toys while Joaquin was babbling nonsense to his uncle Nico while sitting in his lap.

"I know, little man," Nico told him, "life is rough at your age."

Joaquin continued to talk to his uncle Nico as if Nico knew what he was saying. Nico nodded and agreed with whatever the baby was trying to communicate.

Sean teasingly played tug-of-war with Diego over a rubber toy. It looked like one of those indestructible rubber dog bones. Actually, I think that's exactly what it was. When Sean pulled it out of the toddler's grip, he blinked up at Sean before turning to his sister and snatching her squishy doll out of her hands. Then he stuffed it in his mouth. Celine instantly started screaming and crying.

"Hey there, dude." Sean took the squishy doll from Diego, carefully extricating it out of his mouth where his pointy canines had put holes in the doll. "You can't just take from other people like that. Especially your sister. You've gotta take care of her. She's your family."

He handed the doll back to Celine, who squeezed it close, red-faced and scowling at Diego. "Now give her a hug and say you're sorry."

Diego looked confused while his sister stared at him murderously. Sean physically put Diego's arms around Celine, who was much smaller than Diego. Of the triplets, he was increasing in size much faster than his siblings. Diego managed to get the idea and babbled something to Celine while he hugged her so tightly they both fell backward onto the plush blanket they'd been playing on. Then they were giggling while Sean tried to get them both upright again.

"A smile on my cousin's face," said Gareth, now standing beside me. "That's nice to see."

"I have a lot to smile about," I told him.

"Indeed, you do. A baby girl, huh?"

"Her doctor confirmed it." I watched JJ helping Clara to her feet, holding the baby in his other arm as he hauled her up. "But Clara was sure already. I knew she was right."

Clara walked toward me, a protective hand on her rounded belly.

"Happy for you both," Gareth said. "Can't wait to meet my little niece."

When Clara reached me, I took her hand and guided her toward the Christmas tree. The sparkling lights glowed on her skin and her hair that she'd worn in a long braid over one shoulder.

"What is it?" she asked, smiling at my secrecy.

"I have an early present for you."

Her sky-blue eyes widened. "For me?"

"No, for my other wife."

She slapped me on the arm. "Give it to me." She bounced in place.

I pulled the box from the inside pocket of my leather jacket. "It's not fancy, and I needed help. Evelyn helped me because I had no idea how to make it."

"A homemade present?" she gushed as she took the box wrapped in red paper and a tiny white bow and tore into it.

"It's not exactly creative. I kind of copied you." I was minimizing it as she unwrapped it, realizing I probably could've come up with something better.

"Shut up, Henry," she said sweetly as she opened the box and gasped while lifting out the bracelet.

It was the same color pink yarn she'd used to make my brace-let, but instead of *Clarenry* in pink on black, I'd had Evelyn put our couple name in black on pink. I'd asked Evelyn to thread the name in a fancier script as well.

"I thought you might want one, too."

"It's our name." She sniffed, happy tears pooling in her eyes. "Put it on me please."

I tied it around her dainty wrist. "I'll have to trim some of the extra. Looks a little big."

"It's absolutely perfect!" She threw her arms around my neck and pulled me down for a tight hug, as close as we could get with our baby girl in between us. "I love you so much I could just burst," she whispered in my ear.

I held her gently but close and rubbed her back. "I love you too, Clara."

"Is that what I think it is?" Violet shouted over the many con-versations taking place in the room.

"It can't be," said Livvy, joining her to peer out the window into the courtyard.

I turned to see what everyone was gathering toward the win-dow to see. Fluffy, fat flakes of snow were drifting down in the courtyard. Everyone was looking except Clara, who continued to stare up at me with that heart-pounding lovely look of love on her pretty face.

"You did this, didn't you?" I whispered.

"I couldn't help it. It just bubbled out of me. I wanted the world to look as beautiful as I feel inside."

"I'm going out front to see!" yelled Violet with glee, streaking through the house toward the front door.

"Grab your jackets and coats!" called Jules, coming in from the kitchen. She took Morgan from JJ, who then took Charlie by the hand and hauled him outside.

Isadora now held Samara, she and Devraj passing us by to follow the others.

"Come on then." I wrapped an arm around Clara's waist, not letting her slip and fall when we made it outside.

Violet and Livvy were twirling in the middle of the street, catching flakes in their mouths. JJ was already scooping a snowball off Gareth's car parked on the street, getting ready to obviously throw it at Charlie. Nico seemed to like that idea and was gathering a snowball of his own off my Mustang.

Mateo held both his sons in his arms and walked out into the yard, Evie right behind him with Celine on her hip.

"Look at that, boys. Your first snow in New Orleans."

They cooed and squealed, holding up their tiny fat hands to touch it.

"*First* snow in NOLA? What are you talking about?" asked Jules from underneath the porch with Morgan and Ruben. The Savoie parents stepped out of the front door just after. "It hardly ever snows in New Orleans. And not like this." She turned back to her parents. "Mom, has it ever snowed in New Orleans like this?"

"No. This looks like the snows we get in Switzerland."

Jules then looked over at Clara, who was smiling up at the sky. "I think that's because this isn't a natural snow. Is it, Clara?" she called louder.

My wife simply laughed. I wrapped myself behind her while she did her magic, giving us all an early Christmas present.

The snow floated down in giant flakes, peaceful and beautiful, already layering the street, cars, houses, everything. Neighbors were now running out and taking pictures with their phones. One of the neighbors' children giggled and laid down in the street to make a snow angel.

"It must be almost an inch deep already," Devraj marveled from next to Isadora and Samara, who were under the protection of the porch covering.

"Oh, goodness," Clara muttered under her breath.

"What's wrong?" I asked, my cheek pressed to hers as I smoothed my palm over her belly.

The baby kicked beneath my palm, more vigorously than usual.

"I didn't think about the roads," she said.

"Don't worry. People won't drive in this weather. The police will be on top of it."

"I know. But I promised you we'd have our first at the hospital."

I froze, realizing what she was saying. "*Now?*"

She pulled from my arms and turned to face me, fluffy flakes caught in her hair. "Now."

As always, she smiled as the joy poured from her body and into me where she held on to my arms. I never tired of my Aura witch and wife giving me heavy doses of her magic through spells of happiness and love, but at this moment, I knew that her joy didn't outmatch mine.

"We're going to have a baby," I told her quietly.

"We are." She blinked quickly when a snowflake caught in her lashes. "Very soon, I believe. She won't wait for the hospital. I'm sorry."

"Don't be sorry. Looks like Dr. Bienvenu won't be the one to deliver our firstborn, though. And you get the home birth I know you really wanted."

"I didn't do it on purpose." A frown pinched her brow. "Maybe Goddess did it."

"It doesn't matter. I know it will be just fine. Better get you inside now, though," I told her quietly, a sense of calm and control sweeping through me. It was my joy to help her through this as best I could. "Let's get Isadora and lay you down in the downstairs bedroom."

"Yes, the one that was my parents' bedroom. She had all six of us in that room."

"You've told me before." I turned her, and with an arm around her waist again, I guided her back toward the porch.

"Seems kind of poetic to have our first baby there."

"Sure does, angel," I agreed, catching Isadora's attention and nodding.

That was all she needed, noting Clara's small, careful steps. "Take Samara, Dev."

Jules noticed, too, instantly passing Morgan over to Ruben. Her mother, Serena, held the door open, a knowing smile quirking her mouth. While the others screamed and played in the snow my wife had made for them, I helped her into her childhood home to have the first child of our own.

EPILOGUE

Years Later...

~HENRY~

"I can't do this, Henry." Clara's face was pink and glistening with sweat at her hairline. Two nurses bustled around the delivery room, prepping for her to finally push. The labor had been longer and harder than any of her other deliveries.

"You can, love. You've done it three times before." I sat on the stool next to her, holding her hand.

"The others came one at a time. This is two of them."

"They will come one at a time. I promise."

She shook her head, a tear streaking down her cheek, fear bright on her face.

"Hey, now. Look at me." I murmured softly and lowered my head till my face was close to hers. "Everything is going to be perfectly fine. Dr. Bienvenu is scrubbing up for delivery. Your nurses are ready to go for the twins. Your entire family is in the waiting room, excited to meet our new baby boys." I pressed my forehead to hers. She closed her eyes, taking the comfort I was trying to impart. "You're an amazing, strong woman. You've got this."

She breathed through another contraction, during which I remained perfectly silent, knowing that's what she needed. When she exhaled a long, jagged breath at the end, her eyes closed. "I can do this?"

"You can. And you will. You can break my hand off squeezing it if you need to."

She swallowed on a little laugh and opened her eyes, bright with more intensity than usual, the fear sliding away. "What would I do without you?"

"You wouldn't. Because I'd never leave you to do anything alone." I lowered my voice so the nurses couldn't hear. "Plus, I'd kill any man who put you in this state besides me."

Then she really did laugh. "Stop it. It makes them move around when I laugh." She winced. "Though I think it's almost time to push."

"Let me check," said the brunette nurse named Emily who'd been with her since early this morning when we admitted. She checked her dilation. "Yep. We're at ten. Get Dr. Bienvenu," she told the blonde nurse who'd been prepping one of the baby delivery beds. "This is wonderful, Clara. Soon, you'll be holding your new sons."

"Yes," she said with confidence, squeezing my hand and turning her focus back to me. "Thank you."

"For what?"

"For calming me down. Making me feel better."

"That's what we do for each other, baby. You've done it for me too many times to count."

Then Dr. Bienvenu entered in all his handsome glory in his scrubs. "Afternoon, Clara. Let's meet the newest Blackwater boys, shall we?"

Pride made me sit up a little taller. I'd eventually accepted him as her doctor. After our second son was born, I got over the fact that she found her doctor so attractive. It didn't matter if he was, in fact, a Henry Cavill doppelganger. I was her mate and her love and the one and only Henry she chose to build a family with, her life with.

After I had my first panic attack while attempting to have sex with a woman at seventeen, I thought I might never be intimate with a woman. Then my thoughts strayed to the fact that I'd never be a father. Not unless I adopted, like Gareth and Livvy had for their first child. Or Charlie and JJ.

"Here we go, Clara." Dr. Bienvenu settled into place to deliver our babies. "I want you to push now, hold it for as long as you can."

That's when the hardest part for me really started, watching my wife's face contort in pain as she screamed and pushed our children into the world. Still, I remained calm and focused, whispering comforting words to her in a soft voice.

"Almost there," I told her. "I can see his head. You're doing so amazing, baby."

She held my gaze, letting me feed her the confidence she needed in her vulnerable state. It was awe-inspiring and humbling at the same time.

Within ten minutes, we had a squealing baby boy. Sebastian.

"Six pounds, five ounces."

And in five more, we had another. Rhys.

"Six pounds, two ounces."

Both of them were perfect and healthy and pink as Clara's cheeks. While the doctor continued to work on Clara, the nurses bundled the babies and set one of each in our arms.

"They've got thick, dark hair like Raven's," said Clara, petting the cap of hair of the firstborn of our twins.

They did look much like their older sister when she was born.

"Hello, Sebastian," she whispered and pressed a kiss to his forehead, then reached over to pet the son I was holding. "Hello, Rhys."

I held him up so she could kiss his cheek. "They're perfect, Clara."

"They are." She admired her handiwork while I did the same.

After the doctor and nurses had finished and the doc told her she had a few minutes before they'd take the babies into the nursery and move her to her recovery room, I handed Rhys over to her and walked out into the waiting room. It was bursting with people. All of them our family. All eyes landed on me expectantly.

"Two healthy boys and a healthy mom."

Cheers and excitement buzzed in the room. Diego stood nearly as tall as his father at thirteen, Joaquin a few inches shorter, and Celine trailing behind both her brothers, standing near Samara and Raven.

"Can we see them?" asked Celine excitedly.

"Soon," I told her. "Clara wants them to meet their siblings first."

"Of course." Celine and Samara hugged our daughter excitedly, the three girl cousins almost like sisters.

Everyone was there. Morgan stood beside his father, less than a foot away from reaching his height. Jules held their one-year-old daughter Lucinda on her hip. Morgan and Diego were the tallest of all the children, both of them talking and laughing with the cousins Drew and Cole from Lafayette.

Nico whispered something in Violet's ear, his hand on her back, her belly as huge as Clara's had been. They were expecting their first children, also twins but girls, in another month.

Gareth gave me a congratulatory wave, then turned back to Charlie. His and Livvy's adopted three-year-old son, Micah—a vampire—stood in front of him. Micah held both of my cousin's hands, still a little shy around the whole family since he'd recently joined us.

JJ was wiping his and Charlie's daughter Elizabeth's face with a baby wipe. Looked like she'd gotten into something chocolaty.

"Two more to go," said Travis, who was the one who'd originally given the prediction that Clara would have seven children. I smiled in return, not ready to put Clara through childbirth again. Unless she wanted to.

I gestured to my eleven-year-old, Raven, to come and see. She took the hands of her two- and three-year-old brothers—Broderick and Benedict. When Clara had told me she wanted to name the rest of our children after her favorite historical romance novel heroes, I didn't argue. Whatever made my wife happy made me happy.

When they reached me, I lifted the youngest, Benedict, into my arms and led the kids back into the delivery room. "Pick up your brother, sweetheart," I told Raven. "I don't want him to jostle your mother, trying to leap on her bed."

Raven, the sweetest daughter a man could ask for, lifted her brother onto her hip. "Is Mom okay?"

She was a worrier, our daughter. I was afraid she inherited my anxious side. "She's perfectly fine."

We pushed into the room. The nurse still there walked past us. "I'll give you guys a little privacy. We'll need to move Mom and the babies in about ten minutes."

"Come see them," beamed Clara, her expression showing no signs of the anxiety she was under a half an hour ago.

When Raven saw her brothers, her beautiful smile lit up her face. Her blue eyes, like her mother's, brightened with wonder. "I keep forgetting how small they are when they're first born."

Broderick said, "Baby bubbas."

"Yes," said Clara, reaching out to stop Broderick's hand, who was trying to whack his baby brothers on the head. They had no concept of *soft* or *gentle* yet. "Just look at your baby brothers."

Benedict giggled his loud, husky laugh. He was the only one so far who had his mother's blond hair. He had her smile too.

"Are you okay, Mom?" Raven asked, because my answer wasn't good enough. But it was fine. I was used to Raven's need for reassurance.

"I feel wonderful. Do you want to hold him?" Raven was petting Rhys's arm.

She nodded excitedly, passing her other brother to me. I juggled these two at the same time often enough.

Raven was a soft, sweet-tempered girl, innately pensive and a little broody. But when she smiled or laughed, she lit up the entire room. Like she did right now. She let out a little laugh as

Rhys grabbed hold of her index finger, his dark eyes gazing up wonderingly at his sister.

"They're so cute when they do that."

"You're the best big sister ever," said Clara, her gaze leaving Raven to catch mine. "Just two more to go."

I chuckled and eased closer, watching Broderick's hands reaching for his mother. "That's what Travis just told me."

"Here, let me have him." She held out her arms.

Broderick was trying to wiggle out of my grip to get to his mom. "You sure?"

"Yes, you take Sebastian."

I set Benedict on the bed next to Raven. He wasn't nearly as wiggly as his older brother and tended to stay put wherever you put him. He did this time, too, looking over Raven's arm. Then he belted out, "Bay-yey."

"Yes, baby," agreed Raven. "Your baby brother."

"This is going to get complicated now," I told Clara. "So few hands for all of them."

"We'll manage," said Clara with her usual confidence, the fear from earlier completely washed away. She scooted over as best she could so I could sit and take Sebastian, tucking Broderick next to her.

The seven of us were piled on that tiny delivery bed. My heart was so full, gazing at all of those sweet faces. My family.

"We don't have to have any more, Clara." I looked down at Sebastian in my arms. "Our family is perfect just like it is now."

"It is. But I know Goddess has two more spirits waiting to join us."

"You *know* she does?" I asked. "For sure?"

Clara's psychic abilities weren't as strong as her sister Violet's, but when she was confident in hearing Spirit's voice, she was always right.

"Mm-hmm." She nodded, smiling at Sebastian in my arms. "When I was in the Vale. While we were waiting for you, there were seven butterflies who visited me there. They were all ours."

I hadn't actually counted them that day. I was more in a manic state of figuring out how I was going to bring her back to life. But as always, Clara had noticed all of the details and communed with her future children in the netherworld.

"Two more then," I added quietly.

"But we can wait a little while, maybe a few years before we keep going."

Reaching over, I cupped her face. "Yes. Momma needs some rest. You're tired."

"Mm-hmm." She placed her palm over mine, cupping her cheek. "But infinitely happy."

That's when I felt a surge of her magic push into me with her joy spell, filling the room with her love.

"I wish I could do that for you when you needed it," I told her.

"Oh, Henry." She laughed. "Silly man. You do. You always do. Every single day."

I love you, I mouthed to her.

Love you too, she mouthed back.

Then we settled in for the last few minutes of quiet and solitude with our little family, knowing the aunts and uncles and cousins would be invading soon enough.

I'd finally ventured into using my necromancy to help others as an official GOA agent in seeking justice for those wrongfully killed. It did give my life a purpose and gave me pride in helping others. But that wasn't the whole of it. No, it struck me clear and true.

It was a lovely moment, grasping the enormity of life's true meaning. I suppose it was different for everyone. But for me, it was the baby in my arms and the one in my daughter's, my firstborn and the two boys between all of us. And without fail, it was my darling, beautiful, amazing wife. My true meaning on this earth was loving these precious people crowded in one tiny hospital bed. And of course, the two more to come.

I couldn't imagine life getting any better, but Clara proved me wrong all the time. I looked forward to a lifetime of her showing me that love can grow and grow until it's too big to hold in your heart and soul anymore. It has to overflow into the people around you. Like those in this room, and the ones out in the waiting room.

"Okay, y'all," said Nurse Emily, entering softly with the blonde behind her. "Time to take the baby boys to the nursery. There's a whole village of people out there who want to see them and you."

Raven passed Rhys over, and I handed Sebastian to Emily. "Raven, can you take your brothers back out there?"

"Come on, you two." She helped them down and took their hands, following the nurses back out.

When it was just the two of us, I took Clara's hand. "Do you want me to hold them off?"

She laughed, my favorite sound in the entire world. "You and what army?"

"I could manage if you want some privacy."

She shook her head. "No, I want to see them."

Without warning, all five of her sisters burst into the room, Violet bringing up the rear. I stepped to the side so they could hug and congratulate her.

"Move over, dammit. Wide load coming through." Violet pushed the others aside so she could hug Clara, then asked, "So tell me, did they rip you open? I need to know. Am I going to need major surgery to put my vagina back together after this?"

Excitedly, all the sisters started talking at once.

Livvy: "Gross, Violet. No one wants to hear about your vagina woes."

Jules: "Ruben and I decided to stop at two or we might test the multiple babies family curse."

Isadora: "It's not a curse. It's lovely. So many babies to hold!"

Evie: "Definitely a blessing. And your vagina will go back to normal, Violet. Trust me."

They all fell into laughing and talking over each other about how beautiful the babies were and how wonderful Clara was.

"I'll leave you ladies alone then," I told them, though no one heard me but Clara.

She caught my gaze and sent me that adoring look she gave me a thousand times a day. A look I cherished every single time.

Quietly, I left the room, closing the door on the loving, overlapping voices of the Savoie sisters.

Author's Note

I can't begin to thank all of the readers of this series. The count-less kind messages I've received about this world has brought me as much joy as I hope I've given to you. To know there are so many who love the Savoie sisters, their adoring men, and extended family as I do warms my heart beyond measure.

There are many people who have contributed to this series as editors, beta readers, sensitivity readers, and cheerleaders. I'm so appreciative to *all* of you. But one person helped bring the Savoie sisters to life and has been with me the entire series. I still remember the moment I walked into her place with a bottle of wine, plopped my ass on her couch, and said, "I have this new idea about some witch sisters in New Orleans." One bottle turned into two as we laughed through our first plot party for the Stay a Spell world. To my niece and my dear friend, Jessen, a sincere, heartfelt *thank you*. Having you on this journey has meant the world to me.

Turn the page for a sneak peek at a sizzling
new Juliette Cross series!

SOUTHERN CHARM. BOOK 1

A
REBEL
WITHOUT
CLAWS

CHAPTER 1

~RONAN~

"I DON'T KNOW SHIT ABOUT BODYWORK."

I watched the vein in my uncle's temple bulge, his jaws clamp tight, and his pulse jump in his throat. His heart rate picked up speed as he glared at me across his kitchen table, eyes flaring bright green with his wolf.

His fury had no effect on me. Nothing had any effect on me. Not for a while anyway.

Since Aunt Sarah had had enough of me in Austin and kicked me out, I figured New Orleans was a good option for my new plans. Thankfully, Uncle Shane agreed to let me crash at his place till I got on my feet again.

Besides, I'd worn out my welcome in more ways than one in Austin.

"Ronan." Uncle Shane blew out a heavy breath, clasping his hands around his coffee mug on the table. "You don't know shit about shit. Except how to get drunk, get arrested, and get your face beat to hell."

I grinned, the cut on my lip stinging. "Don't worry. No matter how bad I look, I won the fight." I win all of them. The legal and illegal ones.

"That's not what I'm worried about," he growled. "You need to find a place in this world, son. A future. One that doesn't include prison."

I'd heard this speech more than once from many different people—my juvie parole officer, my high school art teacher, my grandfather, my aunt, and now Uncle Shane.

"No offense"—I leaned back in the kitchen chair—"but my dreams never included getting greasy working in a garage."

"You got other options I don't know about?"

Not yet. But I would soon enough. My lengthy pause seemed to answer his question.

"That's what I thought. As long as you're here, you'll work for your room and board." His scowl deepened. "And we do more than fix cars. Our custom paint jobs are the best in all of Louisiana. From what Sarah told me, you're pretty talented."

"I don't do that for customers," I snapped.

That was for me, and me alone. My muscles locked, tension straightening my spine.

I didn't like people knowing or talking about my artwork. It was private. I sure as fuck wasn't going to dance to some rich dude's tune who wanted skulls and flames on his three-hundred-grand Harley.

"Fine." He stood and set his cup in the sink. "You'll work with Ty. He's in charge of the engine work." He grabbed his Blood

Moon Body Shop cap off the counter. "Be there in ten." Then he slammed the door behind him.

Heaving a sigh, I let my new reality sink in. I knew enough about mechanics that I was comfortable with cars. But I'd never done bodywork, and I had no interest in learning a new trade.

What I wanted to do was scout out New Orleans for their ring and find partners for my own team.

Later.

Now I had to get my ass in gear and make Uncle Shane happy so he didn't kick me out before I had another revenue stream coming in.

I splashed my face and checked out the purple bruise on my eye that was fading to green, then ran wet fingers through my hair.

After pulling on my jeans and a Bad Omens T-shirt, I headed out the door. Uncle Shane had built his house on the property next to his body shop. The rest of the pack lived close by on the Westbank of New Orleans, though Ty had told me yesterday when I met him that he lived in the city.

I strode across the two acres to the shop, a radio playing Puddle of Mudd in one of the open bays. The sun was barely up, but it was already around seventy. Summers in Louisiana weren't much different than Texas, it seemed.

As soon as I stepped into the first bay, Ty popped up from an open hood. "Morning. I heard you're with me today."

"You'll probably be holding my hand for a while." I headed around the old Camaro he was working on.

Ty smiled, wiping his hands on a rag, wearing the BMBS coveralls with the howling wolf emblem. "You know anything about cars?"

"Enough. I refurbished my Bronco." I gestured toward the white house where my '71 Ford Bronco was parked.

"Still needs a paint job." He leaned over the engine of the '68 Camaro. "We could do it here."

"Not sure I could afford the shop's prices." I'd seen some of the invoices stacked on Uncle Shane's kitchen counter.

"I'm sure you'd get the family discount."

I wasn't so sure. I peered out the open bay at my Bronco with its worn, rust-brown paint job. "She looks rough but she rides like a dream."

"Good to know you're good on engines." He walked to the wall of tools that stretched across two bays in the back of the garage. "That's mostly what I handle. A lot of the jobs we get are for bodywork only—interior and exterior finishing. But nine times out of ten, we'll find that they're in need of work under the hood too."

I walked around to the open hood. "What's the issue with the Camaro?"

"The guy swapped out the two-thirty engine for a three-ninety-six and the radiator can't handle it."

"You'll need to change out the transmission, too, with an engine that size."

"Exactly." He glanced at me appraisingly. "I just got the radiator in and was changing it out. Transmission won't be in for a few days."

"Cool."

I settled in beside him and helped though he didn't really need me. Still, I was going to do what I was told to make Uncle Shane happy.

Contrary to what my family might think, I didn't enjoy disappointing the people I cared about. Seeing that hurt look on Aunt Sarah's face when she told me I had to leave had gutted me. She didn't want to kick me out, but she had two young pups to raise. And I wasn't exactly the role model her boys needed. I just didn't care enough to change who I was. Moving on was always easier.

"What happened to your face?"

"I ran into a fist or two."

"Do that often?"

"Often enough."

Ty was tall and lean-muscled, built like a welterweight. The deep claw-shaped scars down one side of his throat told me he'd been in a fight before. Or something worse.

In the wolf ring, fighters could unsheath claws and use teeth. Their opponent just had to be fast enough to get out of the way. The fact that I'd never used either and was the champion of south Texas proved I was the best.

Knowing Louisiana had yet to outlaw wolf cage fighting opened a door when Aunt Sarah kicked me out and Uncle Shane agreed to take me in. After a search on the SuperNet revealed there was an established ring in New Orleans with a statewide undefeated team, I knew what my next goal was.

"Damn, man." Ty glanced up at me, pliers in his hand. "I can hear your wheels turning. Something on your mind?"

"Always."

He didn't push for more. I'd known Ty less than twenty-four hours, but he seemed a trustworthy guy, and I had to trust someone to get the information I needed.

"Hey, so where do the younger wolves hang out? Bars and stuff."

"How young do you mean?"

"Like our age."

He grinned and walked back to the workbench behind us. "I'm fifty-one."

That shouldn't have been shocking. Werewolves aged slowly, our life spans five to seven times longer than humans.

"You don't seem it," I told him.

Ty carried himself like a younger wolf in his twenties, like me.

"I've been told."

He leaned under the hood again. "I'm not a club scene guy. The Cauldron is a cool place. Live music on weekends. It's owned and run by our local Enforcer."

"It's a bar?"

"A pub and restaurant actually. Lots of our kind frequent there."

"Good to know." Because I would *not* be going to this Cauldron place. I'd rather stay off the radar of the Enforcer of this city.

"Zack and Bowie are always dragging ass when they work early-morning shifts. I've heard them mention a club called Howler's."

"Let me guess. Werewolf owned."

He laughed under his breath. "Yeah. Bowie has a paint job to finish this afternoon. You could ask him about it then, see if it's what you're looking for."

I helped him replace the radiator on the Camaro while he rambled about a Corvette we had coming in tomorrow when a scent caught my attention. Sweet and warm like the desert rose that grew back home.

I peered around the open hood and—*holy fucking shit.*

Standing right inside the second bay in the sunshine talking to that guy Rhett was the most stunning woman I'd ever seen.

She held a tablet, showing something to Rhett with a stylus in her hand, her brow pinched in concentration. Her heart-shaped face was tipped up, freckles sprinkling her nose and cheeks. A pile of wavy, copper hair was twisted in one of those knots, a curly strand blowing across her lips.

Rhett studied her tablet, saying something I didn't give a shit about. All I could do was stare at her. Inhaling a deep breath, I tried to catch her intoxicating scent again. She was a witch, for sure. I detected that particular designation right away. Usually, that would be enough to have me dismissing her. Witches didn't typically give werewolves the time of day.

I closed my eyes, focusing on the way my bones suddenly felt heavy, my skin too tight, my blood thick and pulsing with a dull throb. I'd never had a visceral reaction to meeting a woman where I felt incapable of looking or moving away. I hadn't met her yet, though. Opening my eyes again, my fascination amplified at the way the sun glowed around her like a halo.

What kind of witch was she? Maybe it was her powers that had captured me so completely. She must be an Influencer. A Warper, some called them. Witches who used their magic to persuade people to do anything they wanted. But I hadn't even talked to her, so how could she be using her magic against me?

She shifted from one foot to another and my body stiffened, readying itself. For what?

Then she tucked a curl behind her ear and licked her lips. I groaned.

"Dude, pick up your jaw, stop looking, and don't even fucking think about it."

"I can't stop looking and thinking. God. *Damn*." I pressed a hand to my sternum, suddenly having heartburn.

Ty huffed and whispered, "You're a dead man if you even try."

"Is she taken?" Something pinched inside my chest at the thought.

"It's not a boyfriend you have to worry about."

"Who then?"

"For starters, her very protective father who would gut you where you stand if he saw you drooling over her. Then there's her two brothers. Diego would rip you a new asshole. Last but not least, there are her many uncles which includes two old and powerful vampires and a grim reaper who could turn you into dust. Literally."

Not one thing he said deterred me from my new mission. If anything, it spurred me on. I liked a challenge. I loved the forbidden.

And that goddess glowing in the sunlight in pink cut-offs and a floral tank top was the most bewitching forbidden fruit I'd ever wanted to taste.

"Don't do it," warned Ty under his breath.

I ignored his warning and walked closer, unable to stop my body from moving toward her. Rhett had just stepped away to the workbench on the far wall.

She sensed my approach and turned her head in my direction. Her emerald eyes struck me near dumb. When I was finally within two feet of her, I forced my legs to lock in place, because my natural urge was to wrap her close and take a deep whiff of her drugging scent. That would certainly not make a good first impression.

She observed me carefully with intelligent eyes, taking me all in. I was at least a foot taller than her, but she didn't step back or look away. I liked that. She didn't intimidate easily, and I was a lot to take.

"You're an Influencer, aren't you?"

"What makes you think that?"

I swallowed hard, tongue-tied, because I couldn't tell her the truth. "You're not?"

"I'm an Aura." She smiled, raising gooseflesh on my arms.

I liked the way her eyes tilted up at the tips when she smiled. I rubbed my sternum. The heartburn was back.

"I'm Ronan," I finally said rather dumbly.

"You're trouble."

I chuckled. "Nothing you can't handle."

"How do you know? Maybe I'm the wilting type."

"No. You're not a type at all."

"What am I then?"

I shook my head, drinking in her beauty. "The kind of woman to make a man's world stop turning."

Her lips parted, pupils dilated, breath quickened, and heartbeat thudded faster. All the signs of attraction. Her reaction curled inside of me, tightening my body, ensnaring me even more.

She tilted her head and held out her hand. "I'm Celine."

I reached out, my hand engulfing hers, brushing my thumb over soft knuckles. My pulse grew loud in my own ears as it raced faster, my head dizzy with desire. And confusion.

Because then something happened that hadn't since that night in Amarillo when I was twelve.

From the deepest part of me, a sizzle of magic warmed my blood, awakening as I held this young woman's hand—stunned and spellbound. I didn't understand what was happening at first, but then he made himself known. I'd thought he was gone forever. But there was no mistaking his presence. Out of the dark, my wolf locked on Celine . . . and growled.